Heart's Desire

Also by Michael Taylor

Eve's Daughter
The Love Match
Love Songs
Clover

Heart's Desire

Michael Taylor

Hodder & Stoughton

First published in Great Britain in 2002 by Hodder and Stoughton
A division of Hodder Headline

2 4 6 8 10 9 7 5 3 1

A CIP catalogue record for this title is available
from the British Library

ISBN 0 340 81826 3

Typeset in Sabon by Palimpsest Book Production Limited,
Polmont, Stirlingshire
Printed and bound in Great Britain by
Mackays of Chatham plc, Chatham, Kent

Hodder and Stoughton
A division of Hodder Headline
338 Euston Road
London NW1 3BH

To Maisie Mae

I

Rhianna Drake had always been able to summon up a picture of the man she might eventually marry. Apart from the essential virtues of tallness, leanness, excessive handsomeness, kindliness and, of course, gentility, he would be reasonably well off and never inhibited about showing her affection – not even in public. He would also be a patient man; patient not only with her but with her family as well. Such high marital expectations for a lowly working-class girl like Rhianna might have been unrealistically optimistic, but her self-esteem was high and she never doubted that such a man existed and would eventually emerge through the Black Country's industrial murk. By the time she was twenty-two however, her imagined bridegroom still had not shown up and the thought had already crossed her mind that maybe she was destined to be an old maid.

Rhianna was born in Dudley in Worcestershire on 18th May 1866 to Titus and Mary Drake. Her father invented her name as a sort of compromise; Mary had wanted the baby named after her own mother, Rhiain who was Welsh, but Titus would have no further truck with anything that came out of Wales. Better to call his new daughter Anna, after his own mother. After some spirited but never serious arguments, when Welsh and English forebears had been equally disparaged, *Rhianna* emerged as the obvious answer – an even-handed combining of the two names. 'There's ne'er another anywheer, our Rhianna, yo'm a one-off,' he used to tell the little girl proudly in his dense Black Country accent, then tousle the dark ringlets that hung down her neck in thick coils. It irritated her to death but she loved him, and he loved her; small, wiry Titus Drake, iron puddler.

Titus told his young daughter unassumingly that while he was at work, sweating over a searing hot hearth, puddling iron, he could sink eighteen pints of beer on a hot summer's day.

'Eighteen pints?' Rhianna queried, wide-eyed.

'Eighteen pints and I never get sozzled! We sweat it out, see. All the blokes drink like fish, working in that heat. The gaffers gi' it we free. We even have a beer boy to keep we topped up.'

'Why don't you drink water, Father?'

'Drink wairter? You couldn't drink the wairter, my angel. You wouldn't dare drink the wairter. It'd gi' yer the ballyache and the squits. Yo'd be off th'ooks for days and lose time at work.'

From the point of view of other folks Titus Drake was nobody special, just an unskilled ironworker. To Rhianna, though, he was everything. On Saturday afternoons he would say, 'Come on, our bab, we'm off somewheer,' and he would take her over the Oakham woodland, known as the Dingle, and show her the bluebells in spring; you couldn't walk anywhere without treading on them. In the autumn, they would take a basket and gather mushrooms and make mushroom soup when they returned home. Everything they saw, every bird, every nervous animal, every swaying flower, every gnarled tree, he had something to say about and made it all so interesting and vivid. Life was always exciting. There was so much to see, so much to learn about. Once, they gathered blackberries to make wine and, when they returned home with baskets full, he asked Rhianna to help him make it.

'Pour the sugar in now, my wench,' he said stirring the must . . .

Unfortunately, the sugar came in blue bags identical to those the washing soda was packed in and . . . well, it was an easy mistake . . . But together they just laughed and laughed.

'What's your earliest memory, our Rhianna?' Titus asked one day, on another blackberry harvesting when she was a little older.

'Oh, walking with Mother to take you a basin of broth for your dinner.' She stooped to reach a cluster of blackberries she'd just spied. 'I remember toddling beside her for miles, holding her hand, on our way to you at the Woodside Ironworks.' She looked up at him and smiled. 'We seemed to have been walking forever.'

'Oh, it's a tidy walk I grant yer, our Rhianna. I hoof it there and back every day, bar Sundays.'

'Yes, but you're used to it. I wasn't. I was only little. I was that thankful when we stopped.' She dropped a handful of blackberries into her basket. 'My little legs seemed so heavy and my poor feet ached. Then all I heard was this terrible roar from inside the factory. It frightened me to death. That, and the clanging of iron and the noise from the steam engines . . .' She stood up to stretch her legs. 'I can even remember the stink. It caught at the back of my throat. I don't know how you could stand it. It can't have done your health any good . . . Anyway, before Mother handed over your basin, you scooped me up in your arms and hugged me. Reuben Danks was with you and you showed me off to him and made me say hello and I was all shy.'

'I remember. And Reuben said, "Titus, yo'll have to watch her when her's a young madam – her'll be a bobbydazzler and no two ways." And he was right.'

Rhianna laughed contentedly.

She also remembered the smell that clung to her father that far-off day, though she did not mention it. It was the sharp aroma of iron and oil and smoke and sweat, all mixed together in some malodorous blend. Yet it was beyond her to actually dislike it, simply because it was his smell, the smell he always carried with him when he came home.

She licked the blood-red blackberry juice that was dribbling between her fingers. 'Something else I remember . . .' She looked at him with all her love in her eyes. 'You giving me donkey rides on your back as well. You used to run about the backyard like a frightened pig escaping from the slaughterman, while I screamed and Mother begged you to be careful lest I fell off and broke my neck.' She chuckled at the memory.

They were not well off, but neither were they poor. Titus Drake earned regular money, sufficient to live on, and he turned it up; he drank only moderately outside of work. They always ate good, nourishing food that Mary Drake cooked in the oven of the black-leaded grate that she cleaned conscientiously until it looked like polished melanite. No neighbour could ever tittle-tattle that Mary wasn't clean. Bacon and pork was plentiful for they kept pigs in those days. Sometimes they'd be given a rabbit or wring the neck of one of the plump chickens that strutted round the yard. They also ate the other things that Black Country families ate; chitterlings, liver faggots with grey peas, lambs' brains with egg, pigs' trotters and grawty pudding. They never went short.

Even at the age of five, it struck Rhianna that her mother was not having any babies. Naturally enough, she was not familiar with the arcane secrets of conception, so it never occurred to her that her father might also have something to do with it. Babies, she had the distinct notion, came from a woman's belly or bottom somehow, but none were coming from her mother's. Friends who were the same age as Rhianna all had at least one brother or sister to play with, and often more. Some even had nine or ten. Why did she not have a brother or sister? Just one would do. It wasn't fair. Then, one day in October 1872, when Rhianna was six years old, Mary Drake announced that she was going upstairs to have a baby. A few hours later Sarah was born, all red-faced and puckered. Rhianna was bitterly disappointed at the sight of her. She expected to see a pretty baby that would gurgle at her, hale and hearty with plump rosy cheeks and wide blue eyes that would smile appealingly.

All she beheld was this ugly, hairless little bundle of wrinkled flesh that struggled to make any sound at all – even when she cried – and slept the rest of the time. Sarah was no fun.

Nevertheless, that ugly little bundle showed early signs of growing into a beautiful princess. When she was five and Rhianna was eleven, Sarah had the most engaging blue eyes, the prettiest little nose and delicious rosebud lips. Rhianna loved to press her cheek against Sarah's and feel the incredibly warm infant smoothness against her own face. It was obvious even then, that given time, all the lads would be chasing her. Already, boys of seven and eight would call for her to come out to play.

Not only Titus, but Mary too, was a great influence on Rhianna as a young girl. Mary was small in stature, slender, and had a natural grace that folk reckoned Rhianna had inherited. Although she was from a poor family she kept a good house and, everything her daughters did, they were made to do properly; a discipline Mary learnt from her days as a servant in a big house in Pensnett. Early on in her daughters' lives, Mary had the foresight to take out a small insurance policy for each in turn, in readiness for the day when they too would enter domestic service and have to pay for their uniforms. She insisted that they go to church every Sunday morning and evening. Because they dwelt opposite the glassworks in Campbell Street, in the parish of St Thomas, they attended Top Church, as it was known. Standing majestically at the top of the town, Top Church was the tallest building for miles with its tapering steeple pointing high into the sky. You could see it piercing the skyline like a saddler's needle from a long way off. It was a great landmark, almost as great as the Norman castle that dominated the other end of the town.

Another good influence on Rhianna was Miss Pope, her schoolmistress at St Thomas's School. Miss Pope taught her common sense and how to do complicated sums. She taught her to read and write, to appreciate the more cultured aspects of life, and vigorously discouraged her from speaking with a broad Black Country accent, correcting her at every slip. Miss Pope's influence stayed with Rhianna.

Rhianna's best friend in those days was Emily Tucker who went to work in service at the house of Mr Charles Ralph Spencer, a highly respected solicitor. He regularly attended Top Church.

'Guess what,' Emily whispered to Rhianna at a moment when the point of Reverend Cosens's sermon was particularly elusive. 'There's a position to be had at Mr Spencer's. They'm after a maid. Why don't you apply?'

'Me?'

'Tha's what you wanna do, in't it? Work in service?'

Rhianna shrugged. 'Yes.'

'So ask about it. Mr Spencer's in church. Ask him about it after.'

Emily was older than Rhianna and far more sensible, Rhianna thought. After fretting all through Matins and taking furtive peeps at the lordly Mr Spencer, to try and judge just how approachable he was, Rhianna finally managed to pluck up the courage to address him after the service as he and his wife were leaving.

'Excuse me, Mr Spencer,' she said apologetically, running beside them down the stone steps that spilled onto High Street. 'My friend Emily Tucker says you have a vacancy for a maid. . . . I wondered if you would consider me?'

Mr Spencer's initial expression was one of disbelief that any girl as young and insignificant as Rhianna could have the brazen audacity to confront him on God's day of rest. But he got over his shock and smiled at her patiently and rather politely, considering her lowliness.

'Your name, Miss?'

'Rhianna Drake, sir.'

'One of our regular congregation,' Mrs Spencer, who was holding his arm, informed him pleasantly.

'Of course, I know your face,' he said with an agreeable smile. 'Well . . . How old are you, Miss Drake?'

'Thirteen, sir,' Rhianna answered, blushing as she realised just how forward she must have seemed. 'Thirteen in May.'

'Do you know where I live?'

'Yes, sir. On Wellington Road, sir. I know just where it is.'

'Come and see my wife at half past four tomorrow afternoon . . . and don't forget to bring your character.'

As he and Mrs Spencer left, Rhianna looked at Emily with open-mouthed disbelief and chuckled at her own audacity.

'There you am,' Emily said. 'Easy. Yo'll get that job and no mistek.'

'But who'll give me a character?'

'Ask the vicar.'

It was July 1879 and Rhianna was just about to leave school. She had been given the job, as Emily predicted, and was thrilled. Naturally, she was sorry to leave her mother and father and little Sarah in that modest terraced house of theirs, but her mother was so proud. She cashed in her older daughter's insurance policy, bought her uniform and off Rhianna went to work. Leaving home to live and work in a strange house was, for many a young girl, a lonely and depressing experience. Rhianna was lucky; she knew Emily. Otherwise, for a time, she might have been lonely even though Mr Spencer was very kind to his staff. She had Sunday afternoons off, when she would visit her family; one night off every week besides, and she was promised two weeks' holiday a year. In addition, she was to be paid £10 a year, most of which she hoped to give to her mother.

Rhianna and Emily joined the St Thomas's Girls' Friendly Society which they attended on their night off. It provided social and religious activities and sewing. They bought material at half the price it was offered in the town shops and a lady came in and taught them how to cut it and sew it, so they could make dresses and other garments. There were Bible readings from Reverend Cosens, beetle drives, and Rhianna made friends with some lovely girls, though not all were in service. She felt a great affinity to that sisterhood of young women who taught her so much, not just about sewing either, but about life . . .

She settled well into working at the Spencer household and enjoyed it. Once, she was taken ill with flu and Mr Spencer paid the doctor to come and see her, then allowed her home for a week afterwards to convalesce. Yet, despite his kindness and commendable charitableness, he docked her a week's money.

When she was sixteen in the summer of 1882, Rhianna realised that the baker's boy was taking an interest in her. Charlie Bills was a good-looking lad with a cheeky grin and she'd secretly been admiring him for some time. One day, when he was delivering, he asked to see her on her night off.

'But I go with Emily to the Girls' Friendly Society at Top Church on my night off,' she told him disappointedly.

'I could meet yer after and walk yer back.'

Her heart started hammering hard at the prospect. 'All right,' she agreed and the tryst was arranged.

When that looked-forward-to time came she bid Emily goodnight and Charlie whisked her away.

'Want to see a wasp's nest?' he said boyishly.

'Not particularly.' Rhianna was not impressed. The thought of being attacked by a million of the humming little devils terrified her.

Yet despite a poor start, Charlie Bills became her first sweetheart. He harboured some exalted plans: he was going to start his own bakery and marry her; they would live in a fine house on Ednam Road, have several children and a top floor full of servants. He was a dreamer and Rhianna took all this in like the immature young girl that she was. Charlie never once considered the difficulties, the sacrifices. To start a bakery business he first needed money. Then he would have to work all the hours that God sent, getting up at two or three in the morning to bake bread ready for his first customers, who wanted it before their husbands scurried off to work. Once Rhianna realised this, she decided she didn't fancy the life.

When you are sixteen and in love, your emotions boil over. They run away with you. Thus it was with Rhianna. She was besotted, early on at least. Sometimes, when Charlie called to deliver the bread, she would contrive to be in the laundry and he would furtively seek her out. He would take her in his arms, press her against the mangle or the stone sink, and she would feel all swoony with pleasure when he kissed her. She could always smell fresh-baked bread on him, a smell she adored. Of course, she never allowed him to go any further than kissing . . . except the few occasions after they got to know each other better, and she allowed him to feel her breasts, but only ever *over* her bodice, never in the flesh. After all, she went to church regularly, she was a regular member of the Girls' Friendly Society and they were always warned about what happened to silly girls who allowed men to take liberties; well, the workhouse was full of unfortunate examples. Yet, when she sat daydreaming, the thought of having her breasts fondled in the flesh, imagining what his lips might feel like nuzzling her nipples, was decidedly appealing. When Charlie kissed her on the lips she would feel her breathing coming harder and faster and was surprised at first when her drawers felt wet, as if she'd dribbled in them.

On summer evenings, on her nights off, they would sit among the limestone ruins of the old St James's Priory. Once, while Charlie was idly poking the ground with a stick, they found some tiles embedded in the dirt and moss, laid originally by the monks that built the place. They had strange, beautiful patterns on them and must have been five hundred years old or more but, at the time, that meant nothing to her. When she went back years later, those old tiles were still there. Then, she could see how beautiful they were, and could appreciate the time and skill that was required to make them and fire them in those long-gone days.

Charlie and Rhianna courted for about two years. He was always talking about getting married but she knew, even then, that he didn't measure up to her notions. When she was eighteen, he asked her seriously to become his wife and she said no – politely, of course. He became resentful at being rejected and told her one day, when he delivered the Spencers' bread, that he had started seeing somebody else. Rhianna was hurt and disappointed but not heartbroken. After that she didn't bother with boys. Those she met all seemed too silly and only interested in one thing, which she, having been tutored by the Girls' Friendly Society, was certainly not prepared to give.

It became manifestly obvious that boys were interested in her by this time. With good reason. She had a shock of dark hair that she wore elegantly pinned up at work and when she went out. When she let it down at bedtime, and when she washed it, it cascaded down her back like a silky, shiny mane. She had a lovely round face too, with high cheekbones. Her blue eyes were big and bright, slightly slanted, with long lashes that swept her cheek as she fluttered them playfully whenever she chose to flirt with those lads that showed an interest. She had inherited her mother's slenderness and grace and was exquisitely constructed. Her skin was an appealing pale olive, smooth and utterly flawless. And, in the same way that a fat person knows when she is fat, a thin person knows when she is thin, an ugly person knows when she is ugly, Rhianna knew she was a thoroughly good-looking young woman with as good a figure as she'd ever seen. Furthermore, she always tried to make the best of herself in a proper, demure way.

Rhianna progressed well in the Spencer household. She did every job that was given her, without resentment or complaint and always to the best of her ability. Fire grates had to be cleaned, including a six-foot range in the kitchen that had to be blackleaded. Fires had to be lit, candlesticks and lamp glasses cleaned. All the water-jugs in the house, all the basins and chamber pots had to be emptied, carefully washed and scalded if necessary. Windows had to be shone. Each week every bedroom had to be cleaned from top to bottom, so there were mattresses to be turned and brushed, pillows shaken and smoothed and, naturally, no dust was allowed to remain under any of the beds. Curtains had to be shaken, brass curtain rods burnished bright, paintwork washed, looking glasses polished and floors buffed. She had to keep a sharp look out for insects and bed bugs, which could enter the house on visitors who had travelled by train or hackney carriage. All hell would be let loose at the discovery of a bed bug.

About a year after Charlie decided he was wasting his time with Rhianna, her father fell ill. It started with gout in his right foot; all that beer, very likely, Mary said. Mary accidentally knocked it once and he called her all the names under the sun. From that day on, he sat in his armchair with his foot in a wicker clothes basket for protection, with a soft cushion to afford some damping if ever it was knocked again. To top it all, he had an abscess up his backside as well. It did not stop him breaking wind, though. 'Abscess makes the fart go yonder,' he said on one such turbulent occasion; despite his acute discomfort, he retained his dry Black Country sense of humour. He had about three months off work and then, as he was about to return, his gout and his abscess having retreated, he began complaining about his chest. He was having difficulty breathing and was having night sweats.

Mary sent for Dr McCaskie and it was evident he was worried about poor Titus. He promised to keep an eye on him, said that he must rest and not go to work. Rhianna was desperate to help and handed over all her wages to her mother, arguing that she needed very little herself since she ate heartily and slept at the home of Mr Spencer. Already she had saved up and bought another uniform, and had made a couple of decent frocks besides for going out in. She was earning £12 a year by this time, not a fortune and certainly not enough to keep her family.

Of course, the Spencers were not so well off that Mrs Spencer had a lady's maid, so Rhianna carried hot water upstairs so they could wash. She worked in the kitchen with the cook and got to know her routine. By the time she was twenty, she was the head maid and earning £15 a year.

Meanwhile, Titus got no better and had to give up work entirely. He was beginning to lose weight, which he could ill afford to do. Mary applied for parish relief. It was always a struggle to find money for coal, for rent and for food. Rhianna tried to borrow money to pay the doctor to treat her father, but realised she had no chance of paying it back, so gave up the idea.

Sarah, by this time, had left school and found work in service. Unfortunately, the family she worked for were not kind to her and she hated her job. Yet she stuck it out, concerned only that she give money to her mother to help keep them.

They all struggled through for a couple of years. Dr McCaskie was sent for again and he warned that Titus might be consumptive. Then, Rhianna had a spot of good fortune. Again, through somebody she had got to know at church, she was asked if she would be interested in the position of housekeeper at a place called Baxter House on the rural north-western side of Dudley. The house was named after Richard Baxter, a long-departed headmaster at the grammar school, famed for having written the words to the hymn, 'Ye Holy Angels Bright'. Baxter House was the home of Mr Jeremiah Cookson. Rhianna had seen Mr Cookson, a business friend of Mr Spencer, before and had occasionally spoken to his wife in the course of her duties, as they were visitors to the Spencer household. Her wages were to be £60 a year, a goodly amount.

Rhianna found it impossible to resist when she realised how

much easier it would be to help support her mother and father and pay for the doctor and medical treatment. Naturally, she was grateful to accept the position. She could scarcely believe that she was to become a fully-fledged housekeeper at only twenty-two years of age. When she went with trepidation and mounting guilt to see Mrs Spencer to terminate her employment, the lady of the house smiled benignly.

'Oh, don't worry, Rhianna,' she said. 'Mr Cookson asked Mr Spencer a while ago for permission to approach you. He and his wife have had their eye on you for some time. They said how much they admire your demeanour and your application to your work.'

Rhianna bobbed a curtsy. 'Thank you, ma'am. I had no idea you'd talked about me.'

'It's a grand opportunity for you, Rhianna, and you deserve it. Far be it from me to hold you back from finer things. I also understand the difficulties you face with your father unable to work any more. It must be a big worry for your poor mother. This new position means you'll be of greater help to her too, I imagine.'

'Oh, yes, ma'am. I already hand over all my wages to my mother. I only want for decent shoes and stockings and she gives me money back to buy those as and when.'

Mrs Spencer smiled sympathetically and touched Rhianna's arm. 'We shall miss you, my dear. But we shall manage, I daresay. Come and see us whenever you have the time. You will always be welcome.'

Rhianna tried hard to stem the tears that were welling up in her eyes but, rather than let them show, she swiftly thanked Mrs Spencer for her kindness and curtsied again before she turned and walked away. When she was out of sight she pulled her handkerchief from her sleeve and wiped the tears that, by now, were streaming down her face. She had been happy at the Spencers' and they had been so kind. She vowed never to forget their kindness.

*   *   *

On 25th May 1888, a week after her twenty-second birthday, Rhianna moved to Baxter House, a fine modern mansion built of red brick. The household was appropriately large too, with many more servants than there were at the Spencers' more modest dwelling. Baxter House was set back from St James's Road, close to where it joined Ednam Road, and overlooked green meadows and grazing cattle. No doubt Mr Cookson preferred it to overlooking the dirty, grey, slag-heaped out-look on the other side of the town. He was immensely rich and spent lavishly. It was said that he employed three hundred men at his iron foundry in Dudley, and had recently invested a great deal of money building a railway siding at the works.

Some of the maids at Baxter House were older than Rhianna and at first she sensed some resentment that they should be told what to do and be given tasks by a girl so much younger. Yet she succeeded in earning their respect. She was never haughty to them, but gave them their jobs as if making a request and with an open smile to which they always responded positively. In so many big houses, girls were unhappy, often abused and sometimes even beaten. The staff of Baxter House were thankful they were well treated and appreciated. Nobody ever took it upon herself to rebel and make things uncomfortable for everybody else.

As soon as there was a vacancy for a maid Rhianna recruited Sarah, her sister. She was fifteen by that time and a good, reliable worker, although not as bright as Rhianna. Rhianna even managed to secure her an increase on what she had been earning but Sarah would have come for less, glad to get away from that house in Holly Hall. Sarah settled in promisingly and Rhianna was happy to have her under her wing. Most nights Sarah would go to Rhianna's little room on the top floor, where they would talk until the small hours, before returning to the room she shared with Hannah Bissell, a kitchen maid the same age as her.

'Have you got a sweetheart?' Sarah asked one night as she lay sprawled across Rhianna's legs.

Rhianna was sitting up in bed attending to her fingernails. 'You know I haven't,' she replied. 'Have you?'

Sarah smiled bashfully and shook her head. 'Have you ever had a sweetheart, Rhianna?'

'Once,' she answered honestly. 'For a while. His name was Charlie Bills. He was the baker's boy when I worked at the Spencers'.'

'Did you love him?'

'I suppose I did. At first, at any rate. Leastwise, he made me feel all sentimental.'

'Did you let him kiss you?'

'Yes, sometimes.'

'Is it nice to be kissed by a boy?'

Rhianna smiled patiently. 'I think that might depend on the boy – and on how much you like him.'

'Would you like a sweetheart again?' Sarah enquired after listening carefully to Rhianna's answers.

'If somebody came along who I fancied.'

'Tell me the kind of man you fancy,' Sarah said dreamily.

'Oh, I have a vivid picture of my ideal husband in my mind's eye,' Rhianna told her, and Sarah's beautiful clear eyes flickered with interest. She sat up on the bed attentively, her back erect, her legs crossed under her cotton nightgown. 'He's very handsome with dark, wavy hair and kind, smiling eyes. He's quite tall, with a straight back, not given to slouching ... He's clever, amusing, and good at making interesting conversation.'

'Ooh, yes,' Sarah enthused. 'You don't want some duffer who can't keep up a decent chat, do you? And will he be rich, Rhianna?'

'Rich enough. Rich enough to afford our own servants.'

'What about Mr Robert then?'

'Mr Robert?' she said with a shudder. 'Are you serious? I

couldn't bear Mr Robert to touch me.' Mr Robert was the middle son of Jeremiah Cookson of Baxter House. Unmarried, he still lived there. Rhianna had already noticed the way Mr Robert looked at her. If he had designs on her, though, he could forget it.

'He's got a handsome friend,' Sarah said, her long eyelashes veiling her eyes. 'I wish I was just a bit older.'

'Oh? And what's his name, this handsome friend of Mr Robert?'

Sarah sighed and picked a stray piece of cotton from her nightdress. 'I dunno . . .' There followed an introspective pause. 'Anyway,' she said eventually, 'how are you going to meet somebody that rich, who'll stoop to marry *you*?'

Rhianna smiled as she realised that Sarah had already got the measure of the marriage market; she knew that wealthy middle-class sons would never demean themselves by marrying below their station, even if bedding housemaids and other girls of the lower classes was not out of bounds.

'Oh, I shall.' Rhianna shrugged nonchalantly. 'I just know I shall. I can put on airs and graces if I need to. I can easily copy the elegant women I see visiting Mr and Mrs Cookson.

'You've set your sights high, our Rhianna.'

'Lord, you sound just like Mother,' she said with mock disdain. 'But if you've got any sense, you'll set your sights high as well. Don't be satisfied with some beer swilling navvy, or ne'er-do-well iron-worker like our father – not that I want to demean him,' she hastily added. 'But just look at our mother . . . You don't want to end up like her, poor as a church mouse, not knowing where the next meal is coming from.'

'I want to get married young and have lots of children, Rhianna.'

The older sister stifled a scornful laugh. 'You'll have lots of children whether or no if you marry somebody who gets pie-eyed every night and makes you do disgusting things with him, whether you want to or not. Marry a man with something about him. Marry somebody who'll respect you.'

'Oh, I wouldn't marry a nobody,' Sarah said, catching on quicker than Rhianna thought she would, for she was often slow on the uptake. 'I'll try to be like you. I'll aim high. I'll marry somebody with some money, or not at all.'

'Good,' Rhianna said. 'Life will be so much easier, so much more comfortable.'

'Mmm . . .' Sarah mused. 'It's just finding somebody . . .'

'Set your cap at this friend of Mr Robert's you fancy,' Rhianna advised. 'He might be a bit older but that can only be to your advantage.'

2

On New Year's Eve, 1888, a party had been arranged at Baxter House and Rhianna had done most of the organising, although Mrs Cookson herself had written and sent out all the invitations. It was to be a grand evening and the Cooksons' immediate family, friends and business associates would be there; altogether, some fifty guests.

'I think informal dining would suit us all better,' Mrs Cookson said as she sat at the table in the breakfast room with a notepad in front of her. To her right was Rhianna, to her left Martha Evans, the cook.

'With so many people to cater for, ma'am, I agree,' Rhianna commented and looked at Cook for her confirmation.

'I'll prepare whatever I'm asked to,' Martha said.

'A buffet dinner that people can eat while they stand and talk. Any suggestions, Rhianna?'

'Well, a variety of meats in dainty sandwiches would be a start, ma'am.'

'I could cook some ham, roast a joint of beef, a few chickens,' Martha suggested. 'Even some venison if we can get it. Then there's smoked salmon, poultry and game birds. I could bake some little savoury pies and tarts as well, ma'am.'

Rhianna nodded her solemn agreement.

'A good selection of cheeses as well, I think, Cook. The men enjoy their cheese after a meal. Oh, and I think a hot soup later, to see everybody homeward, would be a very satisfactory touch. Don't you think so, Rhianna?'

'Yes, that would be very well appreciated, I believe, ma'am.'

Rhianna had never seen so many varieties of cheeses when

the grocer's boy delivered them. For dessert Martha prepared syllabubs, fools, hot fruit tarts and pies, egg custards, creams and even ice cream. It was all to await the hungry revellers in the dining room, where lavishly dressed trestles had been laid out to accommodate it. Everything looked and smelled mouth-watering. The staff, of course, had their own cache of food in the kitchen, which they picked at when they had the opportunity. A trio of musicians had been hired to perform in the function room of the house, where a hearty coal fire burned in the opulent marble grate.

At eight o'clock the first carriage arrived and emptied out Alderman Jukes and his wife, who was appropriately bedecked in all manner of jewellery. The town's Clerk of Works, Thomas Bakewell, and his wife followed them shortly after. Then a middle-aged couple entered; the wealthy and highly respected socialites, Mr and Mrs Alexander Gibson. He, once seen, was not to be forgotten, immaculately dressed, with a superior bearing, like a duke. Thereafter, a veritable procession of carriages and hansom cabs halted in turn on the drive that ringed the front garden, disgorged their passengers and moved on.

Rhianna hovered discreetly in the hall, trying to blend with the fashionable William Morris wallpaper, overseeing the servants who politely divested the guests of their hats, gloves, topcoats and scarves, while others handed them welcoming drinks. She had assigned Sarah to work in the kitchen and help serve the food later.

The house was filling up, and she could hear the chink of glasses, the reassuring sound of laughter. She could smell the rich aroma of cigars as smoke pervaded the air from the function room. The early signs portended a hugely successful evening and Rhianna began to relax a little . . . until a well-dressed man was let in. He was about thirty she guessed, tall with a well-groomed head of dark hair and handsome beyond belief, with eyes that exuded the coolness and clarity of sapphires. As soon as she saw him she could not take her eyes off him. It was love at first sight.

He matched absolutely the image she had fondly carried in her head all those years of the man she believed she was destined to marry. He had to be the one. There were merely three obstacles to a union between them that she could perceive: his obvious wealth, her position as a servant and, not least, the fascinating young woman who accompanied him.

Of course, he did not so much as look in Rhianna's direction. However, she studied him and the girl, watching with bated breath to see whether she wore a ring of any sort as she removed her gloves. She did, but it was neither a wedding ring nor an engagement ring. Stupidly, Rhianna was encouraged. She scrutinised the girl carefully for clues as to her background. People intrigued her and always had. She observed them habitually, noticed their behaviour, their facial expressions, their reactions when spoken to, their body movements. One didn't always have to hear a conversation to know what somebody was saying when the rhetoric of their movements and mannerisms said so much. The first thing that struck Rhianna about the girl was her looks. She was not beautiful in the classical sense – she lacked the finesse, the innate elegance of a well-bred lady – but she had such a pretty face, enhanced by a smooth, cared-for complexion and sleek, fair hair. Rhianna could not help but notice her bare shoulders either, or how her creamy breasts nudged at her décolletage with a youthfully firm resilience that defied both gravity and the constraints of corseting.

'Lawson!' It was the voice of Robert Cookson, Jeremiah's son. 'You made it. For God's sake, grab a drink, man . . . Hetty, would you see that Mr Maddox's hat and coat are looked after . . . and those of Miss, er . . . ?'

'Lampitt,' Lawson Maddox informed him by way of introduction. 'Miss Fanny Lampitt.'

As the maid took the girl's hat and coat, Robert took her

hand and put it gently to his lips, parodying the gallantry of a bygone age. 'Miss Lampitt,' he said admiringly. 'Any friend of Lawson's is a friend of mine. Especially one so beautiful. May I call you Fanny?'

Rhianna continued to watch unobserved in the shadow of the broad, sweeping staircase as the girl, evidently overawed, either by Robert's gushing manner or the opulence that surrounded her, fluttered her eyelashes, and looked up into Lawson's twinkling eyes for reassurance and encouragement. And there Rhianna gained another clue about her. This girl, this Fanny, was unsure of herself. She seemed out of her depth with those affluent people and in such unfamiliar, sumptuous surroundings.

'Oh, please call me Frances,' the girl replied, an entreaty in her voice.

Frances? Fanny? Of course. Rhianna smiled to herself. No wonder this girl would rather they didn't call her Fanny. *Fanny* was reserved for a woman of a different calibre. To Rhianna, it seemed this girl was endeavouring to give the impression she was something she was not. To her credit, the way she was dressed would never have given her away. She wore a good blue satin dress that matched her eyes, with a tight bodice and puffed sleeves. The height of fashion.

'I think . . . In fact, I'm sure I prefer Fanny, if you don't object,' Robert said with a wink to Lawson. 'It has a certain ring to it.'

'All right. Fanny, then,' Fanny answered with an acquiescent smile. 'If you'd rather.'

'That's settled then . . . Amy, would you pass Miss Lampitt a drink? What would you like, Fanny?'

'Oh, a glass of port, please.'

Amy, who was looking after the welcoming drinks, handed Fanny a glass of port, then a glass of whisky to Lawson. They moved on, into the main room, chatting amiably.

Rhianna sighed, envious of the girl despite her name. She

had done well for herself to attract the attention of somebody like this Lawson Maddox. And yet she felt sorry for Fanny as well. Fanny was on tenterhooks lest she make some awful social gaffe that would reveal her true status. She was brave and yet, the way she looked at Lawson so adoringly, it was obvious she would walk barefoot through burning coals for him.

When the last of the guests had arrived and had been welcomed Rhianna went to the kitchen to check how things were progressing there. Martha the cook said everything was under control. So she went upstairs to her room simply to check herself in the mirror. Oh, it was for *him*. Certainly, it was for him. A wisp of stray hair tickled her neck and she tucked it back into place. She pinched her cheeks and bit her lips to redden them and inspected the overall effect. She was not displeased. She had been given permission to wear an unpretentious dress that suited the evening and she had bought it specially. It was midnight blue, very plain, made up of separate bodice and skirt, with a modest décolletage. Mrs Cookson had also permitted her to wear a little plain jewellery, so she wore a thin silver cross and chain and matching earrings that had been given to her by Charlie Bills once as a Christmas box. With her hair piled up she looked appealing and yet demure. Her demeanour was entirely different to Fanny's. Although they came from similar backgrounds, out of uniform Rhianna knew she did not betray her true beginnings and, wearing that tasteful though inexpensive dress, nobody would be any the wiser who was not already aware she was the Cooksons' housekeeper. It occurred to her then to try a little experiment and put her theory to the test.

So she walked slowly, confidently downstairs, practising her poise as she went. The party was getting noisier and the trio was struggling to be heard over the buzz of conversation and laughter. Skeins of blue smoke were drifting through the hall and being drawn up the staircase by the lure of an open window at the top. She made her way to the main room and entered unnoticed. For a while she stood and watched with interest the couples who were already dancing a military two-step. She must have been there for about ten minutes, excusing herself with a smile if she found she was inadvertently standing in the way of couples trying to get past her . . . when Mr Robert Cookson sidled up.

'Rhianna! My word, you look ravishing. Won't you have the next dance with me?'

It would have been impolitic in the extreme to have refused so, when the trio embarked on the next dance, a polka, she joined him and whirled around him nimbly.

'You dance very well,' he said when they met face to face for a few seconds.

'Thank you,' she replied with a broad smile at the next conjunction. 'It's what servants do sometimes in their spare time.'

'Dancing is not the activity *I* heard they do,' he said with a provocative flick of his eyebrows and a smug grin as he twirled around.

Her skirts rustled as he brushed uncomfortably close to her at their next turn.

'Indeed, Mr Robert?' she said, retaining her smile. 'If you mean what I think you mean, I am not aware of any unsavoury goings on at Baxter House.'

'Fiddlesticks, Rhianna! It goes on everywhere.'

'Oh, in some houses, maybe . . . But not here. In any case, it's a subject I'd prefer not to discuss if it's all the same to you.'

'Quite the lady, aren't you?' he commented, and she could not make up her mind whether he was being sarcastic or complimentary. 'How old are you now, Rhianna?'

'I was always led to believe it impolite to ask a woman her age,' she answered, avoiding his eyes.

'I suppose it depends on the eminence of the woman,' he

said cuttingly, putting her roundly in her place. 'So what is your age? Twenty-one? Twenty-two?'

'About that,' she replied, humiliated and yet determined not to give him the satisfaction of a direct answer.

'And not married yet. Nor even courting, I am led to believe.'

Rhianna could scarcely believe his outrageous directness. As they tripped across the dance floor she looked directly into his eyes. 'Mr Robert, I can assure you that no man I have ever met has made me yearn to be married to him, either for love, money, or convenience.'

'My dear Rhianna,' he guffawed, overlooking or failing to note the rebuff.

Thankfully, at that moment, the dance ended. At once Rhianna made a move to leave him and he unhanded her. She stood for some minutes, her head down, dejected at Robert's disparaging attitude.

When she looked up she saw that people were once more dancing, though she had not noticed the trio strike up again, nor the sound of skidding feet marking the polished wooden floor as couples whirled graciously around each other. So many straight backs and elegantly inclined heads. This throng, apart from the uncaring Mr Robert, was the cream of Black Country society. She scanned the sea of faces as they danced, and she spotted him on the floor again. His back was towards her and his partner was Fanny. Was he trying to make a cuckold of his friend?

'Pardon me for saying so, but any man who would leave you standing on your own at the edge of a dance floor clearly doesn't deserve you,' a man's voice whispered very close to Rhianna's ear. 'Especially since you're standing directly beneath a sprig of mistletoe.'

She turned her head to see who had spoken. At the sight of Lawson Maddox and his twinkling eyes she gave a blushing smile, and looked up at the mistletoe optimistically.

'May I introduce myself?'

'No, please,' she replied with breathless ambiguity at being taken by such a pleasant surprise.

'Lawson Maddox. I hope you'll pardon me but I've been watching you and, apart from the polka you danced with my friend Mr Robert Cookson, you've been standing alone. I assumed therefore that you are unescorted. Don't you know anybody here?'

'Oh, yes, yes,' she said recklessly. 'I am with others.'

'Are you a relative of Mr or Mrs Cookson?'

'No . . . But I am connected,' she added obscurely. Obviously, he did not know she was merely a servant. And why should she confess it?

'Connected by trade, then? Through your parents, perhaps?'

She gave an indefinite half nod. She had no wish to lie and, she thought, the best way out of answering directly, which would certainly turn her into a liar, was to turn the conversation.

'Isn't that your lady friend dancing with Robert now?' she remarked.

'How do you know she's *my* lady friend?'

'Because I saw you enter with her earlier.'

'Ah. May I dare to hope that you have already been watching me then?'

She smiled enigmatically, to preserve her self-respect, for she could not allow him to think such a thing. 'I've been watching her . . . admiring her dress.'

'Oh.' He returned a dazzling beam that made her insides churn. 'Why is life always so full of disappointments?'

'Is it?' she queried. 'I would have thought life was full of delights. Especially for a man like you.'

'I don't know your name.'

'Rhianna Drake.'

'Did you say *Rhianna*?'

She nodded, and her pleasure at his attention showed in her big blue eyes.

'Now there's a name I've never heard before. It's beautiful. But not half as beautiful as you ... As if you didn't know already.'

Her smile stretched from one ear to the other, showing off her even teeth to good advantage. 'I'm sure it's not true, Mr Maddox, but it's nice of you to say so.'

'Oh, call me Lawson. And it *is* true. You know it is. You and your lovely name are a fine match. You are far and away the loveliest young woman here tonight.'

'Oh, how can you say that?' she answered modestly. 'Your lady friend is very pretty. Far prettier than me.' She was fishing, of course. She was not only fishing for a further compliment, but for information about his relationship with that girl.

'Fanny,' he acknowledged. 'She's not really my young lady, as you call her, in the sense that we are a couple. There's no marital intention, you understand. We're not even romantically linked.'

'But she seems to think the world of you. I've seen how she looks at you.'

'Fanny?' he said incredulously and laughed. 'You're mistaken.'

Well, Rhianna was not about to argue with him, even though she believed he was plainly wrong. Maybe he was just too blind to see it.

'Listen,' he said. 'The band is playing another waltz. Would you allow me the honour?'

She smiled acquiescently and he led her to the floor. He put his hand to her waist and again she felt that surge of blood through her veins that made her temples throb and tied her stomach in knots. Off they went. He was an adept dancer and led her expertly. As they swirled around together he nodded, grinning, to Robert and Fanny as they swished past.

What was it about him that induced this physical reaction

in her? She wanted to curl up in his arms and be pampered by his caresses. She wanted to feel his arms around her all night – every night. She surreptitiously sniffed at him to familiarise herself with the scent of him, something she could remember when he was gone, for she had no doubt at all that she would never see him again after that night.

'Are you local?' he asked as they glided around the floor.

'Oh, yes, can't you tell?' She was in no hurry to pursue the question. 'Are you?'

'Dudley born and bred. I live in a cardboard box under one of the market stalls.'

Rhianna laughed out loud. 'As long as it's warm and comfortable.'

'Oh, all modern conveniences. A tarpaulin to throw over it to keep out the rain and snow, a candle to warm myself by. What more could a man want?'

'Do you live with your family?' she asked seriously.

'In that box?' He kept a straight face while she laughed again. 'As a matter of fact, I've got no family, save for a distant aunt. No, I live by myself. All alone.'

'Oh, I'm sorry.' At once she felt guilty at laughing at what he'd said. 'I had no idea. What happened to them?'

'It's a long story,' he said evasively. 'Maybe I'll tell you when I know you better.'

The dance ended. Two of the trio put down their instruments and began supping their beer, while the other left the pianoforte. Rhianna looked at the clock on the wall. It said ten o'clock. The food was due to be served.

'Will you excuse me?' she said apologetically. She hated parting with this man, but duty called.

'If I must. If you'll promise me a dance later.'

'Oh, I'd love to.'

'So why don't you accompany me in to eat, Rhianna?'

'Oh, er . . . do you mind if I don't? . . . I'll see you later.'

He nodded, looking disappointed. While he waited for

Fanny and Robert to leave the dance floor and rejoin him, Rhianna made her way at once to the dining room. Sarah was there with two other girls, standing behind the trestles, starting to serve the sandwiches, the pickles and the hot pies.

'Is everything all right?' Rhianna asked discreetly.

'Fine,' Sarah said and pressed on with her work conscientiously.

'Good. I'll go to the kitchen and see if Martha needs any help.'

It was the excuse she needed to make herself scarce because she did not want Lawson to see her supervising the maids. It would be obvious that she was employed at Baxter House and thus ruin any chance at all she might have with him. So far, her experiment to pass herself off as a lady had brought a very satisfactory result. In the kitchen Martha had brewed a cup of tea although she had already been supping sherry with Gerald the groom-cum-handyman. Gerald called himself a coachman but Rhianna knew he wasn't paid coachman's wages even though he drove Mr Cookson to and from the iron foundry in his brougham. She poured them each a cup and, while they chatted, began putting the puddings on trays, ready to be taken to the dining room.

After a further quarter of an hour Rhianna gave the instruction to take the puddings to the dining room and stayed chatting with Martha and Gerald. He had to remain on duty to convey certain important guests home afterwards. When Rhianna returned to the party, Mrs Cookson was the first person she saw, red-faced from the heat and too much alcohol.

'Oh, Rhianna, it's all going so well, my dear,' she said excitedly. 'Everybody seems to be enjoying themselves so much.'

Rhianna smiled graciously perceiving it as a compliment. 'Thank you, ma'am. I agree, your efforts don't appear to have been in vain.'

'Is everything under control?'

'Oh, yes, ma'am. Everything's running like clockwork.'

Mrs Cookson looked Rhianna up and down approvingly. 'Then relax a little and enjoy the party.'

'Thank you, ma'am.'

She was not sure quite how far Mrs Cookson meant she could go, for the woman was aware Rhianna had no escort and no other member of staff was allowed access to roam. Parties that involved staff tended to take place below stairs. But, a nod's as good as a wink, she thought, and swept through the guests as if she was one of them.

Lawson saw her enter and intercepted her. 'Rhianna . . .' She smiled warmly at him as he spoke her name. 'Won't you join me with Robert and Fanny?'

'Oh.' She was taken aback at the suggestion. Mr Robert was sure to blow her cover, especially since he had already scorned her. And Miss Fanny Lampitt was hardly likely to welcome her as a sister-in-arms when she'd been dancing closely with the man she so obviously adored despite Lawson's denial. 'Do you mind if I don't?' Rhianna asked. 'I would rather not be in the company of Robert.'

He glanced over his shoulder at his two companions, and shrugged. 'I reckon they can keep each other entertained, don't you? Shall we dance together a while?'

She smiled, lowering her lids. 'If you think they won't mind you abandoning them.'

His eyes sparkled with the reflection of the gas lights that shone so brightly. 'I would ask you to accompany me outside to take a walk, but I suspect the weather would incline you to decline that offer as well.'

She would have gone out into the cold night gladly, just to be alone with him, but the prospect of fetching her hat and coat from her room and sneaking out of the house without permission presented too many potential pitfalls.

'So let's dance,' she said, tilting her head girlishly, and allowed herself to be led onto the floor again.

She was in his arms once more. They were laughing and he made her feel as if she were the most important, most desirable girl in the world. She forgot about Fanny, she forgot about Mr Robert; whether he and Fanny were dancing together she did not know and cared even less. She was entirely focused on Lawson. He was so amusing and so direct. She hung on his every word, laughed at his every quip, and began to feel possessive, even so soon after they had met.

'I'd love to see you alone sometime,' he said and, all of a sudden, her legs felt wobbly and she feared she would lose control of them. 'Is there any chance of that?'

Was there any chance! 'That would be lovely.' She rapidly considered the options. 'I would be free next Sunday afternoon.'

'But Rhianna! So long to wait.' He looked sullen with disappointment. 'I don't know if I can stand it.'

'I'm not free before then.'

'How elusive you are! Are you in such demand? Ah, well. They say good things are worth waiting for. I'll collect you Sunday then, in my cabriolet. You must give me your address.'

She smiled agreeably. 'So how long have you known Fanny?' Rhianna was perceiving her more as a great rival with every minute that passed.

'A year, maybe longer.'

'How did you meet?'

'We were introduced.'

'But she can't be any more than nineteen,' Rhianna suggested.

'Eighteen, if you want to be precise.'

'So she was seventeen when you met her?'

'Yes, I suppose she might have been. Possibly even sixteen. I forget.'

'Where did you meet her?'

'Oh, at a Band of Hope temperance meeting, I think . . .'

She looked at him with disbelief. 'Honestly?' She saw

humour dancing in his eyes. 'You're mocking me. I've seen you drinking . . . and her.'

'Well, I've already told you we're not romantically linked, but you persist in asking questions as if we are.'

'*You* might not be romantically linked,' Rhianna replied, aware that her jealousy was surfacing, 'but *she* is.'

'So you said before. Well, if she's got such preoccupations, that's her concern.'

She was happy to hear it. It confirmed that Fanny had no prior claim on him.

All too soon their dancing was interrupted. The New Year was about to be greeted and everybody was expected to link hands and sing 'Auld Lang Syne'. They lost each other in the mêlée while everybody was hugging the person closest to them, shaking hands and giving their sincere best wishes for a happy and prosperous 1889. Rhianna decided she must go and check on the soup that would already be heating up in the kitchen to be served later . . . until she realised in a blind panic that she had not finalised the arrangement to meet Lawson. She spotted him, shoved through the noisy crowd of revellers and tapped him on the shoulder.

'I'm sorry, I have to go.'

'You're leaving already?'

'I have to. Do you still want to meet me on Sunday?' Maybe she was being forward, but she was desperate not let him go now she had found him.

'I'll call for you. Just tell me your address.'

'It would be better if I met you somewhere . . . You know . . .' She wanted him to think it might be embarrassing with her family, or even frowned on to be seen going out without a chaperone. 'Can we meet outside the police station?'

'All right. Shall we say three o'clock?'

'Three o'clock, Sunday.' She turned and made her way to the kitchen, extraordinarily pleased with herself.

*   *   *

By the time they had cleared up after the party it was nearly four o'clock in the morning but it had been a huge success for the Cooksons and a personal triumph for Rhianna. She had met the man of her dreams and was euphoric. She couldn't sleep, of course she couldn't. She lay awake for what remained of that cold night thinking about him, going over and over in her mind every word they had spoken to each other. After she'd bid him goodnight she made it her business not to be seen again, staying in the kitchen till everybody had gone. It peeved her beyond endurance to know that Lawson must, out of etiquette, deliver Fanny back home and she imagined with resentment those big, soft pleading eyes, begging for a goodnight kiss. She tossed and turned imagining them kissing, imagining her trying to lead him on. How come a girl of eighteen was allowed out, alone with him, without a chaperone?

Then she remembered her assessment of Fanny. Fanny was not from polite society. Fanny was a working-class girl. It was even possible that her mother and father neither knew nor cared where she was, or whom she was with. But if so, what was somebody so obviously well-bred and well-educated as Lawson Maddox doing with her? She had to be a cousin or a niece whom he considered worthy enough to reward with such an evening out. Perhaps he had even invited her just to introduce her to Mr Robert. After all, they danced together quite a lot, and certainly seemed to laugh a lot. Rhianna felt happier with this perfectly rational explanation.

3

New Year's Day fell on a Tuesday in 1889. Following the party as it did, it promised to be busy. A few guests had stayed the night so there were more people than usual for breakfast. The beds they slept in had to be stripped and remade, chamber pots emptied and scalded, the rooms they occupied cleaned and dusted. But, after lunch, when the visitors left, things were expected to settle down. Lots of sandwiches and pies remained uneaten from the previous evening and Mrs Cookson asked Rhianna to organise one of the girls to take the leftovers to the Dudley Union Workhouse in Burton Road. There would be many a poor soul there glad of the extra food. Rhianna offered to go and requested an extra hour besides, so as to visit her mother and father.

'As long as you're back here by five I have no objection, Rhianna,' Mrs Cookson said kindly. 'Do you think your sister might like to accompany you?'

'Oh, I'm sure she would, ma'am, if you could spare her.' Rhianna was forever surprised at how generous and thoughtful that lady could be.

'I hope your father's feeling better. No doubt it'll perk him up to see his two daughters on New Year's Day. Give them both my very best wishes and compliments of the season.'

'Oh, I will, ma'am, and thank you.'

So, at about half-past two, she and Sarah set off. They huddled into their coats and pulled up their collars to protect themselves from the cold. Shaver's End, on the way to the workhouse, was one of the highest ridges in Dudley and a cold east wind, howling in with unhindered keenness directly from the Urals of Russia, penetrated their layers of clothing and chilled their skin.

As they walked they talked about the party and discussed some of the guests.

'Did you notice that friend of Mr Robert's I told you about?' Sarah asked, clutching her collar to her throat to keep out the cold, a basket of food hanging in the crook of her arm.

'Oh . . . er . . . Which one was that?' Rhianna hedged.

'The tall, handsome one. You must've seen him. I told you about him. Remember?'

It suddenly dawned on Rhianna that she meant Lawson Maddox. It had never occurred to her that Lawson might be the same friend of Mr Robert Sarah had mentioned before. She feigned ignorance.

'I don't recall,' she lied. She wanted to say he was far too old for Sarah but could acknowledge nothing about him.

'Oh, you'd remember him all right. I served him his food. He's a dream . . . He had a girl with him, though.'

'Oh,' Rhianna said trying to affect disinterest. 'Hardly surprising if he's so handsome.'

'A pretty girl, I thought, with lovely fair hair. But he wants to watch out because Mr Robert was all over her.' Sarah shrugged and a smug grin spread across her face. 'Still, I don't mind if he pinches her off him. Then he'd be free to marry me.'

'You know gentlemen don't marry servants,' Rhianna said impatiently and, as soon as she had said it, she realised that this sage remark applied equally to herself. Her unwitting wisdom depressed her. Of course gentlemen didn't marry servants. Oh, they would bed maids at every opportunity, but marry them? . . . 'Which basket have you got there, Sarah?'

'The one with the pies and sausage rolls in.'

'Right. We'll swap some over. Mother and Father can have some of this stuff. They're just as deserving.'

They stopped and, resting their baskets on a wall, sorted out the food so that they had a decent selection to give to their folks. By this time they were only a couple of hundred yards from the workhouse.

'I'll take this stuff in, our Sarah. You wait at the gate.'

Rhianna asked to see somebody in authority. Unless she handed over the food to somebody trustworthy the poor folk in care might never see it. Eventually she let it go to a shy young man in a frock coat who was unsure of her at first, but who thanked her liberally when he realised she was not a gypsy trying to peddle something.

She returned to Sarah. It was a long walk to their home and unbearable in the biting cold. They took it in turns to carry the basket of food that also contained some oranges Rhianna had been able to sneak out. Sarah didn't mention Lawson again but it was evident she was taken with him. How could Rhianna have confessed to Sarah that he already had an interest in her and she in him, despite her private realisation that any liaison was doomed from the start? She hoped that Sarah's was just a young girl's infatuation which she would forget as soon as the next handsome young man appeared. In truth, she hoped her own interest was an infatuation just as silly, and that she would get over it as quickly.

At last they arrived and walked up the entry to the back door, their cheeks red, their noses cold and shiny, and their breath coming in steamy wisps. As they opened the door and walked in, their father was nodding in his armchair, his gouty foot in his washing basket. He roused when he heard them greet their mother.

Rhianna bent down and kissed him on the cheek. 'Happy New Year, Father,' she said. 'How are you feeling?'

'Bloody lousy,' he replied grumpily.

'It's your age,' Mary remarked without sympathy.

'Is it snowing yet? There's snow in the air, I can bloody well feel it.'

Rhianna placed the basket of food on the scrubbed table. 'Not yet, Father. We've brought you some food left over from the party last night at Baxter House.' She turned to her mother, tilting her head in his direction. 'How is he really?'

'Miserable as sin.' She was darning several pairs of socks and had a darning mushroom thrust inside one of them as if she was about to draw the innards from a rabbit. 'I daren't get near him for fear of kicking his washing basket. I've a good mind to kick him up in the air.'

'Pity yower damn nose ai' throbbing like my blasted foot,' Titus protested, feeling very sorry for himself. 'Then yo' wouldn't keep pokin' it where it ai' wanted.'

Both girls chuckled at this bickering, which they knew was mostly pretence and nowhere near as venomous as it sounded.

'Well tomorrer morning I don't know what you'll do wi' yer God foot, but I shall want me basket back for the washing.'

'But it's Wednesday tomorrow,' Rhianna said. 'I thought washing day was Monday.'

Mary chuckled. 'Oh, ain't I a blasted fool? It's 'cause you've come. I was thinking it's Sunday today.'

Titus, typically casual, lifted one cheek of his backside, grimaced and broke wind raucously. 'There, catch that and darn it,' he said scornfully.

'Father!' Sarah and Rhianna complained in unison.

Their mother picked up a cushion and fanned the tainted air back in his direction. 'Dirty varmint.'

Sarah rolled her eyes and giggled. 'Shall I put some coal on the fire for you, Mother?'

'If you've a mind, my wench. Mind how much you put on, though. There's on'y another bucket or two left in the cellar.'

'But it's bitter cold out,' Rhianna said. 'You need to keep warm.'

'We'll have to wrap up then. We'll have to put an extra ganzy on apiece.'

As Sarah made up the fire Rhianna felt in her pocket for

her purse, opened it and sorted through the coins. 'Here's a shilling.' She offered a sixpence and two silver threepenny bits to her mother. 'It's all I've got for now. Take the handcart to the coal yard in the morning and get half a hundredweight at least. Promise me you will.'

'I don't need a shilling for half a hundredweight of coal.'

'Then buy some bread or cheese or something with the change.'

'The rent's due Monday . . . But I'n got a bit put by in me jar to pay for that.'

'Are you short?' Rhianna asked.

'We'll manage.'

'Look, I shan't be able to come on Sunday but I'll give Sarah some money to bring you.'

'Oh? What you doing on Sunday then?' Sarah asked.

Rhianna cast her a guilty glance as Sarah passed by on her way outside to the brewhouse to wash her hands. 'I've been asked to tea somewhere.'

'Oh, very nice,' her mother said with pride in her tone. 'So when shall we see yer?'

Titus started coughing before Rhianna could answer. He hawked blood into a piece of newspaper, screwed it up and tossed it into the fire. She noticed it with horror.

'Has the doctor been lately?'

'We got no money to pay for doctors, our Rhianna,' Mary replied flatly. 'Not since you paid last time.'

'I'll pay again,' she said without hesitation. 'Coughing up blood means his consumption's no better and might even be worse. He needs medicine.'

'You've paid enough. Rest, fresh air, fresh fruit and vegetables is what he needs. That's what the doctor said last time he come. It's senseless paying to be told the same thing over again. It's senseless to waste money.'

'But he needs to go into a sanatorium out in the country . . . to clean air.'

'I'm a-gooin' into ne'er a sanatorium,' Titus mumbled, opening his eyes then shutting them again.

'I thought you was asleep,' Mary said.

It was time to turn the conversation, so Rhianna passed on Mrs Cookson's good wishes and told them about the party at Baxter House. Mary was enthralled, but Titus drifted back to sleep again. Sarah made a pot of tea and they drank it while Mary related her gossip. Darkness was falling and Rhianna lifted the lamp off its hook. She gave it a shake to discern whether there was any oil in it, then lit it with a spill that she had kindled in the fire.

'Have you got any more lamp oil?'

'I think there's a drop in the brewhouse, in a can.'

'I'll see if I can bring you some more. Have you got any candles in case you run out?'

'Oh, hark at her,' Mary complained. 'Have you got this, have you got that. Course I got candles. I ain't altogether helpless, you know.'

Rhianna sighed. The last thing she wanted was to appear fussing like some nuisance busybody. 'It's just that I don't want you to be without. I worry about you two. It's cold out there and it won't pick up for months yet.' By the light of the lamp she could just see the hands of the clock on the mantelpiece; it was nearly half-past four. 'Lord, look at the time. It's time we went, Mother. Sarah and I have to be back by five.'

Sunday seemed forever in coming. Every time Rhianna thought about Lawson and their tryst her stomach churned. She worried about what she should wear, when her only choices to keep out the cold would be her best Sunday dress, her warm winter coat, her scarf and her hat. Whether she should confess from the outset that she was a servant at the home of his friend Robert Cookson also bothered her, but she decided she would confess no such thing – not yet, at any rate. She was intent on first being driven like a lady in his beautiful two-wheeled cabriolet he'd mentioned. She really wanted to play the part of a lady, wanted to be wooed like a lady and held in great esteem, if only for the short time she might be able to deceive him.

On Sunday mornings Rhianna always went to church, walking to St Thomas's with those maids whose turn it was to go also, while the family travelled in their smart brougham. That Sunday it was damp, misty and cold but the snow her father predicted had not materialised. As they walked and talked their breath hung like steam in the still winter air. Rhianna sat in the pew at the back of the church with the other girls and Gerald the groom. She heard barely any of the service. Her eyes were fixed on the huge and colourful rendering on glass of the Ascension that was the east window, but her thoughts were focused solely on Lawson Maddox. Like an automaton she stood up for hymns, knelt for prayers and sat down for the lessons. She was still reliving the dances they'd enjoyed, the words they'd exchanged, cherishing every blessed moment, nurturing the beautiful memory, hopeful and yet apprehensive about their rendezvous, which was still nearly four hours away.

They returned to Baxter House, served dinner and the family retired to the drawing room. Rhianna's eyes were riveted to the clock. She was feeling all jittery inside. At half past two she went to her room unnoticed, adjusted a curl, reset a couple of grips in her hair and reddened her lips with a few hard bites. Then she put on her hat, her coat, her scarf and her best gloves and, at ten minutes to three, left the house by the back door.

The police station where Rhianna was to meet Lawson faced an open square where a market was held regularly. On the adjacent corner, where it met Stone Street, stood a public house called the Saracen's Head. As she waited, it occurred to her that Lawson might not turn up after all, especially if that bounder Mr Robert had enlightened him as to her true status. But, when she looked across the road and saw a beautiful black horse between the shafts of an immaculate black cabriolet standing outside the Saracen's Head, she prayed that it was his and that he was intending to turn up after all.

He did. Rhianna saw him leave the public house and he scanned the street. When he saw her he smiled and beckoned her over. She hitched up her skirts a little and hurried to him, picking her way over the cobblestones to avoid the slurry that ran murkily between them. Her heart was in her mouth, but there was a smile on her face as she presented herself before him and stood transfixed.

'Been waiting long?' he asked and his smile was warm on her.

Rhianna shook her head, the smile never leaving her face. She was so happy to see him. She had waited so long for this moment, with such trepidation. But just seeing his face, just experiencing his warm glow of friendship, made her feel quite at ease.

'What are we going to do?'

'Hop in,' he said and handed her up onto the cabriolet.

He clambered in beside her, and the two-wheeled carriage rocked gently on its springs. He clicked to the horse, flicked the reins and they set off towards Wolverhampton Street.

'Where are we going?'

'I thought you might enjoy a little run out,' he replied turning to her and she caught a whiff of alcohol on his steamy breath. 'I have a bit of business to attend to.'

'Oh?'

'Tenants of mine . . . One owes me three months' rent. I know I'll catch him with his feet up at this time of a Sunday. You don't mind my mixing business with pleasure, do you, Rhianna?'

He'd remembered her name. She swelled with satisfaction.

'No, course not . . . Is it far?' Secretly she hoped it would not be; she was cold and damp already from the dismal January mist and drizzle. But she did not mind so much, just as long as she was with him.

'No, not far. So . . . what have you been doing with yourself all week?'

'Oh, not much,' she answered with the nonchalance of a lady of leisure.

She realised she must have sounded inanely boring. She could have told him she had been on tenterhooks the whole time waiting for this moment. She could have told him about going to the Union Workhouse, visiting her mother and sick father. She could have told him how poor Martha the cook had scalded herself when she spilled boiling water on Friday, or how her sister Sarah had crowed all week about how wonderfully handsome he was. She could have told him about the problem they'd had at Baxter House with a young maid who had been employed on her recommendation last November, who was connected with a burglary they'd had on Thursday. Nothing much had been taken but that which had required knowledge of the house and that knowledge had come from within; it had to be from her. The maid admitted she had given information to the young man, her beau, who was already known to the police. But Rhianna told him none of this, of course.

'What about you?' she asked brightly. 'Been working hard?'

'Working?' he said, as if it were a dirty word. 'I don't work. At least, not in the sense that I own a factory or a farm that needs running. I purport to be a gentleman, Rhianna. I keep busy. I do business. I let others work.'

She smiled, too reticent to ask more.

Lawson turned to look at a young man and woman who were walking in their direction. 'Well, I'll be damned. So *he's* stepping out with *her*.'

'Should I know them?'

'I sincerely hope not,' he replied.

He offered no explanation as to who the two people were

but flicked the reins and the horse broke into a trot. She could hear the dabs of slurry flung from the horse's hooves hitting the underside of the running board.

'Has anybody ever told you you have the most beautiful, kissable mouth?'

'No,' she answered coyly and smiled. She was aware of seeming to be forever smiling when she was with Lawson.

'Honest? I'm surprised. You have, you know.'

'I never thought about it,' she responded.

'So what would you consider your best feature?'

She shrugged and giggled with girlish embarrassment. 'I don't know. I'm not even sure it's the right thing to ask a young lady.'

'Oh?'

'Well, whatever I answer, you could say I was being conceited. I don't think I'm conceited.'

He laughed at that, not mockingly, but genuinely pleased. 'I applaud that answer, Rhianna. You're a smart girl.'

'Thank you.'

'I'm serious. I do admire intelligence in a woman.'

They turned into a road called Southall's Lane, a ramshackle street of old red-brick buildings. Rhianna anticipated that they might drive past the Spencers' house in Wellington Road. She wondered what the Spencers would make of her if they saw her beside this handsome man in his smart cabriolet. She was sorry when they turned left again into Stafford Street.

'We're here,' Lawson said as he headed the horse into another narrow lane called Albert Street. On the left was a terrace of small houses, not very old. 'Wait in the buggy. I won't be long.'

Rhianna nodded and smiled and settled herself in the seat. She adjusted her scarf to benefit from the warmth and waited. So he owned a house here. A man of property. How many others did he have? As she waited, two boys ambled past, scruffy, dirty. They kept turning to look at her, making Lord knows what comments and giggling.

Lawson was about five minutes.

'That bastard!' he rasped when he returned, and there was a look of thunder on his face. 'He owed me thirty-nine shillings. All I could get out of him was a sovereign. But I'll be back next week. And he knows he'd better have the money by then or he'll be evicted.'

He jumped agitatedly into the cabriolet and flicked the reins. They went forward no further than twenty-five yards and stopped again.

'Now for that Molly Kettle.' He jumped down again. 'She owes more than is good for her. Spends it all on gin, the sot. Shan't be a minute.'

Maybe he owned all the houses in the terrace. Rhianna determined to ask him, even though it was none of her business. But if he was putting on this show of ownership to impress her, he would not mind her asking. A young girl of about thirteen appeared from the house Lawson was visiting, obviously come out to inspect her. She was very dainty, with long, dark hair that framed a lovely, angelic face. The girl smiled appealingly but soon went back into the house, clutching herself around the shoulders to ward off the cold. Rhianna felt an affinity with her, recalling her own youth before she went into service. The girl reminded her so much of herself at thirteen.

'Who was that young girl?' Rhianna asked when Lawson returned.

'Oh, one of Molly Kettle's daughters.'

'She's very pretty.'

'Yes, I suppose she is.'

Rhianna said, 'Do you mind if I ask you something?'

'Depends what it is?'

'How many houses in this terrace do you own?'

He laughed. 'All of them. And more besides.'

'Well, well. Lawson Maddox, the great landlord,' she commented. 'Are you a kind and understanding landlord?'

'Am I hell!' he guffawed. 'There's no sentiment in business – and that's what it is – business.' Once more he flicked the reins and the horse hauled them away. 'And these wretched peasants will try and fleece you for the last penny . . . But enough of them. Now I'm going to take you somewhere warm. I bet you're frozen solid.'

She nodded and shivered at the same time.

'Thanks for being so patient . . . Giddup!'

The horse broke into a trot once more and they headed back towards the centre of the town. Eventually, they drew up at the fountain in the market place and Lawson let the horse drink before he tethered it. He handed Rhianna down and took her arm as he led her towards the Dudley Arms Hotel.

'A drink will warm you,' he said. 'And there'll be a good fire in the saloon.'

He saw that she was reticent about going in there but he smiled reassuringly. She needed little persuading; the thought of a warm fire and a drop of some smooth, warming drink inside her was very appealing.

'What would you like?' he asked as he sat her at a table close to the fire.

She remembered that Fanny had asked for port when she arrived at the party. 'Port, please.'

Lawson went to the bar and came back with her port and a glass of whisky for himself. He sat beside her and looked into her eyes.

'I've been looking forward to this,' he said in an intimate whisper. 'Getting you on your own and having you all to myself.'

Rhianna smiled happily. She held his admiring gaze while her legs seemed to turn into jelly.

'I can see now it's not just your mouth that's beautiful. Those eyes . . . Good God, they sparkle more brightly than fine-cut

46

sapphires. I was trying to remember what it was about you that first attracted me. I think it was your whole demeanour but especially your mouth. I just wanted to kiss your lips, to taste them, to feel how soft they were on mine. Do you remember, I warned you you were standing under the mistletoe?'

Her stomach started to churn as if a belfry full of bats was flitting madly about inside when she thought about him kissing her. Then he put his hand on hers and her heart started thumping against her ribs, just to augment the internal agitation. And, just to top it off, her face reddened at his words.

'Such a virtuous blush,' he said, squeezing her hand.

She coloured even deeper and sipped her port to try and hide her face. She felt its rich, sweet smoothness as it slid down her throat. 'I imagine it's not the first time you've said that to a girl,' she suggested.

He shrugged. 'Maybe not. But I've never meant it more than I do now. Tell me about your family, Rhianna. I'm dying to find out about you.'

'I'd much rather hear about you,' she replied deliberately trying to sidetrack him. 'You promised you'd tell me what happened to your family.'

'I said I'd tell you when I knew you better. I can't honestly say I know you any better now than I did on New Year's Eve. I've only spent a half hour with you yet. Tell me about yourself first.'

Rhianna sighed, a deep heaving sigh. What should she tell him? That she was a working-class girl from the terraced houses of lowly Campbell Street and in the service of his friends the Cooksons – and lose him? Or should she lie and say she was the only daughter of a wealthy ironmaster and heiress to his fortune, and maintain the deception for what little time it took to be found out, and then be deservedly cast aside for it? Despite her romantic fancies, she always believed that it paid to be honest. Her father told her once that in order to keep up deceit you need a damned good memory. So she decided to tell Lawson the truth. If he was about to rejected her because of her working-class status he might as well admire her for her honesty. And this early on her aching heart would more easily mend after the rejection.

'I'm a nobody, Lawson,' she began, gazing blankly into the ruby depths of the port. 'My father was an iron puddler at the Woodside Iron Works . . .' She felt herself trembling. 'I'm just a housekeeper at the house of your friends, the Cooksons. My younger sister is a maid there. That night we met I was on duty but . . . but Mrs Cookson said I could stay and enjoy the party.' She looked earnestly into his eyes. 'I really enjoyed your company, Lawson . . . I so enjoyed dancing with you . . .'

He let go her hand and her heart sank into her boots. To disguise her embarrassment she sipped her port. But when she put her glass back on the table he took her hand again. She looked forlornly into his eyes.

'It's all right,' he whispered with his easy smile. 'I already knew.'

'So you were testing me.'

He nodded.

'Oh,' she said.

'It makes no odds to me who you are, or who you ain't. At least you're honest. You're not like the others. You're different. You're chaste, you have honour. Many of those who consider themselves well-bred lack those very virtues.'

'But now I feel naked in front of you,' she said self-consciously. 'I feel exposed and vulnerable.'

'Then let me denude myself. Let's be naked together . . .'

His steely blue eyes seemed to pierce hers and she could barely hold his gaze at this astonishing innuendo. An erotic picture materialised in her mind's eye of the two of them standing naked in front of each other, and it seemed he could see into her head and read what she was thinking with that steady, unnerving look of his.

'I have no breeding either,' he said frankly. 'So I'm not shackled by the constraints and prejudices of the gentry. I'm the son of a corn merchant, Rhianna. My mother died giving birth to me and I was brought up by my father till I was ten. Then he died. Fortunately for me, he'd been an enterprising soul and he left me half a dozen properties in trust. His executors made sure that the income from them paid for my schooling and my board. When I was twenty-one I took control of those properties and, by being enterprising myself, I've added to them. Now I earn a pretty penny, and my enterprises have brought me into contact with many wealthy families, such as the Cooksons.'

'Thank you,' she breathed.

He looked at her puzzled. 'You're thanking me? For what?'

'For accepting me for what I am. For being honest about yourself. I was afraid to tell you the truth about myself for fear you . . .'

'For fear I what?'

She shook her head. She could not say what she wanted to say because it would have sounded too presumptuous.

'For fear I would reject you?'

She nodded and looked into her port again.

'I'd be a fool if I did, Rhianna. You're a gem.'

4

Rhianna's life had suddenly changed and she existed in a delightful romantic dream. Oh, she was profoundly in love, and no mistake. And the first signs were brilliant. Lawson seemed as taken with her as she was with him. She could hardly believe her good fortune. They'd only met a few days earlier – but already she had an illogical yet compelling fancy that they might indeed progress further. She would not let herself think beyond that, however. She did not have the courage to contemplate herself as mistress of her own home, supporting him in his business enterprises, ordering about her own servants, choosing new furnishings and smart new clothes for herself; it was all too much to hope for. It was too much to envisage herself in a position where she could materially help her mother and father. To have wished for all that and ultimately have it denied would have been too great a disappointment to bear.

So she tried to look no further than their next assignation. It was to be on her evening off, on Wednesday. Like the Sunday before, it seemed an eternity coming. It was a cold evening but dry. As she walked up St James's Road to meet him she looked up at the sky and saw how clear it was. There would be a hard frost that night.

Once again she had arranged to meet Lawson outside the police station and once again his cabriolet was standing outside the Saracen's Head, the fine black horse tethered to a gas lamp. Once again he beckoned her to join him and, once again, she skipped biddably across the road to be at his side, her heart in her mouth.

'Maybe we should arrange to meet outside the Saracen's,' she suggested lightly.

He smiled genially. 'Or even inside.'

Once again she could smell drink on his breath.

'Where are you taking me?'

'Jump in.' He handed her up into the carriage. As she settled herself, he untethered the horse, got in beside her, flicked the reins and turned the carriage around in the street. 'Fancy some cockfighting?'

'Cockfighting?' At once she was suspicious. 'I thought cockfighting was illegal.'

He laughed irreverently. 'Lots of things are illegal, Rhianna. That doesn't stop 'em going on.'

'Are you serious? You're not serious? You're going to take me to a cockfight?'

'You'll love it. It's great sport. Great fighting spirit those birds have . . . I'll let you into a secret . . . I have a financial interest.'

She wanted to ask in what way but thought it best not to poke her nose in. For a few seconds she was quiet, wishing to be taken anywhere but a cockfight, for she knew she would loathe it.

'I've missed you, Rhianna,' he said, and his welcome remark was the direct hit of an arrow from Cupid's bow. 'I've thought about you a lot since Sunday.'

'Have you honestly?' Suddenly, her eyes brightened, delighted that he should admit it.

'The only problem was that I couldn't picture your face in my mind's eye. Let me have a good look at you.'

As he drove he turned to look at her in the puny light from the town's gas lamps. She tilted her face towards him with a self-conscious smile and was aware of involuntarily blinking.

'Your eyes,' he said. 'So beautiful. So clear. I've been dreaming about your eyes.' They turned right, into High Street then came to a halt by the crossroads. 'Here we are.'

'It was hardly worth getting in the gig,' Rhianna commented. 'We could have walked.'

'Why walk when we have a fine trap like this?'

They stopped outside a drab coaching house called the Old Bush. Rhianna looked at it with apprehension. She recalled when she was a child her father telling her that the 'Tally-Ho' coach used to leave this inn every day for Birmingham and London. It was not the sort of establishment a wholesome young woman would consider frequenting and she mentioned this to Lawson.

'You're with me, Rhianna. People respect me. They won't think any the less of you for being here. Anyway, it's likely you won't know anybody anyway, so it won't matter.'

Thus chided, she followed him inside. In the public bar he asked her what she would like to drink.

'Port,' she said.

'A port and brandy – your best,' he ordered from the bartender.

'I only asked for a port,' she protested meekly.

'It's cold out there in the yard. The brandy will keep you warm.'

'In the yard?'

He looked at her patiently and smiled. 'Yes, in the yard. There'll be a ring for the birds to fight in, with seats all around. There's no room inside suitable for cockfighting . . . Thanks,' he said, turning to the bartender. 'And a large whisky . . .'

'But if it's outside in the yard, won't some bobby hear what's going on when he does his rounds?'

'Be assured, Rhianna,' he said, whispering into her ear, 'the beat bobby will turn a deaf ear.'

He handed her the port and brandy, which she sipped gingerly, then he took the watch out of his waistcoat fob and looked at the time.

'We'll finish these then go into the yard. Proceedings are due to start at eight.'

Rhianna could feel the brandy warming her and was thankful for it. She looked around her. She felt grossly out of place in that smoke-filled bar, even with Lawson at her side. Although she was working-class herself she did not feel any empathy at all with the folk that surrounded her. They were not her equals. Most were ill-kempt, ill-mannered and rough. They yelled at each other across the room, they coughed asthmatically and spat rudely into spittoons that lay at strategic locations on the sawdust floor. Those folk closest to her stank, as if they hadn't had a decent wash down for months. She longed to go outside into the fresh air of the yard, cold or not, so finished her drink much sooner than she normally would.

'Another?' Lawson asked kindly.

She nodded. 'Please. Then can we go outside? I don't like it in here. Some of these folk smell.' She wrinkled her nose to emphasise her point. 'There must be a big opportunity to sell tin baths in this town, but nobody's addressing it, I reckon. Maybe you should, Lawson, since you're so enterprising.'

He laughed at her derision and paid for the drinks. She was led through a door at the back of the room, down a dismal passage and through another door. Already, about forty men and women were assembled, some standing, some sitting, arguing, laughing, hooting and bawling, nearly all smoking. As soon as one of the men saw Lawson he stepped up to him, shook his hand and led him to a bench that was evidently reserved for him. Other men acknowledged him deferentially as if he were the local squire, then looked Rhianna up and down curiously. She could feel men's leering eyes following her as she followed Lawson to their bench.

'Tasty bit o' fanny that,' she heard one man say.

'Trust Lawson Maddox to come up with the goods,' his companion replied venerably.

She smiled to herself as she sat down. Never had she considered for a moment that Lawson was entirely without sin. He was too good-looking and far too outgoing to have led a sheltered life. Perhaps he'd left a string of broken-hearted lovers behind him. That didn't bother her at all. Men were men and the more women they knew before marriage, the better. It was the way of the world. Even she understood that. The thing that pleased her was that right now Lawson was with *her*, nobody else. However many women he'd known, *she* was the one in his company that night. It was a stimulating thought. She thought of Fanny who wore her heart on her sleeve. Of course Rhianna wanted Lawson to want her more than he'd wanted all the others, Fanny included, but the greatest stimulation came from knowing that all those other women must have desired him as much as she did herself, and that confirmed her own good taste. It also strengthened her determination to make him her own for all time, to make certain he wanted nobody else.

She turned to him and smiled, her eyes sparkling with adoration. 'Tell me about cockfighting,' she said. 'Explain how it works.'

'You'll soon catch on. It's just fowl trying to tear each other to shreds. Mind you, you have to realise they're bred for it. Tonight it's a Welsh main—'

'Main?'

'Contest. In a Welsh main we pair off sixteen birds. The eight winners are then paired off to decide the two semi-finals. Then there's a fight between the best two birds left, to decide the ultimate winner. There'll be plenty of betting going on, especially as we approach the final. I shall be taking bets.'

'You?'

He leaned towards her and put his mouth to her ear. 'Easy money.' He pulled out his watch again and checked the time.

Rhianna saw men carrying their birds in wicker baskets, like the ones pigeon fanciers used. One or two opened the lids and she saw them attaching what looked like knives to the backward-facing claws of the birds.

'What are they fixing to the birds' feet?' she asked, nodding in the direction of the handlers.

'Gaffs. They're like spikes. Sometimes they use knives . . . To try and cut the other cock to pieces.'

'Ugh, that's terrible!' Rhianna protested. 'No wonder it's illegal. You surely don't expect me to sit and watch it, do you?'

'I told you, you'll be all right.'

She had not noticed a queue forming in the gap between the benches at Lawson's side. Those men who could write, and women too, were handing him slips of paper and coins. The money, he pocketed, the slips of paper he handed to Rhianna with an aside to sort them by the name of the bird and to keep a tight hold of them.

'That'll keep your mind off the cockfight,' he said.

There were such names as Vulcan, Phoenix, Golden Eagle III, and others, all stupidly pretentious names as far as she was concerned. She sipped her drink and accepted another slip of paper; Razor Bill was the name written on that five-shilling bet.

Very soon the meeting was called to order by the pitmaster, who sat astride a chair, facing the wrong way. The chair's back had a lectern like a desktop attached to it. Rhianna realised it was a library chair, but the incongruity of its use that night, compared with the more cultured purpose for which it had been made, struck her. He announced the commencement of the spectacle and the first two cocks were brought into the ring by their owners. The shinning metal gaffs were already strapped to the birds' legs. The two men held the cocks face to face, bill to bill, for a few seconds and the poor birds quickly became very agitated. A sudden murmur from the crowd told her that the men had let go the cocks. As they attacked each other ferociously there was a roar. Feathers flew as they flailed at each other, jumping in the air, wings flapping, as they each tried to inflict fatal injury to the other with those deadly metal spikes. At the first sight of blood the men and women screamed even louder at the two victims, which was how Rhianna viewed both birds, irrespective of which one might survive. One bird fell over and seemed to submit. There were groans from some of the crowd and frenzied cheers from others. The handlers stepped into the ring again, picked up the birds and thrust them together once more, breast to breast, until they were both agitated enough to continue fighting. One of the cocks was badly cut and bleeding but it did not curb his will to overcome his opponent. The handlers let go the birds and they went on as before, squawking and thrashing in a rain of feathers. After another minute or so, the injured cock collapsed. The first fight was over.

'I can't watch any more of this,' Rhianna complained.

But Lawson affected not to hear her as people swarmed around him to collect their winnings. He took the slips of paper that bore the name of the winning cock from Rhianna and smiled affably as he paid out to those who had won. Another queue formed, of people wanting to place bets on the outcome of the next fight.

'Do you want a bet on the next fight?' he asked her and she wondered whether he was joking.

'You're not taking my money,' she answered defiantly.

'Take my advice and place a guinea on Razor Bill. And let it ride in an accumulator.'

She had no idea what he was talking about but it all sounded very foolhardy. 'I haven't got a guinea, Lawson. And if I had, I wouldn't squander it on a bet. And certainly *not* on one of those poor birds.'

He smiled equably. 'Then I'll lend you a guinea. If Razor Bill wins – and I reckon he's got a good chance – you can pay me back.'

'Do I have to pay you back the winnings as well.'

'No, course not. You can keep the winnings.'

Rhianna smiled at him. This sounded more interesting. 'Then I've got nothing to lose.'

He nodded, his eyes warm on her. 'You're catching on. Of course you've got nothing to lose.' He handed her a blacklead pencil. 'Write yourself a slip for a guinea accumulator.'

She did as she was bidden.

Razor Bill was next on, his first fight against Vulcan. To her utmost surprise, she found herself watching with interest. Razor Bill, his little eyes gleaming, attacked several times, found his mark and drew blood. But before the other bird could use his gaffs Razor Bill knowingly withdrew. Poor Vulcan was game enough but not in the same league. Eventually he collapsed and Razor Bill was declared the winner.

'The money you've won will go on his next fight, and so on,' Lawson said.

'What if he loses his next fight?'

'You've still lost nothing.'

Between fights Rhianna saw people go inside the house and come out eating hot pies, the aroma of which drifted across to her and made her feel hungry on that cold, frosty night. But she could not eat, not with all that blood and gore from those poor mutilated fowl. And yet, with each fight her horror diminished. She was becoming desensitised to the horrifying ruin the cocks inflicted on each other. She even found herself on the side of certain fowl and actually cheered them on along with the rest off the bawling spectators, to Lawson's great amusement and satisfaction.

She could hardly wait for Razor Bill's next fight. When it came, he won that as well and she was cock-a-hoop. He won the semi-final too and she could scarcely believe it. When the big fight came, the final, she was on the edge of her seat with excitement.

Bets were coming in fast and furious and, despite her own elation, she diligently retained all the betting slips, putting those for Razor Bill in her right coat pocket and all those for Jet Red, his opponent, into her left pocket. The crowd was wild with excitement, clamouring for blood, but nobody was more excited than she was. The appeal of this cruel and bloodthirsty sport, the nature of which she loathed, became clear; it was betting. Betting, the thrill of the gamble, was the fuel that fed it.

The final was a long and equal fight, accompanied by a protracted chorus of ranting and shouting. Rhianna's heart went in her mouth when she saw that Razor Bill was down, with Jet Red on top of him, and she looked questioningly at Lawson. But Razor Bill was up again just as quickly and striking back, his head down, his neck feathers out. Both birds were tired and in a sorry state after four encounters. Neither seemed capable of finishing off the other. Then Razor Bill took the initiative and charged, steel spurs glinting in the gas light. Jet Red was down on the floor, weak and desperately trying to shake off his adversary, but he could not do it, and he lay, gasping for breath until he was picked up by his owner.

Razor Bill had won and Lawson reckoned he owed Rhianna two hundred and fifty-six guineas.

'Two hundred and fifty-six guineas?' she repeated in utter astonishment. 'I can't take that much money from you.'

'Course you can. That was our agreement. Razor Bill won. I told you he might.'

'But it's a fortune, Lawson.'

'I'll say it's a fortune.'

'I don't think you understand. It's more than four years wages for me ... Four years ... It's probably more than you've taken the whole evening.'

He winked artfully. 'Before I met you tonight I placed a bet myself with another bookie. I had a five-guinea accumulator on Razor Bill.'

'Five guineas? So you've won ... more than twelve hundred and fifty guineas.'

'Not a bad night's work, eh?'

'But how did you know that Razor Bill would win?'

'Oh, I didn't. You can never be certain. But he has good form. He's in fine condition and he has a good trainer . . . But there was a sentimental motive that made me bet on him . . .'

'I didn't realise you were sentimental.'

'I am about cocks,' he said, with a twinkle in his eye. 'He belongs to me, you see. I own him. I just had to have a bet on my own cock . . .'

Suddenly Rhianna was rich. She had money enough to spend on a doctor for her father. And it was all thanks to Lawson Maddox. She blessed the day she met him and thanked God for it nightly in her prayers. The trouble was, it turned out that Dr McCaskie had been right in the first place. Her father's illness was incurable by medicine.

'For a patient who is consumptive I prescribe not medicine but a new mode of life,' he told them on the day of his visit. 'We cannot cure anybody of consumption. Endless steadfastness, courage, self-discipline and self-denial are the key. If I can get Mr Drake to alter his mode of life I am giving the correct treatment in some measure.'

But how far could her poor father go in altering his way of life? He would need the support of not only her mother, but Rhianna and Sarah as well. Well, Rhianna would give hers to the absolute best of her ability, for as long as her windfall lasted. She wanted to pay for her father to enter a sanatorium but, not surprisingly, he refused. Oh, he flatly refused. They argued with him, they cajoled, they tried gentle persuasion. All failed. So her mother's care and application of a rigid, monotonous discipline was what they depended on for him.

Doctor McCaskie also decreed that Titus Drake was to be given three good meals a day. 'No special diet is necessary,' he explained, 'but the food has to be thoroughly masticated and digested. He is allowed a little alcohol – rum in warm milk. He should have a little cod liver oil every day, for it will be beneficial. As many hours as possible must be spent in the open air and, when he is indoors, the windows are to be widely opened, or even taken out of their sashes . . .'

'In this vile January weather?' Mary queried, looking at him as if he'd lost touch with reality.

Dr McCaskie ignored her look. 'Your husband has to be made to rest and he must maintain a cheerful attitude of mind . . .'

That amused Rhianna; she hadn't seen her father smile in years.

'Additionally, he must carry a special receptacle to spit into, which should contain disinfectant fluid or a solution of mercury salt. He must never swallow his phlegm. Also, he has to sleep by himself. All this is necessary,' he went on. 'Mrs Drake, you must breathe through your nose at all times to avoid picking up the infection, and wash your hands every time you handle anything of your husband's—'

'Pah! I never touch him,' Mary interjected with distaste.

'And if they can stand to do all this, will his health improve?' Rhianna asked sceptically, because it all sounded rather like shutting the gate after the horse had run off.

'Truly, I cannot say for certain. But it is the only chance he has got. If he is foolish and lapses, then it will not.'

Lawson and Rhianna became regular companions over the next few weeks although her evenings off and Sunday afternoons were the only times they could be together. Every other Sunday she was given the whole day off and it was on the mornings of those days that she visited her mother and father. Sometimes, during the week, her duties took her into the town and then she would make a quick diversion to their house in Campbell Street, less than five minutes' walk from the market place.

There was not a profusion of eating houses in Dudley but,

on a couple of occasions, Lawson entertained her at the Dudley Arms Hotel and at the Fountain Dining Rooms. He made her feel like a princess. He never failed to bring her a gift; some trinket that she could wear or place on the mantelshelf in her little attic room at Baxter House. Lawson was becoming increasingly attentive, to Rhianna's great satisfaction.

One evening towards the end of February, he took her to Lloyd's Circus, which had pitched its tent in Porter's Field by the Roman Catholic church. Lawson had reserved seats in the stalls at three shillings apiece and they watched three athletic sisters, Ala, Ava and Aza perform dare-devil stunts on a trapeze while singing a haunting love song called 'Speak to me, love, only speak'. A group of seven acrobats, the Carlo Troupe, performed wonders on triple bars, and a comic called the French Barber was full of continental absurdity, and then they listened to somebody known as Craven, the singing clown.

The weeks passed in a haze of tantalising romance and sweet talk, and Rhianna began to wonder whether Lawson loved her enough to make her his bride. She had thought long and hard about it. The very fact that she was contemplating the possibility told her how much she wanted already to be his wife. She pondered all aspects. At night she went to bed in her attic bedroom in a reverie of romance, imagining delightful evenings curled in his arms on a sofa in front of the fire, weaving dreams and planning what names to give their children. She imagined laughter ringing through the house as they decided how they would design each room. She imagined trips to the shops to choose new furniture, bone china dinner sets, tea sets and silver cutlery for when they entertained his influential friends. Oh, she would love being married to Lawson.

She had not failed to consider their love life either. Lawson was always sweet and attentive. He made her ache with desire with his delicious, lingering kisses, but he had not made the suggestion or contrived to manipulate her into the situation where he might have tried to take advantage of her. She was still intact of course, yet here was the one man for whom she would gladly lose her virginity without a second thought, so much did she love him.

Each time they met, she wondered if this was the occasion he would take her to his home. She was dying to see his house, to assess its potential, to plan what she would do to improve it when she became Mrs Lawson Maddox. But never did he suggest that he might one day take her there. Rhianna wondered, anxiously, if it was because he was already married. It would explain a lot. The thought made her grossly unhappy. She was hooked like some poor fish dangling on the end of a line and the possibility that she might actually be sharing him with another woman began to worry her.

One Wednesday evening Rhianna and Lawson were invited for supper at the house of one of his well-to-do friends. They played whist and the lady of the house played piano and sang very pleasantly for them. It was a convivial evening and Rhianna drank port. She was becoming very attached to port; it seemed to boost her confidence. Lawson never embarrassed her by letting on to any of his high-class friends that the lovely young lady who accompanied him was merely a servant; but that had more to do with his own self-esteem than hers.

When they left and were in the cabriolet, she asked him the question that was consuming her. 'Are you married, Lawson?'

He guffawed and almost spooked the horse. 'Good God, no. Whatever gave you that idea?'

She shrugged in the darkness, but felt anxiety slough off her like a constricting skin, since he was manifestly not lying. 'Because you've never taken me to your home. I wondered if you were hiding a wife there. I just wonder if you are serious about me, if you really care for me.'

'Oh, I'm in dead earnest, my love,' he answered directly,

looking into her wide eyes. 'But my home is like the Sack of Carthage and you would not be impressed . . . Besides, there are two more reasons why I ain't taken you there. Firstly, whilst I can hardly wait to lure you into my bed, I want you to look upon me as a gentleman. Secondly, despite this ardent desire to bed you, I respect you and regard you as a lady, even though sometimes you don't quite see yourself as one.'

'Oh, Lawson . . . I appreciate I'm not a lady born and bred, but I do try . . . I do try to be like a lady,' she protested. 'I try—'

'Would you like me to show you my home?'

'I'd love you to.'

'Right. I shall make a very determined effort to have the house cleaned up and made very presentable. Then I shall invite you to dinner and you will dine like a lady. We shall have a very romantic evening of it and I might even ply you with strong drink . . .'

'Strong drink?' She chuckled at the innuendo. 'Shall I need strong drink?'

The following night, Sarah went to Rhianna's room for a gossip and to have a moan about another of the girls. They dispensed with those trivialities quickly and Rhianna saw this as an opportunity to confess what she should have confessed weeks ago.

'Sarah,' she began quietly, taking Sarah's hand and holding it gently. 'There's something I have to tell you. I hope you won't despise me but it's been worrying me exactly how to tell you. So I've decided to come straight out with it . . . I've been seeing Lawson Maddox regularly, in my free time . . . I know how you've admired Lawson yourself, Sarah, so I think it's only fair I should let you know . . . We're in love and very serious about each other. In fact, I wouldn't be surprised if—'

'You're courting Lawson?' Sarah said tersely. 'Even though

you know I fancy him? That's not very nice, our Rhianna. That's not a very nice trick to pull across your sister.' She withdrew her hand from Rhianna's, aggrieved, and shuffled agitatedly on the bed.

'There was no intention to slight you, Sarah.' Rhianna was struggling to state her case without seeming insensitive. 'It just happened. We met and suddenly there was this magic . . . Oh, I love him dearly . . .'

'And does he love you?'

'Oh, yes. He says so – often . . . Oh, please don't be resentful Sarah. I had hoped for your good wishes.'

'You told me once that gentlemen don't marry servants.'

'And what I said holds true. But Lawson is not gentry born and bred. His father was only a corn merchant. But Lawson's done well for himself. For all his hob-nobbing with the well-to-do, he doesn't see any distinction between us.'

'Lucky you,' Sarah said scornfully and made as if to rise from Rhianna's bed.

Rhianna took her hand again to prevent her going. 'Wish me well, Sarah,' she pleaded. 'You know that Lawson is too old for you anyway.'

Sarah shrugged but remained where she was. 'All the same, it doesn't mean to say you can't fancy somebody older.'

Rhianna could see from the look in Sarah's piqued eyes that she was coming round, that she just wanted a fuss made of her. 'You're such a beautiful creature, men will be falling over themselves to win you. I bet the boys are already lining up.'

The compliment elicited a smile from Sarah. She shrugged again, shyly. 'There is one lad who comes to the kitchen most days. One of the delivery lads.'

'Oh? How old?'

'Eighteen.'

'That's more the age for you, our Sarah. Far more sensible. What's his name?'

'Roland.'

'So who does he work for?'

'Parker's.'

'And you like him?'

'Yes. He makes me laugh.'

Rhianna nodded her assent, glad that they'd got that one big hurdle out of the way, content to condone Sarah's flirting with a grocery boy. 'Well, that's nice. But don't get too serious at your age. There'll be plenty more, I promise.'

5

Lawson Maddox had arranged for Molly Kettle and her pretty young daughter, Flossie, to do some serious cleaning at his house in preparation for the redecorating that was to follow. Flossie was the pretty girl who had cursorily inspected Rhianna as she sat in his cabriolet in Albert Street while he wheedled seriously overdue rent out of her mother. The cleaning was in lieu of part of the rent that Molly owed.

Lawson did not, of course, employ a live-in maid-of-all-work, for such an arrangement would have been unseemly for a bachelor of his standing. He chose not to employ a man-servant either, or a married couple to look after him. Hence, he lived his life alone. Although he had some respect for his surroundings, it was only when he sent for Molly Kettle to clean for him that the house became truly tidy. His laundry he sent out regularly and usually he dined at whichever hostelry he happened to be in when he was hungry.

This particular series of cleaning events and the decorating took about a month and Lawson, whenever he saw Rhianna, would enthuse about how fine and dandy it was all turning out.

Rhianna was completely overwhelmed that he was going to all this trouble to impress her. The very thought made her smile with satisfaction. Marriage had to be his intention. If he merely wanted to seduce her he could have rented a room at the Dudley Arms Hotel or at any number of inns in the area. But he wouldn't do that. Already he'd told her he wanted to be gentlemanly; he wanted to treat her like a lady and she relished his consideration.

Not that she would have baulked at being seduced before her wedding night. She knew that a girl's initiation must happen sooner or later, and suspected that it would be memorable wherever and whenever it happened. She imagined that farm girls who lost their maidenhood in some dusty hayloft recalled it just as readily and with as much pleasure as if it had occurred in the warmth and luxury of their master's and mistress's soft featherbed. Rhianna knew from talking to girls that some of them used the graves of the dear departed in the town's bone yards as a bed. But such licentious shenanigans were not for her; they were hardly the antics of a lady.

A dinner party had been planned of the Cooksons', for 16th March, a Saturday. Invited guests were the wealthy and very eminent Mr and Mrs Alexander Gibson, Alderman and Mrs George Folkes, whom Rhianna had never seen before, and Mr and Mrs Ernest Bagnall of Tipton, whom she had. The best silver was of course to be used. On the morning Rhianna asked one of the maids, Elsie Morpeth, to make sure every piece was all cleaned and ready. As noon approached she was stopped in the passageway to the kitchen by the same Elsie.

'Oh, Miss, some of the silver's a-missing,' she informed her, wringing her hands as if anticipating being blamed for it.

'Missing?' Rhianna queried incredulously. 'How can any be missing?'

Elsie shrugged. 'I don't know, Miss, but they bain't nowhere. I'n searched high and low.'

'Which pieces can't you find, Elsie?'

'At fust, I thought as it was just two servin' platters, but when I come to fill the salt cellar, I could see as the cruet's gone an' all.'

'They have to be somewhere,' Rhianna said calmly. 'Things don't just go missing.'

At that point, Mrs Cookson came along. 'Good morning, ladies.' She always greeted her girls as ladies. 'Is everything all right?'

Rhianna naturally felt obliged to report what Elsie had just told her and did so. 'I wonder if it has anything to do with that burglary in January,' she suggested.

'No, Rhianna. I think not. We have used the silver since then and nothing was missing.'

'Yes, you're right, ma'am. I'll have a proper search made.'

'Please, Rhianna. And let me know the outcome.'

'As soon as I can, ma'am.'

Rhianna went into the kitchen, which was always the centre of activity when meal times were due. She asked if anybody knew anything of the whereabouts of the missing silverware. There was a general shaking of heads. 'Perhaps we can all double-check cupboards and sideboards,' Rhianna suggested. 'Before lunch.'

As they all dispersed, leaving Cook and a kitchen maid who had been hired just for the day to help out, Sarah beckoned Rhianna to one side.

'I think I know where the missing silver plates and cruet are,' she said.

'Thank God. Then you'd best tell me, our Sarah, before Mrs Cookson blows her wig.'

She took Rhianna's hand and led her out of earshot, through the heavy door of the kitchen. 'I think they'm at the pawn-brokers in the town.'

'At the pawnbrokers? How come they're at the pawn-brokers?'

'I can explain,' Sarah bleated defensively in a pathetic little voice.

'I think you'd better.'

'Roland . . . You know, that lad I told you about . . .'

'Parker's the grocer's boy?'

She nodded. 'He asked me if he could borrow some silver. He asked me if I would get some for him.'

'What the devil did he want with Mr Cookson's best silver?'

'He said he was going to pawn them to get money to wager on a horse. He said he needed the money desperate and he pleaded with me to help him. He said that if the horse won he would be well off and be able to buy the silver back and pay me some money for my trouble besides. I remembered all that money you won on that bet, our Rhianna, and thought it would be a good idea. I mean, he was going to bring it back.'

'Oh Sarah,' Rhianna rasped angrily. 'Are you out of your mind? Do you know how serious this is? Didn't you realise it wasn't your property to lend in the first place? Do you understand what this could mean? For both of us?'

Rhianna saw tears tremble on Sarah's long lashes. The poor, innocent, beguiled child. She had never been as canny as Rhianna, nor would she ever be. 'I'm so sorry, our Rhianna,' she said sincerely. 'I didn't mean any harm. I just thought I would be a shilling or two better off when he brought it all back.'

'And can he get it back? Can he get it back quick? Before Mrs Cookson finds out?'

'Shall I run up to Parker's and see if he's there?'

'I think you'd better . . . Right now. This minute. And don't come back without it.'

Rhianna waited on tenterhooks, concerned that Mrs Cookson might come seeking news and she would have to lie. She waited half an hour. Three quarters. An hour. Eventually, Sarah returned. She was carrying nothing and her eyes were red from crying.

'He said he sold the pawnbroker's ticket, Rhianna,' she whined breathlessly. 'I went to the shop and had a look. I asked them not to let go of the silver, as we would be back for it. But they said as it ain't there any more. It's already gone.'

'Oh, my God. You know what this means.'

'Oh, Rhianna, I'm so sorry,' Sarah blubbered. 'Have I got you into trouble as well?'

'I sincerely hope not.' Rhianna sighed gravely. 'I just wonder what's the best way of handling it to save you getting into trouble . . . If I can get away with denying that I know who's responsible I will. I'll try and protect you. But Mrs Cookson isn't stupid . . . Oh, I know you're not the brightest of God's children, our Sarah, but you're no criminal. I'd better go and see Mrs Cookson.'

Rhianna found Mrs Cookson just as she was about to take lunch.

'Any news on the silverware, Rhianna?'

'Bad news, I'm afraid, ma'am. It was lent to somebody – on the strict understanding that it would be returned, of course. Sad to say, the person who borrowed it pawned it.'

'Pawned, did you say?'

'Yes, ma'am.'

'Why would anyone want to pawn my silverware, Rhianna?'

'To raise money, ma'am. The idea was to gamble the money, then win enough to buy it back and return it safely here.'

'And who was that person?'

'I'm not certain, ma'am. One of the trades people, I believe.'

'Rhianna, you are being evasive. I want chapter and verse. If the police need to be involved, I want them here. Do you hear?'

Rhianna let out a great, troubled sigh, and nodded.

'But who from this household has been impertinent and stupid enough to lend my best silverware to one of the tradesmen?'

'I cannot say, ma'am.'

'Does that mean cannot, or will not?'

'I cannot, ma'am.'

'Very well. Then every servant in this house is under suspicion. What has happened here is tantamount to stealing and no employer will tolerate it. Lord knows, enough of this kind of thing goes on, but I thought we had earned sufficient respect from our staff to prevent such things happening in this house.

I will not tolerate it and neither will Mr Cookson. We try, as employers to be fair with everybody. We go out of our way to be fair.'

'Indeed you do, ma'am. I have to agree. You are model employers.'

'Does anybody below stairs have any genuine cause for complaint about how they are treated?'

'I don't think so, ma'am.'

'Then why are we treated so shamefully?'

'I can't imagine, ma'am,' Rhianna said resignedly. 'I suspect whoever it was saw no harm in what they were doing if the silver was to be returned. Certainly, they wished you no harm.'

Mrs Cookson eyed Rhianna suspiciously. 'And I think you know more about this than you are admitting, Rhianna.'

Rhianna did not respond.

'Of course, I cannot conceive that you had any hand in it.'

'Indeed I didn't, ma'am,' she said indignantly.

'All the same, I want the police here. I shall send Gerald with a note at once. It is the course of action my husband would take. It is the only course I can take.'

'I understand, ma'am.'

'They will resolve this if you cannot. If they have to arrest each and every one of the staff. Please send Gerald to see me at once.'

Rhianna was hopelessly torn. She did not know whether to come out with the truth just to clear her own name. But she could not point the finger at poor Sarah and condemn her to the possibility of several years' penal servitude when there was a chance she might still escape blame. So she said no more and went to look for Gerald.

Half an hour later, with lunch postponed, a police officer sporting a huge moustache arrived. He had everybody assembled in the kitchen and Rhianna explained broadly what had happened, without naming Sarah.

'So who was responsible for letting go this silverware?' he asked pointedly.

Nobody answered, nobody moved.

'Well, somebody must know.'

Everybody seemed preoccupied with looking at their shoes and not at the policeman. It was clear that nobody was going to snitch on their workmates.

'Well I'm sure everybody wants their dinners,' the policeman said ominously, his moustache twitching. 'But there'll be no dinner till I get an answer. And if I have to troop you all up to the police station, throw you in a cell and clap you in irons, I will . . .'

'It was me,' Sarah said meekly, and then began to wail.

Mrs Cookson looked at Rhianna studiedly. She had read Rhianna. She knew that Rhianna had deliberately tried to shield her sister, knowing all the time she was responsible for this senseless error of judgement. Rhianna's heart sank as, with dawning clarity, the implications of her obstructive vagueness intensified.

She went over to Sarah and wrapped her in her arms. 'There, there,' she whispered. 'You are no criminal. You didn't understand what you were doing, did you? Just tell the police officer exactly what happened then everything will be all right.'

Eventually Sarah ceased her weeping and, when the others had been dismissed, she told the policeman all she knew, naming Roland, the grocer's lad. She apologised profusely to Mrs Cookson and made a formal statement admitting her part in the affair.

After lunch, Mrs Cookson sent for Rhianna again. 'Sit down, Rhianna.' Her voice was as sharp as a shard of glass.

'Thank you, ma'am,' Rhianna said, trying to keep her voice even, quaking with apprehension.

'Rhianna, I am profoundly disappointed in your younger sister but, quite frankly, I am even more disappointed in you.

Sarah has shown incredible stupidity in being persuaded by some scallywag to part with silver that is the property of Mr Cookson. Of course, she must be punished for it. I appreciate that she was duped and she is not wilfully criminal. However, I am unable to allow her to continue her employment here. Furthermore, I am certain that my husband might well wish to press charges. We must not set any precedent and appear to the rest of the staff to be too lenient. If we were, we would risk others' further exploitation. Do you see, Rhianna?'

'Yes, I see, ma'am. But do you really have to press charges?' She sat without moving as a shaft of weak sunlight was suddenly cast across the table between them. 'I think that is being rather harsh, if you'll pardon me for saying so. After all, she was not the criminal element, as you have yourself implied, ma'am.'

'And I suspect that *that* is the reason you tried to shield her, Rhianna.'

Her eyes dropped to the floor and she looked absently at the rug that lay beneath her feet. 'Sarah is just a poor misguided girl who failed to use her common sense, ma'am. She's young and innocent. She's not a felon. She's made a silly mistake. You could hardly expect me to betray her when there was a chance she might not be blamed.'

'So you betrayed me instead, your employer. That really doesn't impress me, Rhianna. Your loyalties should lie with those who provide your bread and butter.'

'Ma'am, I am sorry . . .' Rhianna could hear the indignation rising in her own voice, but was unable to control it. 'But if you think that you, or any employer for that matter, should come before any member of my family, then you neither know nor understand me. Certainly I will never stand by and see my sister's regretful lapse blown out of all proportion. That can only mean resentment and mistrust are going to fester between us. I don't believe I could work here in such circumstances, ma'am.'

'Do I understand then that you wish to resign as house-keeper?'

'I honestly don't believe I have an alternative, ma'am,' Rhianna said.

Rhianna left Baxter House that evening and so did Sarah. At first she thought she was in a bad dream and that soon she would wake up and escape the sudden shame and anxiety. Sarah was beside herself with humiliation and remorse, mostly that her blind stupidity had cost Rhianna her position. She was not so concerned about herself. They deposited themselves upon their mother and father and shared the tiny boxroom that Sarah used to sleep in before she started work. Rhianna still had most of the money left that she had won on her bet, but it would not last forever. Finding as good a position in another house would not be easy, especially if Mrs Cookson was reticent about giving her a decent character. But she decided to put such worries behind her until she had talked things over with Lawson next day, the evening of which they had laughingly, frivolously, agreed would be so romantic as he wined her and dined her at his renovated house. The last thing on her mind by this time, however, was romance.

She met him as usual at three o' clock outside the Saracen's Head. They headed for the Dudley Arms Hotel, a Sunday after-noon routine they had slipped into since their very first tryst.

'I've got some bad news,' she said as soon as he delivered their drinks to the table. She explained in detail what had happened while he listened carefully, twisting his whisky tumbler around in his fingers.

'Well, well,' he said thoughtfully. 'What a to-do.'

'But do you think I was right to put Sarah first, even though she'd done wrong?'

'Blood's thicker than water, Rhianna. It's no surprise that you did.'

'But I couldn't see the poor child hurt more, Lawson. She's

the world to me. If she hasn't got me to stand by her, who has she got?'

He drew his mouth down at the corners and nodded pensively. 'Well, it seems to me we have something to celebrate.'

'Celebrate?' She looked at him curiously. 'What on earth is there to celebrate?'

'The fact that you're a free woman. That's what there is to celebrate.'

Rhianna continued to look puzzled.

'You know what I reckon we should do?' he said.

'What?'

'Get married.'

She gasped with pleasure. 'Get married? Oh, Lawson, I'd like nothing better.'

'So will you marry me?'

'Yes, oh yes. Of course I'll marry you.' Her eyes sparkled with happiness. Not only would her future be assured but it would help alleviate so many problems at home. Then she frowned with apprehension as another thought struck her. 'You're not teasing me, are you?'

'Course I'm not teasing you. You're a free woman, I've just had my house cleaned and redecorated from top to bottom . . . and, what's more, we could employ Sarah as a maid.'

She sighed at his overwhelming but welcome impetuosity but there was a smile on her face again. 'You, Lawson Maddox, are so unpredictable. You've been a bachelor all these years, yet suddenly you suggest marriage and you haven't known me three months yet.'

'I know. It's madness. But I'm in love with you. I'm besotted. I told you.'

She laughed joyously. 'When shall we do it?'

'What about Easter? I shall make all the arrangements. So, I propose that you come with me now to see your future home, Rhianna.'

'You mean your house?'

'The same. I've hired a cook for the night as you know, and she is there right now preparing that lavish meal I promised. I don't see the point in wasting it. Do you?'

'Not really.' Rhianna's lips curled into a smile of contentment.

'I shall merely behave like the gentleman I am and, out of respect, refrain from seducing you afterwards.' He laughed out loud.

'Well, I'm glad you've not asked me to marry you just as an excuse to seduce me, Lawson. You obviously think it's important that I should remain a virgin until my wedding night . . .'

A smile spread across his handsome face and she could see a warm light in his eyes. 'Oh, yes . . . Of course you have to be a virgin on your wedding night. Oh, without doubt . . .'

He had speculated about her deflowering before, half serious, half joking, in very intimate and sensual whispers, and just talking about it had warmed her to the prospect. She knew Lawson would be gentle and considerate, and the very thought of all that tender intimacy made her temples throb. She would never admit as much, but she had been looking forward to it like nothing else. Because they were getting married so soon she would not have so long to wait.

Rhianna chuckled with delight. Her life had suddenly switched from catastrophe to unbelievable good fortune in just one day. She was being delivered from spinsterhood, to become the beloved wife of one of the Black Country's most eligible bachelors.

Lawson's house was situated on Himley Road, in the area called Sunnyside in the parish of St James. It was not a grand house – nothing like Baxter House – but it was a substantial family home nonetheless, a gentleman's residence. It stood in its own grounds with a drive that ran in a wide sweep from the front gate to the stables at the rear. The garden was unkempt, as one might expect from a bachelor with no family ties, but its interesting lie offered good potential. Inside, Rhianna envisaged filling each of the bedrooms with their children. Lawson had spent a small fortune on the interior, that much was obvious, including tasteful new furniture. Everywhere smelled of new paint and wallpaper. He'd even gone to the trouble and expense of having new linoleum laid all through and had bought some fine rugs that graced the floors. He led Rhianna to the scullery and introduced her to the hired cook. At sight of them, the cook put a pan of water on the hob to boil, ready for the potatoes, and hung the kettle over the fire on a gale, ready to brew a pot of tea. She was very deferential. She curtsied when she saw Rhianna and already Rhianna felt like the lady she was about to become. The glorious aroma of roast beef was already embracing her and she could hardly wait to be mistress in what was to be her own kitchen.

Lawson took her upstairs to show her the bedroom that would be theirs. It was large and airy, with a clean and inviting feather mattress on an intricate brass bedstead. The window looked out onto the road at the front and had an extensive view southwards over the innumerable pits and grey, miserable slag heaps of Russell's Hall. The corporation catch pound was uncomfortably close. Beyond it, the middle distance was alive with locomotives huffing and puffing to and from a wharf on the mineral railway that connected it with the vast Himley Colliery at Old Park. Oh, it was a decent enough house, but the view ... She was not going to live here for the view, though; she would happily live in a pigsty for the privilege of being Lawson's wife.

'As you might have expected, this was my father's house,' Lawson informed her as he showed her another bedroom. 'Sarah could sleep in this room when she becomes our maid.'

'We can't have our Sarah as a maid, Lawson,' Rhianna said flatly. 'It's impossible.'

'Why is it impossible? It's not impossible. I want her as our maid.'

'No lady of any house would ever employ her own sister as a maid, Lawson. It would betray her own roots. Don't you see?'

'My God!' he exclaimed. 'You've turned into a snob already.'

'I'm no snob, but we have to protect our social standing. *Your* social standing. What would your friends think?'

'Well, that's settled then.'

'I presume there are proper servants' quarters, Lawson?'

'Yes, on the next floor. In the roof. My father had servants. A full complement, even after my mother died.'

'Can we see?'

He took her up another flight of stairs to the second storey, to rooms that were small, bare and cold, typical of the garrets servants normally occupied. Suddenly, Rhianna could see the situation of a servant from both sides. She had lived in rooms like this. Only yesterday she resided in one such. Now she was viewing this garret from the perspective of an employer . . . Well, not quite. She doubted she would ever lose sympathy for employed servants.

'We'll need to make these rooms a bit more welcoming,' she said. 'I wouldn't like to sleep in rooms this dingy.'

He laughed. 'You're the expert, Rhianna. Do as you see fit when the time comes.'

When she had seen enough of upstairs, including a quick peep at Lawson's study, he escorted her back downstairs and into what he called his sitting room, where a welcoming fire burned in a low, stone grate. Rhianna was drawn to the oil painting that hung above it, in which two beautiful young women, clothed in diaphanous attire that purported to be in the style of classical Greece or Rome, reposed languidly on a bench constructed of smooth white marble veined with the most delicate grey and blue tracery and draped with tiger skins. Rhianna had no idea it was possible for anybody to paint marble with such realism and skill. Never had she seen such perfection. The artist had seemingly painted every individual hair of the tiger skin too, had captured every last detail of the bright poppies that adorned the lush garden in which it was all so tantalisingly set. Umbrella pines stood out against a sea and sky of vivid blue and a mysterious, mountainous land on the distant horizon. It all looked so idyllic, so enchanting that she could not help but gasp.

'This is beautiful,' she said simply, unable to draw her eyes from it. 'I've never seen anything like it. Just look at the skill that has gone into painting this . . . Just look at the skin of these girls, their clothes. It's all so unreal and yet so perfectly realistic.'

'I'm glad you like it,' Lawson said indifferently.

'Who painted it? Where did you get it?'

'It was painted by a young artist called John Mallory Gibson, the son of Alexander Gibson, whom you might even have met at the Cooksons' home.'

'You mean *the* Alexander Gibson, the bigwig? One of the guests at Baxter House last night?'

He nodded. 'The same. He and I do business from time to time.'

'You know him well?'

'Yes, I know him well. His son sent him this. Thought he might like it. And Alexander gave it to me.'

'Why would he give you such a painting when he must have treasured it? I mean, he would treasure it if his son painted it, wouldn't he?'

'He gave it to me because he wanted me to have it, presumably.'

'I've never seen anything like it,' Rhianna repeated. 'Mr Gibson's son is a fine artist. Where does he live, this John Mallory Gibson?'

'In London, I believe.'

She nodded. 'The sea and the sky are so blue. It gives me

the impression of endless sunny days, of carefree girlhood. It's beautiful . . . Where do you think it's supposed to be?'

'Italy, I suspect.'

She looked outside at the drab, grey landscape, then with large, almost pleading eyes at Lawson. 'I wouldn't object if you wanted to take me to Italy for our honeymoon.'

He laughed at that. 'I wish I could. But since I can't, where *would* you like to go?'

'Oh . . . I'd love to see London. The Tower, Buckingham Palace, the Houses of Parliament.'

'And I'd love to see Bath. So we'll stay a few days in London, then move on to Bath. How does that sound?'

'Oh, Lawson,' she cooed. 'You're too good to me.'

The hired cook presented a very palatable meal that evening. While Lawson and Rhianna dined like a lord and lady, planning their marriage, she skivvied in the scullery. Before she left, Lawson announced to her that he and Rhianna were to be married; she wished them well. Afterwards, they decided to break the news to Rhianna's mother and father and to Sarah. It would be a welcome relief from the cataclysmic events that had overshadowed and shamed them since yesterday. He had not met her parents, nor been to their house, and at once Rhianna started making excuses, telling him not to expect anything grand.

'Don't worry. I'm marrying you, not your parents,' he said.

She needn't have worried. Lawson took it all in his stride, studying the property with an expert eye. Mary Drake fussed over him like a she-cat with a prize kitten and Titus was on his best behaviour, not breaking wind once. (Titus's health had improved a little, thanks to Dr McCaskie's arduous regime.) Sarah was as fidgety as a kitten with its first mouse in Lawson's company and her long eyelashes swept down every time he glanced in her direction. Lawson, conversely, seemed entirely at home and quite taken with Rhianna's family.

They ended up in a little public house in the market place called the Seven Stars. It was heaving with men, swearing and spitting and coughing and smoking and God knows what else. Rhianna could not imagine why Lawson persisted in dragging her to such sleazy town bars, populated by men reeking of stale sweat. There were three other women in there, not the sort she would associate with by choice. It troubled her that everybody seemed to know Lawson, including the unsavoury women, and they in particular looked Rhianna up and down with curiosity. One of them, no older than herself, seemed as if she wanted to speak to Lawson; she kept edging forward and hovering around them. But Lawson, to his credit, turned his back on her and smiled at Rhianna with love in his eyes as he gulped his whisky. Then, to her complete surprise, he announced to everybody that he was about to be married and introduced her as his bride. There were a few whoops of surprise, and some comments as well that were none too savoury from the more inebriated, but when he said the next round of drinks was on him, everybody congratulated them both and placed their orders at the bar.

Later, when he delivered Rhianna to the bottom of the entry in Campbell Street Lawson was slurring his words idiotically.

'Are you sure you're going to be all right?' she asked, concerned.

'Yesh. Don' worry.' His eyelids were lazy and she was worried that he might fall asleep as he drove home.

'I hope the horse can find his way,' Rhianna said. 'Because I doubt if you will.'

He grinned stupidly. 'Docker'sh a fine horshe. He knowsh hish way around.'

She planted a kiss on his cheek then slid down from the

cabriolet. 'Thank you for everything, Lawson. Don't forget you're supposed to be calling for me tomorrow night.'

'How could I forget that?' he replied.

She stood and waved as he drove off at a rapid rate, oblivious to everything in his drunken stupor.

6

Arthur Hayward, a long-standing friend and drinking partner of Lawson Maddox, had died of pneumonia at a devastatingly young thirty-two. Arthur had inherited his father's prosperous lamp-making business. He left a grieving young widow and three small children. The funeral was held at St Thomas's church on a bitterly cold and blustery Thursday at the end of March in 1889. The churchyard was surrounded by appropriately black-painted iron railings. Afterwards, everybody was invited to the assembly rooms at the Saracen's Head. It was well attended and convivial, with family who otherwise seldom met brought together with friends to reminisce on the highlights of Arthur's short life. At first there was just a murmur of respectful voices but, after a drink or two, those same voices grew more voluble, and laughter began to pervade the reverential gloom. Although the service had been attended only by men, a few women now joined the gathering. They individually threaded their way across the room, with a rustle of long black skirts and clicking heels, stopping to offer their condolences to the bereaved widow who was sitting in state ready to receive them. Then they exchanged courtesies with this or that group as they glided in solemn mourning towards the fire that was burning consolingly in its grate.

Lawson found himself standing at the bar with Robert Cookson and Jack Hayward, the deceased Arthur's younger brother. All had started the commemoration by drinking pale ale but, as the afternoon wore on and dusk inexorably cast its grey mantle over the town and the lamps were lit, they had shifted onto harder stuff and the late Arthur became further removed from their thoughts.

'I've got some news to share with you,' Lawson said, as he casually picked up the last of the ham sandwiches that were now curling at the edges and dried on top. 'I'm getting wed.'

'*You're* getting wed?' Jack Hayward queried incredulously. 'When?'

'Good Friday.'

'Jesus! What madness has seized you?'

'I'm in love,' Lawson answered nonchalantly and took a bite.

Jack flashed Robert a quizzical look. 'Did he say what I thought he said?'

Robert shrugged a limp, inebriated shrug and drew up a high stool, scraping it harshly along the linoleum floor. 'He just said he's in love, Jack.'

Jack turned to Lawson, his glass in his hand. 'The only person you're in love with, Lawson Maddox, is yourself. Who's the poor, unfortunate wench? She should be warned about you.'

'She wouldn't listen. She's in love with me.'

Robert, resting his backside on the stool, was suddenly struck by the light of realisation. 'Don't tell me it's that Rhianna Drake who used to be our housekeeper. I'll wager it is.' He took a gulp of his whisky and held it in his mouth to savour it while Lawson nodded and grinned.

'You mean he's marrying a servant wench? Bloody hell, Lawson. You can do better than a servant wench.'

'She's a treasure,' Lawson said, his affability enhanced by the banter he always enjoyed with his friends. 'Servant wench or no, I'd be mad not to marry her. She's a gem. And I defy anybody to tell she ain't from the upper classes.'

'I trust you've sampled the goods already, Lawson,' Robert leered. 'Indeed, I take it she's up the stick already if you're marrying her so quick?'

Lawson put the last piece of sandwich into his mouth casually, chewed it and picked up his glass.

'Come on, Lawson. Since when have we had any secrets? You're generally very forthcoming with information about your conquests.'

'Well, she ain't up the stick. And I ain't ashamed to say that I ain't even sampled the goods yet. The truth is, I don't want to sully her before the wedding night. She's pristine, Robert. Intact. You know I like my women intact. And as sure as hell I ain't about to marry a woman who ain't.'

'Hang me, but I ain't a bit surprised she's intact,' Robert said.

'Saved herself all these years, she has. Just for me. I'd have to be a right vandal—'

Jack called the bartender. 'Three more whiskies, my man. We've a celebration here.' He turned to Lawson. 'I can see the attraction in marrying a virgin, Lawson, and I understand that finding one over the age of twenty-one must be a bit of a novelty, especially among the working classes. But if she's a looker to boot . . .'

'Oh, she's a looker all right. And honest with it. Straight as a die.'

'But, hang it all man, why d'you want to get married in the first place? I've never known you short of women.'

'I'm taken with her, Jack. She amuses me, she's intelligent . . . and like I say, she's beautiful.'

'Oh, she's worthy and no mistake,' Robert Cookson said resolutely. 'I expect you'll have a lot of fun with her between the sheets. Always quite fancied her meself, but she'd have no truck wi' me.'

'Because she's got the good taste of a born lady.' Lawson parried. 'In any case, I get fed up with the sort of women I've been mixed up with. Rhianna's like a breath of fresh air. She's bright. I can talk to her.'

'But who wants to just talk?' Jack remarked, full of bravado. 'How long have you been courting?'

'Three months, give or take a day or two.'

'You dark horse. And you ain't touched it yet? No horizontal exploits? Christ, you'll be getting boils on the back of your neck.'

'Unless, of course, he's been getting it elsewhere on the quiet . . .' Robert suggested, winking and tapping the side of his nose.

'Ah . . . That's more like it,' Jack agreed. 'You've been dipping your wick elsewhere, eh, Lawson?'

'The duty of every Englishman,' Lawson replied with a roguish gleam in his eye.

'Anybody afresh?' Robert enquired. 'Anybody you'd like to pass on?'

Robert looked at the women in black, still standing in front of the fire, talking. A couple of them were young and attractive and their perfume mingled with the smoke and the sweet aroma of whisky, a sensual cocktail for Robert who had been drinking all afternoon and, by now, had an exaggerated sense of his own desirability. 'I wonder if any of those women are wearing drawers,' he said fancifully.

'They're no nearer you, whether or no,' Lawson said. 'You're fuddled.'

Robert sighed and took another swig from his drink. 'You're right, Lawson, I am. I reckon we could do with a change of scenery. Granted, a couple of those fillies are worthy, but it strikes me they've taken this funeral a bit too much to heart. This is supposed to be a sort of celebration of Arthur's life, for God's sake.'

'One happens to be Arthur's broken-hearted widow, Robert,' Lawson reasoned.

'All the more reason for us to go out and find a bit of *lively* female company.'

'I'll drink to that,' Jack said. 'Is there still a cock and hen do of a Thursday night at the Castle and Falcon? There'd doubtless be some likely wenches there.'

'Let's have a look,' Lawson replied. 'But let's get something to eat first. I'm starving.'

So the three men bid farewell to their hostess, walked to the market place and entered the Railway Vaults. There, they ate hot pies and reverted to pale ale to pace their drinking. They talked about women, about venereal disease, about Salisbury the prime minister and the Irish question, then, inevitably, about women again.

As it approached nine o' clock, the trio ambled boisterously to the Castle and Falcon in Wolverhampton Street with its brass-bound barrels piled up behind the bar. As they went upstairs to the assembly room, a band was playing, the fiddler sawing unequally as he tried to be heard over the squeals and the guffaws of the rag-tag folk already in there. The appeal of cock and hen clubs was that men of all classes could move between women of all social groups at will, even different races since so many had been drawn to the Black Country seeking work. Gentlemen mixed freely and uninhibitedly with the working-class girls of the town. Indeed, some of those girls thought they had done rather well for themselves when they managed to attract the attention of a swell, although it was seldom more than one encounter, unless they genuinely liked each other.

'What shall we drink?' Robert called to his companions over the noise.

'Stout and gin,' Jack suggested in jest.

Lawson laughed incredulously. 'I'm game. Stout and gin it is.'

'Three pints of stout with a large measure of gin in each,' Jack shouted to the barmaid, a plump girl of about nineteen. 'And have a drink yourself.' That last comment drew her attention. She smiled at Jack and began to pour.

'The thing I like about these cock and hen nights is seeing

the lower orders at play,' Robert said into Lawson's ear. 'They really enjoy themselves, you know. And they drink like fish. Just watch.'

'It's not surprising. They must get thirsty from their exertions.'

'They don't worry about their mode of dress either, 'cause they don't have the money to buy decent, I suppose.'

Jack passed them their drinks but continued to charm the plump barmaid.

'I see the working class in action at our ironworks,' Robert said having quaffed his drink and pulled a face of disapproval. 'They're so bloody anxious to get away from it that their only ambition once outside is to get fuddled out of their small minds and enjoy themselves.'

'And who can blame 'em, poor sods,' Lawson remarked.

Robert surveyed the sea of animated faces. He nudged Lawson. 'I fancy that . . . She's my target. See her? That fair-haired one standing by the stove.'

'The best of luck,' Lawson said.

'See you later . . . maybe.'

Lawson watched with detached amusement as Robert made his way over to the girl, hesitant at first lest he was gatecrashing some existing arrangement; then, when he was fairly sure she was not spoken for, he struck. The girl smiled and received him cordially, if slightly abashed as he took the floor with her.

Lawson sensed somebody else at his side. He turned to look and met two smiling eyes that were green and wide, gazing back at him. The girl's lips were full, her mouth clean and appealing. Her hair was a rich auburn, pinned up in a fashionable style. She was trying to attract the attention of the barmaid.

'It's my friend that's occupying her with his glib talk,' Lawson said apologetically over the background noise. 'I'll see if I can attract her attention for you . . . If it goes on much longer we'll need a crowbar to prise 'em apart . . . Jack, can you let go your poppet a minute? There's a delightful young lady here waiting to be served . . .'

The barmaid smiled apologetically and turned to the girl.

'Allow me, miss,' Lawson intervened. 'What's your fancy?'

She looked at Lawson's drink. 'Stout will do fine. What you're having.'

'I wouldn't recommend it. It's stout and gin mixed.'

'I'm no stranger to stout. Nor gin for that matter.'

'Here . . . Try it first . . .' He allowed her a sip.

'Oh, I thought the gin might spoil it,' she said with a lilt in her voice. 'But it makes it dance on your tongue.'

He turned to the barmaid. 'Another pint of this stuff for my lovely friend here.'

Jack turned to look the girl up and down approvingly, then smiled knowingly at Lawson.

'So what's your name?' Lawson asked.

'My friends call me Kate. What's yours?'

'Oh . . . Percival.'

'Percival? Lord! I'd never marry anybody called Percival and that's a fact.'

'Hey, you're taking a lot for granted, Kate.'

The girl chuckled amiably. 'Have I not seen you here before?'

'I don't know. Have you not?' he mimicked good-naturedly.

She shrugged. 'What's a masher like you doing in here, though? Don't you have a pretty little wife to go home to?'

'Do you wish to apply for the vacant position? I can tell you, there have been a lot of applicants.'

'Well now . . . looking at you, I'm not surprised.' She sipped her drink and licked her lips sensuously as she looked into his eyes. 'Are you a man of vast experience then?'

'I've been known to dabble here and there. To be honest, I might even fancy a dabble with you later.'

'You're cocksure, Percival,' she quipped pertly. 'I wouldn't lay money on you getting your way.'

'Then I won't,' he replied, humouring her. 'But then you don't seem that sort of girl.'

'Nor am I indeed.'

He raised his glass. 'Then here's to the challenge.'

'A challenge, am I?' She raised hers and took another drink.

'Why don't we dance, Kate? Then we'll finish our drinks and I'll take you for a ride in my gig.'

She smiled coquettishly. 'Your gig? You have a gig? Fancy! All right then. Why don't we dance?'

On 19th April, Good Friday, less than a month after his proposal, Lawson Maddox and his bride signed the register at St Thomas's church – Top Church. Although Lawson had sent out invitations to many of his top-drawer friends, some had not accepted. The redoubtable Mr Alexander Gibson, father of the artist whose work Rhianna had admired so much, sent his regrets and Lawson wondered whether it was because Gibson had discovered he was marrying a woman who had been a servant; worse still, the dishonoured servant of his good friend Jeremiah Cookson. Well, that was up to him; Lawson knew Alexander would not hold it against him once he met Rhianna. Jack Hayward was best man and Sarah was vividly beautiful as the bridesmaid. Mary Drake had all hell's game trying to get Titus to attend and, in the finish, he didn't. He would not shift, mainly for fear that somebody might kick his gouty foot, and no amount of cajoling worked.

So, in the absence of her father, Rhianna was given away by her solitary uncle on her mother's side. After the ceremony, however, she insisted that Lawson drive her home so that her father could see her again in her lovely satin dress, otherwise he would not catch sight of her again till she had returned from honeymoon.

'Wish me well, Father,' she said earnestly, and she could see he was pale and fatigued.

'I wish yer the very best of everything, my angel,' he replied from his armchair, his throbbing foot lodged safely in its wicker basket. 'And I'm just sorry as I couldn't be there to gi' yer away, but I daresay as your mother's enjoying herself . . . Lawson, just mek sure as yer look after this babby o' mine.'

'Have no fear, Mr Drake.'

The wedding breakfast was held at the Dudley Arms Hotel. Jack Hayward gave a witty speech and Lawson replied, lauding the qualities of his new wife with equal wit. Sarah giggled with wide-eyed admiration at Jack's conversation. Jack seemed dangerously taken with her, and Lawson felt obliged to quietly warn his best man to quell any fantasies he was nurturing about the bride's young sister.

'But she's interested,' Jack complained.

'I don't care,' Lawson said firmly. 'Leave her be. She's my wife's sister.'

Rhianna looked around her, hardly able to comprehend that these people assembled were celebrating *her* wedding. She had hardly had a chance to get used to the idea herself; with all the work and organising she'd had to do, she'd hardly had time to think about it. She had been in a whirl ever since Lawson had proposed. Now, she scanned the guests, drawn mostly from his acquaintances and those of his family who still remained: his Great-Aunt Hannah whose necklace of jade did not suit her donkey-brown dress and made her look austere. The Reverend William Reyner Cosens, slim and clean-shaven except for his handsome sideburns, looked his usual aristocratic self, clinging to a glass of warm ginger beer. Her own Aunt Lucy was there, dowdy and old-fashioned, with nobody talking to her, especially not the well-dressed lady friends of Jack Hayward and Robert Cookson bubbling in their modish dresses and full of themselves. Then she saw her mother with tears in her eyes because her older daughter had married so well.

A male quartet appeared, sporting identical, well-clipped moustaches and shiny hair, and entertained the guests for half an hour with some novelty songs and sparkling harmonies. After that, the bride and groom changed for their journey. Rhianna wore a new outfit in the fashionable nautical style and a flat, sailor-style, broad-rimmed hat perched on her head.

Outside, on the steps of the Dudley Arms, Rhianna turned her back on the carriage that was to convey them to the station and waved to her guests. Everybody smiled at her and waved back and the stylish lady friends of Jack and Robert threw rice. It had occurred to her earlier that Robert's lady friend, whom she had thought might have been Fanny, was not indeed. She had been introduced as Miss Amelia Lester.

Lawson handed Rhianna into the carriage and they were driven away.

'I've got a confession, Lawson,' she said as she arranged the folds of her skirt.

He looked at her ominously, not knowing what to expect. 'Oh? What's that, my darling?'

'I've never been on a train before. Will it be crowded?'

He smiled, relieved it was something so trivial. 'I doubt it. Not in first class anyway.'

'How long will the journey take?'

'We should be in London by about eight.'

'So soon?'

'I know. The wonder of modern railways. We'll be in time to take dinner in the hotel.'

Was this really happening to her? How could she have been so fortunate? What great goodness had she performed in her life that she was being rewarded thus?

In Castle Hill she stared out through the weak afternoon sunshine at the passing traffic. A troupe of bare-footed urchins squatting at the gate of the Castle Grounds seemed incongruous next to the pristine white statue of the Earl of Dudley erected only the previous year. A steam tram huffed asthmatically up the hill from the opposite direction. Old women wearing black shawls carried baskets as they trudged towards the market place. Rhianna glanced at Lawson, at his magnificently handsome face beneath his expensive, shiny top hat, and again she could not believe her good fortune. Less than four months ago they were strangers. They had met with polite words, given each other polite attention and admiring glances. He had not guessed then that she was merely a servant. As their affair blossomed and she nervously received his first kisses, she could never have guessed he would choose her to be his wife. She would endow him with all the love and affection it was possible for one person to give another. He deserved it. It was his due. He never so much as looked at another woman in her company. Never had she met anybody so focused on her, so generous, so affable, so pleasant to be with. And she had yet to experience the ultimate expression of love between a man and a woman. But it would not be that night, nor the next, nor, she suspected, the one after that.

She took his hand. 'Lawson, I have another confession . . .' She smiled into his eyes apologetically.

'What this time?' he asked.

'I've started my . . . you know . . . My monthly visitor arrived. On Wednesday.'

'Hang me!' he said, piqued. 'I think the gods are conspiring against us. Ah, well, there's nothing to be done. We'll just have to wait.' He squeezed her hand affectionately and she didn't feel so badly about it.

'You don't mind?'

'It's not a question of minding.'

'I wouldn't have wished it for the world, Lawson, not on our wedding night, but what's a girl to do to stop it?'

He laughed at the irony of her words. 'What some girls wouldn't do to start it . . .'

'But we shall most likely be at Bath before we can . . .'

He patted her hand. 'Then roll on Bath, eh?'

They reached Paddington Station as it was getting dark. In the noise and bustle a porter close by was lighting gas lamps while another took their baggage to a line of hansoms. Rhianna tripped along behind, astounded by the number of private carriages and horse-drawn buses that screamed advertisements from every side. The roads seemed jammed full of them and everywhere the street noise was unbelievable. More than four million souls inhabited that vast city, and it showed.

They reached their hotel. Once she had unpacked, Rhianna suggested that they have dinner, then take a walk in London's bright gas-lit streets. In the comfortable dining room they sat at a table next to a young man and two elderly ladies, one silked, one velveted. The young man, she noticed, kept looking at her through rimless spectacles and made her feel uncomfortable. She felt the urge to do what she would have done in her early years – bob her tongue at him – but she could not behave thus now she was a lady. So she listened and spoke more attentively to Lawson, and held his hand across the table to confound the young man.

Lawson ordered a bottle of champagne and a bottle of red burgundy. She had tasted champagne before at Baxter House and told him so.

'And did you like it?' he asked, humouring her.

'Once I got used to the bubbles tickling my nose.'

Talk of Baxter House set them conversing during their meal about the people that Lawson knew who had visited the house.

'What happened to Fanny?' Rhianna asked. 'Did she and Robert not hit it off?'

'Fanny? Oh, I think he still sees Fanny from time to time,' he answered dismissively.

'He plays the field, doesn't he?'

'Robert? No more nor less than any other single man in his position. His father is pressing him to wed, but he doesn't admire the girl his father would have him marry.'

'Oh? Who is she?'

'Some mine-owner's daughter.'

'Wealthy, I presume.'

'Why else would he want them to marry?'

'And Jack?'

'Jack will now be running the family firm. I daresay he'll need a good woman to anchor him down.'

Time passed quickly. Before they knew it they had finished their meal and the bottle of wine and the bottle of champagne were both empty.

'I know I suggested we go for a walk,' Rhianna said, 'but I'm so tired. Shall we go up?'

'You go on up, my love,' he answered. 'I think I'll go to the saloon and have a whisky . . . and maybe a cigar as well. Even a game of billiards if I can find somebody to play against. Do you mind?'

'No, course not.' She truly did not mind. It was considerate of him. It meant she would be able to undress without that first embarrassment and awkwardness she was sure to feel if he was there to watch. She could be in bed, covered up in her nightgown by the time he came up. Possibly asleep. There would be no deflowering anyway. Not tonight.

'I'll see you later. I'll try not to wake you if you're asleep.'

She stood up but hesitated to go. 'Oh, I'm so sorry, Lawson . . . To be such a disappointment on your wedding night.'

He smiled tolerantly. 'It doesn't matter,' he whispered. 'I can wait.'

Reassured, she went up and he headed for the saloon. He ordered himself a whisky, bought a cigar and meandered into the billiards room. There was no other soul in there. He set up the three balls and cued a few casual shots, potting the red, then making a couple of cannons but, uninterested in playing alone, he returned to the saloon. He sat down and contemplated events. The significance of what he had done that day in marrying Rhianna was beginning to dawn on him. This delightful, innocent young woman depended on him. She trusted him. Like any gem, she was beautiful; the most beautiful woman he had ever set eyes on. Not that her beauty overawed him. He could handle it. Certainly he would be the envy of all his friends with a wife so lovely and so delightful. But it was not just in outward beauty that she outshone everybody else. She was blessed with a serenity that most other women lacked.

But did he love her?

Whether or no, she was a prize worth the having. He admired and desired her. But love? Love, surely, tended to be associated with need. The greater your need for somebody, the more you seemed to love them. Much depended on what your need was. If you needed somebody to cook and sew you could hire a maid, of course. If you needed somebody just to fornicate with, you could hire a prostitute and have a different one every night of the week so long as you could afford it. If, on the other hand, you needed somebody to enhance people's perception of you, then your need was based on vanity. A beautiful woman, somebody you could wear like a glittering piece of jewellery, was hugely effective in gaining the attention and respect of others. And the more beautiful the woman – the more desirable – the higher your peers would esteem you. Was not that the way of the world? Did it not come down to personal vanity or personal well-being in the long run? Did not vanity and well-being fuel need, and thus our self-regard, which we pretend is our love for somebody else?

But a woman's needs . . . They were subtly different to a man's. A woman needed security, somewhere comfortable and safe to raise her brood. When she met a man who declared his love – which was the irresistible hook that caught any and every woman – would she not surrender herself to him and trade her sexuality to acquire his security and protection? Then, would she not justify her submission by convincing herself that she loved him?

Love. Need. Vanity. Sex. Marriage . . . Children.
Children . . . Ugh!

The prospect of children horrified him. The prospect of witnessing the physical beauty of his wife marred by the disfiguring ugliness of pregnancy was abhorrent. But he would see how it went, this marriage lark – without children. In the long term he had no doubt it would not change him. He was a realist if nothing else. In bed, in the dark, one woman was much like another. Poking the same fire, night in night out, tended to become a chore, whoever's grate it was and however beautifully constructed. And if it was his own grate . . . Well, he was going to be master in his own house; he could pick and choose if and when he would poke his own fire and liven the flames that burned in it. But tonight, he would honour his bride with his presence, if only a passive, admiring presence.

He stubbed out his cigar and drained his glass. He stood up and walked out of the saloon and headed towards the stairs. At the front door, two young women, flightily dressed and flaunting smooth, rounded bosoms, bantered with each other in their strange cockney accents and giggled. One of them saw him through the glass and she nudged her friend. With big eyes, she beckoned Lawson to come to them. Prostitutes. He never went with prostitutes. Why take the risk of catching something incurable? Nonetheless, it was tempting. They were young. They might be clean.

He smiled at their vivacity and, with a great effort of will, turned his back and walked upstairs.

7

Lawson had not seen Rhianna with her hair down before and he looked at her for some seconds as she brushed it, savouring the sight. He unfastened his cuffs, took off his necktie and removed his collar.

'Tomorrow we'll hire a hansom and have a look at the Houses of Parliament and Westminster Abbey,' he said. 'Then we'll have a bite to eat and go to the Tower of London and see how they're getting on with that Tower Bridge they're building.'

'I wouldn't mind spending a whole day in the National Gallery,' she answered as she got up from her stool. 'You know how I enjoy nice paintings.'

'We'll go there on Monday. On Sunday afternoon we'll go to tea at Buckingham Palace, eh? I bet her blessed Majesty Queen Victoria would be keen enough to hang the kettle over the fire, lay her best chenille cloth over the table and bring out her home-made fruit cake.'

Rhianna laughed happily as she pulled back the bedclothes and slid between the sheets. She looked at him and sighed. 'Oh, I love you so much, Lawson . . .'

He sat beside her on the bed and put his arm around her. He kissed her on the cheek affectionately. 'I love you as well, Rhianna. With all my heart. Now get some sleep.'

'But I want to feel the warmth of your body next to mine,' she breathed. 'I've been dreaming about it for weeks.'

He shook his head and chuckled. 'I want to feel *your* body next to *mine*, my love. I want nothing more. But I'm not about to get myself worked up into a lather if I can't have you because of your . . . If I take my beauty sleep instead and appear to ignore you, you won't be offended, will you?'

'Oh, Lawson, I'm so sorry about tonight . . .'

Paddington Station was overtly grand and pungently aromatic, as well as being excessively noisy with the hideous roar of steam locomotives and their ear-splitting whistles. Porters and guards hurried to and fro, opening carriage doors, stowing luggage and giving other unmistakable signs that the departure of the 9.45 to Bristol was approaching. A footplateman was leaning out of his cab, routinely watching, waiting for the signal to depart. Lawson hurriedly gave a silver threepenny bit to the porter who was leaving them, having stashed their luggage inside their first-class carriage just in time. A whistle blew and the great blast of steam from the locomotive's funnel was like Krakatoa erupting.

'We only just made it,' Rhianna said, feeling the first forward movement of the train as she got her breath back.

'Well, you were in no rush to get up and have breakfast.'

She chuckled. 'I'm on honeymoon.'

'The honeymoon begins at Bath,' he proclaimed. 'In earnest.'

She smiled and nodded acquiescently, then looked out of the window at the dismal hulk of a gasometer and the lines of drab houses along the Paddington Canal.

'How long is this journey likely to take, Lawson?'

'About two and a half hours. Sit back and enjoy the scenery.'

In no time they had travelled through the pleasant suburbs of New Kensington and Notting Hill, through fields verdant in their new spring greenery, and had reached Ealing Station. Rhianna sat with her head against the soft squab of the headrest as they crossed over the Thames at Maidenhead. They traversed some spectacular countryside adorned with villages, farmsteads and quaint church towers that peeped over the tops of trees like lookouts. The river appeared again as soon as they pulled out of Reading Station. Rhianna was fascinated by the ever-changing vista of a countryside she had never expected to see.

At Pangbourne an elderly gentlemen entered their compartment. A profusion of untrimmed hairs sprouted from his nose and ears. He raised his hat to Rhianna and offered a polite good morning to Lawson, then settled down to read his newspaper. His presence inhibited their intimate discussion of the treats she could expect in Bath but not her affectionate smiles that flashed across the compartment from time to time. Lawson tried to strike up a conversation with the man, but he was more interested in his newspaper. However, they did glean from him that the train would stop at Swindon long enough to visit the refreshment rooms.

The first-class side of the refreshment room was exquisite, elaborately decorated in arabesques and supported by columns painted to imitate inlaid woods. The mirrors, the hangings and the furniture would have done justice to the dining rooms of nobility. Rhianna sat at a table while Lawson went to the counter and was rapidly served by an obliging young woman. He bought a selection of sandwiches, two Banbury cakes, a pot of tea and a pint of pale ale. Soon they were back in their compartment and on their way.

Rhianna knew they had arrived at Bath when the train slowed down as it emerged from a deep, beautifully landscaped cutting. The line of carriages, like a regal procession, sedately crossed a castellated viaduct built in yellow stone, high above the River Avon. Rhianna beheld a striking panorama of the city, a profusion of golden buildings bathed in sunshine like some new Jerusalem, she thought, spreading up the surrounding hills. She enthusiastically nudged Lawson.

'Oh, look at the view.'

Lawson smiled indulgently and patted her hand.

'Oh, please can we take a walk, Lawson? I'm dying to see the shops.'

'As soon as we can. But first things first. We'll have to find a hansom to take us to our hotel.'

They alighted from the carriage, a porter took their baggage, and they headed for the row of hansom cabs already lined up outside in Dorchester Street.

Rhianna gasped when she saw the imposing façade of the Grand Pump Room Hotel. Inside, she was amazed to be taken to their third-storey room in a lift. At once, Lawson decided to take a swim in the Royal Baths attached to the hotel, foregoing their walk.

'Why don't you come and watch when you've unpacked?' he suggested. 'I understand there's a balcony for spectators.'

The bedroom was large and ornate, with a red patterned carpet. The wallpaper was maroon with an overpowering floral theme and a huge stone fireplace burned logs that gave off a pleasant outdoor aroma of leaves burning in autumn. The four-poster seemed high and when Rhianna sat on it to take off her hat, it was comfortable enough.

When she had unpacked and spruced herself up, she decided it was time to watch Lawson swim. Apprehensively, she entered the lift once more and was taken to the ground floor where she was directed along a spacious corridor that took her past private bathrooms and dressing rooms. She noticed a sign that announced a Cooling Room for Ladies and deduced that ladies were indeed allowed to use the baths. As she turned around, she could see the magnificent swimming bath below with its classical marble statue at the far end. Lawson saw her and waved.

When they returned to their room, Lawson, tired from his exertions, slept. Rhianna went to one of the private bathrooms and drew herself a hot bath. As she undressed she pondered the absolute luxury of hot running water. The bathroom filled up with steam and she slid her plain lisle stockings down her legs and slipped off her new drawers. She ran hot water into the wash basin and thoroughly laundered the rolled-up napkin she had been wearing for use another day, and saw that it had been unstained. Her heart leapt with joy at the realisation that she and Lawson could at last consummate their marriage. Relieved, she stepped into the bath with a smile on her face and slid into its comforting warmth, contemplating her forthcoming initiation.

At dinner, they sat opposite each other in the elegant dining room. They started with salmon in a shrimp sauce and then roast lamb with mint jelly and fresh vegetables. Lawson requested a bottle of Beaune and drank most of it himself. But he messed about his food, something he always seemed to do, and refused any pudding.

'Aren't you hungry?'

'Oh, I've had enough. I'm not a big eater.'

'It surprises me, Lawson. I mean, you're tall and . . . I would have thought you needed your food.'

He made no comment.

'I enjoy my food but I can be excused for not clearing my plate. I don't want to get fat. What do you think of the food here?'

'It's a bit plainer than it was in London. But it's tasty enough.' He quaffed his wine. 'What would you like to do tomorrow?'

She half smiled. 'After we've seen all the shops, you mean?'

'We're not spending all day walking from shop to shop.'

'Well, we could wander around the abbey, if you like. And I'd love to see that place that's built in a half-moon.'

His eyes creased into an attractive smile. 'You mean the Royal Crescent.'

His look warmed her a little. 'If that's what they call it. It's near a park as well, according to the guide book. If the weather holds fine, we could take a walk there in the afternoon.' She sipped what remained of her wine and glanced across the room. The fender's brasswork flickered in the firelight and a waiter collected plates from another table. She looked into Lawson's eyes. 'My darling, I've had a lovely time so far . . .' Her hand found his across the table and squeezed it.

'Good. I'm glad.'

'What about you?'

'Well . . . I've been trying to come to terms with my new situation. This being a married man all of a sudden.'

She felt her pulse quicken and her face flush with apprehension. 'I hope you're not going to tell me you're regretting marrying me already?'

'Not regretting it. But it's suddenly come as quite a shock to the system. My life will be different . . . I'll have to get used to it, won't I? I'll have to come to terms with it.'

She frowned into her empty glass. 'We could get unmarried, Lawson, if that's what you want,' she said quietly. 'I believe you can have a marriage annulled if you haven't consumed it.'

'The word is *consummated* . . .' He chuckled momentarily at her mistake, but instantly became serious again, irked by her oblatory self-sacrifice. And yet, at the same time he was touched by it, for he imagined it would break her heart if she had to face such a trauma.

'Please tell me that's not what you want, Lawson.'

'That's not what I want, Rhianna, be assured . . . Let me order you another drink. I could certainly do with one.' He hailed a waiter. 'Two glasses of your best brandy, my man.'

'Brandy?' she said. 'You'll have me drunk. Still, I don't care as long as you still want me.'

'Yes, I want you.'

The soft crescent of her mouth transformed into a relieved smile. 'I'm glad. You had me worried.'

'Look, I haven't married you because of some lark or some

bet with my friends. I've thought this thing through . . . What I wanted to say is this . . . As well as my love for you, I want you to understand that my being married will give me more social respectability—'

'So you're only interested in social esteem. You don't really love me.'

'Of course I love you. How many times must I tell you? But love isn't everything. There are other considerations, less romantic, and I want you to understand them. Greater acceptance in society, by virtue of being married, is one of them.'

'Then you should have married an heiress, not an unemployed domestic servant.'

'Don't demean yourself, Rhianna. Oh, I know you're neither an heiress nor the daughter of some nabob, but you have the look and the bearing. And I need you. I need you to keep me on the straight and narrow.'

'You need me,' she repeated with some disenchantment. She wanted him to love her, not just need her. Love must be the overriding feature of their marriage.

'Yes. I need you. I have many faults and I'm aware of them. If you don't know them yet, I daresay they'll manifest themselves soon enough.'

'Such as?'

'I'm erratic and moody, I know this. I can be as high-spirited as a pig with a potato one day, and down in the dumps the next—'

'Drink can do *that* to you. Too much drink . . . You do drink too much, Lawson, I hate to tell you.'

'You're nagging me already.'

'I'm your wife,' she sighed. 'I want to help you. I want to look after you. I'm trying to keep you on the straight and narrow . . .'

'But you don't have to nag me. As I said, I know my faults.'

'Sorry.'

'As I was saying . . . I have a vile temper as well, I'm excitable, impulsive, I couldn't care less what my friends or anybody else—'

'Lawson, you are the most intelligent, the most generous, the *nicest*, the most interesting person I've ever met in my whole life.'

'Yes, I'm all of those things . . .' He smiled with a sham smugness that amused her, but was almost immediately sombre again. 'I'm sometimes over-emotional. Intellect and emotions seem to rule me, Rhianna. I also get very jealous, you know . . .'

'You've no reason to be jealous where I'm concerned.'

'No, I don't think I have. But I want you to know what I'm like under the veneer of brashness that you see. I need you to understand me and, when you understand me, to direct me.'

The waiter brought their brandies and deposited them on the table with a flourish and Lawson thanked him.

'You're untidy,' Rhianna proclaimed when the waiter had gone. 'I've noticed that already.'

'And you don't mince your words . . .' He smiled again and tasted the brandy. 'We shall have a successful marriage, Rhianna, you and I,' he said expansively. 'You are the exact opposite of everything I am. I envy you your virtues, you know. Your innocence, your warm-heartedness, your affability . . . You'd give away your last penny if you thought it would help the person you were giving it to, whereas I wouldn't – I'm far too selfish. You're patient. I'm not. You're organised, I'm generally in utter chaos. I'm volatile, I've never once seen you flustered. You're even-tempered—'

'I'm also free of my monthly scourge,' she said quietly and dipped her nose into her brandy glass without looking at him.

He guffawed and his eyes brightened. 'Then why are we sitting here? Come on, let's go upstairs . . . Lord, I've got a stirring in my loins already. Take the brandy with you . . .' He rose from his chair eagerly, then went round to Rhianna and drew back her chair as she rose, a radiant smile on her face. 'Why didn't you say so sooner, save me rambling on the way I did.'

'At least I know you better because of it,' she said as she took his arm. 'At least I know what to expect in future.'

'Oh, ignore me, Rhianna. It was the drink talking . . .'

They undressed by candlelight. As she lay naked awaiting him, the dipping flicker of yellow light added warm colour to her pale skin and threw dancing shadows on the wall behind him as he got into the right-hand side of the bed and lay beside her. At once they were in each other's arms. He was instantly aroused as he savoured the sleekness of her body, the feel of her soft, silky skin pressed lightly against his. It was a once-in-a-lifetime experience this, the very first time with a virgin wife, and he was not about to rush it.

'Aren't you warm enough?' he whispered. 'You're trembling.'

'I'm not cold, Lawson. Just a bit nervous, that's all.'

'There's nothing to be nervous about, sweetheart. I love you. I'll look after you.'

Her baptism of sexual experience was upon her as he traced faint lines all over her body in gentle strokes with the tips of his fingers. She shuddered with delight at the sensations and this new experience of intimacy incited a warmth of desire that welled up inside her. With his eyes shut, he found her mouth and kissed her tenderly, but eagerly and there was no mistaking his hunger, his need for her. While they kissed, his right hand explored more of her, sending fresh, delectable shivers up and down her spine. He pressed himself against her and cupped one round, yielding breast in his hand and felt her nipple harden between his fingers. Then he left a trail of kisses down her neck and across her breast till he found that nipple and nuzzled it like a suckling child.

His tongue flicked delectably across it and the sensations

astonished her. She had tried to imagine all this before of course, alone in her bed in Baxter House and in the boxroom at Campbell Street. But she had not expected that his warm, firm flesh against hers would be so stimulating. She could feel that familiar wetness between her legs and, when he touched her there, she was surprised at how utterly pleasant was the contact. His fingers caressed her so skilfully that she couldn't help but utter little sighs and groans at the pleasure of it. After a while, he rolled onto her and slid down her body, between her legs, leaving a moist trail of tender little bites that went rapidly cold across her belly. He slithered lower until his face was snuggled in her dark, moist curls. His tongue lapped inside her and around her, and the sensations were mesmerising. She arched her back and held his head to draw him further into her and, when he gave her tender little bites she lay and wriggled, and gasped in a crisis of ecstasy and stupefaction. Her heart was pounding hard as he slid his body up over her again and she received his wet, lingering kiss with a hungry, open mouth. He raised himself up on his arms to relieve her of his weight, then looked down between their bodies to where he was nudging her, to where he was pressing for entry.

'I'll try not to hurt you,' he breathed. 'But it might, for a second or two.'

'I don't mind, my love. I want you . . .'

Her hands were on his hips, half expecting to have to hold him back if the pain was too great. She felt him enter, winced as he seemed to stretch her, and she whimpered at the sudden, sharp but anticipated twinge at his first thrust.

'I'm sorry . . .' He halted.

'No . . . It's all right,' she cooed. 'Don't stop . . . Slowly . . .' Holding her breath, she gripped his buttocks and, without further thrusting, he allowed her to pull him into her at her own pace. She let out a little groan as slowly, cautiously, he filled her up. In some distant recess of her mind she could hear herself quietly sighing as she felt him moving gently inside her, against her . . . So this was lovemaking . . . This was how it felt . . . Well, it was not at all unpleasant, this ultimate expression of love . . . In fact, the longer it went on the more pleasant it became, the more heightened became her emotions . . . Soon, she felt Lawson pulsing within her and he let out a great grunt . . . and then he ceased to move any more, to her disappointment. He slumped, relaxed, spent.

'Are you all right,' she asked unsure whether this was normal.

He nodded, his face in the pillow. 'Never better.'

She hugged him. 'Have I made you happy, Lawson? I haven't disappointed you, have I?'

He shook his head, then rolled off her onto his back and closed his eyes. She ran her fingers gently across his chest, moist with perspiration. By the flickering candlelight she glanced adoringly at his handsome face, at his dark hair all ruffled, at his pulse beating fast in the hollow of his neck.

'I love you, Lawson Maddox,' she whispered. 'Oh, I love you so much.' She had given herself eagerly, earnestly, and now it was all over. 'Hold me, Lawson,' she sighed, snuggling up to him. 'Love me . . .' She wanted to share with him the spiritual closeness, this newly reinforced bond. It had been a wonderful experience, far better than she had expected.

He stirred slightly, his breathing steady as she waited for his response. She realised with frustration that he was asleep already and she drew the bedclothes up around them. She blew out the candle and lay awake for ages, overjoyed that they had consummated their marriage, that it was much nicer than she had dared hope . . . Yet she felt there should have been something more . . . She was disappointed as well that Lawson was not awake to talk about it, to tell him how she felt.

Then he stirred again.

'Don't forget to wash yourself out,' he muttered, and rolled over onto his side.

* * *

Next morning they awoke early. She greeted him, her eyes bright with tenderness, her lips smiling her commitment. He made love to her again. This time, there was no lengthy foreplay to make her squirm with desire, and Lawson's whiskery growth was scratchy against her smooth face as he thrust inside her more urgently than he had last night. But afterwards, she held him lovingly and was pleased to see him contented.

Bath was wonderful. They visited everywhere there was to visit, saw everything there was to see. That day they managed a tour of the city centre, peering in the shop windows of Milsom Street. They visited the recently discovered suite of Roman baths, they took tea in the Pump Room and tarried to listen to the fine band that played some beautifully serene music. When they had satisfied their curiosity as to the peculiar taste of the warm mineral water, they returned to their hotel and made love again.

Next day, Rhianna was enchanted by the King's Circus with its exquisite relief carvings, and thrilled to learn that some of the houses had been owned and occupied by such legendary figures as William Pitt the Elder, Clive of India and David Livingstone. They saw the Assembly Rooms, sadly dilapidated, but she imagined the genteel balls of a bygone age, the tea-parties, the card-playing. Queen Square fascinated her with its houses which were on one side the mirror images of those on the other. She was amused at the Bath chairs and the people who used them. Pulteney Bridge was a treasure trove of little shops and tea rooms that fooled her into thinking she was on a street and not walking over the river. Only when they walked along Grand Parade and she could see the bridge did she marvel at the illusion.

Every day they made love, usually more than once – at times of the day her mother would have frowned on – and Rhianna was content that her husband found her so desirable. But she remained disappointed that always, afterwards, she yearned for some tenderness, some show of added affection, while Lawson always seemed oblivious to her needs, usually dozing off. When he touched her, when they laughed and teased and it was obvious they were going to make love, she was always excited, always eager to give herself. Always there was the promise that some scandalously astounding pleasure was about to explode within her, though it had not yet. Oh, lovemaking was nice, to be sure. It made her toes curl . . . But surely there was more to it . . .

And why did he expect her to wash herself out afterwards? Surely he realised she wanted his children?

8

On their first full day back at home in Himley Road, Rhianna got up, washed, and dressed before Lawson, to the disturbing reality that there was no food in the house to make breakfast. While she waited for him to venture downstairs she explored the cellar and foraged for coal. She lugged a bucketful up the stone steps to light a fire in the scullery range. Using a draw-tin, the coals quickly ignited, so she would soon be able boil a kettle and brew a pot of tea. Having returned too late the previous evening to do anything about it, there was no fresh milk in the house. Pondering whether she should don her hat and coat and rush to the nearest corner shop, she stepped into the sitting room. At once she was drawn to the magnificent painting of the young girls draped over their Italian marble bench and could not help pausing to look at it for a few seconds, before turning to the bleak, uninspiring landscape outside her front window. As she peered out, she saw a milk float coming down the hill. She rushed to the front door, waited for it to approach then hailed the milkman. He stopped, touched his cap and alighted from the cart.

'Morning, ma'am,' he greeted her cordially. 'Can I be of help?'

'I take it you don't deliver milk here?' she said.

'No, ma'am. Never bin axed.'

'Could you? In future?'

'Cerpaintly, ma'am. Am you the missus?'

She smiled at this description of herself. 'Yes, I'm the missus. And could we have a couple of pints this morning, do you think?'

'No trouble. I generally carry extra milk. Yo' never know who'll be wanting extra.'

'I'll fetch a couple of jugs. I won't be a minute.'

When she returned the milkman was making a new entry into his well-worn record book.

'Maddox is the name, in't it?' he queried.

'You know it already,' she remarked with some surprise.

'I've heard it mentioned.'

'Well I'm Mrs Maddox. To tell the truth, I'm new over this side of town. We were only married a little while ago.' She held out the enamelled jugs. 'It's our first day back from honeymoon.'

He ladled milk into both of them. 'Honeymoon, eh? Bin somewhere nice?'

'London and Bath.'

'London and Bath. Very nice. Yower husband must be as wealthy as folk mek him out to be then, eh?'

'Wealthy? I wouldn't know. I'm not privy to his financial affairs.'

'Well, ignorance is bliss, or so they say. Eh, Mrs Maddox?'

'I daresay you're right, Mr . . .'

'Turner. At your service. Would yer like me to call tomorrer?'

'Please. Every day, if you would.'

'No trouble. I collect me money of a Saturday.'

'I'll have it ready . . . Tell me, Mr Turner, is there a butcher locally you could recommend. And a grocer?'

'There's Randall's in Salop Street.' He nodded in the direction he'd come from. 'Top of the hill and turn left. They say his meat's all right. Next to him there's a grocer and greengrocer.'

'Thank you, Mr Turner. I'll see you tomorrow.'

Mr Turner returned his ladle to his milk churn, touched his cap and stepped up onto the float again.

Back inside, the fire had caught nicely. Rhianna filled her kettle from the tap in the brewhouse outside and hung it on a gale hook over the fire. She looked around the freshly whitewashed scullery. It was all new to her and she had to find her way around. She located the teapot, the caddy, and spooned tea leaves into the pot ready, then searched the cupboards and the cellar head for food. There was nothing she fancied; only stuff she would have to throw away. She made a note of the kitchen utensils, which were a legacy from Lawson's father's days, and decided she would need everything new.

Lawson came down and stood in the door frame, smartly dressed.

'I see you've lit a fire already.'

'There's not much coal in the cellar, Lawson. We'll need more. We've nothing for breakfast either, save for some milk. I just saw the milkman and asked him to call every day. I think I'd better run up the road and get some bacon or something.'

'There's some ginger biscuits in a biscuit barrel in the sideboard,' he said. 'They'll do for now. I'm not particularly fussed about breakfast, to tell the truth.'

'I'll need some money, Lawson,' she said apologetically. 'For meat and bread and provisions. I could do with finding a hardware shop as well. We don't have any pots and pans to speak of. Nor knives and scissors and such like. Lord only knows how that cook you hired managed.'

'How much do you want?'

She shrugged. 'Hard to say. But I do need to stock up.'

He fished his wallet out of his pocket and rummaged through the coins. He began picking out gold sovereigns. 'Will ten pounds do?'

'Ten pounds? Good God, yes. Ten pounds should be plenty.'

He handed her the coins.

'Are you able to drive me there and back, Lawson?' she asked. 'I'm only thinking about carrying all that stuff.'

'Not today, Rhianna. I've got a busy day today. First I've got to fetch the horse from Jones's stables. Then I've got business to attend to, people to see. I've been away more than a week, remember. You'll have to manage as best you can.'

'What time shall you leave?'

'As soon as I've wet me whistle.'

The kettle started boiling, spitting water into the fire and hissing impatiently. She took a cloth and lifted it from the gale hook and poured water into the teapot.

'So when shall I see you back?' she enquired pleasantly.

'I'll be back for tea, I daresay.'

She stirred the pot, put the lid on and smiled at him. 'And I'll have a lovely hot dinner ready for you . . . Now, let me see if I can find that biscuit barrel . . .'

When she returned, Lawson said, 'I can see that you're going to need a maid, Rhianna. Remind me to see to it.'

'Oh, I can see to it. I'm used to it. I'll put a notice in the window at the post office or something. A maid-of-all-work is what we need.' The thought of having a maid enthralled her. A maid would underline her own uplifted social status. 'A maid-of-all-work would be very useful, Lawson . . . and wouldn't cost a fortune either.'

A long queue of women waited to be served in Randall's, the butcher's shop the milkman had told her about, and Rhianna just managed to squeeze through the door at the end of it. Rabbits, chickens, and half pigs hung stiffly from galvanised steel hooks attached to the ceiling on the other side of the counter. In the window was displayed a pig's head made of plaster and painted in glossy paint, with a painted plaster apple in its mouth and surrounded by sprigs of real parsley, all on a white enamelled tray. Near it were some plaster representations of pork pies and sausages. The chopping block, a cylindrical section of a thick tree trunk, stood upright in a corner behind the counter, its top scrubbed and uneven with wear, but now spattered with blood, flecks of meat and shards of bone from the day's butchering. Sheets of lights and tripe draped the far wall like thick curtains, and two strips of fly paper, dotted with dead flies, hung three feet apart above the wooden counter. The wooden floor was strewn with sawdust.

While waiting to be served Rhianna watched the butcher's obsequious way with the ladies and his technique, which seemed so laborious. 'There y'am, Maude, my lover,' he said with feigned warmth to one customer. He counted the change into her hand as if it were a personal gift. 'Three an' nine, four shillin', four an' a tanner – an' a tanner for yerself meks five bob.' Rhianna wondered why he couldn't be quicker.

He served another woman, packing two pounds of cooked tripe into a quart jug she'd brought with her specially for the purpose. The next customer eventually left with a pound of sausage, a skinned rabbit with the head still on, and some lights which, she claimed, were for her cat. Rhianna shuffled nearer the front of the queue in the sawdust with the other waiting customers while the butcher continued his theatricals. By this time she had most definitely decided that she did not like him. He was an actor if ever there was one, and he brandished his meat cleaver with a casualness that made her wince. She watched his tedious patronising with increasing contempt. Her frustration grew at his lack of system which was keeping her from the important duties that her new marriage imposed upon her.

The next customer bought a pair of cow heels and some lambs' tongues. Another asked for a pig's trotter for her husband's tea and a quarter pound of lamb's liver for his dinner tomorrow. Then, at long last, Rhianna's turn came.

'Yes, my flower?' the butcher said with his professional smile, about to embark on another performance for the benefit of customers filling the little shop behind her. 'What can I do for you?'

Rhianna realised she was being watched now. 'Three lamb chops, a pound of sausage, three liver faggots, and a pound of streaky bacon, please.' These were the preferences of her mother and father and her sister, whom she intended visiting later that day.

The butcher sliced and chopped, weighed and wrapped the meat in greaseproof, and placed it all in a neat heap on a pile of newspaper he used for his outer wrappings. He jotted down the prices on a corner of the newspaper, ready to reckon up, then stuck his blacklead behind his ear. 'Anything else, my flower?'

'A small joint of pork, please, and a pound of best back bacon.'

'You'm fresh round here, in't yer?' he asked, unable to contain his curiosity any longer. 'I in't sid yer afore. And I'd have noticed *you.*'

'I've just married and moved to this area,' she explained economically, enormously self-conscious. She blushed intensely as the butcher's audience listened, for she imagined he would be tempted to make some unsavoury comment or other.

'Just married, eh? Well yo'll need all this meat to keep yer strength up, eh?' He winked at one of his regular customers and leered, and everybody in the shop grinned. 'Who've yer married? Anybody we know?'

'A gentleman by the name of Mr Maddox. From Himley Road.'

'Yer mean Lawson Maddox?' he asked.

'Yes. Do you know him?'

The butcher shook his head. 'Only by reputation, my flower.'

The shop went quiet and the butcher seemed strangely stuck for further conversation. He scanned the rows of meat hanging up, reached for a leg of pork far bigger than she needed, and placed it on his wooden chopping block. He deftly sharpened his fearsome carving knife, and made an incision into the meat as deep as the bone. Then he took his cleaver and chopped straight through it with one hefty but very precise blow. Rhianna knew the routine by now. He placed a sheet of greaseproof paper onto his scale, and put the cut meat onto that. Then he turned around, picked up the piece of bone he'd hacked off the end, together with a thick strip of fat, and placed them on the scale with the meat. He tried an assortment of weights till the whole ensemble balanced exactly.

'That joint's one an' eleven, Mrs Maddox,' he said, scrutinising the conversions on the scale.

Rhianna coloured up again and felt hot. She hadn't expected bone and fat to be charged at the same rate as best pork, and she didn't like what he'd done. She was about to appear a very silly and gullible young bride in front of his regular customers if she stood for it. But why should she stand for it? Why should she allow him to swindle her? Inside she was boiling with resentment, yet she hesitated to say anything. If she took issue with him he would have some glib, well-rehearsed answer to make her look even more foolish. Her sense of diplomacy told her she should say nothing, but she could not allow this to go unmentioned. She had to say something. Already people must be thinking she was stupid.

She felt herself trembling. 'I don't expect to pay the same for bones and scrag ends of fat as you charge for best pork,' she said at last, trying to check the waver in her voice.

There was a loud silence.

Rhianna sensed she had thrown the butcher off balance; she had disrupted his routine. She felt the people in the queue behind her were waiting for her next move with increasing interest.

'The cost o' the pig to me includes the bone. That's the way we do it in the butchery trade.' No hint of an apology.

'Not with my money it isn't. Not with my husband's money, if you don't mind.' She sensed she had the upper hand when she heard murmurs of approval from behind.

'Huh! 'Ow'm we poor butchers ever supposed to mek a livin' then? Any road, yer need the fat to mek it nice an' tasty. Your mother must've told yer that afore yo' left 'um.' He wrapped the meat, complete with bones and fat, in a sheet of newspaper, then disdainfully handed her the parcel. Haughtily, he held his hand out for the money.

'How much did you say?'

'One an' eleven for the joint. Plus two an' eleven for the rest.'

She fumbled in her purse for one of the sovereigns that Lawson had given her, allowing him to believe for a few seconds that she had capitulated. But she had not. 'Would you take the bone off and weigh it again, please?' she asked politely, much to his surprise. There was another murmur and some shuffling of feet behind.

'Yo'm a contrary madam,' he muttered irritably. 'Let's hope yo' ain't as contrary wi' yer new husband.' Rhianna wondered if she'd dug herself into a hole. However, sensing the silent condemnation of his other customers if he refused, he unwrapped the meat and did as she requested, removing the fat as well before weighing it. 'One an' sevenpence,' he said at last.

Despite his concession, Rhianna handed her money over with great reluctance. She was certain he had still overcharged her – for everything.

'Perhaps you'd like to recommend another butcher,' she said as she took her change and left the shop.

'Yes, there's one along the road,' he replied. 'Goo to 'im next time.'

She went in the grocery shop and had no trouble there. She bought food enough for the next few days, including lard, suet, sugar, tea and fresh vegetables. She bought washing soda, starch and tablets of soap, candles, matches and spills. Laden down she took everything back home before she went shopping again for cooking and kitchen utensils, lamp oil and other household goods she could only get from the ironmonger's. When she had taken that home she collected everything she had bought for her parents and set off again, this time on the long walk to Campbell Street.

'So how was your honeymoon?' Mary Drake enquired as she poked the fire to liven it up for her newly-married daughter.

'Oh, we had a lovely time. Waited on hand and foot, we were. The hotels were lovely – nothing was too much trouble. The food was tasty and there was plenty of it.'

'How was London?' Sarah asked. 'Is it as busy as they say it is?'

'Busy? It's bustling,' Rhianna replied.

'So what am the shops like?'

'Well, you can't imagine, Sarah. Everything you could ever want you can buy in London shops. And the fashions . . .'

'Babylon,' Titus put in contemptuously from his threadbare armchair. 'They reckon there's anything up to sixty thousand prostitutes in London.'

'Hark at him,' Mary complained. 'You should be ashamed, talking about such things in front of your daughters. Get back to sleep and mind your filthy mouth.'

Titus shrugged. 'I on'y know what's in the papers . . .'

'It's disgusting what they print in the papers.'

'How's he been?' Rhianna asked.

'Same as ever,' said Mary.

Sarah brewed a pot of tea and made cheese sandwiches. While they supped, Rhianna was keen to tell them all about London and Bath and, once she started, there was no stopping her. Sarah listened with wide-eyed enchantment.

'Oh, it sounds beautiful, our Rhianna,' she said. 'I'd love to go.'

'Then yo'd best find a rich husband,' her mother advised.

'It's time her fun' work,' Titus muttered. 'Never mind a bleedin' husband.'

'I'm *looking* for work, Father.'

'Not very bloody hard, yo' ain't. Get off your arse and start looking proper.'

'Don't *you* want a maid, our Rhianna?' her mother enquired.

'As a matter of fact we do . . . But how could I employ my own sister? I mean, when Lawson invites friends to supper or to dinner, I can hardly present my own sister as a servant when I'm supposed to be the lady of the house, can I?'

'Folk needn't know I'm your sister,' Sarah suggested.

'No, Rhianna's right,' Mary conceded, sympathetic to Rhianna's reasoning. 'It's obvious she can't hazard her own standing. But if you hear of any positions going, our Rhianna . . .'

'Of course, I'll let you know. As a matter of fact, I could always give our Sarah a character. We have different names now. Prospective employers wouldn't connect us.'

'That would help,' Sarah said.

Rhianna looked at the clock on the mantelpiece. It was after three.

'I'd better go. I've got Lawson's meal to get ready. It's my first. I have to give myself time to get it right.'

'Well thanks for the meat and stuff, our Rhianna. How much do I owe you?'

'Nothing, Mother. Lawson can afford it.'

'I'll have to thank him when I see him.' She got up to see her daughter out.

'No, don't mention it. I don't want him to know.'

When she returned home, Rhianna settled down to cooking the joint of pork. She prepared her vegetables and decided she would have it all ready by six o' clock. By then, the meat was done to perfection and the vegetables were cooked. She had the choice of plating their dinners or leaving the stuff in the pans and reheating when Lawson returned. She decided to serve the dinners and keep them warm under upturned plates in the oven, till he arrived.

By seven he still had not shown up and Rhianna was

beginning to get anxious. She checked the dinners to make sure they had not spoilt. She was beginning to feel hungry herself and wished he would hurry. By eight o' clock there was still no sign of him and she took to standing in the sitting-room window, looking up and down the road for sight of him until it was too dark to see. Nine o' clock, and still he had not come back. She felt slighted as well as ravenously hungry and decided to sit down and eat her own dinner. Already it had started to dry out but it was tasty.

Ten o'clock arrived but no Lawson, and Rhianna, angry and deeply hurt that he should avoid their first meal together, a meal she had painstakingly prepared, decided that she should get undressed, ready for bed. She was loath to go to bed without him, so she sat up and waited.

She waited till well after midnight. The first sign of his return was the clip-clop of the horse's hoofs at the back of the house. She heard Lawson unharnessing the animal and then shutting the stable door, and his voice as he spoke to the horse. She opened the back door ready for him and heard him curse as he tripped over a loose cobble.

'You're late,' she said evenly. 'I expected you earlier than this.'

'I couldn't help it,' he responded, and there was impatience in his tone. 'I got caught up in some business.'

'But you said you'd be back for tea.'

'I might have said I'd try . . . And don't you bloody nag me.'

She could smell whisky on him and saw his eyes were heavy-lidded. 'Have you eaten, Lawson?'

'Course I've eaten.'

'Then I might as well throw your dinner away.' In a fit of pique, she opened the oven and, with a cloth, lifted out the plate with his dinner on. She uncovered it and defiantly scraped it into a newspaper to throw away.

'Yes, you can damn well throw that in the rubbish – or

burn it,' he commented. 'You didn't expect me to eat that, did you?'

'Well, when it was cooked it was beautiful, although I say so myself. It's ruined now.'

'I'll have a bit of pork pie.'

'We haven't got any pork pie. How am I supposed to know you like pork pie?'

'I gave you a cartload of money this morning, and you didn't get me any pork pie? What have you spent it on, for God's sake?'

'On other things. On things we needed . . . For all you seem to care.'

'I'll have some cheese,' he said quietly, as if reluctant to pursue an argument. 'Have we got any pickled onions?'

'No, but there's some fresh onion. I'll cut you some. Go and sit down and I'll bring it to you.'

She made a cheese and onion sandwich and a pot of tea, then took it on a tray into the sitting room for him.

Lawson was asleep.

Aggrieved and annoyed, she left him there with his sandwich and went to bed.

Lying alone in bed, Rhianna could scarcely believe Lawson could be so inconsiderate on their first full day of living in the house that was to be their marital home. She pondered how hard she had worked, so full of enthusiasm to get things right, to make things work, to please him. She was profoundly hurt and prayed that this was not the beginning of a pattern of behaviour she would not be able to endure. She was worthy of better and she had not counted on being treated like a maid. Even though she had been a servant in somebody else's house, her self-esteem was high and she would not accept the unacceptable, however much she loved him. Where had he been? Who had he been with, out till this hour? Well, better not plague herself with stupid speculations. It must have been business. He'd said so. So it must have been important business, else he would have come home when she expected him.

Rhianna cried herself to sleep that night, alone in her new marriage bed.

But, in the morning, Lawson was lying beside her. They awoke at the same time and he smiled at her as if nothing untoward had happened. He went to put his arm around her, but she turned away. Why should she reward him for being so thoughtless? She quickly slipped out of bed and began washing her face at the wash stand.

'Come back to bed,' he said and his voice was as smooth as butter.

'It's time to get up, Lawson,' she said indifferently. 'There's work to be done.'

'You're not in service now.'

She wanted to suggest that she was; that she was in service to him, that she was his wife and, after the way he'd treated her last night, was there really any difference. But she thought better of it. 'How do you feel this morning?' she asked instead. 'You were the worse for drink last night.'

'I know. I'm sorry, Rhianna. I fell amongst thieves . . .'

'You mean business thieves?'

He laughed ironically. 'Oh, yes, business thieves . . . Come on back to bed. I want you.'

'I'm sorry, Lawson, but I haven't forgiven you. You can't butter me up with sweet talk.'

He sat up and ran his fingers through his hair. 'Ooh, my head . . .'

Rhianna dried her face, ears and neck with a towel. 'It serves you right. I've got no sympathy. Fancy leaving me on my own all night in this house when it was our first full day of marriage . . . the day that was to have been the start of our normal married life. Well, I hope *that* was not normal . . .'

'So you're not coming back to bed so's I can make passionate love to you? Look at this for a whopping doodle, all ready for you.'

'I don't want to see, Lawson. Anyway, why should I reward you?'

He shrugged and lay down again but unable to settle, he slipped out of bed, washed and dressed and followed Rhianna downstairs. She did the things that she envisaged were about to become her domestic practice, stoking the fire, boiling the kettle, preparing to make breakfast. He stood facing her, holding his arms out and took her upper arms gently.

'Don't touch me . . .'

He let go of her and felt in his pocket. 'I have this for you . . . Close your eyes and hold your hand out . . . Here . . .'

Resignedly, she did as he bid.

'Now open them . . .'

She looked at the open palm of her hand. 'It's a key.' Her expression revealed the extent of her puzzlement.

'It's the key to a cottage I own.'

'Are you throwing me out?' she asked, bewildered.

'Throwing you out? Of course not. It's for your mother and father and your sister.'

'Oh, Lawson,' she said quietly, her resentment, her bewilderment blending into gratitude and admiration. All at once she felt humble, having castigated him for being inconsiderate. How wrong she'd been. She stood on tiptoe and kissed him full on the lips, then nestled her head against his chest as he held her to him. 'Oh, Lawson, what can I say? . . . You're so *generous* . . . Thank you . . . Oh, Mother and Sarah will be beside themselves with joy. Where is this cottage? Maybe I can show them while you're out today. Does it need any work done on it?'

'I've seen to it that it's in perfect condition, Rhianna,' he stated proudly, entirely pleased with her gratitude, however predictable it might be. 'It's what occupied me most of yesterday.'

'So where is it?'

'In Paradise.'

She laughed. 'Well it would be, compared to the house they live in now.'

'No. I mean that's the address – Paradise – that place surrounded by fields and allotments that overlooks the Buffery.'

'Oh, there! Well that's not so far from Campbell Street. And it'll be good for Father's health. All that fresh air. Oh, Lawson, I'm so grateful to you.'

'Kiss me then, and tell me you're sorry for ticking me off about being home late.'

'Not just late – drunk . . . And I'm not sorry for ticking you off. You deserved it.'

'If I'm drunk, I'm almost bound to be late. You have to be more tolerant when I err.'

'I'll try. But you told me to keep you on the straight and narrow.'

He hugged her tightly, affectionately, and sighed . . . 'I've got to go away for a few days, Rhianna.'

'Oh?' she exclaimed, disappointed. 'Where to? How long for?'

'A week. Maybe a little longer. I'm going to Brussels and Paris.'

'Can't I go with you? I'd love to see Paris.'

'It's business, Rhianna. It won't exactly be a grand tour.'

She looked up at him kittenishly and pouted. 'But I shall miss you.'

'I shall miss you too, sweetheart. Kiss me.'

She kissed him.

'Now come to bed with me.'

'I've just got dressed.'

'So have I. So what? We can get undressed.'

'Oh, Lawson, you're impossible,' she said as he led her back upstairs.

9

Rhianna, Mary and Sarah visited the cottage in Paradise on the same day that Lawson had handed her the key. The row of cottages stood in a hollow on open ground, away from the town. The front of the houses faced north-west onto a field that was divided up into allotments. There had been talk of developing the waste ground to the south and east into a park which would partially surround the row, but also make it a fine location.

Not much more than two hundred and fifty yards away stood Netherton station and they could hear the locomotives as they hurtled from the tunnel that had been constructed by the Oxford, Worcester and Wolverhampton Railway some years earlier. Through the cottage's upstairs window they could see palls of steam and smoke rising from the cutting in thrusting white clouds that dissipated in the wind. Adjacent to the station, but side-on to the cottages and therefore unseen, stood a pair of huge gasometers, five or six storeys high when charged, and a sickly waft of gas inevitably issued from that direction when the wind was south-easterly; but they could smell the gasworks in Campbell Street as well.

Excitedly, the women stood together in the cottage's newly decorated small front room, and made their plans as to how it should be furnished and curtained. From her winnings from the cockfighting, Rhianna would buy them a new table and chairs for the scullery and armchairs for the front room, a new chenille fringe for the mantelshelf and a matching tablecloth to be laid on Sundays. They would choose bright new linoleum for the floors and Mary said she would podge a hearthrug out of Titus's old jackets. Upstairs: new curtains, lino and bed linen. Outside in the yard, which they would share with three other cottages, the brewhouse had running water and there was a two-seater privy, which Rhianna thought could turn out to be spectacularly sociable.

Full of enthusiasm, they walked back to Campbell Street to report the purpose of their outing to Titus and to embellish their findings.

'Lawson has found we a better house to live in, Titus,' Mary began on their return.

'A better house?' Titus queried, looking suddenly bemused.

'Yes. Not a new house, but a better one.'

'Well, that's right noble of the lad. What's it likely to cost a wik in rent?'

'Nothing,' Rhianna answered proudly. 'It's rent-free.'

'And where is it, this house?'

'Down Paradise.'

'Huh! It'll be overrun wi' mice, mark my words.'

'There's no mice, Father,' Rhianna said. 'There's no sign of mice.'

'No mice, eh? And rent-free . . . down Paradise . . . Well . . .' Titus shook his head pensively. 'But I'm hanged if I'll accept charity, our Rhianna. I couldn't. And any road, what's the sense in we flitting? We'm all right here.'

Rhianna looked at her mother as much as to say she expected this response. She turned to her father and kissed him on the cheek. 'Well, hard luck, 'cause you're moving and that's that.'

'Listen,' Titus said, wagging a long, thin finger at them. 'I can see what yo' three am up to. Ganging up on me, yo' am. But it's no good trying to railroad me into doing summat what's agin' me nat'ral inclination. Especially without due consideration. I'd sooner stop where I bin.'

'*I've* gi'd it due consideration, Titus,' Mary replied defiantly, removing her hat and placing it on the scrubbed table, 'and you'll do as you'm told. It'll be better for your health than stuck sitting in this damp hole like a flea in a dishcloth. And it'll be better for me an' all. It's me what has to look after yer, remember. It's me what has to walk half a mile to the nearest blasted water pump. There's running water in the brewhouse down there.'

'Sometimes our Sarah fetches the wairter,' Titus said defensively.

'Sometimes her does,' Mary conceded. 'But when her's at work again, her won't be hereabouts to fetch it. So I suggest you gi' that some of your due consideration.'

Titus rubbed his eyes and sighed. 'Well, tell me all about it, then.'

The women looked at each other acknowledging that Titus had as good as conceded defeat. Eagerly, they extolled the virtues of Lawson's property, describing it vividly in turn. Eventually, Titus grudgingly agreed that if it was as good as they claimed, then it might be all right.

'So when am we flitting? We'll have to borry an 'oss and cart to carry all our trankelments.' He was attempting to put one last obstacle in the way. 'And how am I gunna get there wi' me foot?'

'On the cart,' Mary said impatiently, 'along with the rest o' the trankelments.'

Rhianna laughed at their habitual bickering. 'Oh, you'll love it there, Father, surrounded by trees and allotments. It'll be quiet as well. There's hardly a factory within a quarter of a mile … And they're talking about making a park right by it with a bandstand. Just think, you'd be able to listen to the band playing of a Sunday afternoon.'

'So when am we flitting?' Titus asked again.

Mary looked at Rhianna for a reply. 'What d'yer think, our Rhianna?'

'As soon as we can. As soon as we can arrange to borrow

a horse and cart. I'll ask Lawson later. He's bound to know somebody.'

'What would we do without that Lawson?' Mary mused.

'Well, the day after tomorrow I'll tell you. He's off to Paris and Brussels for a week.'

'Oh? Doing what?' Mary enquired.

Rhianna shrugged. 'Business. How should I know?'

'Well, you should, our Rhianna . . . Anyway, why don't you use his curricle while he's away?'

'If only I knew how to handle the thing . . .'

'Ask him to learn yer. Think of the shoe leather you'd save.'

'That's not a bad idea, Mother. Maybe I will . . . Listen, I think we should go and choose some furniture. Why don't we go now up to the town? Father will be all right for a couple of hours. Won't you, Dad?'

'Have I got any choice?' Titus said acidly.

'Well, Sarah could stay here with you.'

'No, I want to come,' Sarah exclaimed, afraid she might miss something. 'I want to go up the town.'

'Hang me, but I've only just took me blasted bonnet off,' Mary complained.

'Well, put it back on again, Mother. And look sharp about it. I want to be back home by four at the latest.'

Titus scratched his head and looked from one to the other. 'When am I gunna get me dinner? I'm clammed. I could eat a dog that's died o' the riff.'

Mary put her hands to her face and chuckled. 'I forgot all about his dinner, poor sod. Shall we have a bite to eat, then, afore we go? Then we needn't rush back.'

The next week was devoted almost entirely to moving from one house to the other. Such things as could be carried on foot they carried, in bags and boxes. Lawson paid for somebody to transport the Drakes' furniture and bulkier possessions by horse and cart, and the move to Paradise went entirely well, even for Titus. Rhianna sat at home at night sewing curtains and nets, pondering what Lawson might be doing while he was away. Maybe her mother was right. Maybe she should get more involved in his business activities, especially if he were to allow her to use his cabriolet. It would take some of the load off him, enable him to get home earlier at night. It would save him getting waylaid by the highfalutin friends and acquaintances whom she had no time for, and returning home late the worse for drink.

And so the Drake family settled in Paradise. Rhianna decided it was oddly named. If the sun shone endlessly, if the sky was eternally blue and everywhere was surrounded by beautiful white marble, bright poppies and umbrella pines, like in the painting by John Mallory Gibson that she loved so much, that would indeed be Paradise. But not here, in this misnamed corner of Dudley, tucked away in waste ground with allotments to the front, the Doghouse Brickworks and the slag heaps of the Old Buffery Colliery visible in the distance at the rear. But at least it was costing nothing in rent. She could afford to pay for their groceries and incidental needs; and Sarah could help when she found work.

Before he left for his trip, Lawson arranged for a decorator to spruce up one of the servant's bedrooms in the attic of their own house and had a new bed and bedding delivered. He returned home after eight days. A hansom drew up outside the house and deposited him with his baggage in the late afternoon, the day before Rhianna's twenty-third birthday. He was tired and flopped wearily into an armchair in the sitting room.

'I'll make you a cup of tea,' Rhianna said, having fussed over him for a minute or two. 'Do you fancy something to eat as well?'

'A bit of pork pie and a few pickled onions wouldn't come amiss.'

She smiled. 'I bought a pork pie only this morning. It'll be lovely and fresh. I won't be a minute. Take your shoes off and put your feet up awhile, Lawson.'

She prepared his drink and his pie and delivered it, teapot and all, to him on a tray. His eyes were closed, but when she walked in and put the tray on the low table in front of him, he roused. She handed him a plate, poured his tea and sat beside him.

'So . . . did you have a successful trip?'

He took a bite out of the pork pie and nodded. 'Oh, you wouldn't believe how lucrative, my love. But those trips to the Continent always are . . .'

'What did you do? Who did you see?'

He waved his hand dismissively. 'I don't want to talk about it now, Rhianna. I'm tired and I need some rest . . .'

'The move went well for Mother and Father,' she said conversationally.

'Ah, good.'

'I don't know how we'd have managed if you hadn't organised that chap with the horse and cart.'

'It was no big thing. Anybody can organise a horse and cart. Folk are glad of the money.'

'Well, they love the house, Lawson. They're so grateful to you, you can't imagine.'

He dismissed her gratitude with a brisk flourish of his hand. 'Pour me a glass of whisky, Rhianna.'

'Whisky?' A wave of disappointment swept over her.

'Yes, whisky.'

'All right . . .' Now was not the time to take issue with him over drinking.

She returned with a measure and handed it to him. He downed it in one gulp.

'I'm going to bed now for an hour,' he said, and put down his glass. 'I need some sleep.'

'You haven't drunk your tea.'

'No matter.'

'Shall I come upstairs with you?'

'I'm going upstairs to sleep, Rhianna,' he said, misconstruing her intention.

'I wasn't thinking of anything else, Lawson,' she said defensively. 'I just wanted to be near you. I haven't seen you for more than a week.'

'Suit yourself.'

She thought better of it. His brusqueness grieved her. Even though he was tired, he could still be civil towards her, especially after having been away so long and married less than three weeks. He was thoughtless when in other ways he was so considerate. But he had warned her what he was like. She should be neither surprised, nor distressed.

Shortly after eight o'clock in the evening she heard him upstairs. He was awake. She put the potatoes on the hob to boil and next to it placed the pan containing the peas she had just shelled. He came downstairs, naked to the waist, and washed himself at the sink.

'Your dinner will be ready in about twenty minutes. I've cooked you a nice piece of gammon. I'll fry you a couple of eggs to go with it.'

'I couldn't eat it, Rhianna,' he replied.

'What? None of it?'

'None of it. Besides, I'm going out. I'm due to meet Jack Hayward.'

'Oh.' Her disappointment was manifest in her voice. 'I did think you'd stay at home tonight, since I haven't seen you.'

'Can't be helped, my love.'

'Well, I'm not very happy about it, Lawson. Couldn't you have arranged to see him some other time? I mean, your friends seem to see you more than I do.'

'It can't be helped, I told you.' He rewarded her with a smile. 'I was looking forward to having a nice quiet evening with my wife, but on my way back from the station this afternoon I called at the Saracen's Head and Jack was there. There's some prizefight on in West Bromwich. I'm running a book.'

'But you could have put him off.'

'Well, not really. There's a fortune to be made. I daren't miss the opportunity.'

'Well, can't I come?'

'It's not a fit spectacle for ladies.'

'No less so than cockfighting, I would have thought. You took me to a cockfight.'

He shook his head. 'This is different. It's men beating seven bells out of each other.'

'But—'

'No buts. That's my last word on the subject. Now tell me, how has the horse been? Have you been looking after him?'

'Course I've looked after him. I've fed him, watered him, mucked him out. He'll be glad to get out of that stable, I should think. He'll be that frisky when you get him on the road.'

'He needs exercising when I'm away. I could pay a lad to exercise him.'

'Why pay a lad?' she said, determined to utilise this God-given chance to mention her mother's suggestion. 'Why not teach me how to handle the cabriolet and I could give him all the exercise he needs.'

'The trouble with that idea, Rhianna,' Lawson said with an amused smile, 'is that I should never get my hands on the cabriolet again. You'd be trotting off to Paradise in it all the time.'

Rhianna went to bed alone, thoroughly dejected. For eight days she had waited for Lawson to return home from France and Belgium. For eight days, sewing curtains, she had pondered his return and how good it would be to see him again, to laugh with him like they did, to lie with him now that making love was becoming so enjoyable. But his sporadic indifference to her she could not credit, it was so disconcerting. One minute he was blowing hot, next minute cold. Why was he so mercurial?

When he finally came home that night and slid into bed beside her, cold and reeking of drink, she pretended to be asleep. He did not molest her or bother her. Within a few minutes she heard his deep, sustained breathing and knew that he was already asleep. How much money had he made tonight on his bookmaking? And why was prizefighting so different to cockfighting? Both were barbaric.

Tomorrow was her birthday. So far, he'd shown no signs of remembering it. Well, on principle she would not remind him, but she would be sorely aggrieved if he forgot.

Next morning, having slept fitfully, she arose before Lawson woke up. If he found her beside him when he awoke he would expect her to lie there submissively while he pumped his seed into her then expected her to wash it out. Well, he did not deserve her. She merited better consideration. Oh, she yearned for some romance, most certainly, but just to be used as an object to satisfy his impulsive lust was not part of her plan. She was his wife; beloved, to be respected. She was not some whore, there to lie on her back and satisfy the sexual urges of male incontinence umpteen times a day, for a shilling a go.

She stole downstairs, washed herself at the sink and prepared breakfast. The postman dropped a letter through the letterbox – for Lawson. Mr Turner, the dairyman, called for his dues and she paid him. Before Lawson was even out of bed she had left the house and had walked to the town for her shopping, and then on to see her father.

While she was at the cottage in Paradise, being given a birthday card by her family, Lawson appeared. Mary made a great fuss of him. She made him a cup of tea and brought out the cake she had made, which she had been saving for Sunday tea. Titus was full of deference, even offering to give up his horsehair armchair in veneration of his munificent son-in-law. Rhianna was naturally pleased to see Lawson, but apprehensive lest he was in brusque mood. She had not yet learned how to read or predict him. However, Lawson was charming, humorous and inordinately polite to his in-laws. His affability rubbed off on her, evoking guilt that she had probably judged him unfairly in her fit of pique. They stayed about an hour before he suggested to Rhianna that maybe they should return home.

'I'm glad you came,' she commented airily as they pulled away in the cabriolet. 'I wasn't looking forward to the walk back to Himley Road with these bags to carry.'

'I was relieved to find you there,' he replied, loosening the rein a little as they climbed the hill that would take them to Prospect Row. 'When it was obvious you weren't at home, I thought you'd run off with that milkman.'

She gave a little laugh at the ridiculous notion. 'You hoped, you mean. You don't really believe I'd ever run off with anybody, do you?'

'I would hope you wouldn't.'

'The truth is, Lawson, I didn't want to wake you. I realised how tired you were.' She wouldn't dream of telling him the real reason. 'Did you do well at the prizefight?'

'Oh, well enough.'

'I was upset that you had to go out. You're not going out again tonight, are you?'

'I thought I might.'

And on her birthday.

No mention of her birthday.

Rhianna fell silent.

She remained silent, brooding again, upset that he had evidently forgotten her birthday after all, that he couldn't care less.

'Brussels is a lovely city, you know,' he commented affably, oblivious to her distress. 'It's got a city square that's surrounded by magnificent architecture. Fifteenth century, I think. Least-wise, it looks like Perpendicular to me – not that I'm an expert.

I had some beautiful mussels in some café there, done in garlic. You can't beat Brussels for mussels.' He looked at her to see her reaction to his glib little rhyme.

Rhianna did not acknowledge it, but looked on expressionlessly at Constitution Hill with its grubby terraced houses and little factories on either side.

'But Paris is something else,' he went on, full of enthusiasm. 'A beautiful city. Oh, the night life there is unbelievable. I was taken to somewhere called the *Champs-Élysées*, and some splendid cafés. I saw the girls at the *Folies Bergères* dance the cancan, I went to *Montmartre* where all the artists live and work. You enjoy paintings, don't you? Well, the work of some of those artists is unbelievable. I would have bought a picture for you but the prospect of carrying it back home was daunting, to say the least . . . And you should see that new tower they've just about finished building. The Eiffel Tower. You wouldn't believe it's possible to build anything so high, especially of iron. It's a wonder the weight of it doesn't make it all come crashing down . . .'

Lawson chattered on with his snippets of information. Rhianna said nothing, listening, resentfully gleaning as much as she could about what he had been doing. They were ascending narrow Church Street and had almost reached Top Church before he said, 'Rhianna, I feel as if I'm talking to myself here. You haven't commented on anything I've said. What's the matter?'

'Nothing.'

He turned to her again and was surprised to see tears in her eyes.

'You're crying. What's the matter?'

'Nothing,' she repeated, more vehemently.

He drew the cabriolet to a halt at the side of the road where it was at its narrowest, outside a small workshop built of red brick and topped with a rusty corrugated iron roof.

'If there's nothing the matter,' he said gently, 'why are you crying?'

'It doesn't matter.' She took a handkerchief from her pocket.

'Of course it matters. Tell me . . . What's wrong?'

'You,' she blurted out. 'You're what's wrong.'

'Me?'

'Yes, you.'

'How? What have I done to upset you?' There was indignation in his tone, as if he was beyond reproach.

'Well, if you don't know . . .'

'How can I know? I'm not a bloody mind-reader.'

She sighed, a profound, shuddering sigh. Here was her chance to tell him. Here was the big opportunity to set things straight and try to steer her marriage along the road she had anticipated it might have taken in the first place.

'Well, first of all, you seem to be more interested in going out at night with your friends than enjoying the company of your new wife,' she began. 'You were away from me more than a week and the very day you come back you're as grumpy as hell, then take off again under some pretext that you are running a book.'

'And so I was. It's business, Rhianna.'

'And could you not afford to forego it, just once, to spend time with me? After being away so long? Is it such a chore to spend some time with me?'

'I think you're feeling sorry for yourself, Rhianna.'

'Oh, I'm feeling sorry for myself all right. How do you expect me to feel, shut up in your house every night while you go off gallivanting? Does being married preclude me from going out with you at night? You used to be keen enough to take me with you before we were married, I seem to recall.'

'You don't enjoy the places I sometimes go to. Look how you hated the cockfighting.'

'Of course I hated the cockfighting, but I enjoyed the bet you made for me. Winning all that money.'

'You wouldn't be getting mercenary, by any chance, would you?' he asked cuttingly.

'Me? Mercenary? I think not, Lawson. Emotional, maybe. But never mercenary.'

'Emotional. Ah! It must be that time of the month. Well, evidently you're not pregnant, and thank the Lord for that.'

She ignored his unwelcome comment about not wanting her to be pregnant; she could pick up on that later if ever she needed to. To discuss it now would only divert her. 'It's nothing to do with the time of the month, Lawson. Have you forgotten what day it is?'

'Saturday,' he answered flippantly. 'So what?'

'So what?' she repeated incredulously. 'I can't believe you said that. It's my birthday and you've forgotten it. It just shows how much you really think of me.' She dabbed her eyes and sat defiantly erect in the cabriolet. Well, now she'd told him. His response would be very telling.

'Oh, now we're getting to the bottom of it,' he said, unabashed. 'Well, as a matter of fact, I haven't forgotten your birthday, Rhianna. I haven't forgotten it at all. But the gift I ordered for you won't be ready till next week. I was going to surprise you with it. I ordered it before I went away but there was a query on it. Obviously I couldn't sort it out until I came home, else you'd have had it today.'

'You've ordered me something? Why didn't you tell me?'

'I was going to. You don't really think I'd forget your birthday, do you?'

She gave a shuddering sigh. 'How was I to know? You haven't mentioned it. You haven't wished me many happy returns, you haven't even given me a greeting card. Why should *I* have to mention it?'

'Oh, Rhianna . . . You know how forgetful I am. Forgive me . . . I tell you what – there's a florist up here by the church. I'll buy you the most magnificent bunch of flowers.'

'I don't want a bunch of flowers *now*,' she pouted. 'The

damage has been done. You could have woken up before me this morning and got some flowers then, ready for when I went downstairs. I would have thought the world of that.'

He took her gloved hand and fondled it. 'It's only now I'm coming to realise how sensitive you are, Rhianna,' he said quietly, consolingly. 'Forgive me. I know I'm often guilty of being thoughtless but, believe me, I do mean well. I love you too much, my sweetheart, to have any intentions at all of hurting you . . . Will you forgive me?'

'I forgive you too easily, Lawson. And that means you go and do exactly the same thing again, knowing I'll let you get away with it. But I won't. I deserve better. I ask you to be more considerate. I ask you to consider my feelings a bit more often.'

He nodded. 'I will, I will. I promise . . . Look, I won't go out tonight. We'll have a quiet night all to ourselves. You can cook us one of your beautiful dinners, we'll open a couple of bottles of that expensive claret I brought back from France and we'll play cards afterwards and . . . and we'll go to bed early. We'll celebrate your birthday all right, just the two of us . . . in our own little love nest . . .'

She smiled up at him, love in her tear-filled eyes. Oh, he could twist her around his little finger, of that she was aware. But she loved him too much to care. At least she had made her point early enough in their marriage. She had made him see. Things could only be better from now on.

IO

On the Monday morning, Lawson visited the works of J. Preece and Sons in Wolverhampton Street, to order Rhianna's birthday gift. He congratulated himself for having handled her crisis of sensitivity so adroitly, hiding, to his satisfaction, the fact that he had forgotten all about her birthday. He discussed his requirements at length with one of the sons and was shown some fine examples of their work. Eventually, back in the office, he handed over a deposit.

'So how soon can you deliver?' Lawson asked Mr Preece the youngest.

'In view of that cancelled order I told you about, Mr Maddox, I can let you have it by the end of next week.'

'Shall we say the Friday morning then?'

'Let me see . . .' Mr Preece consulted a calendar. 'That'll be the 31st. I think we can manage that. Would eleven o' clock suit?'

'It would suit very well. But not a word to my wife as to when I actually placed the order, if you don't mind.'

'Naturally.'

Lawson gave the man a knowing wink. 'I think this will more than make up for her disappointment last Saturday, and keep her off my back for some time to come.'

Mr Preece chuckled, content to connive about womenfolk and the deceiving thereof with such a worldly and well-heeled client. 'Oh, I'm sure she'll be entirely happy, Mr Maddox . . . Now, when may we remit you?'

'I'll pay cash on final inspection.'

*   *   *

The weather was set fair and had been for a few days. The hazy sunshine lent a warmth to the air, quite still now after some raucous May winds a week earlier. Unaccountably for a Friday, Lawson had stayed at home, lounging about the house, getting in Rhianna's way.

'How come you haven't gone out?' she asked. 'You've normally disappeared by this time of a Friday morning.'

He pulled out his watch and checked the time. 'I haven't got to go out this morning.'

Rhianna held a tin of furniture cream in one hand and a duster in the other. 'Would you move your legs while I polish this table?'

'You shouldn't be polishing tables.'

'Well, I'd like to think that too,' she said with an ironic little laugh. 'I really should advertise for a maid.'

'Had you forgotten?'

'No. I just haven't had time. I'll put an advertisement in the *Dudley Herald*. I'll do it on Monday.'

Lawson looked at his watch again, stood up impatiently and went over to the front window. He parted the nets and peered to his left, looking up the hill.

Rhianna continued with her chores, dusting the mantelpiece and the frame of her favourite picture. She had finished and was just about to leave the room to work upstairs when Lawson spoke.

'Quick, take your pinafore off and smooth the creases out of your frock. I don't want you looking like a maid. We have company.'

'Company?'

He smiled at her mysteriously. 'Don't ask questions. Just do as I say.'

As she took off her pinafore she heard the sound of horses and the rumbling wheels of a carriage at the side of the house where the driveway stood.

'Who is it?'

He grinned. 'You'll see in a minute.'

There was a knock on the front door. Lawson answered it and she heard him greeting somebody. 'Rhianna!' he called.

She went to him. A man was standing on the doorstep wearing a top hat and a fine tail coat. He looked as if he was from a funeral parlour, except that he was smiling pleasantly.

'This is Mr Preece, Rhianna. He's delivered your birthday gift. A little belatedly, I know, but better late than never.'

Rhianna smiled at the man. 'Good morning, Mr Preece.'

Mr Preece tipped his hat. 'And a beautiful morning it is, Mrs Maddox.'

'So what is this mystery gift I've been promised for so long?' she asked, looking into Lawson's eyes.

'I think you'll find it's outside, my love,' Lawson said. 'Come on. Let me show you.'

Parked on the hill was a smart, two-horse phaeton with another man sitting in the driving seat. He was waiting for Mr Preece, to return him from whence he had come, or so Rhianna imagined. Then, as Lawson led her into the drive, she saw a magnificent cream-coloured gig and a palomino horse as beautiful as a fountain sparkling in sunshine. She put her hand to her mouth and gasped.

'This?' she queried, incredulous. 'This gig?'

'And the mare.'

She stood and looked with open-mouthed disbelief. 'They match perfectly,' she said eventually. 'Oh, Lawson, I can't believe it . . . How can I thank you enough? Oh, you're so generous.' She flung her arms around his neck and hugged him while Mr Preece self-consciously averted his eyes. 'But where did you get such a beautiful horse?' She went to the mare and patted her shoulder experimentally. She had never had much to do with horses until she'd been required to tend Lawson's while he was away, and was only now beginning to acquire some confidence with them. The beautiful tan-coloured mare gently flicked her head and the creamy mane tousled and fell back into place perfectly. Rhianna faced her and stroked her nose and spoke quietly to the animal. 'Oh, you *are* beautiful,' she murmured and the palomino's ears flickered interestedly. 'Do you have a lump of sugar, Mr Preece?'

'Indeed I do, ma'am.' He felt in his pocket and handed Rhianna three lumps.

'If she's to be mine, then I must curry favour with her from the outset.'

'Very wise, ma'am,' Mr Preece said.

She held her palm up and the horse nuzzled it, taking the sugar. 'Her mouth is so soft, so gentle.' Enthusiastically, she turned to Lawson. 'Oh, I think she and I are going to get along famously . . . What shall we call her?'

'You decide.'

'Oh, I can't think of anything pretty enough right now . . . Maybe Blossom . . . Yes, Blossom. What do you think, Lawson?'

'Blossom it is.'

'Let me show you the gig, ma'am,' Mr Preece suggested.

'All right.' She patted the mare again, gave her another lump of sugar and stood at the side of the gig.

'This is a Stanhope gig, ma'am. Very safe, very stable, something a lady can handle with confidence. As you can see, it has a hood in case of foul weather but, with the summer coming along, let's hope you won't need it.'

Rhianna turned to Lawson and smiled again contentedly. 'I'm going to need some tuition on how to handle it, aren't I?'

'Yes, your husband has thought of that, Mrs Maddox. Hence, the presence of my brother in the phaeton. He and I will teach you all you need to know.' He beckoned the other Mr Preece to join them. He obliged and reversed the gig out of the drive and onto the road.

'You get into the gig using this step,' the second Mr Preece said, indicating the iron plate that hung suspended from the coachwork. 'Would you like to try?'

Lifting her skirt a little, Rhianna stepped up and took her seat for the first time in her own gig. She giggled like a little girl with a new toy as she admired the immaculate coachwork and the shining, hand-stitched leather seat. Mr Preece handed her the reins and gave her her first instruction on how to communicate her intentions to the horse.

'Flick the reins and call "Giddup", Mrs Maddox.'

Rhianna did as she was bidden and the mare moved forward obediently.

'Oh, she's moving,' she said with some surprise.

'Because you told her to, ma'am. That's all you need do to get her moving. She's very well trained. To get her to stop, pull firmly on the reins and call "Whoa".'

'Whoa! . . . She *is* well-trained, isn't she?'

'A beautiful animal, ma'am. Your husband chose well for you. Now, let's go for a little ride up the hill and see how you fare.'

'I'm going to need some tuition on how to harness her as well, Mr Preece.'

He smiled with approval at her enthusiasm. 'Oh, one step at a time, Mrs Maddox.'

That afternoon Lawson also took Rhianna out, allowing her to drive, giving her tips on how to handle the rig. Naturally, she was keen to show her new acquisition to her family so they headed finally towards Paradise. The Drakes, even Titus, filed outside to admire the new Stanhope and the beautiful palomino.

'I think you'm ever so lucky, our Rhianna,' Sarah remarked enviously in an aside, while Lawson chatted to Mary and Titus. 'You really fell on your feet when you met Lawson.'

'Yes, I suppose I am fortunate,' Rhianna replied. 'In so many ways . . .'

'And my luck's a-changing, our Rhianna,' Sarah said excitedly. 'I found work this morning. At Hillman's in Trindle Road.'

'You mean the leather works?'

'Yes. I start Monday.'

'Well, that's good. In some ways, it's better than being in service. You'll earn more money. *And* be free to do as you like at nights.'

'I hope as there's some nice chaps there,' Sarah said. 'It's time I had a sweetheart.'

'Sweethearts will appear soon enough, won't they Lawson?' Rhianna replied.

Lawson made a great show of looking Sarah up and down. 'Be sure of it.'

'Don't be in a rush and take up with any old Tom, Dick or Harry,' Rhianna continued. 'You're a good-looking girl. You'll always be able to take your pick of lads, a girl like you. Just be a bit choosy, like I've told you before.'

Rhianna was soon handling the Stanhope competently and within only a few days she was confident enough to drive it on her own. As she travelled through the streets of Dudley, passers-by stopped in awe to watch this elegant and beautiful young lady swish past in her cream gig with its sleek, matching horse. Those who were unaware soon learned that this was the recently installed wife of Lawson Maddox, the well-known borough rake, and that she really must have something extra special to commend her if she could captivate such a profligate womaniser, to the extent that he was prepared to lavish extravagant gifts like a horse and trap on her.

On one trip, she visited the offices of the *Dudley Herald* to insert an advertisement in the Situations Vacant column. Lawson had decided that as well as a maid-of-all-work, they also needed a boy to act as groom – especially now they had two horses to care for – somebody useful who could also turn his hand to gardening; it was certain the lad would never be idle. In their elevated social position they needed servants, and postponing the hiring of suitable staff would reflect badly.

Naturally, on her way home, she called to see her mother and father as she did most days. Rhianna stepped off the gig and bid good morning to an elderly man who was digging in one of the allotments opposite. As she tethered the horse, the incongruity of the opulent rig and the row of working-class terraced cottages struck her. But it was the rent from working-class terraced cottages like these that provided the wealth whereby Lawson could afford such luxuries . . . Well, that and his bookmaking . . .

'I'm glad to get our Sarah from under me feet,' Mary declared as she peeled potatoes at the stone sink. 'Thank God her's started work. Her's done nothing but sit about daydreaming ever since her left the Cooksons.'

'She needs a sweetheart, Mother,' Rhianna said. 'She needs to fall in love.'

'Her needs my foot up her backside,' Titus muttered from the miserable depths of his chair. 'I'll gi' her bloody sweethearts at her age.'

'It'd hurt your foot more'n it'd hurt her backside,' Mary scoffed. 'Even if you could kick her wi' yer good foot you'd never stand on yer gouty un. Talk about a one-legged bloke trying to kick somebody's arse . . . He does spout some tripe, our Rhianna.'

Rhianna sat down and chuckled. 'I've just been to the *Herald* offices. I read in the last issue as how Mr Watkins, the hairdresser in Union Street – who'd got gout as bad as yours, Father – rubbed something called St Jacob's Oil on it regularly. After three days he could walk normal, with no pain. Don't you think it's worth a try?'

'St Jacob's Oil, did you say? Shove it up St Jacob's arse. It's an advertisement, our Rhianna.'

'No, it was an article, Father.'

Titus shook his head. 'A wik or two ago I read the same thing about a vicar in Liverpool what was using it. It's wrote like an article but it's an advertisement.'

'But don't you want to try it?'

'What's the point? If it was any good the doctor would've prescribed it.'

'He'd rather suffer,' Mary said stoically, drying her hands on her apron. 'He'd rather drive me to drink with his moaning than try summat as might help him. It's a pity he never went in a sick and draw club when he was at the ironworks. Anyroad, what yer bin to the *Herald* offices for?'

'We want a maid. And a groom for the horses. I went to place an advertisement.'

'A groom and all now, eh?' Mary said proudly, placing a pan containing the potatoes on the hob. 'I can scarcely believe as how you've come up in the world, our Rhianna. He's one in a million, that Lawson. Just you look after him, my wench.'

'I *do* look after him. Too well.'

'Never too well. He looks after you as well. And see how he's looked after us and we'm only his in-laws. I don't know what we'd have done without him and his kindness. Such a bostin chap. If our Sarah does half as well I'll be that proud of her.'

'She'll do all right, Mother. She's young yet. I didn't start courting till I was twenty-two, remember.'

They chatted on for another hour or so, until Rhianna said she must go. She drove back home, unhitched Blossom from the shafts of her gig and tacked down. She fed and watered the mare, talking softly to her all the time as she would talk to a child. She brushed her down and was surprised at how naturally all this came to her. She would be sorry to leave caring for Blossom to a groom when she enjoyed it so much herself. There was something about the smell of the mare that was so sweet, something about her nature that was so appealing.

Back in the house, Rhianna changed and set about her domestic tasks. Yes, she did need a maid. There was so much to do. Fortunately, she sent the weekly wash to the laundry; thank God there was no sweating in a steamy brewhouse, no turning a heavy mangle, or getting cracked hands. But their bed had to be changed regularly, the floors swept, the windows cleaned, the range blackleaded, the front doorstep reddened, and every other domestic chore that, while she was housekeeper in the Cooksons' household, she organised others to do. Well, she would soon get some applications, and the sooner the better.

Lawson returned home for his tea that afternoon earlier than she expected. He took off his boots, picked up the newspaper and sat down to read it. Brooke Robinson, the town's Conservative MP, was still making defensive comments about the young Earl of Dudley, who had been found in a gambling hall in London at two o' clock one morning during a police raid. The furore had still not died down . . .

A gambling house, Lawson thought. Well, what was wrong with gambling? It was just as well they didn't trawl the London brothels for notable persons; nobody would be in the least surprised who they might find in such places, royalty included, as events not so long ago had demonstrated. And the authorities worried about gambling . . .

'I saw Alexander Gibson today, Rhianna,' Lawson said, looking up from his newspaper as soon as she entered the room with a tray of tea and dainty cakes. 'He says he'd like to meet you.'

'Does he not recall me from Baxter House?'

'I haven't reminded him that you were in employment there. It hardly seems appropriate now. That life is behind you. He invited us to dinner a week on Friday evening.'

'To dinner? Goodness. What will I wear?'

'I turned him down.'

'Why? What for?'

Lawson smiled, amused at her apprehension one second and

disappointment the next. 'Because I've enjoyed his hospitality enough already, without ever being in a position to return it. Now that I have a beautiful and capable wife to show off, and my home is presentable at last, I reckoned it was time he and Ruth enjoyed some of our hospitality.'

'So you invited him here?' she said, horrified. 'But it's little more than a week away and we haven't got a maid yet. How shall I cope? How shall I be able to cook a meal, serve it and be hostess all at the same time? Oh, Lawson, What am I going to do?'

'Well, you can hire maids just for the evening.'

'But I could do with an experienced cook to prepare a meal such as they would expect.'

'Give 'em a cheese sandwich,' Lawson said flippantly.

'Oh, it's all right for you to make jokes, but it's me they'll be judging. I have to get a cook straight away. And a maid. I'll have to plan a menu.'

'It's not going to be a formal dinner party with eight or ten guests for a seven-course dinner, my love. Nothing so elaborate. You know what to do. I'm content that I can leave it in your capable hands. Are you going to pour the tea?'

As she poured, she said, 'I wouldn't mind, but he's such a supercilious swine from what I remember. Full of his own importance. Oh, Lawson, I wish you hadn't asked them.'

'It seemed only fair that I should. You'll cope. I know you'll cope. I have every faith in you . . .'

Next morning, after pondering the problem most of the night, Rhianna drove up to Salop Street, to the grocer she enjoyed dealing with best. She got on well with the grocer's wife and they chatted amiably, interspersing their conversation with items she asked to be added to her order.

'I'm looking for a cook, Mrs Bowater. Urgently. If you know of a good cook seeking a position, please let me know, or ask her to contact me. Would you?'

'As a matter of fact, Mrs Maddox, I do know somebody,' Mrs Bowater replied, cutting a segment of mature Cheddar from a round. 'Been a cook years, she has. Respectable woman. Pleasant. Middle-aged. The only drawback as far as I can see is that she's a Catholic.'

'That makes no odds to me, Mrs Bowater. She could be a Shaker for all I care.'

'Would you like me to mention you?'

'Oh, I'd be that happy if you would. If only to help out one night, although I am looking for somebody permanent.'

'She should be here tomorrow for her grocery. I'll mention it.'

'You know where I live, Mrs Bowater. Just ask her to call on me. I'll be forever in your debt.'

Next day, just before noon, there was a knock at the front door. Rhianna went to answer it and saw a woman, small in stature but inclined to plumpness. She was plainly dressed, had a round face and a twinkle in her eye.

'Mrs Maddox?'

'Yes, I'm Mrs Maddox.'

'I had a message off Mrs Bowater in the grocer's shop to say that you're looking for a cook, ma'am.'

Rhianna breathed a sigh and smiled openly. 'So you're the lady she told me about.'

The woman nodded, returning the smile. Rhianna at once liked the look of her.

'Won't you come in so we can talk?' She stood aside and the woman entered. 'Let's go in the sitting room . . . Please, have a seat . . . I take it you live locally?'

'In King Edmund Street, ma'am. Five minutes' walk.'

Rhianna sat down in one of the armchairs, realising the woman would take her cue from her. 'I understand you are free at the moment?'

'I've not worked for six weeks, ma'am.' She sat on a high-backed chair and turned to face Rhianna. 'I was in the employ of Mr Nicolas Archer in Bagley's Lane, ma'am, until he passed away just before Easter, God rest his soul. He was a widower and his married daughter lived elsewhere. She closed the house up and now it's for sale.'

'I take it you have a character reference?'

'Indeed, ma'am.' The woman felt in her pocket and withdrew an envelope which she handed to Rhianna.

Rhianna studied it. 'Well, Mrs O'Flanagan,' she said eventually, taking the name from the document. 'this is a fine testimony to you and your work.'

'Thank you, ma'am.'

'I take it you're not from these parts?'

The woman laughed pleasantly. 'I know . . . The accent, ma'am. There's no hiding it, and that's a fact. I'm from Donegal. Came over with me husband five years ago. For the work, of course.'

'And I take it you've settled here?'

'Oh, yes, ma'am. Despite the muck and the smoke we love it. The folk are mostly good and kind.'

'But if you're married and your husband's here, I take it you'd want day work only. You wouldn't want to live in?'

'That's so, ma'am. I'd have to go home at night. I've a family to look after. But I wouldn't be dashing off till the dinner was done.'

Rhianna smiled. 'Well, that's not a problem. We have only one other bedroom made up as yet and we're hoping our maid will occupy that – when we've found somebody suitable.'

'You don't have a maid?' Mrs O'Flanagan sounded surprised.

'My husband and I are only recently married. I've only just begun finding servants.'

'Oh, please, ma'am, I meant no disrespect. 'Tis just that . . . if you are looking for a live-in maid, I have a daughter, nineteen years old. She was with me at Mr Archer's. She's a fine girl, ma'am. A willing worker. Gets on with the job without having to be told all the time.'

Rhianna's face lit up. This could be the answer to her prayers. 'And she has a character reference as well?'

'Oh, yes, indeed, ma'am. A fine character. Like I say, she's a fine girl. A very fine girl. The apple of her father's eye.'

'Then I'd like to see her, Mrs O'Flanagan. Can you ask her to call?'

'Oh, with the greatest of pleasure, ma'am. I'll get her to call this afternoon. We could both start work right away.'

'That really would be most convenient, Mrs O'Flanagan . . . I'm certainly satisfied with your credentials. Perhaps I should show you the scullery and the brewhouse . . .'

Mrs O'Flanagan had a good look around and made some gestures and noises that registered her approval. 'I think we could work together, ma'am. Don't you?'

'I believe we could. Tell me, how does fifty pounds a year sound? I'd be happy to pay you every week. Say, a pound a week?'

Mrs O'Flanagan looked disappointed, and Rhianna's heart sank. Yet she knew this was a fair rate of pay.

'If you can stretch it to a guinea a week, ma'am, I'd say yes straight away. Remember, I don't require board and lodgings.'

Rhianna also remembered how desperately she needed her. 'Very well then. A guinea a week. That's settled.'

Mrs O'Flanagan smiled, a broad smile. 'Thank you. When would you like me to start?'

'Let's say Monday, if you can.'

'Monday it is. And I'll send my daughter round this very afternoon.'

'I'll be waiting, Mrs O'Flanagan.'

11

The young woman that stood on the doorstep when Rhianna answered the door that afternoon was strikingly lovely, with hair that was a dark shade of titian pinned up neatly under her hat. She had large green eyes that creased into an appealing smile like that of her mother, Mrs O'Flanagan. She was tall and slender with an air of self-esteem about her that Rhianna admired in a maid. Evidently, she was not ashamed of the lowliness of her station.

'You must be Miss O'Flanagan,' Rhianna said with a welcoming smile.

The girl returned the smile. 'At your service, ma'am.'

Her brogue was not as pronounced as her mother's, but was still unmistakably different to the Black Country accents Rhianna was used to hearing.

'Won't you come in?'

The girl stepped inside deferentially and, as with Mrs O'Flanagan, Rhianna found that she instinctively liked her. She led the girl to the sitting room and gestured for her to sit down. When the small talk about the weather had been dispensed with Rhianna said, 'Your mother tells me you were in service at the home of—'

'Of Mr Archer, ma'am, in Bagley's Lane.'

'How long were you there?'

'Oh ever since we came over, ma'am. About five years.'

'And what sort of work did you do?'

'I was general maid, ma'am. I did everything, apart from cooking, of course. Mr Archer was very particular about his food. Only my mother was allowed to cook for him. I did the cleaning and dusting, carrying the coal up and laying fires, laying table and waiting on table. Everything, ma'am. I sorted myself a routine and stuck to it.'

'My husband and I are only recently married, Miss O'Flanagan. As and when we grow into a family we shall no doubt increase the staff. But as yet there will be just the two of us. I have already engaged your mother as cook, as you know, and my husband will be engaging a groom-cum-handyman very soon. The duties I would expect you to perform would be in line with what you were doing at Mr Archer's. I need you to live in, of course.' Rhianna was aware that she sounded slightly pompous, rather like Mrs Cookson at Baxter House. 'I take it you have no problem getting up in a morning?'

'Oh, none at all, ma'am. I'm up like the lark.'

'Good. May I see your character?'

The girl handed over an envelope. Rhianna opened it and read the reference.

'You were evidently thought very highly of, Miss O'Flanagan.'

'I believe so, ma'am.'

'We have a room all ready on the second floor. I'll show you.'

'Yes, I'd like to see it, if I may.'

'May I enquire as to what you were paid at Mr Archer's house?'

'Fifteen pounds a year, ma'am, all found.'

'Then if you will take eighteen, the position is yours, Miss O'Flanagan.'

'Oh ma'am, thank you very kindly. Of course, I accept.'

'Then I'll show you your room and around the house. I take it you can commence work on Monday?'

'Oh, yes, ma'am.'

Rhianna smiled at the girl reassuringly. 'I'm pleased that you can. I hope you'll be very happy here.'

She showed Miss O'Flanagan all there was to see. After the tour, they stood at the front door, the girl ready to go.

'I'll see you on Monday morning, then, ma'am.'

'Yes. Can you get here for ten? My husband will be out of the way by then and we can get you settled in properly and talk in detail about your routine.'

'Ten o'clock's fine, ma'am. I'll come with my mother.'

'By the way . . . You haven't told me your Christian name, Miss O'Flanagan . . .'

'Oh, Caitlin, ma'am.'

'Caitlin. What a lovely name. It's Irish, I presume?'

'As Irish as meself, ma'am.' Caitlin curtsied as she turned to go. 'See you Monday,' she called over her shoulder.

Rhianna naturally told Lawson that she had employed both a maid and a cook, mother and daughter, but was careful not to mention that they were Irish in case he held some prejudice against Catholics that she was not aware of, although she doubted it since religion did not impress him. There seemed little sense in jeopardising their positions by making their nationality or religion an obstacle. She liked Mrs O'Flanagan and her daughter, and was certain they would prove to be good, reliable servants. Only if they ultimately proved otherwise would she dispense with their services. But she doubted that would ever be the case. Their characters were spotless.

On Monday, the two women arrived and immediately got down to work. Rhianna discussed the daily routine, first of all with Mrs O'Flanagan, and then with Caitlin. While Caitlin explored the house and made herself useful, Rhianna began planning her menu with Mrs O'Flanagan, ready for the visit of Mr and Mrs Alexander Gibson on the Friday. They decided on slivers of smoked salmon with onion rings and imported tomatoes as a first course, and roast beef cooked to perfection for the main course. Pudding was to be a syllabub, and followed by cheeses.

At last Rhianna was confident that she could give a good

account of herself as the wife of Lawson Maddox to any visitors he might invite. She began to relax.

Lawson returned home that evening at ten minutes past six. He unhitched his horse from the cabriolet and stabled it with a bale of hay and clean water for its trough. Curious as to how Blossom was faring, he opened the door to the next stable and patted the mare on the nose. All was well. Rhianna was making a good job of grooming her. Well, this very day he had met a lad who was keen to start work looking after the horses, the gigs and the garden. There was room over the stable for him to live and it just remained to make it liveable. A clean up, a coat of whitewash, a lick of paint on the woodwork, a new bed, a chest of drawers and maybe a rug on the floorboards would suffice. He would get Jimmy Costello in to spruce it up later in the week.

Lawson entered the house through the front door. That way he would avoid meeting the new cook until Rhianna could introduce her properly later. Rhianna was in the sitting room, embroidering a pillowcase.

'What's this new cook of yours going to delight us with tonight?' he asked as he sat down. 'It smells good.'

'Roast pork with apple sauce,' Rhianna replied, looking up from her work.

He nodded his approval. 'Do you fancy beer with that, or wine?'

'Oh, wine would be lovely.'

He stood up again. 'I'll see what's in the cellar.'

Two minutes later he returned. 'Chablis,' he announced. 'I fancy some Chablis. I've taken it to the dining room. Your new maid can uncork it when she deigns to grace us with her presence.'

Rhianna smiled. 'She's very willing. Quick to learn. I think you'll approve of her.'

'Good,' he said. 'So how long before we eat?'

'I told Cook seven o'clock. Are you going out again later?'

'Not tonight. I thought I'd have an early night . . . By the way, I'm off to the Continent again. Thursday of next week.'

'Again?' Rhianna regarded him with disappointment. 'So soon after the last time?'

'Lucrative business, Rhianna. Lucrative business. Oh, and I've found a groom. I'll seek out Jimmy Costello tomorrow and ask him to get the room over the stables up to scratch. Can I leave it to you to get a bed and a bit of furniture organised?'

'You know you can.'

'Good. With any luck we can have him installed on the weekend I return.'

'Oh, that will be good, Lawson. Then we'll have a full complement.'

Lawson went upstairs to change. Meanwhile, Rhianna went to the kitchen to check on Mrs O'Flanagan and Caitlin. By the time he came down, dinner was ready. Lawson sat himself at the table. While he waited he contemplated the novelty of being served dinner in his own house by his own servant at last. He was beginning to enjoy these trappings of respectability. And in his line of business, he needed that impression of respectability which marriage endowed. Oh, there was no doubt Rhianna had made a difference to the way he was being perceived. Because she was his wife, and as able a woman as he could have met, he was on the edge of becoming a fully-fledged member of society, no longer merely a well-off bachelor who hung about on the peripheries with the randy and effervescent sons of the wealthy. Marriage, in that respect, had been the right move. He had chosen his wife well. The visit of Alexander and Ruth Gibson would confirm it.

Rhianna returned and sat opposite him. 'Dinner will be served in a couple of minutes,' she said, and sounded excited at the novelty of it.

'I think you're enjoying being the lady of the house,' he remarked, amused. 'See how excited you are.'

'I am,' she replied. 'It's a complete change of position for me.'

'A role reversal, Rhianna. I knew this one would suit you better.'

'Things have happened so quickly,' she sighed. 'And there's still the groom-cum-gardener to arrive. Once the garden's all spick and span we'll be able to hold garden parties. Oh, I can't wait.'

'Well, maybe not in time for this summer,' he said realistically. 'But next year.'

The door opened and Caitlin appeared carrying a tray stacked with serving dishes. Lawson was sitting with his back towards her and Rhianna smiled reassuringly at the new maid. The girl placed the tray on the sideboard and began unloading the serving dishes. Rhianna glanced at Lawson, seeking his approval and saw, to her surprise, that his face was set hard like granite.

'Lawson, this is Caitlin,' she said. 'Caitlin, let me introduce you to—'

Caitlin turned around. 'Percival!'

There was a silence that seemed to last forever but was, in essence, little more than a second. Rhianna sensed some acute discomfort, either with Lawson or with Caitlin, and tried to understand what was happening.

'Are you mixing me up with somebody called Percival, miss?' Lawson asked pointedly.

'Percival?' Rhianna repeated with bewilderment. 'Who on earth is Percival?'

'I'm so sorry, ma'am,' the girl said coolly, catching a glimpse of Lawson's hard look. 'Your husband is the image of another man I know. For a second I was taken off guard. I'm such a fool. I'm very sorry . . . I'll serve dinner now, ma'am.'

'Please do, Caitlin.'

Caitlin left the room with the same self-assured poise she had when she entered. But once on the other side of the dining room door she felt her legs go weak and tears stung in her eyes. She lifted her skirts and ran up two flights of stairs, rushed to her room and slumped on her new bed in a fit of desolation. She took a rag from the pocket of her pinafore, wiped her eyes and blew her nose. Why had he not told her he was married? But to find out like this . . . To actually be employed in his very household, unwitting . . .' And his wife such an obliging young woman. Had she known this was where he lived she would never even have consented to come for an interview. She prayed fervently that she had successfully covered up her utter shock at seeing Percival Harrison, as she knew him, at the table she was about to wait on. Percival Harrison indeed! Well, she knew now his name was Lawson Maddox. And he knew hers was Caitlin and not Kate.

But what should she do now? Should she try and forget that she loved this man? Should she simply forget, cast from her mind the number of times they had lain together in that little terraced house in Netherton he took her to on those nights they met? The house she had believed was his bachelor home? Impossible. She could not forget. How could she? Her feelings were too real, too intense to ignore. What if she was pregnant as a result of all those heady nights of lovemaking? All these thoughts ran through her mind. And she was working here now for him and his wife. Well, she could either tell Mrs Maddox that she could no longer work here and leave, or brazenly stick it out and pretend she had not previously known Lawson as Percival. But how could she leave without a lot of unwelcome questions being raised? How could she leave and not upset that decent, obliging Mrs Maddox? How could she leave and implicate her mother who was so relieved and delighted to find this position – for both of them? They needed the money to live – desperately.

There seemed only one solution – to brazen it out, just so long as Lawson was able to. Well, she would soon discover how great a thespian he was, how well he could carry off the deceit. She swilled cold water over her eyes, dried them, tidied her hair and set her cap straight. She smoothed the creases out of her uniform and straightened her shoulders. Then, with all the confidence and poise she could muster she went back downstairs. There was work to be done.

Caitlin did not look directly at Lawson again and he did not look at her. He engaged Rhianna in bright, amusing conversation to divert her although she did think that Caitlin's eyes were just slightly puffy when she returned to collect the dinner plates, as if she had been crying. But she made no comment.

Later, when the meal was finished and everything cleared away, Mrs O'Flanagan bid them goodnight and Rhianna told Caitlin the rest of the evening was her own.

'Thank you, ma'am,' Caitlin said. 'I can use the time to do some mending.'

She handed the maid an oil lamp to light her way upstairs. 'And I'm going to get on with my embroidery in the sitting room.'

'I'm going to the stables to check the horses, Rhianna,' Lawson said.

He went outside. It was dusk and the first bright stars had just made themselves visible in the northern sky. When he reached the stables he opened the door of the first loose-box and checked the horse. Of course, the animal was fine; it had been less than three hours since he last attended it. He came out, closed the door, turned to enter the next loose box. He looked up at the window of the servant's room that Caitlin was occupying. He could just make her out standing there, watching him. He beckoned her to come down, indicating she leave the house via the back staircase and door, hoping she could read his gestures in the twilight. He opened the door to Blossom's stable, checked her water and her feed. He closed the door behind him as he went out and turned the corner of the building. Caitlin was stealthily making her way across the yard.

'What the hell are you doing here?' He grabbed her wrist and yanked her behind the stable, out of sight of the house.

'I work here. Your pretty young *wife* engaged me.' There was acid in Caitlin's tone at the word. 'If you'd told me your real name in the first place I'd never have even shown up for the interview.'

'Well, you're here now, by God, and we need to get this straightened out. Whatever happens, I don't want her finding out about us. Do you understand?'

'I don't particularly want her finding out either. To be sure, she's been very kind. She's paying me a very fair wage. My mother too. Especially my mother. I don't want my mother to find out. Why should she lose her situation?'

'There's no reason why either of them should know,' he whispered. 'Neither your mother, nor my wife.'

'It's just a bit of a shock to discover some other woman has got a prior claim on you,' Caitlin said, regaining her composure. 'If only you'd told me you were married. It wouldn't have made any difference.'

'I intended to. But we just can't acknowledge each other in Rhianna's presence, except in the normal way of servant and master. Do you understand?'

'Of course I do . . . Well now, Percival, that was a close call in there. When I first set eyes on you, I had the shock of me life. Do you think I carried off the deception?'

'By the skin of your teeth. And you can stop calling me Percival now.'

She leaned against the wall coquettishly now and looked at him under her long lashes, with the intention of testing his resolve. 'I can't get used to calling you anything else . . . I'm sorry. But I'll try to remember to call you *Sir* . . .'

'Sarcasm doesn't become you . . . *Kate*.'

Caitlin sighed, a heartfelt sigh. 'I love you, Lawson. And because I love you so much I don't have a choice. Of course, I'll be respectful in the course of my duties. But that won't stop me secretly wanting you.' She felt for his hand and squeezed it with all her devotion and edged closer to him. 'It won't stop me thinking about how we make love,' she whispered. 'God, Lawson, you're so close. *So* close that I can almost feel the warmth of your body through my frock . . .'

He felt a stirring below at her potent words; images of their previous encounters filled his mind, of her submissive nakedness as she lay on the feather mattress of that little house for him the very first time – a virgin, there for the taking . . .

'How can I turn and go when I want you so much, when you're so close? Is it the same for you, *Lawson*, when you feel the warmth of my body against yours? The smoothness of my skin . . .'

He took her by the waist and thrust himself against her. He bent his head to kiss her, and she pressed herself against him.

'Oh, I can feel you all hard against me,' she breathed into his ear in her soft Irish lilt when they broke off. 'Sure, I can tell you want me now. And I want you inside me, Lawson. I'm all ready for you . . .'

'Up here . . .' He took her hand and dragged her up the outside staircase that led to the room above the stable. He opened the door and pulled her inside. It was too dark in there to see the cobwebs of years hanging in grey strands from the rafters. It was too dim to see the untrodden dust of more than two decades lying on the floor. He pulled her to the hard wooden floor, lifted the hem of her skirt while she fumbled to unfasten the buttons of his fly. When they were each divested of sufficient garments he rolled on top of her and, when he entered her, they rolled from side to side in a frenzy of desire.

When they emerged into the moonlight they dusted each

other off and Caitlin crept back safely to her room via the back staircase. Lawson went to the bedroom he shared with Rhianna by way of the hallway, changed into his night attire and climbed into bed. By the time Rhianna went upstairs, wondering why he had not returned to the sitting room after having been to the stables, he was fast asleep in bed.

The incident at dinner bothered Rhianna. It made no sense. Both Lawson and Caitlin had looked concerned just for an instant, but long enough to render the instant bizarre. She wished she could read people better. Maybe they had met before somewhere. Maybe it was just a combination of unrelated circumstances which coincided at that moment. Caitlin had explained it easily enough when she said Lawson was the image of a man she knew. Well, everyone seemed to have a double, so her explanation was plausible. It was also instantaneous; not a struggle to search for an excuse. Being reminded of a loved one called Percival might have induced her tears, for Rhianna was sure Caitlin had been crying when she came to collect the crockery. Maybe she would refer to it again when a suitable opportunity arose, just to get Caitlin's further reaction. Perhaps when Lawson had gone to Belgium and France.

Next day Rhianna was sorting through their clothes to decide what should go to the laundry when she noticed Lawson's suit and how dusty it was. She took a clothes brush and, hanging the jacket and trousers in turn out of the window she brushed them so that the breeze took the debris. When she saw Caitlin later, she saw she had smudges of dust on the back of her frock also.

'You have dust all over you, Caitlin,' she remarked, trying to sound casual.

'Oh?' the girl queried and Rhianna saw how she blushed unaccountably. 'Oh, it must be from the coalhouse, ma'am. I must have brushed up against it when I filled the buckets first thing.'

'Be more careful, Caitlin. We don't want dust coming into the house on your clothes.'

'Sorry, ma'am.'

Lawson's excuse when she tackled him was that he had stumbled against the wall in the stable when his horse had nuzzled him too enthusiastically.

Friday arrived and Rhianna spent most of the afternoon preparing the flower decorations for the table ready for the visit for dinner of Mr and Mrs Alexander Gibson. When they arrived Mr Gibson handed Caitlin his hat and his gold-handled cane. He was in his late fifties – difficult to judge – had a full head of grey hair, well groomed, and he wore spectacles. Evidently he had an eye for the women since he kept looking Caitlin up and down when Ruth, his wife, was not watching. Ruth seemed oblivious to him, or was used to his covert fancies. She was of average build and Rhianna could see the elderly vestiges of what must have been a very attractive woman. She had a good bone structure with high and well-rounded cheekbones that afforded her a beauty that defied ageing. Her eyes had been large and were still bright. But, like her husband, she had adopted the outwardly pious air that wealth and position brings, and Rhianna felt it was a great pity they should be so pretentious.

All went well and the food Mrs O'Flanagan cooked was fit for a king. The impression of Alexander Gibson that Rhianna had formed at Baxter House was certainly not confirmed at close quarters; he turned out to be not pompous at all. And she noticed he was looking her over as well; his eyes lingered on her as he sat opposite. No doubt he was aware she had worked at Baxter House but, to his credit, he did not mention it.

'It didn't take Lawson long to propose to you, Rhianna,' Alexander said when they were taking cheese and biscuits.

'Because it was love at first sight,' Lawson answered for

her. 'I knew from the moment I saw her that she was the only woman for me. Have some more port, Alex.' Rhianna smiled self-consciously. It was a comment she wanted to hear after the doubts and strange coincidences of the last few days. 'And I believe she loves me equally, despite all my faults.' He took her hand and squeezed it, which drew a look of devotion from Rhianna.

Alexander helped himself to the port and passed the bottle. 'You're a very lucky fellow, Lawson.' He turned to Rhianna. 'Did you follow the events surrounding that Jack the Ripper fellow, my dear?'

Rhianna looked bewildered at the sudden turn in the conversation.

'Oh, Alex, do spare us talk of Jack the Ripper at the dinner table,' Ruth said, looking at Rhianna apologetically. 'Especially when we are guests in somebody else's house.'

'Nonsense, my dear. The Ripper is a most interesting phenomenon. Pity they never caught the blighter, tearing up innocent women like that. But there you are.'

'Innocent women indeed,' Ruth exclaimed contemptuously.

'Innocent is perhaps an ill-chosen word,' Alex conceded. 'But they did provide a valuable service within the community.'

'Who do you think did it, Mr Gibson?' Rhianna asked, at once absorbed. 'Do you have an opinion?'

'Well, some say Sickert was behind it.'

'Sickert the artist?'

'Yes, Walter Richard Sickert. Studied at the Slade – worked with Whistler – chum of Degas and Lautrec. That Sickert.'

'So how might he have been involved?'

'Well, another of his chums was Prince Eddy, the Duke of Clarence. Eddy, for his sins, is said to have fallen in love, poor chap, with one Annie Crook who modelled for Sickert. She had Eddy's child in Marylebone Workhouse afterwards, although it is speculated that they later married secretly.'

'You never mentioned this before, Alex,' Ruth said and sipped her port.

'You've never allowed me to explain, Ruth,' Gibson replied. 'Not a fit subject for discussion, you've always maintained.'

'And I'm right. All the same, it is jolly interesting. Do go on.'

'Well, Mary Kelly, the Ripper's final victim, worked with this Annie Crook behind the counter of a tobacconist in Bloomsbury, it appears. She also worked the streets, of course. Rumour hath it that she tried blackmailing Prince Eddy through Sickert, whereupon Sickert reported the business to the Prime Minister, who ordered her elimination. And, merely as red herrings, three other women had to become victims.'

'Ridiculous!' Ruth proclaimed. 'As if the Prime minister would embark on such wickedness.'

'To protect the Crown, my dear.'

'I never heard such nonsense, Alex. Where did you hear of such a thing.'

'Our son knew Sickert, Ruth, during his time in London. He told me about it.'

'John knew Sickert?'

'It's not beyond the realms of possibility that he might, Ruth. Let's face it.'

'All the same, it's a preposterous story.'

'Never substantiated, naturally. Nor ever likely to be . . . Which reminds me, Lawson . . . My son John . . .' He turned to Rhianna. 'Do you like art, Rhianna?'

'Oh, I do. That picture in our sitting room . . . The one your son painted . . . I think it's the most beautiful painting I've ever seen. We went into the National Gallery in London when we were on honeymoon but I didn't see anything I liked anywhere near as much.'

Alexander smiled and nodded his understanding. 'I agree. His work has an undoubted charm.'

'I'm baffled as to why you'd want to part with such a

beautiful painting, Alex,' Rhianna remarked. 'Especially since it's the work of your own son.'

'A gift to a friend, my dear . . .' He turned to Lawson. 'Something I wanted to discuss with you, Lawson, old man . . . John is returning home. Due back next Saturday. Naturally, we don't want all his mucky artists' paraphernalia around us at Paganel House – not that we have suitable space – not that he wants to be with us in any case. He'll want to work, of course, unimpeded by us. I wondered if you have a property available that I could rent for him. Not that he needs much in the way of accommodation. A bed upstairs to sleep in, a decent sized room downstairs he can use as a studio.'

'As a matter of fact I have the very thing. A good sized house with a conservatory on the back that benefits from facing north. The only vacant place I have, as a matter of fact.'

'And it's available?'

'Yes, it's available. I could have it readied by next weekend. I'll be away – another trek to the Continent as you know – but Rhianna would be happy to show him the property, wouldn't you my dear?'

Rhianna shrugged. 'If you say it's all right, Lawson. Of course.'

'I must say, Rhianna,' Alexander said leaning towards her as if to impart a great secret, 'I have never condoned his becoming an artist. Far too bohemian an existence to be respectable. We've had many an argument. Many an argument . . . However, he's my son, I feel a responsibility towards him, and he does possess an undeniable talent.'

'Would that he painted pictures that *I* found less offensive,' Ruth remarked. 'So many scantily-clad gels.'

'Oh, I don't find them in the least offensive,' Rhianna declared. 'Just the opposite, in fact. They give me an impression of such peace and tranquillity. I think they're beautiful.'

'Quite right, my dear,' Alexander said. 'Ruth is a little over-sensitive to such subject matter. She had a very strict religious upbringing, you understand. Nowadays, it manifests itself in prudery – decrying young ladies who flaunt what attributes they have. She forgets that she was young once.'

'I certainly do not, Alexander. But when I was a young woman modesty was considered a virtue.'

Rhianna decided it was time to change the subject. She rang for Caitlin and ordered coffee to be served in the sitting room, where Alexander lit a cigar and proceeded to fall asleep in an armchair, to the further embarrassment of his wife.

12

The entrance to Windmill Street, Shaver's End, Dudley was an astonishingly steep but thankfully short climb that caused the horse to struggle as the gig turned into it from Salop Street. Beyond the troublesome hill it became a cart track of black dirt, with potholes and random, jutting stones to trip people up if they didn't look where they were walking. A patch of waste ground lay to the right; the sooty, red brick ends of five rows of terraced houses abutted the left side. Anyone reaching the crown of that little rogue hill would realise just how high this place was.

As the rig progressed, the street opened out into what looked like a communal yard, shared by eight more small houses in a cluster around a rusting water pump. Another assemblage of dilapidated outbuildings, belonging to a worked-out coal mine, stood on the opposite side. Past the two groups of sorry constructions, the track narrowed again, funnelling into a rain-riven path that skirted the slag heaps, dismal and depressing even in the sunshine. Lawson's vacant property, formerly a mine manager's dwelling that he had acquired cheap, stood alone on the right in front of the mine. The sweeping view over Shropshire, with the Wrekin and the Long Mynd breaking the far distant horizon like the backs of sleeping animals, was the place's only redeeming feature.

Ragged children, snotty-nosed and dirty-faced, stood barefoot and watched in awe as the handsome couple drove slowly along in a shining black cabriolet drawn by a glistening black horse. When the gig drew to a halt the children tentatively edged nearer until Lawson Maddox shooed them

away as if they were animals. He fumbled in his pocket
for the key and opened the door. Rhianna followed him
inside and her footsteps on the cold flags echoed in the
emptiness.

So this was to be the home of John Mallory Gibson.

'This place isn't furnished,' she commented with disappointment. 'I imagined it would be furnished.'

'He can provide his own furniture,' Lawson replied indifferently. 'Why should I have the expense of furnishing it? I
imagine he'll use the floor for a bed and eat off his lap in
any case. Queer lot, artists. Used to living in squalor. And,
as I recall, John Gibson is particularly queer.'

Rhianna felt an illogical pang of sympathy for the poor
artist, however peculiar he was, travelling all the way from
London and ending up alone in a cold, rambling, empty house.
'It's not the prettiest of spots here, either,' she said. 'Especially
for an artist. I mean, look at that slag heap and that derelict
monstrosity looming over that coal shaft. I doubt whether he'll
get much inspiration from that.'

'It's not my problem, Rhianna. Alex asked for a property
to use as a studio. Well, that's what I'm providing. Oh, I'll
get Jimmy Costello to give it a lick of paint here and there
and sweep it out, but that's it.'

Upstairs, their footsteps on the floorboards echoed in the
hollow silence. Rhianna looked through a side window at
the immediate landscape, tragic and desolate. Beyond the slag
heaps stood the chimney stacks of the London Fields Fender
and Fire Iron Works, pushing out columns of grey, swirling
smoke. From a rear window she saw the expanse of waste
ground with its stunted tufts of green grass that struggled
to thrive but looked bright against the grey spoil of the old
coal mine. She was filled with apprehension for poor John
Gibson, and hoped he would turn out to be resilient enough
to withstand it.

'If I give you the key now,' Lawson said, 'I won't have to

remember to do it later. I mean, God forbid that you wouldn't be able to let the poor bugger in.'

As she took it Rhianna said, 'While you're away, do you want me to collect any rents for you? Now I've got Blossom and the gig it's a pity not to let them earn their keep.' Since there was little for her to do now that she had a maid and a cook, the thought of idleness while Lawson was away filled Rhianna with dread.

He smiled. 'Good idea. Yes, I'll make a list of where to collect from, and how much. That should keep you occupied.'

Outside her home in Albert Street, little Flossie Kettle sat alone on the step that led into the entry and wistfully picked moss from the criss-cross pattern moulded into the pavement bricks. The sky was overcast, causing the extended daylight of that June evening to fade early. She had been playing hopscotch with her friends in a rough grid they'd chalked out on the ground but, one by one her friends, mostly younger than her, had been called in for bedtime or had drifted away in the relentless search for mental stimulation. Flossie had no wish to go inside yet and be bawled at for no reason by her mother, for Molly would be well down a bottle of gin by this time. Why did her mother have to drink so much gin? It made her so clumsy and bad-tempered.

A black and white cat stole down the entry and slipped, unseen and unheard, down the step beside Flossie onto the pavement. When it brushed its sleek body against her bare shins, she gave a startled cry and jumped up, and the cat darted back into the entry. Sorry that she had scared the animal, she peered after it and saw its green eyes gazing suspiciously back at her. It was a friendly, inquisitive little thing. Flossie approached it with soft, friendly noises and put out her hand as if offering it a morsel. Uncertain what to do next, the cat arched its back slightly, eyes torn between distrust and a desire to reciprocate the attention. Flossie touched it cautiously and managed to stroke its silky coat with the side of her forefinger, whereupon the cat, at once won over, rubbed its head against her hand, closed its eyes and began to purr.

'Am yer hungry?' Flossie cooed, gently rubbing the animal's neck. 'I wish I could find you a drop o' milk. D'you want some milk?' But she knew there was no milk in the house and, in any case, she was not going back in there yet.

She picked up the warm bundle and as she walked through the entry with it to the backyard, she pressed it to her bosom, then bent her head to rub her cheek against the soft fur. The cat continued to purr, content with its new-found friend.

Flossie heard footfalls in the entry and turned around to see a well-dressed young woman emerging. She wore a white summer dress, the skirt of which was narrow and tight at the waist, with a short jacket. Wisps of fair hair escaped from under a fine hat that was adorned with flowers. She looked elegant, and vaguely familiar.

'It's Flossie, isn't it?' the woman said with a friendly smile. 'My, you're quite the young lady now, and that's the truth.'

Flossie blushed at the compliment, smiled politely, and lowered her long lashes to hide her self-conscious eyes. She hoped that she would grow into womanhood as well-dressed as this young woman and appear so pampered.

'Is this your cat, Flossie?'

'I just found it,' Flossie responded. 'I think it wants some milk but we ain't got none at our house.'

'Well, what a shame. But cats are well known for being able to look after themselves, you know. So I shouldn't worry. Is your mother in?'

'Yes, I'll take you to her.' Still holding the cat, Flossie opened the back door and preceded the young woman into the house.

Molly Kettle was slouching in a dilapidated chair in front of a dying fire, lost in a haze of nostalgic recollections of her youth. From the chair's upholstered arms coarse tufts of horsehair sprouted riotously. A glass was in her hand and a half-consumed bottle stood on the hearth near her feet. She looked up at Flossie with eyes that glinted resentment at being disturbed.

'Tek that bloody cat out,' she yelled at her daughter. 'Yo' know as I caw't abide cats.'

'There's somebody to see you,' Flossie protested, and escaped outside with the cat.

'Mrs Kettle . . .' the young woman began.

Molly squinted in the half light to focus on whoever it was that had the lack of consideration to call at this time of a Wednesday night when she was trying to reach gin-soaked oblivion. 'Why, it's Miss Underhill.'

'I hope I haven't called at an inconvenient time, Mrs Kettle.'

'No, sit yer down and mek yerself at 'um. I'll light a candle so's I can see yer better. I was just having a tot o' gin. It helps me sleep, yer know. Would yer like a drop?' she asked grudgingly.

'No, no, thank you Mrs Kettle. I seldom drink.' Miss Underhill sat down on a rickety wooden chair at the side of the equally rickety table.

Molly stood up, then leaned over the fire to light a candle she'd taken off the mantelpiece. She sat down again and stood it on the table in a holder. 'Struth, has it bin twelve month since last time yo' was here?'

'Thereabouts.'

'Doh the time fly? I s'pose it's our Flossie again?'

'Having just seen her after a year I'd say she was ready, wouldn't you? There are some golden opportunities for girls like Flossie. The well-to-do, especially in London, are still clamouring for good, hard-working girls for domestic service. And in London the rates are so much better. I'm certain I can place her in a very comfortable position where she will be well looked after.'

Molly sighed. 'I still bain't so sure as I want her to go. Her's still on'y just fourteen.'

'The ideal age. The best houses like to train their domestic staff from an early age, you know. Flossie is such a pretty girl as well. With a bit of grooming she'll be very presentable. She could end up working in the home of some duke or earl.'

'D'ya really think so?'

'I really do.'

'So how much am yer offering for her?' Molly asked and took another slurp of gin.

'She's worth three pounds, I should fancy, Mrs Kettle. A handsome sum.'

'Three pounds? No, you'm pullin' me leg. You'm not getting her for three pounds, Miss Underhill. Double it, and I'll begin to talk.'

'Six pounds?' Miss Underhill shook her head. 'Too much. I have to take into account my expenses, Mrs Kettle. I have to provide her board and lodgings till we find her somewhere to work. No, six pounds is far too much.'

Molly looked ruefully at the dwindling gin in the bottle at her feet. It was her last and she had no money to buy any more till another cleaning job came along, for nobody would let her have anything else on tick. To make matters worse, Flossie was growing up and requiring clothes that fit, shoes that fit and even stockings, when there was no surplus money for anything. And even if Flossie went into service locally, whatever money she earned would be her own. She, Molly, would see precious little of it. Neither would she see Flossie for that matter. So she might just as well make some money out of her daughter's going.

'Five then.'

The younger woman tightened her lips to signify that five pounds was still a hard bargain.

'She is pretty,' Molly urged. 'Yer said so yerself. And a fine temperament. Yo'll find her a place easy enough.'

'All right then. Five pounds it is. But I must take her now.'

'Tonight?'

'Yes, tonight. As soon as she's ready. I'll wait.'

Molly lurched slightly as she got up from her chair. She teetered towards the door, opened it and called Flossie.

'Come inside and get you ready, our Flossie. You'm a-goin' with Miss Underhill. Her's gunna find yer a position in service down in London at the big house of some fancy duke or other. It'll mek a lady of yer and no mistek.'

Flossie put the cat down outside and entered the house, all of a sudden excited and yet uncertain at what this meant. 'Do I have to go tonight?' she said as if it was no more than a minor inconvenience. 'Can't I go in the mornin'?'

'Miss Underhill wants you tonight. Go and fetch yer clean clothes from upstairs and put 'em in a bag. And don't forget your brush for yer hair.' She turned to Miss Underhill. 'Will her need any soap?'

'We have soap, Mrs Kettle. All she needs is clean underwear and something to travel in.'

Flossie went upstairs. As she collected her meagre belongings together, she pondered what this new life, which was being thrust upon her out of the blue, would offer. More than what life now offered, surely. She was about to leave school. She was expected to go in service anyway. London would be perfect. As far away from her drunken mother as she could get. Within two minutes she came downstairs carrying her clothes in a bundle. Molly stashed them carefully into a brown paper bag and handed them back to her.

'There y'am. All ready to go then. Be a good wench and do as you'm bid for Miss Underhill, our Flossie. And write to me as soon as you get to London.'

'I will.'

'Thank you, Mrs Kettle,' the young woman said. She took out her purse and handed Molly five gold sovereigns. 'I'll see as she comes to no harm.'

Flossie smiled to herself. The prospect of this new, unanticipated adventure was growing in appeal. She would meet other girls, learn how the rich and wealthy lived. Maybe some of their wealth and good fortune might trickle down to her. She might even meet a nice lad – a groom or something – and marry well . . . And there would be no more being shouted at by her inebriated mother.

Flossie stepped outside with her bag. The cat was sitting at the top of the entry waiting for her. When it saw her, it glided towards her, its tail up, and looked at her appealingly. Flossie stooped down and stroked it once more. 'Can I tek the cat wi' me, miss?'

'No cats, I'm afraid, Flossie.' Miss Underhill said.

'It's not usual to see somebody in your position cleaning, ma'am,' Caitlin observed standing on a wooden box as she reached up to clean the tall windows of the house in Windmill Street. 'You should let me do that.'

Rhianna was on her hands and knees scrubbing the floor and, although Caitlin felt some resentment towards her, simply for being Lawson's wife, she was inclined to admire her.

'Oh, I'm not above a spot of cleaning, Caitlin,' Rhianna replied, wringing out a floor cloth. 'But Mr Maddox seemed content to rent this house in what I think is an unacceptable condition. It's no hardship to me to do something about it on his behalf.'

When she had mopped the floor to her satisfaction she went over to the maid who had just finished work on one casement. 'I could easily make some curtains for these windows, you know, Caitlin.'

Caitlin stood, contemplating the next room's windows, unwittingly fingering a silver cross on a thin chain around her long, girlish neck.

'Tomorrow, we'll come back with a tape measure. When we've measured up I'll go to the market and buy some material . . . Is that a new cross and chain you're wearing, Caitlin? I've not seen it before.'

'Oh, er . . . yes, ma'am.' Rhianna noticed how she coloured up. 'I decided it was time I wore it. I hope you don't mind, ma'am. It was given to me a while ago.'

'It's very nice. Very distinctive. Is it silver?'

'I believe so, ma'am.'

'You know, I couldn't make my mind up whether you had a sweetheart,' Rhianna said with a knowing smile. 'And I didn't like to ask for fear of embarrassing you. But it seems that maybe you have.'

Caitlin shrugged non-committally.

'Is it that Percival chap you mentioned the other evening?'

'Oh, no, ma'am,' Caitlin replied emphatically, shaking her head and blushing to the roots of her hair. 'It's nobody called Percival.'

'So who is Percival?'

'Oh, er . . . nobody . . . I mean, just somebody I knew . . . Your, er . . . your husband bears an uncanny resemblance. That's all, ma'am.'

'You mean there's another man like my husband?' An answer was unnecessary; Rhianna turned and walked towards the door. 'I'm going to clean the windows upstairs, Caitlin. When you've finished the downstairs rooms, if you'd clean the windows in the conservatory and generally give the quarries a good scrub, I would appreciate it. I'm sure Mr Gibson will too, when he arrives. It's likely he'll use it as a studio.'

'Very well, ma'am.'

Next day, without telling Lawson, Rhianna took Caitlin to measure the windows for curtains and bought some inexpensive material. During the next couple of days she worked unstintingly on them and finished them on the Thursday after Lawson had left for the Continent. She delivered them to the house where she met Costello, who was to do the painting and maintenance work and got him to fit poles over the windows for the curtains.

On Saturday, as arranged, Rhianna drove over to Paganel House in warm sunshine to meet John Mallory Gibson and to take him to inspect his new abode. She was greeted cordially by Ruth who introduced her to her son.

'I'm an admirer of your work, Mr Gibson,' Rhianna said affably. 'As a matter of fact, one of your paintings has pride of place over the mantelpiece in our sitting room. I love it.'

John smiled reticently. 'Thank you for the compliment. So which painting would that be?'

'It has two very pretty young girls lounging on animal skins on a marble bench and overlooking the sea.'

'That sounds like "The Daughters of Paradise".' He looked at his mother questioningly. 'I thought I'd sent it to my father.'

'So you did,' Ruth confirmed. 'But he gave it to Rhianna's husband.'

'I see,' he said, and Rhianna thought he seemed displeased at the revelation.

John Mallory Gibson was about five feet ten, or so Rhianna estimated. Leastwise, he was not as tall as Lawson. He was wiry, with a worried look about him, but not dirty and scruffy like she imagined some painters to be. He was conventionally dressed in smart, sombre suit with a collar and necktie that belied his profession. She could not conceive of this man producing such scintillating paintings. His hair was short and curly when she had expected to find it long and lank. She'd expected to meet a man with a bushy, bohemian beard, but he was clean-shaven. He seemed very mild-mannered, with soft brown eyes that appeared warily incapable of meeting hers, hinting at a shyness that she found inappropriate in a man of such monumental talent.

'So are you ready to inspect your new home, Mr Gibson?' Rhianna asked pleasantly.

'Yes, indeed, Mrs Maddox.'

'Maybe I should accompany you?' Ruth said. The suggestion was directed at Rhianna, and Rhianna guessed the reason for it.

'Unfortunately, Mrs Gibson, I have only room for one passenger.'

'Such a pity that Alex is out in the phaeton. He would have asked Nock to take us.'

'Well, please don't worry. I'm sure I won't need chaperoning, if that's your concern.'

'I'm merely concerned for your reputation, Rhianna.'

'My reputation is as precious to me as to anybody else, Mrs Gibson,' she responded with a reassuring smile. 'But my husband is aware of my taking your son to the house today, since he asked me to do it while he's away, as you know. I think he understood that I would be unchaperoned.'

'If you're quite sure.'

'Oh, quite sure, Mrs Gibson.'

As Rhianna drove the gig down the long, sweeping drive of Paganel House, she looked at John and smiled, trying to elicit some eye contact. 'I really am a great admirer of your work. I'd love to see more of your paintings.'

He acknowledged her comment by glancing in her direction, but his eyes again failed to meet hers. 'You're very kind. I'll happily show you more.'

Rhianna turned the gig into the road. A middle-aged woman in a strange hat was pushing a handcart loaded with salt, a salt-seller from Gornal. The woman stopped to admire the gig as it drove by.

'What's Italy like?' Rhianna flicked the reins and the mare broke into a trot. 'I get the impression from "The Daughters of Paradise" that it's all bright sunshine, clear blue skies and blue seas. Is it really like that?'

'Yes, it is. Most of the time. In summer at any rate.'

'Were you in Italy long?'

'About a year, that's all. Long enough to fall in love with it.'

'Fancy . . . Well, it seems to me that your love for Italy spills out into your pictures.'

'All my paintings are actually classically inspired, Mrs Maddox. Have you heard of Sir Frederick Leighton?'

'Yes, I think so.'

'One of our great artists. I draw a great deal of inspiration from his work. The classical and High Renaissance aspect of the paintings. He's a master of the genre. Queen Victoria owns at least one of his paintings.'

'Oh, it must be lovely to have a talent like yours, Mr Gibson. I do envy you.'

'Everybody has a talent, I believe,' he said awkwardly. 'Not everybody discovers it, unfortunately.'

They fell silent for a while. Rhianna tried to think of something to say. She was finding it difficult to make conversation with this man. When he responded to a question he offered little in the way of a thread she could catch hold of, something that might elicit a further comment.

'I hope you'll like the house,' she said eventually, groping for a topic that was of mutual interest. 'It's quite big really but it's unfurnished. I have managed to make some curtains, though, and had them put up at the windows for you.'

'Well, thank you for that.' A smile flickered across his face at her obvious thoughtfulness. 'I'm sure it will be very suitable. I'm told there's a decent conservatory I can use as a studio.'

'Yes, attached to the scullery. The surroundings aren't very inspiring, though.'

He smiled again politely. 'No matter. The surroundings in the paintings I did when I was in London came largely out of my head. From memory.'

They drove on and very soon arrived at Windmill Street. Neither commented on the drabness of the surroundings. Rhianna let him into the house and invited him to explore it while she adjusted the fall of the curtains in several of the downstairs rooms. Soon, she heard his footsteps as he descended the wooden staircase.

'It's a fine house,' he said. 'Plenty of room for my paraphernalia. Couldn't be better. My studio tends not to be the tidiest of places. So much stuff to work with . . . I must say, the views are magnificent, Mrs Maddox.'

She laughed with surprise. 'You think so?'

'Oh, I know the slag heaps and the old colliery workings aren't very pretty, but beyond them in the distance, all I can see are green fields and rolling hills.'

'Shropshire, I believe.'

'Well, once I have some furniture and my studio set up I shall be as happy as a king here. You won't hear a murmur of complaint from me. I can't wait to start painting again.'

'Well, that's good to know. Shall I take you back home now?'

'If it's no trouble. But I could walk . . .'

'Oh, I wouldn't dream of letting you.'

She handed him the key to the house, they stepped outside and he locked up.

That afternoon, Rhianna spent some time in Lawson's study with the intention of familiarising herself with the properties he owned and, from the list he had made, the names of those tenants who were due to pay rent. Come Monday morning she would begin the task and she looked forward to it with enthusiasm. She sat perched on the high chair and idly lifted the lid of his desk to see what else she could learn. Typically, it was untidy, but after rummaging about for a few seconds a large sheet of ledger paper, folded in half, came to hand. She opened it up and saw it was written in Lawson's swirling hand. This, too, was a list of properties with the tenant's name beside each. Two properties stood out, in that neither had a name written alongside them. The address of one was given as Windmill Street, obviously the house John Gibson was about to occupy; the other, noted as being furnished, was at a location called Meeting Street in Netherton. No name was written alongside it, as if it too was without a tenant. Strange, since Lawson had already said that the old house in Windmill Street was the only untenanted house he owned. This one in Netherton had obviously slipped his mind.

So, had he listed everything? She counted the number of properties on the list he had given her, and compared it with the number on the ledger sheet. They differed by five. So not all appeared on the list Lawson had given her. Rhianna wondered whether he had sold these since she had known him. Then, she noticed that three of those on the ledger had a string of numbers written next to them instead of a name. What those numbers meant she had no idea.

On the wall behind her was a board with hooks screwed into it. Each hook bore a key or a set of keys with a tag attached showing the address. Spare keys, Lawson had told her. In case of emergency. She counted the sets of keys. The number corresponded with the larger number on the ledger sheet, not with her new list. She became very curious.

Monday came and, after breakfast, Rhianna set out to collect rents as she had promised she would. The weather remained fine. As she drove up Himley Road in the June sunshine she pondered the dramatic changes in her life in just a few short months and how fortunate she was. How many other women, let alone former servants, had the unrestricted use of their own horse and gig? She smiled and waved self-consciously, even guiltily, at a neighbour she saw frequently around the shops of Eve Hill. Was there something too ostentatious about this elegant mode of transport, about the whole flamboyance of her life these days?

Albert Street, appropriately, because it was the very place Lawson had taken her on their first tryst, was her first port of call. She stepped down, tethered the mare to a post and tapped the door of the first house. She introduced herself but the tenant, a Mrs Blocksidge, refused to hand over any money.

'Yo' could be anybody, for all I know.'

Rhianna smiled in admiration. 'You know, I don't blame you, Mrs Blocksidge,' she said. 'It's something I never considered. You're right to refuse me. I do need proof of who I am.'

'Well, if yo' can provide it, I'll pay me rent.'

'I'll be back in a few minutes.'

Rhianna had had an idea. She rushed to the house occupied by Molly Kettle. Molly would surely be prepared to confirm her identity. She knocked on the door. No reply. Of course, it was washing day. Perhaps Molly was in the backyard pegging out washing. She made her way up the nearest entry and hoped that Molly's was one of the houses that used this yard. Between the billowing sheets and towels and fluttering undergarments that festooned the washing lines, Rhianna could see a couple of brewhouses bustling with activity. The cackle of women's laughter leaked out with the steam. She caught sight of Molly through the door of the one furthest away, and feeling conspicuously out of place in her fine clothes, made her way towards her through the wet, dangling washing.

'Mrs Maddox!' Molly exclaimed through the wheel of the mangle.

'Hello, Molly. You look as if you've seen a ghost. Is anything wrong?'

'Seeing yer so unexpected, like . . .'

'I need your help, Molly, when you can spare me a minute or two.' Rhianna explained she was there to collect rents. 'I imagine the tenants in this block will know you well enough to accept from you that I'm the wife of Lawson Maddox.'

'Wall-eyed Sam mightn't,' Molly conjectured. 'The miserable old bugger. Even Mr Maddox has trouble getting money out of him. Like getting manure out of a rocking horse. I'd leave him to Mr Maddox, if I was you. But let me get these frocks on the line fust and I'll gladly come wi' yer. It'll gi' me a bit of a break.'

'And I'll give you sixpence for your trouble,' Rhianna said and folded one of the garments for Molly that she passed through the mangle so as to squeeze the excess water out. 'It promises to be a good drying day . . . You seem down in the dumps, Molly. What's the matter?'

'Oh, it's our Flossie.'

'Is she all right?'

Molly shrugged and offered another garment to the mangle. 'I wish I knew.'

'Why, where is she?'

'I needed money desperate, Mrs Maddox. I sold her.'

'You sold her?' Rhianna could not hide her astonishment. Oh, she knew that some young girls were sold by their parents for a tidy sum, but she could never have imagined Molly doing it.

'I don't know if I did the right thing. The young woman what bought her said as how her'd be going into service. Her said how some of the big houses in London – you know, them as am owned by the well-to-do – was always on the lookout for sprightly young wenches like our Flossie.'

'Well, who took her? If we could find out who took her I'd buy her back for you if you're that worried.'

'Oh, it was somebody as I'd met afore. A woman. An 'andsome young woman. Last year her asked me if I'd sell our Flossie and I told her as her was too young to leave home. I trust the woman, you know, Mrs Maddox . . . She seemed decent . . . Anyhow . . .' Molly sighed heavily. 'I 'spect as Flossie's far from here by now. In London somewhere, I 'spect. I just hope as her's all right. I hope as I hear from her soon.'

'So when did she go?'

'Last Wednesday night.'

'I expect you'll hear from her soon enough, Molly. I shouldn't worry. To tell you the truth, I'd thought about offering her a position as maid for Mr Maddox and me, but I thought she was a bit too young yet. We needed somebody with a bit more experience. Somebody already trained as a maid-of-all-work.'

'Oh, I'd have bin that happy if she could have worked under you, Mrs Maddox. Now I'm just mythered to jeth.'

Rhianna took the next garment that Molly mangled and folded it. She placed it in the washing basket at her feet, ready to hang out, and pondered poor Flossie's plight. 'I'm sure she'll be all right, Molly,' she said reassuringly. She dearly hoped the girl had gone into service in the home of some kind gentleman and his family, but not all were kind. It was best not to say anything lest poor Molly worried more.

'Let me peg these out, Mrs Maddox, and I'll come with yer,' Molly said and picked up the washing basket.

Rhianna spotted a pile of wooden clothes pegs on the window sill and collected them up. She followed Molly out into the sunshine and began pegging washing out.

'There's no need for you to be doing this, Mrs Maddox,' Molly said guiltily. 'Don't trouble theeself.'

'It's no trouble, Molly. I'm really quite used to it.'

In no time, the washing was hanging out to dry and Molly wiped her hands on her pinafore. 'I'm ready then.'

'Right. We'll go to Mrs Blocksidge first, Molly.'

It took more than two hours to collect the rents from those houses in Albert Street. At each one, Molly introduced Rhianna and Rhianna made it her business to befriend each occupier she met, passing the time of day, gossiping unhurriedly. She felt that they liked her because she was not aloof, not prepossessed with an assumed air of superiority. For all they knew, she might have been one of their class. Of course, she did not let on that she was.

When they had finished, Rhianna collected the dues off Molly as well, but gave her a shilling back for helping her to get to know the tenants in Albert Street.

13

Rhianna took almost a week to collect the rents from all the properties on Lawson's list. She saw no point in rushing but spent a couple of hours each morning doing the rounds, familiarising herself with the locations, the actual dwellings and, of course, the folk who inhabited them. Most took her on trust, reluctant to appear sceptical to so genteel a lady, unlike the distrusting Mrs Blocksidge.

Jimmy Costello spent two days making the upper room over the stables inhabitable. The walls were distempered, the iron window frame painted and the floorboards thoroughly cleaned and varnished. On the Thursday a bed was delivered, along with a chest of drawers and a chair. Rhianna asked Caitlin to make up the bed, and so it was furnished in readiness for the new groom.

On the Friday, prior to grocery shopping in preparation for Lawson's return home that weekend, Rhianna decided to call on John Gibson to make sure that all was to his liking. She drove the gig into Windmill Street's steep entrance, tethered the mare outside the old mine manager's house and tapped on the front door. After a longish wait, John answered.

'Mrs Maddox. Nice of you to call.'

'Good morning, Mr Gibson. I was passing so I thought I'd make sure everything is to your satisfaction. I hope you don't mind.'

'Of course I don't mind,' he said, as if there could be any doubt. 'Will you come in?'

'Only if I'm not detaining you.'

'Not at all. Please.' He was soft-spoken and sounded most sincere. 'I was just sorting out my studio.'

He held the door wide open for her and she followed him through the hallway to the back of the house, into the studio.

'It's lovely and warm in this conservatory with the sun on it,' she commented. 'I hope it won't get too hot for you.'

He smiled. 'I'm sure I shall get quite used to it. One benefit is that it will dry the paint quicker. Can I offer you something to drink, Mrs Maddox?'

'Oh, I don't want to put you to any trouble. If you have work to do . . .'

'Really, it's no trouble. Unfortunately, I have no coal for the fire yet so I can't offer you anything hot. Just some wine.'

'Wine? Well, maybe just a small glass.'

'I have to apologise again, Mrs Maddox,' he said ruefully. 'No such luxury as glasses here either.'

That made her laugh. 'Do you want me to drink out of the bottle?'

He smiled apologetically. 'If you wouldn't mind drinking from a mug . . . I hesitate to offer such a meagre vessel, but not all of my belongings have arrived yet and it never occurred to me to ask to borrow any from Paganel House. It never crossed my mind that I might be entertaining somebody so soon.'

He seemed so much more at ease with her compared to their first meeting, so much warmer. She decided she did not dislike John Gibson after all.

'I hope I'm never too pretentious to drink wine from a mug, Mr Gibson.'

He rummaged through an old tea chest and withdrew a dusty bottle of red wine. 'I have a corkscrew somewhere . . .'

'Please don't open a bottle just on account of me,' she pleaded. 'I feel guilty—'

'But you're my first guest, Mrs Maddox.' He found the

corkscrew and forced it into the bottle, twisting it deftly. 'I do feel obliged to mark the occasion.'

She laughed again. 'If you insist.'

'Indeed I do. Would you be so kind as to pass me those mugs? . . .' He pulled out the cork, poured an ample measure of wine into each mug and handed her one. '*Salute!* Please, won't you sit down?'

Rhianna sipped the wine, glanced around for the chair that she knew was somewhere behind her and sat down. 'So where did you train to become an artist?' she asked.

'Well, to start with, my father didn't want me to become an artist. He was dead against it. We had some terrible arguments. He had some egotistical notion,' John Gibson said scornfully, 'that I should be like him. Nothing could have been further from the truth. He's the last person I would model myself on.'

'You don't like your father, then?' Rhianna sounded surprised.

'I'm very grateful to him for supporting me while I was learning my craft – he still supports me to some extent. But . . . let's say I just don't want to be like him . . . Anyway, when he finally accepted that art was my destiny, he grudgingly agreed to pay for me to attend the Royal Academy of Art school in Piccadilly. I loved the school, Mrs Maddox. I had not only the great Lawrence Alma-Tadema tutoring me, but Frederick Leighton also.'

'I'd really love to see more of your work, Mr Gibson.'

'I remember you saying so.' He got up from the stool he was sitting on. 'I have a couple of paintings here that I brought in my luggage. I intended selling them in London but . . .' He began to undo the string around a brown paper parcel. 'As you can see, they're not that big.' He pulled the brown paper off the parcel and turned the two gilt-framed pictures towards her.

Rhianna got up from her chair and went to inspect them

more closely. She gasped. 'Oh, they're absolutely beautiful, Mr Gibson. How serene those women look.'

'This one here . . .' he gestured to the painting on her left, 'is called "A Priestess of Bacchus" . . .'

Rhianna scrutinised it closely. 'The way you paint marble is so clever,' she said brightly.

'Thank you. It's a technique I picked up from one of the school's visiting artists – Edward John Poynter. He taught me.'

'So what's this other painting called?'

'"Expectation".'

A slender young woman wearing a flowing, diaphanous robe was peering expectantly down a plunging marble staircase as if waiting for her lover to run to her from the sea below that reflected the brilliance of the late afternoon sun. In the marble pillar at the head of the staircase Cupid was carved in bas-relief and John's representation of it was exquisite.

'Which do you like best?' he asked.

'This second one – "Expectation",' she said with certainty.

'You can have it.'

'Good gracious! How much are you asking for it?'

'Nothing. I'm giving it to you.'

'But you said you wanted to sell it. I'll only have it if you'll let me buy it.'

'I don't want money from you, Mrs Maddox. Your thoughtfulness alone is payment enough.'

'But I couldn't.'

'It's my gift to you. You are not allowed to refuse it.' He smiled and she saw how his brown eyes crinkled appealingly. 'It would be thoroughly bad-mannered of you to refuse.'

'Well, now I feel well and truly chastised,' she quipped. 'I don't know how to thank you . . .'

He smiled again, an affable smile, and their eyes met at long last – and held for just a second. In that brief moment she already perceived some warmth for her, and was just a little disconcerted by it.

They sat down again, drank more wine.

'What sort of people buy your work?' Rhianna enquired.

He laughed self-consciously. 'This type of painting – with the pretty girls in revealing robes – tend to be bought to adorn the walls of billiards rooms and gentlemen's clubs, I suppose. The more classically acceptable subjects . . . well, I imagine they find their way into the homes of the same gentlemen.'

As he spoke Rhianna was all the time weighing him up, assessing him. He seemed such a kind, gentle soul, anxious to please, and at ease now in her company.

'Tell me about your life in London.'

He sipped more wine, then smiled again, evidently pleased that Rhianna was taking an interest in him. 'Artists tend to herd together, Mrs Maddox. First of all I lived in an artists' colony in an area called St John's Wood. I mixed with a whole host of artists, all brilliant in their way. I had my first picture accepted for the Royal Academy Summer Exhibition in 1887 and I began to do well enough to rent a studio in Kensington where I met lots of other well-known painters. Then I went to Italy for a year.'

'What did you do in Italy? I'm fascinated.'

'Again, I lived in an artist's commune – in Rome.'

'And you enjoyed it, of course.'

'I loved Italy. The light is so . . . oh, the light inspires me even now.'

'And all that marble,' she suggested with an impish grin.

He laughed self-consciously. 'Yes, all that marble . . . But after a year I returned to London.'

'So what decided you to come back to Dudley?'

'Oh . . . lack of funds . . . A temporary setback, I hope. I've been seeking a dealer to handle my work, to save me the worry and effort. I intend to settle and be as prolific as I can be here, at home in the Black Country. I hope to produce a lot of good quality work.'

'I wish you well, Mr Gibson. I'm sure you'll succeed.'

'Thank you. Would you care for more wine?'

'I'd better not, thank you. Already it's gone to my head and I've got so much to do. I really should be going.' Rhianna emptied her mug and placed it on the workbench he'd installed. 'Thank you for the drink – but especially for the painting. I'll treasure it. When you are very famous and it's worth a fortune I shall be able to swank and tell everybody how I knew you.'

'I'll wrap it for you, shall I? Save damaging it.' It took him only a few seconds, and he handed it back to her. 'Please call again, Mrs Maddox. I've enjoyed talking to you no end. Next time, I hope to have some proper wine glasses.'

'Next time I hope you have some means of boiling a kettle,' she replied teasingly. 'I don't normally drink wine during the day. In any event, it would be a privilege for me to see your work as it's being created.'

'Conversely, Mrs Maddox, it would be a privilege for me to show you my work.'

On Saturday, when Rhianna had finished attending to the horses, she ascended the outside stairs to the room over the stable to check Caitlin's work. The new bed was neatly made with a fresh crease visible on the sheet that was turned over the quilt, and the pillow was nicely plumped up in a white, freshly-laundered pillowcase. She looked around. It was very spartan still, and she wished to make the new groom's accommodation a little more welcoming. Having lived in servants' quarters she knew how inhospitable they could be, and she didn't want that for her own servants. A new jug and bowl was needed, a towel rail, a rug for the floor. Maybe a stove. In winter it would be unbearably cold in here with no fire and she did not envy the poor lad who was to occupy it. Let him have some home comforts. First thing next week, she would purchase those few items that would make it more like home.

On Sunday, Lawson returned from his travels. Of course, he was tired and hungry and glad to take off his boots and sit with his feet up while Rhianna told him of her week.

'I take it you haven't missed me then?' he said.

'I've been too busy to miss you,' she replied blithely. 'But I've really enjoyed myself keeping busy. Having Blossom and the gig is a godsend.'

'How have Mrs O'Flanagan and Caitlin been behaving?'

'They seem to have settled in well. Mrs O'Flanagan is certainly queen of the kitchen now and Caitlin seems a willing worker.'

'You've had no trouble with either of them, I take it?'

'Indeed not. Nor do I expect to. Why should I?'

'Just checking . . . I see we have a new painting by John Mallory Gibson.'

'I know. Isn't it beautiful? I called on Friday to see how he was settling in and he gave it to me. I wanted to pay him for it but he wouldn't accept anything.'

'How do you find him? Is he still as odd as I remember him?'

'I don't think he's odd at all, Lawson,' Rhianna said protectively. 'He seems very pleasant.'

'A bit of a milksop, though, eh?'

'I wouldn't have said so.'

'Certainly anti-social. He can never look you in the eye.'

'I think he's just very reserved, Lawson. Shy. A bit unsure of himself . . . a loner. I certainly wouldn't call him a milksop. I think he was glad of a bit of company, to tell you the truth. He likes the house anyway, which is a load off my mind. He likes all that space.'

'Another satisfied customer then.'

'Yes. Anyway, how was the Continent?'

'Oh . . . Paris was crammed. Never seen it so busy. They've

got this thing on, they call the Centennial Exposition, to mark the centenary of the French Revolution. It's what they built that Eiffel Tower for. I actually had lunch on the first stage one day.'

'I've seen photographs of it. It looks magnificent.'

'Paris is magnificent.'

'D'you like it more than London?'

'I tell you, Paris makes London seem dreary.'

'I wish you'd take me sometime.'

'One day, I promise. You'd love the fashions. By the way, is the room over the stable ready?'

'Well, the bed and the chest are installed and ready. It just needs a jug and bowl set and a towel rail – and the lad to occupy it, of course.'

He nodded his acknowledgement. 'And did you collect the rents I asked you to?'

She laughed. 'Yes. But I had to take Molly Kettle with me to prove who I was to some of those doubting Thomases in Albert Street.'

'How was Molly?'

'Worried . . .'

'Oh? What about?'

'About little Flossie. She sold her.'

'Oh? Who to?'

'To some woman who said she would find her a place in some gentleman's residence in London. She was bitterly regretting it. You know, Lawson, I'd buy the child back for her if I could find out who she went with and where she was. I don't suppose you've come across anybody buying young girls?'

'Me?'

'It was just a thought. You socialise a lot. How do I know who you might meet?'

'Well nobody who buys young girls that I know of,' he answered dismissively. 'Anyway, I'm going upstairs now to have a rest. What time's dinner?'

'Seven.'

'Good. Get Caitlin to fill a hot bath for me in an hour.'

'All right. Do you intend to go out later?'

'Are you joking, Rhianna? I'm tired. I've just got back from Paris.'

It didn't stop you last time, she wanted to say, but held her tongue.

That night, Lawson retired to bed before Rhianna. When she went up he was sound asleep and she looked at him lovingly. Well, there'd be no lovemaking tonight, even though he'd been away more than a week. Perhaps in the morning . . .

In the night Rhianna was woken by the fretful sounds of the horses in the stable. She reached a hand out to Lawson to alert him that something might be amiss, but discovered that he was not there and his side of the bed was barely warm. It must have woken him too; he must have gone down to investigate. She got out of bed, closed the sash to shut out the noise and dived back under the covers. Presumably, he had the commotion under control. Within a few minutes she was asleep again. When she awoke in the morning, Lawson was already up and dressed.

'You're up early.' She was disappointed that he had not woken her first.

'Busy day,' he said economically.

'So what was causing the horses to be so fretful in the night?' She swung her feet out of bed and onto the rug at the side of the bed. 'They woke me with their whinnying.'

'Oh, it was nothing. A couple of drunks from London Fields spooked them with their hooting and bawling.'

'You'd think people would have more consideration.'

'It's not something you ponder intensely when you're fud-dled.'

'Oh, listen to the voice of experience . . .'

After breakfast, when Lawson had gone out, Rhianna tacked up Blossom and guided her between the shafts of the gig. She was already becoming expert in handling the mare and it was a source of great satisfaction to her. She drove into Dudley and bought a large rug for the floor of the room over the stable and some other things she thought might be useful for the lad when he started work; a soap dish and a mirror. She called at Paradise briefly to see her mother and father and learned that Sarah continued to enjoy working at Hillman's leather works. Before lunch she returned home and, as soon as she had unhitched Blossom she ran up the outside staircase to the groom's room to lay down the new rug and hang the mirror on a nail that had been hammered into the wall years before and since whitewashed. She unfolded the rug, an inexpensive, home-podged affair she'd bought from the market, and placed it on the floor at the side of the new bed. She got up, stepped back and inspected the overall effect. Much better. Much more homely.

Then she noticed the bed.

The bed was not in the same pristine state as it had been on Saturday. The sharp, ironed crease down the middle of the sheet that turned over the quilt was not so sharp anymore, and there were small creases everywhere as if it had been lain in. The pillow, though tidy and set straight, had been slept on. Oh, the bed had been remade expertly, but it did not look the same as before. At once she thought about the horses being disturbed in the middle of the night. Had somebody slept in here unbeknownst? Was that the reason they were so agitated?

Puzzled, she drew back the covers. A silver cross and chain lay curled on the bottom sheet. Caitlin's. A cold shudder ran down her spine. Rhianna had noticed at breakfast that the maid was not wearing her cross and chain, but had thought nothing of it.

She picked it up and inspected it. On the obverse of the cross, on the horizontal bar, the word 'Percival' was engraved. She sat down on the bed, trembling a little, trying to understand its significance. Something was not right. Too many strange coincidences had cropped up lately, coincidences that by themselves were inexplicable and meant little. But each, when considered as part of the same phenomenon, began to make some sense. She did not like what it suggested, so she had to think it through very carefully. Percival was at the bottom of it, whoever Percival might be. This Percival had given Caitlin the silver cross and chain – and it *was* silver, for there was a hallmark stamped into it – and a man doesn't give a girl such an expensive personal item of jewellery if she means nothing to him, or he to her. And yet, Caitlin had claimed that Percival meant nothing to her. It did not ring true. Look how the girl reacted when first she saw Lawson. She'd believed Lawson *was* Percival. She'd admitted as much. But she'd tried to trivialise the incident.

Could Lawson have met her before? Could she have been one of his former conquests when, to preserve his true identity, he'd told her his name was Percival?

There was no doubt that Caitlin had been in this bed. The fact that her cross and chain was here was testimony enough . . . And Lawson had gone down to these very stables last night . . . and his side of the bed was cold when she felt for him. How long had he been gone? She wished now that she'd lit the lamp and looked at the clock. She wished now that she'd stayed awake to see just how long he was away. She wished now that she'd followed him down here . . . Maybe . . . Oh, God, it was too distressing to even contemplate . . . What if it was Lawson and Caitlin together who had disturbed the horses? . . . Dear God, let it not be . . . Not Lawson . . . Please God, make it not so . . . Please, please, God . . .

Rhianna looked up to the vaulted roof of that little room without seeing it and tears filled her eyes at the realisation of what she had discovered. Just what had she stumbled upon? How long had it been going on? What unspeakably cruel quirk of fate had impelled Mrs O'Flanagan and her daughter Caitlin to become part of her household and in her employ? How cruelly ironic. It was not fair because she instinctively liked them. It was not fair at all.

Rhianna and Lawson had been married little more than two months. Two months that, apart from a couple of instances, had been the happiest, the most eventful time of her life. If this thing was true . . . If there really was something going on between Lawson and Caitlin . . . Oh, it was too horrible to think about . . .

But think about it she did. She could not help it. It gnawed at her insistently. Yet, typically, she wondered how Caitlin felt. If the girl had come to work here in good faith and discovered to her surprise that Lawson, whom she had believed was called Percival, was her employer, how would she feel? How would Rhianna feel in the same circumstances? Naturally, she would feel hurt, she would feel betrayed. She would also bitterly resent Lawson's wife, who might have been just as big a surprise if he'd formerly denied her existence.

Rhianna gripped the cross and chain tightly in her hand, pondering what to do for the best. Well, she would take it to Caitlin, face her with it, ask her what it was doing in the new groom's bed. She would ask who, in the absence of a groom, had been in bed with her. It was at that point Rhianna felt compelled to look for harder evidence that adultery had been going on in that bed. She needed proof, some dried-out stain; as a former maid she knew the signs . . . She found her proof and her heart sank many more fathoms into the sea of misery in which her happiness was already drowning.

But wait. Why declare this discovery to Caitlin? This cross and chain lying here might have been placed. Its presence was just a little bit too contrived. What if Caitlin had planted it? What if she actually wanted her to find it? It could be her way of letting her know that Lawson enjoyed her too? No, she would not return the cross and chain. Let it remain here in this bed. Let Caitlin retrace her steps and retrieve it herself, and be unaware that her mistress knew. Rhianna would see just how soon Caitlin was wearing it again. In the meantime she would say nothing. Then nothing could get back to Lawson. He mustn't know that she knew. It would be the most difficult thing in the world to appear ignorant of such heart-breaking shenanigans, but she was still not entirely certain. She needed more proof yet. There was a great deal at stake. She needed unassailable evidence that the things these events and coincidences suggested were actually going on.

14

For the rest of that day Rhianna suffered the unbearable agony that half knowledge can bring. Before dinner she made her excuses. While this vile uncertainty hung over her she did not want to dine at the same table as Lawson and be waited on by his whore. Her self-esteem would not allow her to. So she pleaded sickness, and he agreed that yes, she looked pale. She retired to bed.

Lawson went out that night. At about nine o' clock Caitlin tapped on the bedroom door and asked if there was anything that ma'am needed before she went to bed herself. No, there was nothing, thank you. Rhianna was hardly able to look at the girl, yet she saw she was now wearing her cross and chain again.

She drifted off into a fitful sleep and was awakened by Lawson returning. He lumbered into the bedroom the worse for drink, clumsily undressed himself and left his clothes in a heap on the floor. She pretended to be asleep and all she could hear was his laboured breathing as he struggled to remove his socks. He slumped into bed beside her and she froze lest he touch her, lest he wanted to force himself on her. But in no time, he was asleep.

Rhianna stayed awake till the first rays of light began filtering into the room through the heavy brocade curtains. She was preoccupied, tortured by the exaggerated notions that the demons of night bring to those already anguished. If he went down to the stables again that night she wanted to be aware of it. She needed absolute proof of his infidelity. He did not stir, however. He snored and snuffled and occasionally twitched in his stupor. But he did not wake up.

Well, if it was as she thought, where did it leave her? She was a married woman, totally at the mercy of her husband. What was hers was his. *She* was his, to do with as he pleased. Trapped, she was. But how could this marriage, which she had fallen into so willingly and so easily, which had held such electrifying promise, suddenly seem so fragile? Did such happiness have to end so quickly? Was she destined to spend the rest of her married life wondering, worrying who he might be bedding next? Oh, she knew he was not lacking in sexual experience; indeed, a woman could forgive it, could expect a man to have philandered before he wedded, but not after. Surely not after he had made his vows.

Already, the trust was all but gone. She just needed that final proof; proof, she was convinced, that would not be difficult to obtain. She realised she had not lived with Lawson long enough to know all his faults, even though he had forewarned her of many. Keep him on the straight and narrow, he had urged. Well, she had expected his fidelity as a right of marriage. Had she been naïve? Had she been utterly deluded to expect him to respect such a basic right?

She fell asleep again in this torment of misery and awoke after a couple of hours. She slipped quietly out of bed, without even casting a glance at Lawson, and parted the curtains. The sun had risen two hours earlier and the aesthetics of dawn, such as they might have been, had long since fizzled out, rather like her contentment. The morning was clouded over but very still. The distant hills of Shropshire were a flat grey, dissolving into the piebald clouds that abutted them. In the middle distance, a locomotive, the only entity yet stirring, huffed on the mineral railway, volleying plumes of grey smoke and steam into the monochromatic atmosphere.

She heard the early morning clatterings of Mrs O'Flanagan in the kitchen as she prepared breakfast, and her muted conversation with her loose-legged daughter. Rhianna had to eat but would not take breakfast with Lawson. When Lawson awoke she would declare that she felt no better and have her breakfast brought to her in bed. One thing she must ensure, however, was to be agreeable towards Caitlin; she still did not want the maid to believe she had discovered her indiscretion and was grieving.

Lawson got up, asked how she was. He washed, dressed, went down and had his breakfast. Caitlin appeared, looking irritatingly pert in her clean uniform. Her lovely face, the youthful set of her head, must be most alluring for a man and Rhianna could quite understand. The girl was at the height of her young femininity; flesh firm, waist small and limbs lissom. But Rhianna herself was no old crone. At twenty-three she too was in her prime, and at the very pinnacle of her beauty. So why had Lawson strayed? Did he find her repulsive already? Or was she merely no challenge any more?

'Good morning, ma'am. Are you feeling better today?'

'Good morning, Caitlin,' Rhianna replied with a forced smile that looked friendly enough. 'I feel much the same, thank you. I daresay I've picked up a chill. I imagine I'll feel much better tomorrow.'

'Best stay in bed, I think, ma'am. Rest is what you need. Would you like me to send for the doctor?'

'Goodness, no.'

'Then would you like me to bring you some breakfast, ma'am?'

Rhianna was ravenously hungry. 'I'll have two soft-boiled eggs on two pieces of toast. And a cup of tea.'

'Very well, ma'am. I'll see to it right away.'

Ten minutes later she ate her breakfast alone and enjoyed it. Lawson came and said goodbye then went out for the day; she did not know where, she never asked. No doubt he would end up at some rowdy public house in the town with his drunken, immature friends and their flighty trollops.

Then a thought occurred to her. Tomorrow, she might just about be able to contrive a conjunction of events with the principal players in this charade. She slid out of bed, put on her dressing gown and tiptoed across the landing to Lawson's study.

There was some serious snooping to be done.

On Wednesday morning, while Lawson breakfasted alone once more, Rhianna took a bath and dressed. Her anger was still simmering but she managed not to show it to either Lawson or to Caitlin. Just before eleven she went into his study again and took the spare key she had located the day before. Then, she went out in the gig and visited her mother and father. She had no obvious purpose in visiting, except to behold how a normal marriage functioned. Mary and Titus bickered always, but Rhianna knew that their minor squabbles were their way of expressing their affection. It was why people found them so amusing and never took it seriously. If they did not care about each other they would hardly bother to communicate at all. In fact, when they were alone, just the two of them, they spoke to each other very normally and discussed all sorts of things. Their verbal attacks were for the entertainment of others. No offence was ever taken.

On the other hand, her relationship with Lawson was somewhat different. They discussed only day-to-day things now, things that were of immediate concern. No longer did he discuss with her grand things, such as his atheistic view of religion, what he thought of the Queen, the Prince of Wales, politics and the prime minister. No longer did he try to astound her with his wit. In any case, she had heard all his witticisms before. Her ringing laughter was no longer commonplace. He himself had become dull and uninteresting; sometimes nowadays he was even morose, especially after drink. Their relationship had changed. Even after so short a time married he seemed to take her for granted, knew she would always be there for his bidding like a faithful dog. Oh, he was generous in the extreme, but she wondered to what extent that generosity was elicited by a guilty conscience and a desire to keep her sweet, unquestioning, tractable. Well, now she was questioning at least. She was questioning what this marriage was all about, what it really meant to him, for it was turning out to be of no cerebral or emotional benefit to her; it brought her no peace of mind. Oh, certainly she had a gig to drive herself about in, her mother and father had a decent house because of his kindness, but they were material things. What did she do before she had a gig? She walked, and she could walk again if need be.

'Look at her, Mary,' Titus said when she walked in. 'Her's gorra face longer than Jacob's ladder. What's up, my wench?'

'Nothing, Father. How's your foot and your string of ailments?' she parried.

'Better than yours by the looks o' yer. I feel like a king today, our Rhianna.'

'Except no king would ever put his foot in the piss pot when he got out o' bed,' Mary said scornfully.

Rhianna laughed, for the first time in ages it seemed. 'He never did.'

'Slopped it everywhere, damn fool. You never seen such a mess. It seeped through the floorboards just as Doctor McCaskie was standing underneath it. He never knew what he'd bin anointed with, thank the Lord. As he wiped his head dry I had to tell the poor bugger as how yer father must've knocked over the water jug.'

'I'm glad as it was me own piddle, seeing as how yo' med me clean it up after,' Titus said. 'Still, me foot feels better for the soaking. How's that Lawson, our Rhianna? We ai' sid him for a while.'

'Well, he's so busy,' Rhianna replied evasively. 'He's not long got back from the Continent. I'll try and get him to call soon. He sends his best wishes.'

'God bless him,' Mary said. 'You'm lucky to be married to such a lovely, hard-working chap.'

'Oh, I know, Mother. Every day that passes I realise it the more.'

Rhianna ate with her mother and father and left just before three. She had set herself a particular task. It was not a task she relished doing, but it was necessary.

In the community of Netherton, Meeting Street ran north to south and was in two sections, divided about halfway along by Church Road. The whole area was a warren of narrow red brick terraces, gullies and high walls crowned with cemented-in broken glass to deter trespassers. Rhianna decided to start at one end of Meeting Street and work her way along. She knew the number of the house she was seeking but had no idea where it was situated. She did not have to look for long; Lawson's gig was standing at the left-hand kerb, further on past Church Road. His horse was busily nuzzling into a nosebag. Rhianna's heart began pounding with apprehension. Cautiously, she halted Blossom well before the gig and tethered her to a post, then, clutching the key she had in her pocket, approached the house.

Lawson was certainly here. But it did not mean Caitlin was even though it was her afternoon off.

She looked around, furtively checking that nobody was watching, though how many snooping neighbours were peeping from behind net curtains was anybody's guess. The house was not the sort that opened up at the back onto a party yard. It had its own private backyard and shared only an entry with the house next door. Warily, with a stealth that surprised her, Rhianna stepped towards the front room window and peered in. She thought her heart was going to rip through her chemise it was thumping so hard. She could see nobody. She took a second to notice what was in the room; a couple of armchairs, a sofa, an Indian rug. The floor was covered in decent linoleum and velvet curtains hung at the window.

Rhianna left the window and tiptoed up the entry. There was a gate at the top. Silently, she lifted the latch and slowly pushed the gate open, bracing herself lest it creaked on its hinges. She peered around it. At some time there had been a garden which was now a wilderness of long grass, thistles and nettles. A brick-paved area formed a broad path between the house and the garden and Rhianna noticed the back door with its dark green paint. She crept towards it, watching the back window for signs of activity, but saw none. She gripped the iron door knob and tried it. It yielded to her turn with a thin metallic chink as the catch disengaged. She held her breath, opened the door an inch. She waited a few seconds, still holding her breath . . .

Nothing.

Slowly, she pushed it open. No challenge from within. She stepped over the threshold silently and put her head round the door. Lawson's hat adorned an occasional table.

She was in the living room. At the far end of it, at the left-hand side, was an open door which led via another short passage into the front room. She guessed that in this passage was the foot of the stairs. Trying to stifle the sound of her breathing she crept to where the stairs ascended to her right. She heard a man's voice upstairs and was in two minds as to whether she should retreat. If Lawson actually saw her and thought she was spying on him he would be hopping mad, especially if he was involved in something totally innocent. But then she heard a woman's voice, a kind of bleat, and her resolve returned.

With cat-like stealth, she climbed the stairs, praying that the wooden boards beneath her feet would oblige by not creaking. At the top was a small landing. She made a calculated guess that anybody using this house for the purposes she imagined, would use the back bedroom, which would be less visible to the prying eyes of nosy neighbours. It was ajar. And this was indeed where the voices were coming from. She pushed it open gingerly and peered around it.

Two naked bodies were writhing together. The youthful limbs of a girl were wrapped around her lover as he thrust determinedly into her. Rhianna watched in disbelief, holding her breath, illogically wondering if she herself looked as ridiculous when similarly engaged. It was all she could do to stop herself from crying out in protest. With an enormous effort of will, she controlled herself and was truly surprised at her ability to accept the inevitable when she was irrevocably faced with it. Although she recognised Lawson, even from such an unlikely position, she could not see who the woman was; her face was hidden behind his broad shoulders. Judging by the slenderness and unblemished appearance of her smooth thighs and upper arms, it was obvious she was young. Then they shifted their position as if to turn over and Rhianna darted back behind the door again. The cavorting couple spoke to each other, but Rhianna could not hear what was said. Then she heard the girl's muted giggle in response to some comment. Warily, she peeped round the edge of the door again and saw that the girl was sitting astride Lawson now, as if he were a horse in some lewd derby, her dark red hair flowing down her back.

Oh, it was Caitlin all right. There could be no mistake.

Rhianna withdrew and, as quickly as she could, she ran down the stairs, out of that living room and out of the house.

'What was that?' Caitlin said in alarm. 'Did you hear something?'

'I did,' Lawson answered agitatedly, and shoved her off.

He ran naked to the front bedroom and peered through the net curtains. He had to open the sash and put his head out of the window before he could see Rhianna scurrying off to his right. He called after her but she ignored his yell. He watched, helpless, as she untethered Blossom, leapt athletically into her gig and turned round to drive off in the opposite direction.

In seconds Caitlin was behind him. 'What was it?'

'Oh, only your bloody mistress. You heard her running down the stairs. She must have seen us. What the hell shall we do?'

Caitlin shrugged her naked shoulders and Lawson noticed how her well-weighted breasts moved up and down in fascinating concert.

'She might not have seen anything,' he said resignedly. 'And even if she did, we might as well finish what we came here to do. We haven't come all this way to do only half a job. We might as well be hanged for a sheep as for a lamb.'

The emotion Rhianna was first aware of was hate. Hate did not come naturally to her, but she hated Caitlin. Her second emotion, more typically, was that such hate might well be misdirected. Maybe, like her, Caitlin was the victim of Lawson's easy charm, of his effortless way with buttery words and tantalising promises. Maybe her hate should be directed at him.

But this was a joint betrayal. Each was equally to blame. Illogically, she wondered if there were some potent refinements of lovemaking that Irish girls were privy to that she herself knew nothing of?

Now the trust was gone. Finally. Irrevocably. And so much else was gone besides. The pride she had in Lawson was gone; he had not only let himself down, he had let her down as well. Gone too was the pride she had in herself, pride that a man like him had picked her for his wife in preference to a woman more socially elevated.

She flicked the reins and the mare speeded up into a fast trot. The gig bounced and rumbled over the uneven cobbled surface of Cinder Bank, the main road from Netherton to

Dudley. Well, if the gig overturned at the next bend and she were thrown out and fatally injured, that would make him see. That would show him. That would shock him into realising what he had done.

But why give him that satisfaction? Why make it easy for him to have Caitlin as a permanent bed partner? She reined Blossom in and slowed her down.

What must she do now? Where should she go? She daren't tell anybody about this, she would look such a fool. Married only weeks and already her husband was bedding the maid. How would it look? That she herself was at fault? That she could not keep her virile husband sufficiently interested in bed to divert him from the indisputable fascination of the Irish maid?

She drove back to the house in Himley Road, left Blossom hitched to the gig and went inside. Perhaps she should go and find Mrs O'Flanagan and tell her she was about to dismiss her daughter. But what reason could she give? Mrs O'Flanagan was the most decent woman, the most able cook imaginable. And she would have no clue at all as to what her daughter had been up to. Was it necessary to upset the poor woman when it was no fault of hers? Rhianna went upstairs instead. She slumped onto the bed and sobbed.

She had no idea how long she had been crying when she heard the click of the door catch. She was lying down and turned her head apprehensively.

'I've brought you a cup of tea,' Lawson said calmly. 'I thought you might be thirsty.'

'How very considerate,' she replied with acid sarcasm in her voice.

He placed the cup and saucer on her bedside table and waited, sitting in a chair at the foot of the bed. After some minutes she turned over and sat up, her legs dangling girlishly over the edge of the bed. Her eyes were puffy and red. She took a handkerchief from the pocket of her skirt and blew her nose.

'I shall drink the tea,' she said piously and sniffed. 'If you have poisoned it, then so be it.'

'Oh, don't be so melodramatic, Rhianna.'

'I'm melodramatic? I suppose what you've been up to with Caitlin was not?'

He looked to the floor, at the fine Kidderminster carpet that lay like an island of dense fur in the room with their bed marooned on it. 'I'm sorry, Rhianna.'

She sipped the tea and savoured the hot sweetness. 'You're sorry?' she queried. 'Sorry for doing what you did or sorry for being found out?'

'For what I did, of course. It was wrong of me.'

'Well, now's the time to admit it – now you've had your fun.'

'Look, Rhianna, it means nothing. I don't love Caitlin, I love you. With all my heart and soul I love you.'

'You have a very peculiar way of showing it, Lawson,' she said scornfully and sniffed once more. She felt tears welling up again and tried to stem them by pressing her handkerchief to her eyes. 'Is that why you married me? Because you loved me?'

'You know it is.'

'And I loved *you*. I idolised you. But now it's ruined. Can you see that? I could never trust you again . . . Never. Besides, how many other women have you had, even in the short time we've been married? Is that why you keep that house in Netherton unoccupied? So you can take all your women there and bed them in comfort, in secret?'

He shook his head. 'No. That's not why I keep it unoccupied.'

'Then why? Tell me that.'

'If you want to know the truth, Rhianna, Robert Cookson and Jack Hayward rent it off me jointly,' he said softly. 'They use it as somewhere to take *their* women.'

She managed a contemptuous little laugh. 'But you're not averse to using it yourself, eh?' Her emotions were fluctuating from grief to scorn – and to anger. Did he really think she would believe such arrant nonsense? Who did he think he was fooling? Ever since she had known him he had beguiled her with nonsense. Well, thank God she could see through it at last. She would not be beguiled again. She sipped the hot tea and looked at him challengingly over the rim of the cup.

'I dismissed Caitlin,' he said. 'She no longer works for us.'

'I bet she was favourably impressed with that.'

'What else could I do? It's obvious you wouldn't want her working here.'

'So when are you seeing her again?'

'I'm not . . . Of course I'm not.'

Rhianna swallowed hard, trying to control her voice. 'Well, you might as well for all I care. Let's hope for your sake she's not pregnant.'

'Rhianna, you're spilling your tea.'

'Well, isn't that a shame?' she said caustically, 'because you could do with your little whore-of-all-work to come and clean it up.' There was within her now a searing, raging anger. Deliberately, she dropped the cup and its contents onto the floor. It bounced on to the linoleum and smashed to smithereens, tea splashing on the carpet and onto the bedclothes. She could have thrown the cup at him, full of tea, had she not already abandoned it to the floor. The saucer too. Indeed, she felt like attacking him with a knife, hitting him over the head with a hand mirror. She wrestled with her boiling emotions, desperately trying to calm herself, for in calmness lay strength. Their eyes met, hers burning into his with all her scorn and disdain. She raised her hand that held the saucer and hurled it at him. As he raised his arms to fend it off she stood up and strode over to the door.

'I shall be sleeping in the spare bedroom from now on. And I swear, Lawson Maddox, that if ever you enter that room when I'm in there, I'll wait till you're asleep and I'll stick a knife between your ribs.'

Mrs O'Flanagan took the news of her daughter's dismissal stoically. She was anxious not to offend Rhianna for fear of losing her own position, and remained deferential. Not that Rhianna would have dismissed Mrs O'Flanagan in any case. Indeed she felt sorry for the woman, shared her disappointment and complete surprise that her daughter had been discovered by Mr Maddox in their bedroom, rifling Rhianna's jewellery box, with a couple of pieces in her pocket already. Mrs O'Flanagan was only too thankful that Mr Maddox, in his kindness and understanding, had seen fit not to prosecute.

On the following Monday, the new groom commenced his employment and Rhianna started a new maid called Emma, who was not in the least alluring.

But all that week a thundercloud seemed to hover over the house. Rhianna remained angry and the depth of her wrath surprised even her. She could not forgive Lawson for what he had done and had no intention of trying. How many other times had he been unfaithful and how many times in the future might he be? If he could have got away with it once he could have got away with it a hundred times. And once he had strayed, she had no desire to be touched by him again. Rather, the very thought she found repulsive.

The only times they met were at mealtimes, and even then they contrived to avoid each other, though it was not always possible or convenient to do so. So when they met, she was icily polite and he struggled to make conversation that sounded normal.

On the Tuesday, when Lawson was out, Rhianna came downstairs to find a white envelope lying on the hall floor, having been shoved through the letterbox. She picked it up and saw that it was addressed to Mr and Mrs L. Maddox. She duly ran her thumb under the flap and opened it. It was an invitation. Mr John Mallory Gibson requested the pleasure of their company at a party to celebrate his return, at the house in Windmill Street on Saturday evening, 13th July, at half-past seven.

Rhianna took the invitation over to the escritoire in the sitting room, pulled out a clean sheet of notepaper from a sheaf and wrote back, saying that unfortunately, due to other commitments, Mr Lawson Maddox would not be able to attend. Mrs Rhianna Maddox, on the other hand, would be delighted to.

15

In all his professional life, John Gibson had never been used to having so much space as he now enjoyed at the old mine manager's house in Windmill Street. There were rooms galore. Besides the conservatory that he had set up as a studio, he had a scullery, a room for formal dining in which he could entertain guests, if only he were outgoing enough to make sufficient friends. There was a large and airy room on the side of the house that would make a superb drawing room. He even had several bedrooms. In the three weeks he had resided in this house, furniture had begun to appear, all acquired cheaply from second-hand shops, since he was keen not to be too much of a financial drain on his father. However, he was no homemaker. He was not about to go around arranging and rearranging these lacklustre, scratched appurtenances. Nor was he about to adorn them with pretty doilies and stick potted plants upon them, even though he had the design sense to do it. Besides, this stuff was utilitarian, intended to serve only its purpose, and was neither decorative nor particularly elegant.

All this space was luxury. In the conglomeration of ateliers called Bolton Studios, he'd moved to in Wimbledon in 1887, that was all he'd had: a studio. And in that studio he had lived and worked. He ate there while he worked, he slept there on the floor. He smiled to himself as he fondly recalled those times. Henry Ryland and Lawrence Bulleid, who also rented studios, were his soulmates. There was no doubt they had influenced each other in their artistic growth. While he and Lawrence Bulleid were socially reserved, Henry Ryland was socially engaged, to John's great envy. But the common thread that bound them together was their love for painting detailed classical scenes that featured pretty girls. It amused John to ponder the descriptions of their work penned by some of the less appreciative art critics; 'togas and terraces', 'painters of the patio' and the like. Well, if Lawrence Alma-Tadema could do it and be praised for it, they could do it, too.

It was the Saturday of the party he was hosting and the post that morning provided some cause for celebration. A letter had arrived from Messrs Thomas Miller McLean of the Haymarket in London, advising him that they were prepared to promote his work, and were confident of realising a very acceptable level of sales among their clientele, to their mutual benefit. In addition, they would like Mr Gibson to submit paintings for their forthcoming annual Winter Exhibition. John was delighted with this news. Not only was the Haymarket an important centre for the fine art trade, but above the gallery's awning, was proudly displayed the Royal crest.

Painting was what John did best. But art was a jealous master. He gave his life to it, but shut out the rest of life from it. He painted from his soul. He was not particularly interested in pandering to either his critics or the public. Technically, he was brilliant. His renditions of marble looked smooth, perfectly veined and weathered, and promised to be uncannily cool if touched. Overall, his pictures evoked the heady aromatic atmosphere of the Mediterranean with its vivid midsummer light and its heat. His subjects were beautiful young women who, despite their perfect, glowing skin, their tantalising figures and angelic faces, never disturbed the serene Elysian environment he created on canvas. And this paradox only served to accentuate his prodigious ability and understanding of things beautiful, without being sentimental, suggestive or improper. These openly innocent, youthful, patrician maidens, conspicuously lovely in their demure, compliant poses, were not only incongruously sensual but, above all, truly eloquent in his halcyon compositions.

John put down the letter from his new dealer and penned a reply. Naturally, he would be delighted to submit his best work, he wrote. Between today and the Winter Exhibition he would be able to produce between eight and ten new paintings. All, he hoped, would be worthy of inclusion. All should sell and give him, he privately hoped, that final independence from his father that he craved.

By late afternoon, Alexander Gibson's phaeton had arrived, conveying three housemaids and the party food they would be serving to the forty or so guests, who happened to be mostly family and friends of his father. Almost apologetically, John explained to the maids where it was all to be set up in the would-be dining room. He had lined the bare walls of the could-be drawing room with his work and they hung from the newly painted picture rail. It had the feel of a gallery, if not a home, but at least there was room for folk to stand and gossip. He had ordered a kilderkin of India pale ale from the British Oak close by, and cases of red and white burgundy from wine merchants Rutland and Lett, as well as a gallon each of whisky, rum, brandy and gin.

At half-past seven, people started arriving and many commented on the novelty of the sudden steep rise on entering Windmill Street. Somebody brought along an accordion and somebody else a fiddle and not many drinks later, they were comparing repertoires. Soon the place was noisy with the sound of chatter and laughter, and foggy with the smoke of cigars and cigarettes. As well as Alexander and Ruth Gibson, the Cooksons of Baxter House were present, including their son Robert who escorted a brassy young woman who might have fallen straight into his arms from the chorus line of some music hall.

Just before eight o' clock, Rhianna appeared, straight-backed, wearing a plain but beautifully cut dress in dark green satin. The bodice was tight with a high neck and the sleeves loose and billowy. The skirt fitted smoothly over her hips without a bustle, the very height of fashion, eliciting mixed comments behind the hands of some of the older women. John saw her arrive in her gig but was surprised to see it driven away afterwards by a groom. He greeted her at the door.

'Mrs Maddox. Please come in. I'd almost given you up.'

'Am I very late?' she asked as she entered. 'If I am, I'm sorry.'

'There's no need to apologise. Not everybody's here yet in any case. It's a pity your husband couldn't make it.'

'Yes,' she replied turning to him, 'but I don't see it as a reason for me to be confined to the house. Do you?'

'As an ardent non-conformist in everything, Mrs Maddox, I'm inclined to agree.'

She smiled. 'I hoped you'd be on my side, Mr Gibson.'

'Let's say there's a streak of unconventionality about you that I don't disapprove of, Mrs Maddox. Look, let me introduce you to some of the people you don't know.'

'Thank you.' She followed him into the neo-drawing-room and saw that it was decorated with vases of summer flowers. She wondered if he had arranged them.

'May I get you a drink first, Mrs Maddox?'

'Do you have any white wine?'

'Hock, or burgundy?'

She shrugged, uncertain which to choose. 'Oh ... you choose, Mr Gibson.'

People were standing around chattering animatedly. Already, the accordionist and the fiddle player were experimenting between themselves with laughter and hesitant tunes. Rhianna gasped with apprehension when she caught sight of Jeremiah Cookson and his wife, her former master and mistress. But it was too late to turn away and pretend she hadn't seen them. Mrs Cookson nodded a greeting and glided over to her.

'Rhianna, how lovely to see you.'

'Mrs Cookson.' Rhianna smiled a broad, open smile that concealed her uneasiness at meeting the lady again, the first time since her departure from Baxter House.

'Well, Rhianna, how are you? I understand that you married my son's friend Mr Maddox.'

'I certainly did.'

'Quite a character, isn't he?'

'Oh yes. He's quite a character, Mrs Cookson.'

'I take it he's with you this evening.'

'Other commitments, I'm afraid.' The urge to call the lady 'ma'am' was almost overwhelming but she assiduously managed to avoid it.

'Oh, yes, Lawson always was a busy bee as far as I could make out. So how have you settled down to married life?'

'Every day I learn something new,' Rhianna replied with an ambiguous smile.

They chatted a while, and there seemed to be no animosity from Mrs Cookson, though she never once enquired about Sarah. John Gibson sidled up to Rhianna to deliver her glass of wine. She thanked him and drew him into the conversation at once, to shift the focus from herself.

'So you two have met already?' Mrs Cookson deduced.

'Oh, yes,' Rhianna replied. 'In fact, this house Mr Gibson is renting belongs to my husband. We met because of it.'

It was immediately evident that John felt as uncomfortable as Rhianna in Mrs Cookson's company. He sipped his drink edgily and she decided it was time to save not only him, but herself as well.

'I'm such an admirer of Mr Gibson's work, Mrs Cookson,' she said, then turned to John without excluding the lady. 'I see you have some more paintings up on the walls that you haven't shown me yet. I'd love you to explain them to me.'

'Of course, Mrs Maddox.' John smiled at Rhianna, then at Mrs Cookson. 'Would you excuse us, Mrs Cookson?'

'Thank you for saving me, Mr Gibson,' Rhianna said when

they were out of earshot. 'I'm not particularly comfortable with Mrs Cookson.'

'Oh, I thought *you* were saving *me*.'

He led her to the first painting, of a young woman sitting in profile on a heavy wooden chair of classic proportions, in a room of white marble walls and floor. Beneath her sandalled feet was a leopard-skin rug, perfectly executed.

'This is entitled "Waiting for the Dance". Painted last year, I think . . . And this next one is called "Sewing Girl" . . .'

In the foreground was a girl in a dark green toga with a gold sash, sewing a length of ribbon as she sat on a tiger skin; in the near distance was another girl, her back towards the viewer, looking out onto a blue sea beyond a marble balustrade.

'Is it very time-consuming to paint every hair of the animal's coat?'

He beamed at her obvious interest. 'It's an illusion, Mrs Maddox. I don't actually paint each and every hair . . .' They moved on to the next painting. 'This one is called "Waiting for an Answer". The man has just asked the girl to marry him . . .'

'Yes . . .' Rhianna mused. 'I can see that . . . That looks like you in the picture, doing the asking.'

'A self-portrait,' he said with a self-conscious grin. 'You recognised me. And I even had a beard.'

'You look very preoccupied. So who is the girl? I presume somebody *real* modelled for you?'

He avoided her eyes when she looked at him. 'Fernanda Carpaccio,' he said. 'Italian. She lived in London for a while.'

'Lived?' she queried. 'Not any more?'

'Not any more, no. She married a Frenchman . . .'

Rhianna looked at him with increasing curiosity. 'Does this painting reflect something of your own personal life, by any chance? Of your own endeavours with this Fernanda, perhaps?'

He gave an embarrassed smile. 'Yes. I confess it's somewhat allegorical, Rhianna. How astute of you.'

'You called me Rhianna,' she said softly, catching his eye.

'Do you mind? I apologise of course. I wasn't trying to be forward. Forgive me, it was a slip of the tongue.'

'No, please, I don't mind a bit. It *is* my name, after all.' She smiled and touched his arm to put him at his ease. 'Yes, please call me Rhianna. And, if you have no objection, I'll call you John instead of Mr Gibson. Agreed?'

'Agreed.'

'So, I take it then . . . John . . . that you and this Fernanda . . . that she was special to you . . .'

He sighed with melancholy. 'Yes, she was rather special to me.'

'Were you in love with her then?' She sipped her wine as she waited for his reply.

'Oh, yes . . . I was very much in love with her.'

'I'm sorry,' said Rhianna, and put a consoling hand on his arm again. 'I didn't mean to pry. It's none of my business but . . . it's so evident from your painting . . . You waiting for the girl to say yes, she'll marry you – while she's looking all wistful as if she has so many things, so many options to weigh up before she gives her answer. When did you paint this?'

'Oh . . . about Easter time. I really was waiting for her answer at the time.'

'And she let you down.'

'Yes . . .' He sighed again. 'She had already agreed to marry this Frenchman – another artist. I had no idea . . . They moved to Paris soon after.'

'Oh, John, I feel so sorry for you,' Rhianna said and it came from the heart. 'Has the pain subsided just a little bit since then?'

He nodded. 'It's the main reason I left London. It wasn't entirely the lack of money. There were too many painful memories. It's not been so bad up here. Quite therapeutic, in fact. I've had things to occupy me that I wouldn't have had in London – like buying this old furniture for instance, organising this party . . . even entertaining my landlord's wife when she decides to drop in on me . . .'

'Be warned. She might drop in on you again . . . Unannounced.'

'Would you, really? You'd be surprised how it helps, talking to you, Rhianna . . .' There was a look of openness and honesty in his eyes. 'I . . . I don't mix easily, you know . . . I have the greatest difficulty making friends . . . I'm uncomfortable with people. But I find you very easy to talk to . . . I think Lawson Maddox is a very lucky man.'

Rhianna smiled sympathetically, almost tempted to tell him about Lawson's intolerable indiscretions, but she thought better of it. If she did, she would no doubt break down in tears, as she had every day since discovering his infidelity for certain. 'Tell me about this next painting, John.'

'It's called "An Idle Hour",' he informed her as they shifted along. In the foreground was an array of red and white sweetpeas that looked real enough to be wavering in a breeze.

'It's the same girl,' Rhianna said. 'And wearing the same headbands. She's beautiful, isn't she? Such a lovely face and figure. Is her skin really as smooth as it looks?'

'Oh, yes,' he whispered.

'I can see why you were so captivated . . . But why did you use an Italian girl? Apart from the fact that she's beautiful, I mean. There must be other beautiful models?'

'Because she had the right colouring, the right demeanour. I want my pictures to look authentic. A fair-haired, pale-skinned woman wouldn't look right in an Italian setting. Others have done it, but it never looks right.'

'Why did you become an artist, John?'

'Oh, I couldn't help it,' he replied as if any other reason was unthinkable. 'I have an inner need to paint. There's nothing else I could possibly do. There's nothing else I want to do. I could never work in my father's business, for instance. I would die of boredom. I'd shrivel up with spiritual starvation.'

The two musicians who had been seriously threatening to bombard everybody's ears, had evidently sorted out a selection of tunes and struck up in earnest. The hips of several of the women present started swaying to the gentle rhythm and some started singing along with the accordionist who, it transpired, was a cousin of John Gibson.

John showed Rhianna the rest of the pictures hanging on the wall in that room and she listened intently to what he told her.

'I mustn't monopolise you any more, John,' she said eventually.

'It's no hardship, I can assure you.'

'But you have other guests. You mustn't neglect them.' She took a sip of wine.

'On the other hand, it would be very ungallant of me to leave you to your own devices when you are here unescorted. Let me introduce you to some of the guests you might find interesting. That way I'll be mingling with them as well.'

'All right.' She was pleased he suggested it, since the only other people she knew there, apart from the Cooksons, were Alexander and Ruth Gibson. John introduced her as his landlady to a besatinned Mrs Guest, his mother's sister. While they chatted, Robert Cookson brushed past her. She turned and smiled at him in polite acknowledgement.

'No Lawson tonight?' Robert queried, and Rhianna could not determine whether he was being facetious or whether he was ignorant of events.

'Not tonight, Mr Cookson,' she responded deferentially. 'I have no idea what Lawson's plans were for this evening.'

'Some meeting of the Puritan Lobby, I've no doubt,' Robert Cookson said with a smirk. He turned to his tart, who wore so many bangles and beads that she clinked as she moved.

After speaking to Mrs Guest for some time, John diplomatically drew Rhianna away again. 'Would you like to see what I've done with my studio?'

She allowed herself to be led away to the back of the house, through the scullery and away from the main party.

John Gibson had installed a workbench that was strewn with tubes of paint, sketches on odd sheets of paper, messy palettes, glass jars with brushes soaking in a browny coloured liquid. It all smelt of linseed oil. Standing against the wall around the periphery of the studio were stretched canvasses, some untouched, some finished. Behind one canvas Rhianna noticed a growth of fungus that looked like a half-cooked rasher of bacon sprouting from the dirt crack between wall and floor. Four marble busts were grouped in one corner like a collection of redundant Roman effigies in a stonemason's yard. Another table was strewn with various rags, candles and a random pile of books.

'It certainly looks and smells different,' she remarked.

'Like an artist's studio.'

'I see you have some more paintings leaning against the wall.'

'Not quite dry yet. I'll show them to you when they are.'

'And another you've started.' Rhianna walked over to his easel and peered at the few lines and rough areas of paint. 'What's this one to be called?'

'I think I'm going to call it "At the Garden Shrine in Pompeii".'

'Isn't that a bit of a mouthful?'

John smiled. 'You know, I think you are right.'

'So, is this to be Fernanda?' she asked, lightly tracing the outline of a female figure with her finger.

He nodded. 'I had her sketched already in this pose, sniffing a rose.' He uttered a little laugh of self-mockery.

'Let's hope she's happy with her Frenchman,' Rhianna suggested.

'Oh, yes, I really hope she is,' John said sincerely. 'I want her to be happy, whichever way she has chosen . . .' He perched his backside on the corner of his workbench, careful to avoid any drips of oil paint in case it was still wet. 'You've only been married a short time yourself, I understand.'

'Not yet three months. We married at Easter.'

'An Easter bride . . .' he mused quietly. 'I expect you looked astonishingly beautiful.'

Rhianna laughed. 'Oh, astonishingly,' she said with self-effacing sarcasm.

'My mother speaks highly of you.'

'That's reassuring. But not your father?'

'Oh, my father makes no comment on anybody. Unless he particularly dislikes them – then he can be rather outspoken. He hasn't said he dislikes you, anyway.'

'Am I to be reassured by that? But then, he's a friend of my husband, isn't he? Some business connection they have. Although I haven't yet worked out what it is exactly.'

'How did you meet Lawson, Rhianna?' he asked, changing tack.

She emptied the glass of wine that had accompanied her from the party room. 'I was . . . Well, to put it bluntly, I was in service at the Cooksons'. I was their housekeeper. We met at their New Year's Eve party.'

'Good God!' he exclaimed, evidently delighted, and burst out laughing. 'You really were their housekeeper?'

'Is it so funny?'

'Oh, it's beautiful. I have to admire a man who shocks his family and friends by marrying somebody from below stairs. For all their stuffiness, I bet they all envied him.'

'Well, he had no family to shock, John. No close family at any rate.'

'Even so, I could just imagine my father in a similar situation. Had I been successful with my suit for Fernanda, I've no doubt I would have incurred his derision and wrath. More especially since she was foreign.'

'But it wouldn't have stopped you going ahead?'

'Of course not. I have no time at all for such petty social

prejudices. One person is much like another to me. There are good and bad in all classes and all races. To my mind, an honest pauper is much preferable to a corrupt nabob.'

'I've always thought so.'

'It must be quite . . . exciting,' he commented. 'The early days of marriage, I mean.'

'Oh, you can't imagine,' she replied evenly, but feeling emotional at his comment; it stirred up again the hurt, the heartache, the anger she still felt about Lawson. She pushed back tears that were pressing for release. 'I think maybe I'd better return to the others, John. People will talk if they see us alone like this.'

'For my part, Rhianna, people can say what they like. But to protect your reputation, you're right. We should return to the party. I mustn't monopolise you. But I've so much enjoyed talking to you.'

'And I to you,' Rhianna said. 'Do you know what time it is?'

He lifted his watch from his pocket. 'Nine.'

'I asked my groom to collect me at ten. I hope you won't regard my leaving early as a slight.'

'Of course not. I understand.'

'Thank you. It's just that I feel I should be back at home before Lawson. That's all.'

'Of course. I quite understand.'

Over the next few days Rhianna began to feel ever more detached from Lawson. Her anger was still rampant within her, and her love for him, like sweet, fresh milk exposed to a heated atmosphere, was turning sour. When she thought about what she had witnessed in that house in Netherton – and the image plagued her frequently – her heart still thumped momentarily and she felt a sickening revulsion. Thank God that she did not know how many other times, how many other women there had been. Judging by the regularity with which he was away from home there must have been dozens, for he certainly had a way with women. Her only wish now was that she herself had never been subjected to it.

She was deeply hurt by his infidelity and did not feel she could ever forgive him. All week they had slept in separate rooms and she saw no reason to alter that arrangement. She had no further physical desire for him; just the thought of him touching her was repulsive. During the day and at mealtimes she avoided him as far as possible. When they had to speak, they were direct and economical with words. This absolute transformation in her feelings for him surprised Rhianna no end. If he found so much pleasure with Caitlin then let him pursue it with Caitlin and leave her alone. Rhianna did not intend to compete, she had no wish to compete. Competing for a man, who was in any case her own husband, was beneath her. Lawson still went out every night and might still have been cavorting with Caitlin for all she knew. Caitlin, however, would doubtless soon be eclipsed by some other susceptible female who, like all the others, would think the sun shone out of his backside till he did the dirty on her as well.

The overriding problem, as she saw it, was that she was irrevocably married to Lawson and there was no escape, whatever he'd done. Divorce was not a remedy easily available to her. Adultery by itself was not enough; she needed another matrimonial crime to bolster her claim, such as cruelty or desertion. But he had been neither cruel nor deserted her. Additionally, the only courts available to sanction divorce were in London and the costs involved in going through with it were prohibitive. In any case, settlements still favoured the husband outrageously, however erring he might have been.

Rhianna was not vindictive by nature, however. She sought no revenge and desired none. If Lawson preferred to find his pleasure in drink and other women, then so be it. Just so long as he left her alone now. She was simply sorry that this marriage, which had promised everything at first, had proved too soon to have no future in it.

She wondered how he felt about it. Whether he felt any remorse for what he had done.

16

Lawson Maddox was genuinely sorry that he had upset his wife. He had married her with noble intentions, with unequivocal if not pure, unbounded love in his heart. He had a problem with women, though; he could not leave them alone. He was obsessed. He moved in circles where women were plentiful. Most were willing enough. Some were of elevated social classes, yet that did not mean he favoured them. The only qualifications they needed were to be very young, very attractive, and untouched. Class was immaterial. Indeed, he had served his apprenticeship in voluptuousness with brickyard and pit bank wenches. Not all were single either. In his formative sprees, he was just as likely to tempt a young and good-looking married woman as a single one. There was less of a risk with married women; if you made one pregnant for instance, it would only ever be her husband's child she was carrying, wouldn't it?

One of the reasons Lawson had not pressed his seduction of Rhianna before they were married was that he found her virginity and innocence something of a novelty in a girl older than eighteen; a novelty to be preserved and savoured on the first night of their marriage. Delaying the pleasure would only increase his appreciation of it later. In the meantime, he was not short of available women. Women fell at his feet.

But for all his philandering, he loved Rhianna in his own capricious way. She was the only woman he had ever really esteemed. She was untainted. For all her lowly upbringing, she was a lady in every other sense and he was quick to spot it. She was endowed with innate good judgement and

level-headedness, and a sense of moral decency that he dis-
tinctly lacked. She knew her own worth and would neither
compromise nor devalue it. He *needed* those exceptional
qualities in her to establish some respectability in society for
himself, to influence him positively; for he knew his failings
well. In his view, *need* was the very thing that engendered
love. If only he could make her see that she was the most
important thing, the only steadfast entity in his life, that he
needed her, that he depended on her for her innate stability,
for her reasoned opinions, for her gentle guidance. The way
he had behaved, however – or rather, the way he had been
found out – she would never believe it.

Lawson knew there was only one way of winning back his
wife, and that was by example, by proving to her that he could
remain faithful. The thought almost made him laugh. How
could he sustain fidelity? He couldn't. Not under any circumstances, and he knew it better than anybody. All his waking
hours he thought about women and the sexual favours they
had bestowed upon him from an early age. He contemplated
them in all their modes of submission, in all their ecstasy
as they writhed with unbridled pleasure beneath him and
sometimes on top of him. Many an afternoon, even as a
youth, he had hired rooms in bawdy houses, where he had
entertained kitchen maids and nursery maids and chamber
maids to an hour or two of unrestrained romping during their
time off. He would never spend money paying for prostitutes
though. Let others do that. Why should he, when he could
have women for free?

He had an insight into women that few other men possessed.
It was a common enough fallacy that women did not enjoy sex.
Well, his experience told him the exact opposite. They relished
it. Some relished it so much they would risk anything, would
go to any lengths for it, no matter how degrading, giving the
lie to their manifest primness, their feigned protestations and
shock at his bawdy talk. While such willing women existed,

he must devote his time to them, even at the expense of his marriage.

It was a fundamental flaw in his character; Rhianna would have to understand and accept this if they were ever to have a successful marriage. Yet there was no prospect at all that she would accept him on such terms. Never. Nor would unlimited gifts and material generosity achieve it. Not now she had discovered what he was really like, not now she had discovered his real weakness. If he was not able to persuade her to change her mind in a short time, however; if he did not quickly win her back, his own impatience at being rejected would turn to vindictiveness.

And only he knew just how malicious that vindictiveness might be.

Lawson thought he saw a chink of light in Rhianna's defences at breakfast on the morning of the following Tuesday. He had almost finished his, and she was under the impression that he had already left the house. As she entered the breakfast room, he was sitting there deep in thought, elbows on the table, a cup of tea held between two hands.

'I thought you might be still asleep,' he said.

She made no reply but, after hesitating a moment, sat at the opposite end of the table as far away from him as she could get. She reached for the teapot and poured herself a cup of tea without looking at him, added milk and a little sugar. The summer sunshine streaming through the window behind her enhanced the rich dark gloss of her hair and lit the edge of her cheek, accentuating its elegant, feminine curve. Lawson saw it and was, of course, moved by it.

'Are you going out today?' he enquired pleasantly.

She shrugged with indifference. 'I might. On the other hand, I might get the groom started on the garden. Lord knows it's a sight.'

'Good idea,' he said unctuously and reached for the teapot

himself. 'But why not do both?' He poured himself another cup of tea. 'Are you still intending to collect rents for me?'

'You mean from your *officially* occupied properties?'

'Yes, I mean those.'

'If you want me to. I don't mind. It keeps me busy. And I like quite a few of your tenants.'

'I was hoping you would.' He smiled agreeably. 'I really appreciate your doing it.'

'Oh, I'll be doing it to please myself, Lawson, not to please you. I'll be doing it to keep myself busy. Otherwise, I'll die of boredom. But don't worry, I shan't pocket any of your precious rents.'

Emma, the new maid, entered and asked what ma'am would like for breakfast. Rhianna said she would like a boiled egg with bread and butter and Emma left the room again to arrange it.

Lawson sugared his tea and stirred it. He wanted to make ordinary conversation, as one would during any ordinary breakfast time shared by an ordinary couple. Even he was finding it difficult. He said, 'How is Emma turning out?' and knew at once that he had said the wrong thing, asked the most tactless question.

'Oh, I thought you were the expert on maids,' Rhianna replied tartly.

'I asked a civil question, Rhianna.'

'I don't know. How is she turning out? Like Caitlin? Though she's not half as pretty, that might not bother you.'

Petulantly, he crashed his cup back in its saucer and tea slopped into it and over the clean white tablecloth. 'I'm going out,' he rasped. 'You do as you please.'

'Oh, I will, Lawson. Be sure of it.'

Two months passed and things did not improve. In those two months, Rhianna's emotions for Lawson had metamorphosed from devastation, through anger, to contempt. It was late

morning on 23rd September, a Monday. The day was bright
and it was warm for the time of year. Rhianna had been
collecting rents from Albert Street and the general area around
Eve Hill as she had been doing regularly. As each week passed
she was growing ever more aware that she was rushing through
the other tenants to get to the old mine-manager's house in
Windmill Street as quickly as she could. She hankered for
the company of John Gibson, looked forward to seeing him
every Monday morning. She was confused as to the reason.
Maybe it was what wronged wives did; sought male company
elsewhere, wished somehow to retaliate, to curry favour with
other men and take their revenge . . . Revenge, however, was
not a word in her vocabulary. At least she had some rapport
with John Gibson. She had come to know him well. He was
like a breath of fresh air. He was so open, so sincere, and so
refreshingly naïve for a man; such a change from Lawson's
boisterous, knowing, abrasive intensity.

She drove into the narrow street and hitched the horse to
the gatepost. A group of very young children were scrabbling
about in the dirt close by while their mothers and grand-
mothers sweated amid the clouds of steam that billowed over
their cast-iron mangles and wooden maiding tubs in their
tumbledown brewhouses. She felt in her purse and gave them
each a penny to keep an eye on her horse, but on no account
to worry it. Then, she walked to the front door, tapped the
cast-iron knocker and awaited a reply.

John Gibson was as usual delighted when he saw her.
He stood aside to let her in and invited her through to
his studio.

'I was just about to make a sandwich, Rhianna. Can I
tempt you?'

'If you have enough. If I wouldn't be depriving you. That's
very kind . . .' She stood and cursorily looked at the painting
on his easel. 'You seem to be getting on very well with
your work.'

'Actually, no. It's not going well at all . . . But never mind that. Come into the scullery and talk to me while I slice some bread.' He took a fresh loaf from a bread bin and a large knife from a drawer in his table. 'Thick or thin?'

'Let me do it, John.'

'I wouldn't dream.'

She laughed. 'I imagine I'm more used to slicing bread than you are. Besides, you have smudges of paint on your fingers. Let me.' She held her hand out for the knife and he passed it to her. 'Thick or thin?' she asked, mimicking him.

'Something in between, I think. Neither thick nor thin . . . Actually, I was contemplating cheese and tomato . . .'

'My next question,' she said, cutting a first slice, 'was to be what are we going to put between the slices of bread?'

He went to the cellar head and fetched out a lump of cheese wrapped in greaseproof paper, and a couple of ripe tomatoes. He placed them on the table in front of her. 'Would you like some wine to drink?' he suggested.

She smiled as she looked into his eyes. 'Wine would be very nice. A bit like having our own little private party.'

She had cut five slices of bread and was buttering them when John returned with a bottle of red wine. 'I don't know if this stuff is any good.' He scrutinised the label on the bottle. 'I'm not an expert.'

'Neither am I. Lawson says that good wine is wasted on me. I'm sure this will be fine. I must say, I didn't expect to be entertained to lunch quite so royally.'

'The spontaneity appeals to me, Rhianna. Does it not to you as well?' He opened the bottle, reached for two glasses and poured. He handed her one. 'I seldom have company, and friendly company permits spontaneity . . . What do you think of it?'

She sniffed the wine and feigned a studied look, parodying the more pompous guests who had sat around the dinner table at Baxter House. 'Oh, exquisite nose, John,' she said in an affected accent, then she sipped it. 'Mmm. Deliciously soft on the palate . . . Good length . . . Absolutely top-hole . . .'

He chuckled delightedly. 'I see you have the measure of such people, Rhianna. You mock scandalously.'

'But isn't that what they say? I wasn't really mocking though. Just imitating.' She opened the package of cheese and began slicing it, laying the slices onto the buttered bread.

'Nonetheless, it bore a striking resemblance to my father. Except that you are beautiful when he is patently not.'

She felt herself go hot when he said that. She was sure that she had coloured up, and cursed herself for reacting like a silly schoolgirl. What did it matter if he thought her beautiful? 'Oh, but I imagine your mother thinks he is,' she said, trying to disguise her discomposure.

The hooter blew at the bucket and fender factory in London Fields at the rear, signalling dinnertime. Rhianna sliced the tomato without further comment and placed that on top of the cheese. John watched while she put the remaining slices of bread on top and cut them all in half. He felt a strange and somehow nostalgic intimacy with Rhianna; nostalgic in the sense that this minor domestic event reminded him of what might have been but could sadly never be, because she was married to another man. For some time he'd been brooding over her. Already, she was breaking his heart and, in the fullness of time, would do so completely. The perfidious Fernanda was fading from his thoughts and was being replaced by this equally enchanting young woman whom he knew instinctively was infinitely more compatible, and yet just as remote.

'Where shall we sit to eat?' Rhianna asked, looking up at him now.

'The weather's so fine, why don't we sit outside in the back yard? It's private enough with that high wall around it.'

'All right.'

'I'll take two chairs out . . . Go through the studio, Rhianna.'

She nodded and carried the two plates out with her as she walked in front of him. Suddenly, she remembered that Blossom was tethered in the street. She asked if he had a bucket that she could use for water. He found a galvanised one and she went to the pump outside the old miners' cottages and filled it. Some of the workers from the bucket works were making their way to the nearest public house. As they deferentially bid her good day, she removed the nosebag and set the water on the ground in front of the mare. As the mare drank, Rhianna patted her and spoke softly to her. She left the bucket for Blossom to finish at her leisure and went back inside where she washed her hands in a bowl of water and dried them.

John had taken the wine to the backyard; her glass and plate were waiting for her on her chair. She picked them up, sat down and took another sip of wine. John asked if the mare was all right.

'She seems so. When I arrived, I asked the children outside to keep an eye on her but I imagine their mothers have called them all in for their dinners. I'll check her again soon.'

They were silent for a few moments while they ate. She looked at the backyard. It was wild and overgrown. At some time it had evidently been a prized and lovingly tended garden, if the ornamentally edged paths and paving bricks were anything to go by. Formal geometric patterns remained, formed by flowerbeds that were now choked with a thick, wild growth of weeds and tufts of twitch grass.

She was enjoying this warm September weather, which seemed to be enhanced by the warmth she felt for her friend John Gibson. She sensed their affinity. But how long would it be before somebody would view their friendship as something more? It seemed impossible in their society of outward respectability, with its rigid marital and moral codes, to have a legitimate friend of the opposite sex without some cynic perceiving that there must be something sordid going on. Such a pity for already, she valued this friendship above any other.

It suddenly struck her how he and she had both been afflicted by the infidelity of the people with whom they had been in love. It had not occurred to her before. She thought about Lawson and an image of his debauched antics with Caitlin vividly flooded back. Funny how she felt no pain any more, how the passing of a few weeks had moderated her emotions so that all she felt now for Lawson was this cold contempt and indifference. Was this cordial and candid friendship with John Gibson responsible? Hardly. How could it be when they were not in love with each other? Surely, only the love that people exchanged could shut out the pain of former loves?

Rhianna finished the wine in her glass and John at once refilled it.

'Thank you, but I really shouldn't drink too much.'

'Nonsense,' he replied with a pleasant smile. 'It's such a beautiful day. In any case, it's customary on a picnic to open at least one bottle of wine.'

'A picnic!' Rhianna exclaimed delightedly. 'Yes, I suppose this is some sort of picnic.'

'Alfresco, the Italians call it. Eating outside in the fresh air, that is. Unfortunately, the weather in this country seldom allows it. It's good to take advantage of it when it does.'

Rhianna had finished her sandwich and put her plate on the ground beside her. She picked up her replenished wineglass and drank. 'How come your painting isn't going so well?'

He sighed and put his sandwich back on his plate. 'I'm missing Fernanda.'

Rhianna felt an illogical pang of jealousy at hearing this. 'Does it still hurt so much?' she queried.

'Oh, no, I don't mean heartache,' he said earnestly, anxious to dispel any doubts. 'No, I mean I'm missing her modelling for me. I have a sketch of her, done specially with this painting in mind, but I need to see the nuances of shade and colour in her skin – in the flesh, if you understand me – to enable me to impart it to the canvas accurately and with some expression.'

'Oh, I see . . . Would it help if I took her place? I mean, if I modelled instead? I could pose like she was supposed to, and you could see how the light falls on me.'

'Would you?' he said and his face lit up like a child's at receiving a surprise gift. 'I'd be so grateful. You have exactly the right colouring, you know. I thought so from the moment I first set eyes on you.' He left what remained of his sandwich, got up from his chair eagerly and beckoned Rhianna to follow him back into the studio through the open door. 'Look, can you see how she's supposed to stand?' he asked as they stood together facing the painting.

The model had her back to the viewer, her head turned in three-quarter profile as she looked out to sea expectantly, her arm resting on a marble balustrade.

'I can do that. The drawback as far as you are concerned though, John, is that Fernanda was lovely.'

'And you are not?' He was incredulous that she should apparently believe otherwise. 'You honestly think you are not?'

'I never try and fool myself that I'm something I'm not.'

'Let me tell you, Rhianna, that you are a perfect artists' model. Your face is as lovely as the dawn in summer, your hair and your colouring are ideal. Your figure is . . . Well, you have an excellent, youthful figure.'

'I'm happy you think so.'

'I do. And beauty is what people want to see. They see enough ugliness . . . This dress, Rhianna . . .' He pointed to the unpainted figure on the canvas. 'I have it upstairs in a trunk. If you'd wear it, I'd be able to capture the folds in it properly, without relying on memory.'

Rhianna laughed. 'That would be novel,' she said excitedly. 'You know how women love to try on different dresses. Something from a different era – a totally different style. Oh, I'd love to, John.'

'I'll dig it out for you and you can put it on . . . You'd better come upstairs.'

She followed him up the wooden staircase, their shoes clumping on the bare boards. She felt elated, inordinately pleased that she was being of some practical help. Not only that, the prospect of seeing herself in a painting, seeing her likeness as John saw her, thrilled her. He led her into a room that was devoid of furniture, a lumber room where his travel boxes lived, together with an old easel, a couple of marble busts, boxes full of God knows what. He went to the trunk and opened it. It was full of the flimsy dresses, ribbons and stoles he used in his paintings. He rummaged through it all and pulled out a plum-coloured garment made of a loosely woven cotton gauze. He held it up as if assessing its likely fit on Rhianna.

'This is the one I intended Fernanda to use. There are some straps as well that tie around the front and back of the bodice. Don't worry about doing them up correctly, they're a bit tricky. I'll do them up when you come down.'

'I hope it fits all right.'

'I don't see why not. You're about the same size and shape as Fernanda. If you'd like to use my bedroom . . . while I go to the studio and prepare my oils.'

He tossed the garment to her and indicated which room was his then went downstairs. Rhianna closed the door behind her and laid the dress on his neatly made bed. As she unfastened her own dress she looked outside and saw that Blossom seemed content standing with the gig. She scanned the room and saw the curtains she and Caitlin had made and put up, and felt a surge of pique as she recalled their friendly conversation, when all the time Caitlin was betraying her. Rhianna was down to her underwear now. She took the flimsy dress, pulled it over her head and lifted the skirt so that the folds fell naturally into place. One of the doors in the wardrobe had a full-length mirror and she looked at herself. The dress was simple but elegant, light and comfortable, the perfect length for her . . . To her horror she saw that it was possible to see through it. That horror, however, was caused by the sight of her underwear. Beneath the dress, it looked incongruous and ridiculous. For this to look authentic, for her to genuinely look like a maiden daughter of the Roman aristocracy, she would have to remove her chemise, her drawers and her stockings. It was going to take some nerve to pose in front of John Gibson in a dress he could partially see through. She'd offered to pose for him though. If she went back on her word, she would appear prudish and feel uneasy that she had let him down. She had no intention of letting him down.

So, unabashed, she removed all of her underwear and her stockings and slipped the dress over her head again. Once more, she looked at herself in the mirror, turning one way, then the other. Then she turned her back to the mirror and looked over her shoulder at herself, and was pleasantly surprised to see how lovely the whole thing looked, even without the bodice straps yet done up. She could discern the outline of her body and a hint of skin tone through the material. It was certainly erotic but hardly indecent. It was elegant and only mildly frivolous. In any case, what was she worrying about? John would not look at her lasciviously. He would only be interested in how the folds of material fell. So, barefoot, she gracefully descended the stairs and presented herself in the studio.

John gasped when he saw her. 'Oh, you look wonderful,' he enthused and she noticed he deliberately avoided looking at her where it would most embarrass. 'Shall I criss-cross those bodice straps now?'

She stepped in front of him and offered herself diffidently. He took the straps and passed them over her shoulder and under her arms, determinedly avoiding touching her. Rhianna was uneasy that he might be able to make out her breasts and her nipples through the material. His consideration, however, made her feel all the more comfortable with him. Here, at least, was a gentleman.

When he had finished, he looked her up and down with a professional eye. 'Perfect,' he said. 'You look magnificent. Now I want you to pose like this . . .' He turned her around so that her back was towards him. He touched her face gently, turning her head to the left. 'Just look directly ahead of you, as if you're looking out to sea.'

'Don't you want me to wear headbands?' she enquired.

'The headbands, yes! Yes, of course,' he said. 'I forgot. I won't be a minute.'

He came back with what she presumed were the same gold-coloured headbands Fernanda had worn. She tilted her head towards him and he put them on for her, adjusting them to his liking.

'Perfect. Oh, Rhianna, you look so right . . . No, just rest your hand on the table . . . Pretend it's a marble balustrade. That's it . . . Are you comfortable? Can you hold that pose without moving?'

'I think so.'

She could feel the sun warm on her shoulders through the glass roof of the studio. It was a glorious feeling. She closed her eyes. She became the girl in the picture he was creating, basking in warm Italian sunshine. The sea in front of her was a deep blue, heaving and sighing, matching her own emotions. The sky, which was of an equal hue, met it at the far horizon. She could feel the glistening white marble beneath her bare feet, touch the smooth balustrade in front of her with her fingers. Her body felt ethereally lifted from the constraints of too many hot and uncomfortable clothes; underwear and corsetry that she had already decided was ludicrous and ugly despite the lacy frills and fancies.

'I wonder what your husband would think if he saw you now, Rhianna?'

'Frankly, John, I wouldn't give tuppence to know what he thinks.'

'You wouldn't?'

'No.'

'I'm intrigued.' He noticed how her eyebrows flickered momentarily, wincing. He was touched. Something was manifestly amiss.

'Can I let you into a secret, John? Swear you won't tell anybody?'

'Of course. I swear.'

'He's been unfaithful . . . I found him with another woman.'

'Good Lord! You poor, poor thing . . . Is he mad? I think he must be mad.'

'I certainly was, I can tell you. But . . . putting two and two together, I can generally come up with four. I think he's been unfaithful quite a few times . . . He's out most of the time, even when he's not travelling on the Continent . . . and he does have a way with women, you know.' She went on to tell John exactly how her discovery had come about, how her suspicions had been aroused. She told him how she felt about it, about the anger that kept her from sleeping at night, how indifferent and resentful of Lawson she had since become.

'But it surprises me, John,' she went on, 'how my feelings have turned around. I mean, in only a few weeks I've gone from being hopelessly besotted to being almost totally uninterested. That doesn't seem right. So I ask myself whether I was really in love with him in the first place.'

'Oh yes, you must have been in love, Rhianna,' John said emphatically as he mixed two colours together with a brush on his palette. 'If you *think* you're in love, then you *are* in love. Love is a state of mind as much as it's anything else. The fact that your emotions tell you you don't love him any more might be a reaction, a sort of protection that possibly comes from being hurt. Maybe you're telling yourself that because he does what he does, means he doesn't love you. So why should you love him? In the same way that you once conditioned yourself to love him, you have since conditioned yourself not to. Do you follow?'

'But I didn't know you could turn love on and off like a tap.'

'It's just an illusion, Rhianna. I'm sure you do still love him, deep down. It's just that you can't admit it to yourself any longer because he's hurt you so much. In other words, you are saying to yourself, why reward him with your love when you so obviously feel he doesn't deserve it? But that's good. It's good because it saves you a lot of pain.'

'Do you still feel pain for Fernanda?'

'Not so much. Not nearly so much.' He wanted to be truthful and add that he felt no pain at all for Fernanda since Rhianna had entered his life, but that would be too presumptuous. Any hopes he might harbour of winning Rhianna were truly pie-in-the-sky. He could never compete with the likes of magnetic Lawson Maddox. He could never hope to win such a prize.

17

Every day that week Rhianna travelled to Windmill Street and sat for John Gibson. When she wasn't posing as 'The Lonely Maiden' in the plum dress, she was making herself useful in other ways. She went to the shops for him and bought groceries, meat from the butcher, lamp oil from the hardware shop. She washed and peeled vegetables and put them into pans of water so that all he had to do was stand them over the fire in the range in his scullery when she had gone. She swept the house, cleaned the windows and found it not in the least demeaning, although John Gibson protested vehemently that she must not do the work of a maid.

'But you don't have a maid,' she replied, 'and I only want to help.'

'There's no need, Rhianna. I am perfectly capable.'

Although she did not confess it, she had nothing else to occupy her, and was doing only what was second nature to her. At home, Emma did all the domestic chores and Mrs O'Flanagan did the cooking. Other than deciding what they were going to eat and giving Emma instructions, there was little else to do. Albert, the groom, was making a fine fist of the garden but she could hardly stand and supervise him all day without getting her own hands and shoes dirty. She was terrified of having nothing to do; time spent in idleness spawned anxiety and self-pity over what Lawson had done, and entertaining such thoughts was not her intention.

John Gibson was something of a godsend during this time of intense emotions and uncertainty in her marriage. He was a calming influence. His unassuming way and his imperturbability were touchstones that seemed to whisk her back to the reality of a more normal life. Oh, he was unsure of himself, irreconcilably a loner, but she felt easy with him, and was flattered that he was so evidently at ease with her. She felt she understood him, and wanted to protect him from his inborn vulnerability. She was taking an avid interest in his work and felt inclined to help all she could to make him successful . . . if he would allow her.

'The Lonely Maiden' was finished and Rhianna inspected it with awe. John had caught her looks wonderfully, albeit in profile, an aspect of her face she was not used to seeing. He had also painted the plum-coloured dress in such a way that there was no trace of her nakedness beneath the folds of material. It could hardly offend even the most prudish viewer. Whether he had done this in deference to her modesty, or whether it actually appeared thus to him, she did not know and did not feel compelled to enquire. The composition of the picture was tight; only the maiden, the balustrade, the sky and the sea, but it was serene, calming, innocent, like all his paintings.

'Would you like to pose for me again, Rhianna, for another painting?' he asked.

'You really think I'm suitable?' she replied, seeking reassurance. Despite all, Lawson's infidelity had shaken her self-confidence.

'If you weren't I wouldn't ask you.'

She smiled gratefully. 'Then I'll do it, John. Course I will.'

'Excellent. Thank you. Of course, I'll pay you.'

'You'll do no such thing,' she replied indignantly. 'Do you see me as one of those gay women that takes money for men's favours?'

He laughed and raised his hands defensively. 'Not at all. You must know I don't. But I am taking up your valuable time.'

'Only because I enjoy being with you.' At once, she was

concerned that perhaps her words conveyed more than she intended. She must play down its suggestion and divert him. 'So what is this next painting?'

'Oh, not unlike the first, except that you'll be more or less facing the viewer.'

'And the dress?'

'Shall we go and choose one?'

In the lumber room, they agreed on a greeny-grey satin dress that this time was not translucent. Rhianna changed into it while John went to his studio. She used the same bodice straps on this dress too, but she knew how to tie them herself by now.

John arranged her pose and asked her to adopt a wistful expression, then painted a draft study in oils to ascertain the composition and colouring of the final painting. It took him about an hour, during which time they talked almost continually.

'How is Lawson?'

'Too attentive for it to be sincere,' she replied.

'He doesn't want to lose you.'

'I guessed that, John. But he's lost me already. Oh, we live in the same house, I'm married to him, but I don't share his bed any more. He's lost me. He's lost my respect, my trust . . . everything.'

John lifted his brush to eye level and held it at arm's length towards Rhianna, peering at it with one eye shut to size her up. 'Do your family know what's happened?'

'Lord, no. I don't want to burden them with my problems. They have enough problems of their own. In any case, they think the sun shines out of his bum. They think he's the most marvellous person on two legs. And with good reason, I suppose, since they live rent-free in one of his houses . . . And my sister Sarah, poor devil, is still secretly in love with him, I'm certain.'

'I didn't know you had a sister.'

'She's sixteen . . . Now there's a stunner, if ever there was one, John.'

'Maybe she'd like to sit for me sometime?'

'Who knows? Maybe when she's a bit older. You'd have to pay *her* though.'

'Of course I'd pay her.' John stepped back from his easel and assessed the completed study. 'Let's take a break.'

'What shall you call this picture?' she asked, gratefully sitting down in front of the easel next to John.

'I think, "Italian Reverie" has a good ring to it, don't you?'

On the first Sunday in October, on their way back from church, Alexander and Ruth Gibson called at the old mine manager's house in Windmill Street to collect their son. John had a standing invitation to dinner at their house on Sundays. The coachman stopped the vis-à-vis phaeton outside, the couple alighted and Alexander rapped the iron knocker. John appeared in a sombre, dark grey Sunday suit, a striped cotton shirt and a necktie. He invited them in.

'Would you like a drink?'

'Don't mind if I do,' his father replied. 'I need a drink, having sat through that interminable sermon. Do you have any port?'

'Sorry. I might have some dry sherry, though. Will that do?'

Alexander nodded resignedly.

'Same for you, Mother?'

'Very well, dear.'

'Why don't you find somewhere to sit?' John suggested.

Alexander strutted into the largest room and looked around. 'If I could find a damned chair, I might be able to oblige,' he called and his voice boomed through the hallway that was devoid of linoleum, carpet, or rugs. 'Don't know how you can live without even the simplest comforts.'

'There are chairs in the studio,' John called from the scullery. 'Come through.'

Ruth moved through the scullery, twisting to avoid snagging her bustle on the rough corner of a chest of drawers, followed by Alexander. They arranged the two cheap wooden seats to face each other and sat down. Alexander peered with a superior expression at the overgrown garden outside and grunted some comment to his wife.

John came in, bringing two decent measures of a pale sherry, and handed one to his mother.

'Pity about the garden,' Alexander commented as he took his glass. 'Couldn't you get young Lawson Maddox to arrange for somebody to renovate it?'

'I doubt if Lawson Maddox would want to spend the money, Father.'

'Don't see why not. It's his property. It's in his interest to see the property's properly maintained, garden and all.'

'Well, you only have to look at his own garden to understand that he wouldn't spend money on another,' Ruth remarked disparagingly. 'I don't know why that poor wife of his tolerates it.'

'Maybe he's expecting her to do it, eh, Ruth?' Alexander chuckled at the thought. 'After all, she is from gardening stock.'

John was suddenly incensed by his father's insensitivity but, typically, would not be drawn to remonstrate. 'She seems very decent,' was the best defence he could muster without creating dissent.

'That she is,' Ruth proclaimed. 'A fine, sensible young woman despite her lowly origins. Though whatever possessed her to marry *him* I fail to understand.'

'Money,' Alexander baited. 'What always decides a woman?'

'I don't think Rhianna is like that,' John said.

'Don't be so bloody naïve, John,' Alexander scoffed. 'They're all like that. Especially those from the lower orders if they believe there's a chance of a leg up the social ladder.'

'Some are, I grant you, but I don't think she is,' John said, determined to defend her, then left the studio to get a drink for himself.

When he came back with a glass of beer, Alexander was poring over 'The Lonely Maiden' which was propped up against the wall on his workbench, drying out.

'Damned if the girl in this painting isn't the spitten image of the aforementioned Rhianna Maddox,' Alexander said.

'It *is* Rhianna Maddox, Father.'

'You mean she's been sitting for you? Here? In this house?'

'Yes.'

Ruth got up from her chair in a state of high concern at this disturbing revelation and stood by her husband to scrutinise the work. 'Sitting for you?' she asked reproachfully. 'You mean, posing in those disgraceful frocks that you can see straight through?'

'They're hardly disgraceful, Mother, and you can't see through the one she's wearing there. In any case, they are perceived to be of their time – classical Roman and Greek.'

'I can scarcely believe she would do such a thing as to pose like that. I trust she was chaperoned?'

'Only by me.'

'Then she's certainly dropped in my estimation. Ever since she brought you here alone that day I've had a sneaking suspicion . . .'

Alexander and Ruth both peered intently at the painting.

'Hang me!' Alexander declared. 'How many times has she been here, posing like this?'

'Several. She was here every day last week and most days this.'

'My God!' Ruth exclaimed. 'Have you no shame? Has *she* no shame, posing without a corset?'

'Does Lawson know she's been posing like this?'

'No, and why should he? He doesn't deserve her, the way he treats her.'

'Doesn't deserve her!' Alexander roared. 'My God, what nonsense you spout! Do you know what you're playing with here, man? Do you? You have the gall to admit you are entertaining a young, recently married woman in this house, she practically naked by the looks of this, and without a chaperone . . .'

'I don't see what all the fuss is about,' John responded quietly. 'She comes here to sit for me. Nothing more.'

'Well, it'll have to stop. I won't have a son of mine dragged into some unnecessary scandal, even if it is of his own making.'

'Well, I won't stop it, Father.'

'Then *I* shall make damned sure it is stopped. Furthermore, if you persist in encouraging her, you may rest assured, sir, that I shall cut you off without a penny. I will not have the good name of Gibson besmirched by scandalmongers.'

'Whether you cut me off or not, Father, I doubt whether you will stop it. She's a grown woman. Old enough to know her own mind.'

'She is a *married* woman, John, and her own mind is of no consequence. She belongs to her husband and she must be ruled by him.'

The following day Alexander Gibson sought out Lawson Maddox in one of his regular haunts, the Dudley Arms Hotel. He was upstairs, drinking in the saloon with two other men and a woman. Alexander drew him aside.

'I am in possession of some information, Lawson, which distresses me no end to recount. However, before I report it, you must realise that I offer it to you in the best possible spirit and to avoid future embarrassment to us both.'

Lawson looked at him with some concern. 'All right, I understand, Alex. So what the devil is it?'

'It concerns my son John and ... I'm afraid ... your wife.'

'My wife? Are you suggesting ... ? What exactly are you suggesting, Alex?'

'I'm not certain that I'm suggesting anything, Lawson. But your wife has been sitting as a model for John. Knowing the kind of voluptuous pictures he paints, you will realise that modelling for them requires her to be ... well, almost completely naked but for some ... some transparent attire, as you well know. During this time, they have been quite alone together. As I said, I am anxious to avoid a scandal. I have threatened my son with disinheritance if it continues but, for your part, I would like your reassurance that you will put a stop to these visits.'

'You may have it, Alexander. Of course I shall put a stop to it. And I appreciate your telling me.'

'I am absolutely satisfied, of course,' Alexander continued, 'that this liaison is totally innocent and that that's all it is – a modelling arrangement. But in our respective positions Lawson, we cannot afford unwanted attention.'

'I agree. And thank you again for enlightening me.'

'My duty, Lawson. My duty as a friend.'

'Good. Will you allow me to buy you a drink?' Lawson cocked a knowing eyebrow. 'Or are you otherwise engaged, Alex?'

'Alexander grinned sheepishly. 'Not presently, Lawson. Of course you may buy me a drink.'

Lawson and Rhianna dined together that evening. Emma served the meal that Rhianna had already organised with Mrs O'Flanagan. When she had finished serving the maid left the room.

'I sometimes wonder if it's necessary to have any staff at all,' Lawson said, salting his meal.

'Oh? From what point of view?'

He took the pepper pot and shook it over his plate. 'The expense for one thing.'

Rhianna picked up her knife and fork. 'Have you hit on hard times?' she asked, her voice tinged with sarcasm.

'I was thinking about it from another aspect. For instance, if we got rid of them, Emma and Mrs O'Flanagan, you would have more to do at home. You could cope with the cooking and the cleaning, couldn't you?'

'I could, but why should I? You want me to be a skivvy now, do you?' She cut a piece of meat and was poised to put it in her mouth.

'Not at all. I'm aware you're unsettled, Rhianna.'

'On the contrary,' she said haughtily, 'I'm quite content. In any case, why should you care?'

'I do care. It seems to me you need something to occupy you.'

'I have plenty to occupy me.'

'Oh? So tell me. What has occupied you today?'

'This morning I collected your rents, as I do every Monday morning.'

'Where from?'

'Where I normally collect them from on a Monday. From Albert Street, from The Dock, from the High Side, from Salop Street . . .'

'From Windmill Street?'

'Yes, and from Windmill Street . . .' Rhianna felt herself colouring. Her omission seemed too glaring. 'After that, I went to the shops, I visited my mother and—'

'Strange. You mother swore she hadn't seen you today. So how was John Mallory Gibson?'

She looked down at her plate, avoiding Lawson's eyes. 'He seemed fine . . . Busy.'

'Good. I'm glad he's keeping well. I feel a certain responsibility towards him knowing he's living in my house, and knowing his father as I do.'

She risked a quick glance at him. 'I daresay he would be comforted to know that.'

'Next time you see him, be good enough to tell him so.'

Rhianna pondered that conversation most of the evening while Lawson was out, and when she went to bed. Had he found out, or did he suspect that she was spending too much time with John Gibson? If so, she failed to see how. Nobody could see the house, let alone the gig, from the main road, and she was always back home before Lawson. In any case, her conscience was clear. Nothing untoward was going on. They were not having a love affair, there was no impropriety; she merely helped him in his work, posing for his paintings. Even if they were having an intrigue it would serve Lawson right. It was no more than he deserved. Even now, after the shenanigans with Caitlin, he still went out every night, he was out all day, every day. What was she supposed to do? Sit in the house and mope? Twiddle her thumbs?

Next morning she avoided Lawson and went down to breakfast after he had left. By eleven o'clock she had readied herself and asked Albert to prepare Blossom and the gig so that she could go out. She made her way to Windmill Street via her usual route. She tethered the mare to the gatepost and slipped the nosebag over its head.

John smiled as he answered the door. Each day she spent with John Gibson, Rhianna admired him the more. While she posed for the 'Italian Reverie' she watched him as he worked and felt a great tenderness for him. There was such sadness in his eyes, such uncertainty, such timidity. Oh, yes, she certainly wanted to protect him, not just from himself but from the rest of society. She realised instinctively that his art ruled him to the extent that he had forsaken society in lieu of it. It was that willing sacrifice that had robbed him of his social skills and rendered him self-conscious, reserved, reclusive, inhibited. He lacked those skills others of his class took for granted. How different he was from Lawson.

She watched his eyes. He was concentrating entirely on his work, consumed with the connection between her as the model, and the image he was magically transposing onto the canvas. He would catch her looking at him and smile self-effacingly, and she would wish that she had averted her gaze sooner. He had such soft, kind eyes, with long lashes that rendered them all the more attractive.

He was anxious to please her; that, she could also discern. On, the other hand, he seemed anxious to please everybody. That night of his party she noticed how he was extremely polite to all his guests, whether he knew them well or not, as if he was worried about displeasing anybody. He responded always with a grateful smile when she told him how much she liked and admired his work, as if he desperately needed that reassurance.

She risked another look at his face. Oh, he was not immediately handsome, yet there was an undeniable attractiveness there. His cheeks were sallow, his nose was straight but not long. His clean-shaven chin was strong but not jutting. She looked at his mouth, how intently he pouted when he was applying his brush to a canvas. He had a well-formed mouth and a set of fine, even teeth; she wondered how his lips would feel on hers, and a strange exhilaration surged within her at the thought . . .

John took a feather from his workbench and dipped its long, bowed edge in a blob of dark paint on his palette. He applied it to the canvas.

'What are you doing with the feather?' she asked, intrigued. 'Are you tickling me?'

He laughed, delighted at her notion. 'I use it to put the fine veining in the marble. Only a feather is suitable. Brushes are too coarse.'

'Fancy. Who ever would have thought it?'

'Tricks of the trade.'

'When can I have a rest, John?'

'Right now, if you like.'

'Yes, please.' She relaxed her pose, stretched and sat down. 'May I see the picture?'

He turned the easel towards her. She nodded her enthusiastic approval. 'Subtle use of colour,' she commented.

'You sound like an expert.'

'Do I?'

'Indeed you do.'

'How much would a painting like this fetch in London?'

He shrugged. 'Eighteen, maybe twenty guineas.'

'For what? Two weeks' work?'

'Thereabouts.'

'That's not bad.'

'No, it's quite respectable.'

'I'm going to write to your dealer in London and tell him you are ready to ship some paintings, and that you expect to get twenty-five guineas each for them.'

'You are?'

'Yes. If I don't do it, I know you won't. You're far too reticent.'

'And you're far too good to me, Rhianna. Why are you so good to me? What have I done to deserve it?'

'I didn't realise I was being good particularly.'

'Nobody has ever taken as much interest in my work. I find it very flattering . . . but very disconcerting.'

'I'm fascinated, that's why. I want to see you do well. If it bothers you, if . . . if you'd rather I didn't come, I won't.'

'Lord, no, you must never think that, Rhianna. I love you to come. I want you to come – as often as you can – as often as you dare . . .'

'Oh, dear . . . Which reminds me . . . Lawson told me to tell you he feels responsible for you as a tenant and because of his friendship with your father.'

'Oh? Does he know you come here now?' There was a sudden look of concern on John's face.

'He knows I collect rent from you each week now.'

'But not that you've been sitting for me?'

'I haven't told him that. Why should I? It's no business of his.'

'He is your husband.'

'In name only.' Rhianna stood up. 'He doesn't care what I do. He doesn't give a damn. He'd rather have his trollops . . . Look, I must go and give Blossom some water.'

She collected the bucket from the scullery and went to the front door. Before stepping outside, she checked to see that nobody was in the street to see her in the grey-green satin dress. All seemed quiet. She had set foot on the path to the front gate before she noticed that neither Blossom nor the gig was there. In panic, she ran to the gate, looked up and down Windmill Street. Nothing. She rushed down the street in a frenzy of anxiety to see if the mare had become untethered and had wandered on, and was now hidden behind some nook further on. There was no sign of Blossom. The horse and gig had entirely disappeared.

With tears streaming down her face, she ran straight back into the house and reported the fact to John. 'She must have been stolen.'

'But by whom?'

'God knows. There are enough thieves and vagabonds about. Oh, John, I'm so worried. Poor Blossom. I hope she's all right.'

'Now, now . . . Don't cry, Rhianna.' He held his arms open for her and she fell into them as easily as a lover. He hugged her sympathetically. 'It upsets me to see you crying.'

'I can't help it. I'm so worried.'

'A fine young mare like that could fetch a pretty penny, I warrant,' John said.

'What am I to do for the best?' She looked up at him with

tearful eyes. 'Should I go straight to the police station and report it?'

He hesitated a moment before answering. 'No, Rhianna . . . I would wait and see what Lawson advises. The horse *is* his property after all.'

'Why do you say that? The horse and gig are both mine. They were a gift.'

'Technically, they belong to your husband. Anything that's yours belongs to your husband. In any case, I wonder if your husband isn't behind this . . .'

She looked at him with alarm. 'Why do you say that?'

'Oh, because my father was here on Sunday. He recognised you in "The Lonely Maiden". He deplored the fact that you had posed for it and said it had to stop. I think he was worried about any impropriety.'

'Do you think he has told Lawson?'

'I suspect that he intended to.'

'Oh, God . . . I wondered what he was getting at last night when he asked me how I filled my days . . .'

'I imagine he'll stop you from coming here again. Especially if he thinks—'

'But what if he comes to you, John? What would you say? Oh, I'm so worried . . .'

'I don't think he will for a minute . . . No. Any anger will be directed at you . . .'

18

Rhianna changed into her normal day clothes and, in a state of apprehension, left John Gibson. She hurried home, walking as briskly as she could along Salop Street, yet preoccupied with the disappearance of Blossom. She turned right into Himley Road and found the long descent awkward in her dainty shoes that were not designed for walking over uneven footpaths and cobbled streets. As soon as she reached the house, she headed for the stables to see if indeed Lawson had taken Blossom and returned her there to teach his erring wife a lesson. She needn't have bothered. There was no sign of the gig or of Blossom. There were, however, some grunts and giggles from Albert's bedroom above the stables, and she suspected that Emma was in there with him, up to no good by the sounds of it. Lewd behaviour between servants would normally mean dismissal for both. She had no inclination to stop and make a fuss, however. More pressing things were occupying her.

She went to the kitchen where Mrs O'Flanagan was peeling carrots at the stone sink.

'Has Mr Maddox been back this afternoon?'

'To be sure, I've not seen him, ma'am. Have you enquired of Albert?'

'I have the feeling Albert is otherwise engaged, Mrs O'Flanagan.'

Rhianna sighed uneasily and went outside again. She had to know if Albert had seen Lawson.

'Albert! . . . Albert!' she called. 'I must speak to you at once.'

Albert eventually appeared at the door at the top of the

outside steps. He looked flushed and his hair was dishevelled as he descended the stairway, tucking his shirt into his trousers.

'Albert, has Mr Maddox been back this afternoon?'

'No, ma'am. I ain't sin him since he took th'oss and cabriolet the smornin'.'

'Did he give you instructions to find Blossom and the gig and take them anywhere?'

'No, ma'am. I ain't sin him, ma'am. Why, ma'am? Where is Blossom?' He looked past her towards the road, seeking the mare.

'I'm not sure . . . You're sweating, Albert. Your hair's a mess as well. What have you been up to?'

'Er . . . digging . . . and pulling weeds, ma'am.'

'Planting seed, more like,' she said with a knowing look. 'Tell Emma she's wanted in the kitchen at once.'

'Yes, ma'am.' The groom blushed to his roots as he turned and went back up the stairs.

Rhianna went into the house and sat in the drawing room, deep in anxious thought. John might have been wrong about Lawson. It was likely that Lawson had had nothing to do with Blossom's disappearance. If that was so, it was common theft and must be reported to the police. All the same, her husband would have to know that the mare had been taken from Windmill Street. Well, her rent collecting was a valid enough excuse for being there . . . But if Alexander Gibson had reported to Lawson that she'd been modelling . . .

She went to her bedroom in a flurry of agitation, concerned for poor Blossom and her own situation. Yet why should she feel so agitated, so guilty about posing for John Gibson? It was Lawson who had been unfaithful. Nothing intimate had occurred between her and John. Her conscience was clear; they had only talked; and why not? They were good friends. They were close friends.

She heard Lawson return home. He settled himself in the

drawing room with a glass of whisky and, there, she encountered him.

'Good afternoon, my dear,' he greeted with a gloating smile. 'I trust you've had a good day?'

'Fine, thank you,' she replied, as if nothing strange had happened. It had suddenly occurred to her that if Lawson was somehow responsible for the disappearance of Blossom and the gig, then she would be merely falling into his trap by mentioning it in the first place. If, however, she avoided mentioning it, he would be quick enough to, for her indifference would drive his curiosity.

So they sat in silence for some minutes, Lawson slurping the whisky, a smug expression fixed on his face, as if savouring some amusing secret. The low October sun was pouring in through the window, creating oblique shafts of orange on the intricately patterned carpet and its loose fringes. It was still warm in that south-facing room, even without a fire. He finished his drink and poured himself another.

'You drink too much,' Rhianna declared.

'Oh?' said he, suddenly indignant. 'And what has it got to do with you?'

She shrugged. 'Nothing. I couldn't care less what you do.'

'Then mind your own business.'

Silence for several more minutes.

'Don't you have anything to do?' Lawson asked pointedly, aware that his wife was lingering, obviously intent on discussing something important when, normally these days, she was anxious to be out of his company. 'Don't you have any novels to read, any letters to write, any embroidery to keep you occupied?'

'Nothing pressing,' she answered.

He took another slug of whisky and looked at her with cold, piercing eyes. His breathing was audible to her, a shallow, rhythmic exhalation. How she hated that invasive sound, a sure sign that he'd been drinking.

'How is Blossom?' he asked, unable to defer the question any longer.

She stared at him with a defiance she did not feel. 'Blossom's fine.' She got up to walk out of the room. This was not the best time to have a rational discussion, with Lawson in his cups.

'You're lying.'

She reached the door, put her hand on the handle, and tried to stem the tears that were suddenly stinging her eyes. 'She was fine last time I saw her, Lawson.'

'Oh? When was that?'

'You mean you don't know?' she said derisively.

'I asked you a straightforward question. Have the *decency* to give me a straightforward answer.'

She turned towards him, looked at him, scornful of his abrasiveness. 'How dare *you* lecture *me* about decency,' she shrilled, her anger rising, for she was sure now that he knew where Blossom was. 'But if you're so keen on straightforward questions, let me ask you one . . . What *have* you done with Blossom?'

He grinned triumphantly and she could have spat at him. 'Well, wouldn't you like to know?'

'So? Are you going to tell me?'

'I'll tell you this,' he sneered and got up from his chair quite steadily. He walked towards her, his face like granite, his cold eyes never leaving hers. 'Nobody crosses Lawson Maddox and gets away with it. Least of all you. Do you think I'm so stupid as to let you go courting John Gibson using a horse and gig I paid for? Did you honestly think I wouldn't get to know about you two?'

He shut the door with a sharp snap, denying her escape. He grabbed her by the upper arm, held on to her with a firm grip and stared at her ferociously, his colour rising with his anger. Then he struck her around the head with the flat of his free hand. 'Maybe that'll teach you.'

She reeled, dazed for a second. 'You are the limit,' she hissed defiantly, tasting the heat of her own anger on her tongue as she rallied. 'Why do you judge everybody by your own disgusting standards? Do you think everybody is as depraved as you are? John Gibson is a decent, respectable man, which is more than I can say for you. But you wouldn't understand gentlemanly behaviour, not being a gentleman yourself.'

'Why should I be, to a woman who was nothing more than a common housemaid?' he taunted. He was poised to strike her again but, anticipating it, Rhianna dodged out of the way.

'Lay a hand on me once more and I swear, I'll swing for you,' she rasped. 'You have no right—'

'No right?' he roared, incredulous. 'You have the nerve to tell me I have no right? I am your husband and whatever you might think of me, make no mistake I have every *right*. I have every *right* when you have been posing naked for John Gibson, lying on your back and spreading your legs for him, like the dirty whore you've turned out to be.'

'Then divorce me, Lawson Maddox, if that's what you think,' she pleaded, perceiving that it would be useless to deny his allegations. 'I'm your wife in name only now. You surrendered all claims on me when I caught you with that Irish slut.'

'Divorce you?' he scoffed. 'If ever I divorce you, it will be to suit me, not you and your pathetic, impoverished little artist. Meanwhile, you can grin and bear the inconvenience at my pleasure. And inconvenient it will be without a horse and gig . . . will it not?'

That night Rhianna locked herself in her room and cried, mostly for herself, a little for Blossom. She cried for having been deceived in the first place into believing Lawson was a decent and honest man. She cried because she had become trapped in a loveless marriage that promised only a lifetime of numb misery. The dream she had nurtured as a young girl of marrying a wealthy man had been realised, but tears flowed more as she realised how much it had cost her. Wealth had certainly not brought her happiness.

Had she been of a more forgiving nature there might, in time, have been a chance of reconciliation between her and Lawson. Not any more. Especially not when he believed *she* was being unfaithful. Of course, it was expected and tolerated that men had their mistresses. But why should she tolerate his philandering? He had made solemn wedding vows to keep him only unto her as long as they both should live. Well, his behaviour amply demonstrated how little those vows meant to him.

Now he thought the same of her.

All the time she had known John Gibson she had been aware of a warm affinity between them. She liked him, admired him, continually found herself yearning for his company, which she found inspiring. Perhaps she was in love with him. Maybe she'd been in love with him from the outset but unable to admit it to herself, unable to allow such a stunning self-confession when it could generate such monumental consequences.

As her silent weeping subsided she lay awake, her thoughts becoming more wrapped up in John Gibson. She knew only that she craved his company again. She wanted so intensely to tell him what had happened, to know what he thought. She had to let him know that Lawson had confiscated Blossom and that he believed they were having an affair. At the very least, she should forewarn him.

She got up from her bed and peered through the bedroom curtains at the night sky. Over to her right, she saw a glimmer of suffused light in the east; dawn was beginning to peel back the first layer of darkness. On impulse, she dressed herself, pinned up her hair and crept onto the landing. The door to Lawson's bedroom was ajar and she heard his snores. Stealthily, she tiptoed downstairs, put on her shoes, her coat and let herself out quietly.

The chill in that October dawn made her shiver, but walking

briskly would warm her. She did not venture up Himley Road. Logic told her that the way she'd always had to travel to Windmill Street in the gig was the long way round. She was sure there had to be a short cut – a footpath. She took the first left-hand turn she came to – Dibdale Street – and, as she reached its crown, she could make out the dark chimney stacks of the London Fields Fender and Fire Iron Works ahead of her, shadowy obelisks pointing into a leaden sky.

She was warmer now and breathing harder from the exertion of the climb. She wondered what John would say when she knocked on the door and disturbed his sleep? Would he send her away, tell her he had no wish to be involved in her marital problems? She thought not but, even if he did, who could blame him?

Dawn was still just a meagre, diffused easing of the night but it was adequate to pick her way along the path that Dibdale Street had regressed into. When she reached the old mine another path joined from the right and she took it, realising it must lead directly onto Windmill Street. In only a minute, she was closing the front gate of the house that John was occupying.

She rapped on the front door with the iron knocker . . . and again. Presently she heard the scuff-scuff of footfalls on the quarry tiles inside, the door opened a couple of inches and a bleary-eyed John Gibson peeped out, wearing a dressing gown.

'Rhianna!' he said incredulously. 'Come in, come in.' He opened the door wide enough for her to enter and stood aside. 'You're the last person I expected to see tonight. What's the matter?'

'Oh, everything. I'm so sorry to have woken you, but I just had to come.'

'I'll light a fire and put a kettle on to boil.' He led her through the passage into the scullery and lit a candle. 'So what's wrong?'

'Just about everything.' Rhianna sighed profoundly. 'It was Lawson who had Blossom and the gig snatched away. Where poor Blossom is now I don't know, but I do hope she's being well looked after. He'd been drinking when he came home . . . We had an awful row.'

'Oh, no.'

'Your father must have told him I'd been sitting for you. He was furious, John . . . He struck me and . . . well . . . he thinks you and I are lovers . . .'

'He thinks that?'

'I'm afraid so. I'm so sorry. I'd give anything not to have dragged you into all this. You of all people.'

'Oh, Rhianna,' he breathed, raking out the fire from yesterday. 'Would that we *were* lovers . . . It would all be worth it.'

'Yes, I know,' she said absently.

After a moment's hesitation John turned to her and said, 'Rhianna, do you know what you said?'

'What?'

'You said, "Yes I know". As if you agreed it *would* all be worth it.'

'Did I?'

'You did. Do you suppose that's what you really meant?'

'I suppose so . . . If there was something between us, I suppose it would all be worth it.'

'Well, I wish we were lovers, you and I, Rhianna. God knows I've thought of little else since the moment I first set eyes on you. Of course, I realise that it can never be. I only torment myself by harbouring such fantasies.'

'But why can't it be?' Rhianna asked.

He shrugged. 'Because you're married.'

'Oh, I'm married all right.' She uttered a little self-mocking laugh. 'But it's the middle of the night and look where I am. Am I in *his* bed? No. I'm here in your scullery. This is where I instinctively came.'

'Where would you rather be?'

She looked into his eyes intently. 'Do you want the truth? Can you take the truth?'

'Only ever the truth, Rhianna.'

'I would rather be here . . . With you.'

'Do you mean that?'

'Oh, yes . . .'

He sat down on his rickety chair and put his head in his hands. 'Do you understand what you are saying, Rhianna?'

She knelt down before him and took his hands tenderly. He raised his head and she saw the anguish, the doubt in his eyes. 'I believe you said, John, that if we were lovers all this upheaval in my marriage might be worth it. Am I not mistaken?'

'You're not mistaken.'

'And I agree with you.'

'Do you mean you would also like us to be lovers, Rhianna?'

'Aren't we already? Don't we already feel so much for each other? Oh, John, the fact that I've come to you at this hour . . . I've only this night been able to admit it to myself, but I feel what you feel . . . From the first time we met I've felt this . . . this pull. I feel as if I've known you all my life, I feel that we've already been lovers a long time . . . A long time ago . . . Does that sound silly?'

He shook his head gravely. 'Oh, Rhianna . . .'

'What, John? Tell me . . .' She could sense his doubt, some innate fear he was having difficulty in overcoming, inhibiting any real commitment.

He held her hands more tightly and she felt him trembling with emotion. 'I'm so afraid, Rhianna . . .'

'Afraid of what?'

'That for all your tenderness and heightened emotions now, you would forsake me for him in the end. He'll win you back, I've no doubt. I couldn't stand that . . . Not again. Not after Fernanda.'

'Please don't think of me being as fickle as that,' Rhianna

said gently. 'If I make a promise I keep it. If Lawson hadn't been unfaithful in the first place I wouldn't be here with you now, whatever feelings for you I might secretly have harboured. I would have been faithful to him. As it is – the way I see it – he's relinquished all claim on me by his own infidelity, and I on him. So I feel justified in making a commitment to you if you want me . . . a commitment I'll stand by through thick and thin, for as long as you want me.'

'Except that you're a married woman and still his property. So not legally free.'

'What's legality got to do with it? It's what's in my heart, not what's written on some legal document. Anyway, if Lawson thinks I'm being unfaithful he'll divorce me. I'm certain of it. It would do his ego no good at all to be married to a woman who preferred to be with somebody else.'

'I suppose not,' John said quietly.

'Anyway, there's only one thing that might change my mind . . .'

'And what's that?' He saw a glimmer of humour in her eyes and wondered what havoc she was about to wreak on his fragile emotions.

'If I don't like the way you kiss . . .'

Suddenly he got up and rushed to the sink. From the cupboard he took a tin of tooth powder and a toothbrush and began frantically cleaning his teeth.

Rhianna laughed. 'Why are you doing that?'

'Because I don't want you kissing me when I've got a dingy mouth. You might not relish it. It might change your mind.'

'You might feel the same about me.'

'Never.'

He dried his mouth with a towel and she stood facing him. They stepped into each other's arms and their lips met, tentatively at first then, after the first pleasurable contact, more determinedly. It was clear to Rhianna that John lacked

Lawson's experience but his parted lips felt perfectly, pleasantly at home on hers. After a long, lingering kiss they broke off and he looked questioningly into her eyes, desperately seeking her approval.

'Well?'

'All I can taste is tooth powder,' she teased, smiling happily. 'But I'll give you ten out of ten for pleasantness of feel.'

He laughed with relief. 'You must think me such a fool, Rhianna. Honestly, I can't believe my luck. I'll wake up soon and realise this has all been a dream.'

'It's no dream, John,' she said contentedly. 'I'm so glad I came. I hadn't the least notion this would happen. I just had to warn you, let you know, that Lawson believed we were . . . you know . . .'

'And now we are.'

'Yes. And now we are.'

'Except that . . .' he said with uncertainty. 'We haven't . . . you know . . .'

'Oh, John . . . I have no qualms about going to bed with you . . .' She laughed, half embarrassed. 'But let's not make a great plan for it. Let it just happen in an unguarded moment . . .'

'Yes,' he agreed. Then he went to add something else, but hesitated.

'What?' she asked, sensing his further uncertainty.

'Nothing . . . I must have no doubts. You said so.'

She smiled and gave him an affectionate squeeze. 'I think I should go now, John. I crept out of the house. I think I should creep back in before Lawson gets up.'

'You said you don't sleep with him any more.'

'It's true, I don't. I sleep in another room. But if I'm out of the house I won't be there to get up. Sometimes we meet at the breakfast table. He'll notice if I'm not there and he'll most likely guess where I am.'

He nodded his understanding. 'Let me give you a key to

this house. You never know when you might need it. Come whenever you want. Never stay in his house with him if there promises to be trouble.' He rummaged in a drawer and found the key. 'I'll always leave the bolt off from now on.'

'Thank you.'

She kissed him again. It was lingering and meaningful, setting the seal on their new relationship.

'I'll come to you later,' she promised.

19

Lawson left the house that morning not having seen his wife, and unaware of her nocturnal visit to John Gibson. He was certain, however, that there was something sordid going on between them. He asked young Albert to tack up Docker and prepare the cabriolet, then left the house for one of his properties, where he knew he would get some comfort and some sympathy.

The house was in Downing Street, close enough to the centre of the town to be convenient, far enough away to afford discretion. It was large, with seven bedrooms, all elaborately furnished. Gas was laid on and there was running water in the bathroom. Downstairs there was a parlour, a drawing room, a small, intimate dining room laid out for beguiling entertainment, and a scullery. Lawson employed four staff there, two of whom were maids, one a cook and, the fourth, a woman he had known some time, whom he could trust.

In an act calculated to deceive, Lawson drew the cabriolet to a halt outside the Malt Shovel Inn in Tower Street, which stood in the lee of the old castle high on the hill above, and walked to Downing Street. When he arrived at the house, he rapped smartly on the front door. A good-looking young woman with a slender figure and sleek, fair hair piled up on her head answered.

'Lawson! You look terrible.'

'Thanks for the compliment. That's all I need to buck up my self-confidence.'

He stepped inside and the young woman closed the door behind him. It was warm and comfortable in there. He made his way to the parlour and sat on a chair with a well-padded seat, at a table draped in a deep red chenille cover.

'Shall I order you some coffee?'

'Something stronger. Bring me a bottle of whisky . . . And bring a glass for yourself. I hate drinking alone. I have enough drinking alone at home. No wonder I'm seldom there. I want to talk to you.'

'Giving you trouble, is she? You should have married me. We understand each other.'

He nodded morosely and the young woman left the comfortably furnished room. She came back with a tray on which stood a bottle of whisky, two tumblers and a jug of water, and poured a measure of whisky into each glass.

'Water?'

'No, straight.'

She handed it to him. 'You should have water with it at this time in a morning. It'll rot your gullet drinking it straight.'

'Don't you start as well. You're sounding like her.'

The woman diluted her own drink and sipped it. 'Have you had any breakfast?'

'Oh, yes, I've eaten. Alone again, of course.'

'Well don't sound so sorry for yourself. She did catch you rogering Caitlin. Did you expect her to applaud you?'

He sighed heavily. 'I just thought she might have been a bit more tolerant, living the life of Riley as she does. Lord above, all men have their mistresses. It doesn't mean they're going to leave their wives. In any case, variety is the spice of life. A man needs a bit of fresh from time to time.'

'If it was only from time to time, maybe some women would turn a blind eye. I wonder you haven't caught the clap or the pox.'

'I'm very careful about such things, Fanny,' he said evenly. 'As you well know.'

'So what's she been up to, Lawson, this wife of yours?'

'I found out she's been modelling for Alexander Gibson's

son. God knows how much time she's spent up there with him. It's obvious they're having an affair. And him such a weedy little bugger.'

'You're jealous.'

'I'm hopping bloody mad, that's what. Makes me look such a fool. But I shall get even. Mark my words. I know her Achilles heel.'

'Why be vindictive?' said Fanny Lampitt. 'Can't you just walk away and admit it was all a mistake? I don't know why you married her in the first place.'

'Because I fell in love with her, silly sod that I am. It was love at first sight. Being vindictive, I can't help. It's in my nature. I can't stand to be beaten. Nor can I stand the thought of somebody else having her.'

'The trouble with you is, you've got a fetish for maids. As soon as I saw you dancing with Rhianna last New Year's Eve at the Cooksons' I knew you wouldn't be able to help yourself.'

'I didn't know she was the housekeeper then,' he said defensively.

'I did. At least I could tell she was a servant. When we arrived she was hovering like a servant, supervising the maids who were taking the hats and coats and giving out the welcoming drinks. I noticed her even if you didn't. And I could tell what she was, despite her elegant dress.'

'I only had eyes for you then.'

'Liar! So . . . if she's having it off with Alexander's son – Alexander was here yesterday, by the way, with that young piece he's been tailing . . . Calls herself Mrs Jones.'

'Mrs Jones again, eh? Interesting. Which room did he have?'

'His usual. The big one on the front.'

'Did he pay?'

'Up front, o' course. I always get the money off him before he goes up.'

'Good girl.' He took a slug of whisky and put the glass back on the table.

'So . . . to get back to your little wife . . . I was about to say, if she's having it off with Alexander's son, it don't say much for your bedtime endeavours.'

'There's nothing wrong with my bedtime endeavours, Fanny, as you know well enough. I've put many a smile on your face.'

'Not lately, you haven't.'

'No, not since you and Robert Cookson started having a fling. I've no intention of following him anywhere. You never know where he's been. You never know what he might have picked up along the way.'

'Oh, and I thought it was because of Rhianna.'

'I've sold her horse and gig, you know. As soon as Alexander told me what was afoot I had it snatched. That's peeved her as much as anything. She loved that mare. Loved it more than she loved me, I'm certain.'

'So are you going to divorce her?'

'Why? So that she can marry him? So that she can marry John Gibson? Besides, divorcing her could cost me upwards of six hundred pounds, plus dragging the witnesses to London for God knows how long. Never. Anyway, she'll come back to me all repentant, I know that much.'

'And you'll take her back?' Fanny asked.

'Why not? I want her back. I still love her.'

'But if you love her, why do you keep going off with other women?'

'Oh, you know me, Fanny . . . I can't help myself, but there's no harm in me . . . You know I'm always surrounded by women, you know I'm addicted to them. I only have to look at a woman and, if I fancy her, I don't rest till I've had her. And they all submit in the end.'

He emptied his glass and Fanny poured him another.

'So why do you love her, Lawson? You've had better.'

'No, Fanny, you're wrong. I've never had better. I've met women of higher class, some of them just as beautiful, but never one better. I know she was only a servant but she's the cream, I tell you. She's got such a lovely nature. She's straight and trustworthy. I need her.'

'She's having an affair with John Gibson. She can't be that trustworthy.'

'Ah, but maybe I've driven her to it. If only she'd never found out about Caitlin, everything would still be all right. Still, she'll have got even now. We can start again with a better understanding of each other.'

'Does she know about this place?'

'No. I've never told her anything.'

'So she doesn't know you rent out rooms to the gentry for their sordid frolics with their mistresses?'

'Why should she?'

'It's just something else you're not being straight about. Maybe it's time you made a clean breast of it and admitted all your business activities. Involve her more. That way you would take her in to your confidence and win her trust again.'

'We'll see . . . So who else did we have here yesterday, besides Alex Gibson?'

'It's in the book . . . Here . . . That Mr Oliver, the church-warden, met his fancy piece here – she's keen – she was here well before him. That James Mundy from the Union offices and his woman, though what he sees in her God only knows. We had a new chap in with his girl – I had the feeling they were a courting couple and couldn't find anywhere for a bit of privacy. Oh, and a very smart, well-dressed woman of about thirty called – gave her name as Mrs Owen but I doubt if it's her real name – wanted to know how much a room was during the day. She seemed desperate, she was anxious that we'd be discreet if she called with her friend. I told her, we specialise in discretion.' Fanny took another sip from her glass. 'Don't you feel sorry for all these poor souls who have to sneak out of house and home to get their pleasures?'

'My heart bleeds,' Lawson replied sarcastically. 'Just don't let me leave here without taking their money. Is there anybody here now?'

'Yes. We've got that Dr Scott in number three with his fancy woman. He's been here since nine.'

'Then let's hope he's got no patients languishing, eh? She's a tasty morsel, though, as I recall. There's a spy hole into that room from the one next door. I think I'll go up to have a peep. I shall be as bawdy as a fiddler's bitch watching her – send your new maid up to me. You can spare her for an hour or two.'

'You mean Caitlin?'

'You know very well I mean Caitlin . . . You know, Fanny, I feel much brighter now, having talked to you.'

'By the way, Rhianna, I had a letter today from Thomas Miller McLean in the Haymarket,' John said as he applied a series of brush strokes to his canvas. 'They've accepted all those paintings we sent. Two have already been sold – one for seventy-five guineas.'

'Seventy-five guineas?' Rhianna repeated, incredulous. 'That's beyond belief. I'm so pleased. Which picture was it?'

' "The Sweet Siesta of a Summer Day". Very Tadema-esque, but so what? They've sent me a cheque already. Minus their commission, of course.'

'You see? It was worth my writing.'

'I'm delighted, of course. We'll celebrate. You must let me take you out to dinner.'

'Oh, if only we could. But I daren't be seen out with you. Perhaps we could celebrate here one evening. I could cook us a lovely dinner.'

'That would do fine,' he said. 'If you can arrange it.'

'I'll try . . . Do you need me to pose any more?'

'No, not today.' He put his brush down and stood back to inspect his work. 'It's all background painting from now on.'

'Then I'll go up and change . . .'

Rhianna went upstairs to doff the grey-green Grecian dress and put on her normal day dress. She undid the bodice straps and pulled it over her head. She had fallen into the habit of wearing nothing beneath it following the first time, and today was no different. As she removed the garment, she was aware that John had come into the bedroom and was looking at her.

'Oh, I didn't hear you,' she said, trying to excuse her nakedness, and sat on the bed to protect her modesty.

'Are you bashful of my seeing you like this?' he asked, his voice gentle.

'Not you, John.' She smiled trustingly.

'You really are beautiful. More beautiful than a Botticelli.'

'I bet you say that to every model who poses for you,' she teased, self-consciously.

He shook his head. 'No . . . I said it to Fernanda,' he answered honestly. 'She was deserving of a compliment, but she was no more lovely than you.'

Rhianna held out her hand to him and looked into his brown eyes. 'Will you hold me?' she whispered. 'Please? I feel very vulnerable . . . I need to feel affection. I need to feel loved . . .'

'Oh, Rhianna, I do love you.' He sat next to her. 'With all my heart and soul I love you.'

He put his right arm around her and she let her head rest luxuriously on his shoulder. He was wearing an old shirt, back to front to protect his clothes from paint. It was daubed with every colour imaginable and she put her hand to it lovingly, savouring its linseed smell. He placed his own hand over hers and when their eyes met again there was no doubting their mutual desire. She offered her mouth to him. Immediately they were in a passionate embrace. Gently, he eased her backwards and she lay down willingly on the counterpane. Their lips joined and she tasted him with delight as she hugged him. His left hand explored her, eliciting little sighs of pleasure as his cool fingers glided over her skin.

'You have such smooth skin,' he breathed. 'I can scarcely believe how lovely you are to the touch.'

'Are you going to get undressed . . . so that I can feel your skin?'

He chuckled, half at her surprising forwardness, half with embarrassment. 'A capital idea. Please don't run away. I won't be a minute.'

Hurriedly, he undressed and resumed lying beside her. They continued where they had left off, their desire for each other increasing immeasurably. Rhianna felt far more at ease with John than ever she had felt with Lawson. Absolute sincerity and devotion seemed to exude from him, filling her with the trust and confidence that had always been lacking with her husband. Only now was she aware of it, now she had this kind and moderate man to compare him with. John's fingers gently probed her, half apologetically, and she parted her legs to allow him easier access. She was aware of her own sweet moistness and wriggled against him to increase the sensual delicacy. She reached out to him and found him aroused and hard, but so soft and smooth was the skin on the outside that she longed to feel him inside her. As he eased himself onto her, it struck her how, just a few short weeks ago, she could never have imagined that she would be making love with any man other than Lawson. How times and emotions changed. How they had changed her. She welcomed John's easy weight on her and he bent his head to kiss her again.

'Oh, my love, I've wanted you so much,' he breathed.

'And now I'm yours.'

She gasped with joy at the sweet redemption created by having him inside her. Slowly he moved, and she savoured every supple, erotic motion. Before long, deep in the pit of her stomach, she began to feel a tingling glow that seemed to wax brighter with his steady rhythm. Her eyes were closed but inside her head a lamp was alight whose flame grew more vivid as the exotic sensation in her groin increased. At last, there was an explosion of brilliance in both places simultaneously. She squealed, squirming at the exquisite agony and the bewildering pleasure consuming her. She wanted this internal commotion to go on and on and on . . . Then John gave a great bellow of release and, after a minute or two, floundered, for the time being, spent.

They held each other unspeaking for some time after, still joined, loath to uncouple. Her thoughts were focused on how much she loved him, on the extreme pleasure they had given each other. She ran her slender fingers gently down his back, over the smooth, firm flesh of his small backside.

'I never knew it could be like *that*,' she whispered at last. There was a smile on her face and she sighed as he began moving inside her again, rekindling the light that had not entirely extinguished.

Lawson went home and asked Emma to fill him a hot bath. Whilst he waited for her to climb the stairs with pails of hot water, he drank plenty of cold water and, by five o'clock when he had finished his bathing, he was relatively sober. As he dressed himself, he mulled over the events of the day. He smiled to himself. What fun Caitlin was in bed. Nothing was beyond her, nothing seemed too bawdy for her tastes. But, it was obvious what should be done with her. The time was right. There were plenty more where she came from . . .

He heard voices downstairs and realised Rhianna had finally returned. Some minutes passed and, whilst he was attaching a collar to his shirt, Emma tapped on the door to say she would empty the bath.

'I take it my wife has returned, Emma.'

'Yes, sir. She's taking a bath as well before dinner.'

'Did you tell her there was water already in it, that she could have bathed in this room?'

'I axed her already, sir, but she says she wants clean water. She says she don't like to go into anybody's dirty bath water.'

'Well, did she now?'

'She did, sir.'

He heard the rustle of Rhianna's skirts as she climbed the stairs, her muffled footsteps on the carpet and the click of the catch as she closed the door to her room. Emma continued in a state of high activity until, eventually, the bath was empty and she dragged it across the landing into Rhianna's room. Lawson went downstairs to the lounge and, seeing the world with a clarity that offended him, he poured himself a whisky. He sat for ages, eyes transfixed on the tall windows, contemplating Fanny, Caitlin and a host of other women he'd had over the years. One by one they entered and exited his mind in a voluptuous procession.

One woman, however, had not acted and reacted like the others, and it puzzled him. That woman was, of course, Rhianna. Oh, she'd been keen enough at first, infatuated like they all were, but she had gone cold on him. She had never even manifested any jealousy when she found out about Caitlin, as other women would. The opposite in fact. She had become indifferent. Sex never seemed to interest her greatly after her initial curiosity had been indulged, and that very perception inhibited him from performing at the pinnacle of his ability. Nothing inhibits a man more than perceiving that his ardent endeavours are being merely tolerated. It was easier on his ego to leave her be and endow some woman more grateful with the benefit of his sexual expertise. It was preferable to favour somebody who really appreciated it. He poured himself another whisky and wondered how long it might be before his dinner was served. He rang the bell and Emma, hot and flustered opened the door.

'Tell Cook to hurry with the dinner, Emma. I'm hungry and I'm due to go out.'

'Mrs Maddox has only just got out the bath, sir.'

'Never mind Mrs Maddox. I'll eat without her. What culinary delights can I expect?'

Emma looked at him in confusion.

'I mean what's for dinner, girl.'

'Oh, beef and onion pie, sir. It smells lovely. I'll tell Cook you'm waiting for it. I'll give you a shout, eh, sir?'

'You mean you'll come and tell me. Thank you.'

He sat down again, meditating. The door opened and Rhianna appeared. Somehow she looked different but he could not determine how. She was simply more beautiful than he had ever seen her before; she radiated a serenity that had eluded her till that moment. Her liquid eyes shone with an indefinable softness and gentleness that had eluded him previously. She seemed more sure of herself, her self-esteem raised and her poise was more elegant in consequence. He watched her with increasing curiosity and a renewed longing for her as she glided through the room and sat in one of the plush armchairs in the huge bay window.

'I wouldn't mind a drink,' she said.

'You're going to join me in a drink?' he queried with a smile that registered how pleasantly he was surprised. 'There's a novelty. What would you like and I'll get it?'

'Oh, a glass of port or sherry . . .'

He got up from his chair and went over to the sideboard where a stash of half-empty bottles stood. There's white port . . .'

'Please.'

He poured her an ample measure and took it to her. She thanked him and sipped the liquid.

'I take it you're going to dine with me this evening?'

'It depends, Lawson. I want to talk to you first. There are things we must discuss.'

'Can't it wait? I'm famished. Let's enjoy dinner together. We can talk over dinner.'

'I'd rather say what I've got to say first. But I want a rational discussion, Lawson. I don't want you to go flying off in a huff if what I'm about to say doesn't suit you.'

He returned to his chair, sat down and picked up his tumbler. 'Is it about John Gibson?'

'Partly . . .'

He rolled his eyes disapprovingly. 'Go on. I'm listening.'

'Promise you'll hear me out.'

'All right, I promise.'

'Well . . . Ever since . . . During the weeks that I've been collecting rents for you, I've got to know John very well . . . and, as you discovered, I've been sitting for him—'

'With no clothes on.'

'That's not true, Lawson. I know it's what you think, but it's not true. Of course I've had clothes on.'

'But not your clothes.'

'All right, not my clothes . . . But you're veering from the point . . .'

'Which is?'

'Ever since I found out about you and Caitlin, I . . . I've felt more drawn to John. Whether, in the first place, it was for sympathy or for support, I don't know. But as we talked we both realised that we . . . that we felt the same way about things, that we had so much in common—'

'That you had an affinity,' he suggested witheringly.

'Yes, an affinity. It was much more than just an affinity though, Lawson. We began to realise that we were in love . . .'

'Pah!' He took a swig from his whisky. 'Why is it that all women think they're in love with whoever says he fancies them? Women are so damned gullible. And you're evidently no different. I thought you were different.'

'You promised not to get angry, Lawson. You promised to listen and I haven't finished yet.'

'I assume that you and he are lovers by now – that he's bedded you,' Lawson said, full of disdain.

Rhianna sipped her port and looked at him challengingly. 'Do I take it from your tone that it's all right for a man to bed a woman other than his wife, but it's not acceptable for the poor injured wife to be so bedded?'

'Of course. There are other considerations than mere poking. What about if the woman gets pregnant because of her affair? The implications for the husband are too great to ignore. Why should he be lumbered with some other man's child, for instance?'

She could have argued but saw no profit in doing so. She could have queried the consequences if a husband made his mistress pregnant. She could have asked the consequences of the husband contracting one of the dreaded venereal diseases that were incurable and all too common, and passing it to his wife. Instead, she asked, 'Isn't divorce a remedy against such an event?'

'If you can tolerate the stigma. If your skin is so thick . . . I take it you would like a divorce?'

'That's up to you, Lawson,' Rhianna answered with a sigh. 'And it's easier for you. Whether you divorce me or not, I intend to go on seeing John. I intend to spend as much time with him as I can.'

'Then go and live with him. Save yourself the bother of a judicial separation from bed and board.'

'I think I might.'

'Good. Go and live with him and be the butt of every lewd joke for years to come. Go and live with him and try to cope with the scorn and contempt that people will pour on you forever more. Go and live with him and see how everybody will ignore, you, even cross over to the other side of the street to avoid you. Just do it and see how you fancy being treated like a pariah. Society doesn't like women who cuckold their husbands.'

Emma came into the room and announced that dinner was ready.

'We'll be another five or ten minutes, Emma,' Rhianna informed her.

Emma curtsied with typical ungainliness and left the room.

'So . . . you are recommending that I do not live with John Gibson?' Rhianna said, resuming the discussion.

'I think you would be a candidate for the workhouse if you did. But . . . if you do – and I'll not stop you – then you wouldn't get a penny from me, nor would I lift a finger to help you . . .'

'I think I know that,' she said quietly. 'Nor would I expect it. You've always been very generous but I wouldn't expect a thing from you if I left.'

'You've apparently already considered all this?'

'Our marriage is over, Lawson, and it was none of my doing. It was over the moment you took Caitlin.'

'Then it was over even before it started,' he answered. 'I had Caitlin some time before I had you.'

Rhianna rolled her eyes in disdain. 'Why am I not surprised? Don't you see? There's nothing left in this marriage for me. No respect, no love, no tenderness, no nothing. Only boredom and indifference. Let me go, Lawson. You don't need me. I can't imagine why you married me in the first place.'

'I married you because I loved you . . . And I still love you. Maybe more than you'll ever know.'

'You love yourself,' Rhianna said with a cynical laugh. 'Far too much to leave room for anybody else.'

Rhianna's mouth was dry and she took a sip from her glass, briefly savouring the intensity and dryness of the port. She looked at Lawson as he projected a hurt expression, designed to elicit sympathy. But she was beyond giving him sympathy. He had hurt her beyond measure, yet always it was somebody else's fault, never his.

'I do believe it would be better for both of us if I left you,' she said at last. 'Whether or not I go to live with John directly.

Maybe I should go and live with my mother and father for a while.'

'Piffle! Of course you'll go straight to live with him. Now you've got the fondness for his doodle. Do you think I was born yesterday?'

She shrugged. She could not gainsay it.

'Meantime, do you think it fair that I should maintain your mother and father in a house I own – at my expense?'

'I was coming to that, Lawson . . . Would you just give me time to find them alternative accommodation? We could pay you rent at the going rate till we find somewhere else. Nobody would expect *you* to maintain them, there in Paradise . . .'

'It would be a fool's Paradise if I did, but I'd be the one living in it. I'll give you a month. No longer.' He stood up and put his glass down. 'Now I'm going in for my dinner. You'll oblige me, Rhianna, by eating elsewhere.'

Lawson went in to dinner alone. Although he had been hungry his appetite had disappeared and he picked at his food fitfully, ruminating on his conversation with his wife. He had already considered threatening to evict the Drakes from Paradise to deter Rhianna from leaving. However, she had anticipated him, neutralising any threat. In any case, ousting them would only succeed in uniting them all against him. Word would spread and he would be vilified; if he acquired a reputation as a ruthless landlord, it could even affect future lettings and thus his pocket. The Drakes would simply end up renting another house where they could all live together happily and spend their waking hours reviling him and his evil ways to their hearts' content. No. There was another way. There was a better way to wreak his revenge upon Rhianna. It would be far more subtle, yet far more hurtful. This way would spoil the miserable lives of each and every one of them. He would find it a singular pleasure to administer too . . . and all was fair in love and war.

Barring her from the dinner table, Lawson had made it plain what Rhianna must do. Stunned at his ostracising her thus, Rhianna went to her room, collected together as many of her things as she could carry and packed them into two large bags. Silently, determinedly, she crept downstairs, put on her coat and, with the bags, slipped out of the front door and onto the drive unseen. In the autumnal darkness, she retraced her steps by way of the shortcut over London Fields to the old mine manager's house.

'Next, you'll be the one to be evicted,' Rhianna said to John. 'Especially when he knows I'm here. Do you really think I'm worth all that trouble?'

'All that trouble and more.' John smiled kindly and squeezed her hand. 'What can Lawson Maddox do to hurt us when we have each other? We'll find somewhere else to live.' He turned to face her, held her gently by the arms and looked into her big blue eyes. 'Oh, Rhianna, this is a dream come true, having you here with me. If we're poor as church mice, living off floorboards and rickety old chairs, it doesn't matter. I swear I'll do my best to make you happy.'

She bent her head forward and rested it on his chest. Tears began to flow; she put her arms around his waist and held him tight. It was not all over yet. Not by any means. But already she felt happier, more at peace. John she could rely on entirely, and knowing it made such a difference. It didn't matter that they must live off floorboards for as long as they were allowed to remain in this house. It didn't matter that the furniture was old and frail. She had had fine furniture, plush carpets, fine bone china and lead crystal glassware on the dining table, but none of it had brought her happiness. She had enjoyed a fine gig with a divine mare to match, but neither had brought her contentment. Only this unselfish man, uncertain of himself, whose only asset was his talent for placing paint on canvas, knew how to make her happy. Only this quiet recluse who was prepared to sacrifice all for her, could make her contented. If only she had known him before Lawson entered her life . . . But then . . . the ways of the world never were quite that simple.

20

Sarah Drake, sixteen years old and as fresh as a summer morning, shuffled along in the queue at Hillman's Leather Works to have her time card stamped. It was six o'clock and time to go home. In front of her was Maggie Butler, of similar age; Sarah's friend and confidante. Behind her, Sammy Wilkes, who was two years older, was trying to gain her affection by intermittently pinching her firm, young buttocks, believing she liked it.

'Stop it, Sammy!' Sarah said, feigning disapproval but gratified nonetheless at the attention.

'Come out wi' me tonight then,' he suggested, not for the first time.

'Why would I want to go out with you, Sammy Wilkes? I want somebody handsome.'

'Handsome is as handsome does . . . And I could do you handsome, Sarah Drake.'

'You'm not getting the chance. Did you hear him, Maggie?'

'Just ignore him.'

'But he keeps pinching my bum.'

'Then lamp him round the yed. I'll hold your card.'

But Sarah could not hit him round the head; the clock intervened and diverted them all. Maggie inserted her card into the machine and pulled down the handle. It made a thud as it imprinted the time. Sarah hovered next to her, blinked in anticipation of the horrid thud as it stamped her card, then put the card in the rack to be stamped again at eight o' clock next morning. They hurried out together, jostling with the hordes of people flowing from the factory in a great swarm.

Outside, away from the unrelenting, cloying smell of leather, the air was cool and the October dusk wrapped all in a grey mantle. Maggie and Sarah hurriedly crossed the street to escape Sammy Wilkes's unwanted attentions but he caught them up, pinched Sarah's bottom again and she shoved him away huffily. They were about to turn into Little Street with its precariously leaning chimneys atop ramshackle houses, with the intention of taking one of the alleys that led to the bright and bustling shops of Hall Street, when a horse and gig pulled alongside them. Sarah looked up alarmed. Unwittingly, she'd almost walked into it, but she smiled as she recognised the man driving the two-wheeler.

'Lawson! Fancy seeing you.'

'Sarah! I was hoping I might see you. Hop aboard. I'll give you a lift.'

'It's all right, thanks. I was going to walk with my friend Maggie.'

'Maggie can come as well. There's room for the two of you if you squash up.'

The two girls looked at each other seeking consensus. But the novelty of riding in a smart gig with a handsome gentleman in a high hat, being seen by all their workmates, was sufficient to warrant their mutual approval. They giggled and Sarah climbed up first, followed by Maggie.

'Squash up to me then,' Lawson said with a warm smile as he flicked the reins.

As they moved away Sarah, from her greater height on the gig, bobbed her tongue out at Sammy, who looked disappointed that his quarry had escaped.

'Right. Let's take Maggie home. Where do you live Maggie?'

'John Street, by the gasworks.'

'Lawson's my brother-in-law,' Sarah announced proudly.

'I like his float,' Maggie said as the horse broke into an effortless trot, leaving behind the hordes of workers trudging home on foot.

The two girls giggled again.

'It's a cabriolet,' Lawson corrected, smiling affably.

'A cabriolet?' Maggie repeated in awe.

'Yes. A float is what the milkman uses.'

'This is nice and plush, in't it, with lovely soft leather seats?' Sarah remarked. 'A float's just plain and there's no hood on a float like there is on this. That's right, in't it, Lawson?'

'I'm not that familiar with milk floats, Sarah.'

'Well sod the milkman. I want somebody with a two-wheeler – a *cabriolet* like this,' Maggie declared, savouring the word on her tongue. 'You can tell that Sammy Wilkes to sod off as well, eh, Sarah? Unless he can come up with a *cabriolet* . . . eh?'

'I know.'

The girls giggled.

'Who's Sammy Wilkes?'

'Oh, just some chap who fancies Sarah. He keeps pinching her bum and she don't like it. Do yer, Sarah?'

'I wouldn't mind if he was somebody *I* fancied,' she replied.

'What's the 'orse name?' Maggie enquired.

'Docker.'

'Docker? That's a funny name for an 'orse, in't it?'

'It suits him,' Lawson said. 'Anyway, what name would you suggest?'

'Dunno . . . How about St Thomas? I mean, you can call an 'orse anythink, can't ya?'

'St Thomas? Yes, that'd be novel.' Lawson roared with laughter. 'What made you think of that, Maggie?'

''Cause I can just see the spire of St Thomas's church poking up over there.' She pointed to it, visible on the horizon through the alleys between the houses as they drove down Oakeywell Street.

They chatted on about anything and nothing until they

reached the end of John Street at the bottom of Constitution Hill, seemingly overpopulated with bawling ragamuffins. Maggie stepped down, thanked Lawson for the lift and walked the rest of the way. Lawson turned the cabriolet around and they set off back up the hill.

'She's funny, your friend.'

'But I like her. She says what she thinks.'

'Do you go out with her, nights?'

'Occasionally. Not very often. She's got a sweetheart she sees most nights.'

'Lucky Maggie.'

'Yes, I know. Lucky Maggie.'

They turned right into Fountain Street, the location for several workshops dotted between blocks of grim terraced houses. Poverty was rife here, that much was evident.

'So you haven't got a sweetheart, Sarah?'

'Not yet.' Her eyes met Lawson's as he turned to look at her in the half light.

'I don't know what's wrong with the young men round here, missing out on a beautiful girl like you.' He smiled warmly.

Sarah dropped her eyelids bashfully. 'I bet you don't mean that.'

'Oh, but I do, Sarah. I most certainly do. You really are a beautiful girl.'

'What? As beautiful as our Rhianna?'

'Even more so . . . I chose the wrong sister . . .'

Sarah felt her heart thump at the extreme compliment. 'Oh, you mustn't say that, Lawson . . .'

'But it's true.' For dramatic effect he drew the horse to a halt and looked into her eyes intently. 'And nobody will ever stop me saying it . . . You have the most appealing eyes, you know, Sarah. Such a pretty little nose . . .' He put his forefinger to it, pressed it gently, intimately. 'And the most kissable lips I've ever seen.'

'Kissable?' A thrill ran up and down her spine. 'Oh, Lawson . . . Do you really think so?'

'Just give me one kiss . . .' He leaned towards her and offered his lips.

She reciprocated without hesitation and their lips touched as gently as the beating wings of a butterfly, making her heart flutter. He slid his hand around her waist and gave her a hug, then withdrew it. She smiled at him perplexed, but her stomach swirled with exhilaration, flattered that this man, so much older, found her so attractive after all.

'Oh, such soft, adorable lips,' he whispered. He covered her hand with his and looked into her eyes. 'Kiss me again.'

She kissed him once more and this time they lingered a few seconds. Never before had her heart pummelled so hard within her; a bass drum thumped heavily inside her head.

'There's something I want to say to you, Sarah . . .' His eyes were two liquid magnets from which she could not detach herself. 'I came directly to find you. You're the first person I thought of. The only person in the world I wanted to see . . . Rhianna has left me, Sarah . . . She's gone off with somebody else . . . Gone to live with him, I believe.'

'Our Rhianna?' Sarah queried, astounded. 'Are you sure?'

'Oh, yes, I'm sure. It's my guess that she'll already have been to let your mother and father know—'

'Lord, I can scarcely believe it, Lawson. Our Rhianna? You ain't bin married five minutes.'

'Five months . . . Anyway, the point is, she believes that because she's left me, I'm about to turn you all out of the house in Paradise . . . I could, of course . . . I'd be within my rights . . .' He turned his gaze away from her. 'Maybe I should, the way she's treated me.'

'But where would we go? Oh, Lawson, don't. Our poor father couldn't stand it, moving again.'

'But don't you think I'd be a fool to allow you all to live

there rent-free while my wife – your sister – their daughter – is living in sin with some ne'er-do-well elsewhere?'

'But . . . I don't know.' Sarah struggled to arrange her thoughts. So much information, so many conflicting emotions needed to be sorted.

'Well, I don't want to do that, Sarah.' Lawson smiled warmly to allay her fears. 'So I thought . . . Well, I thought, I've always actually fancied you, I'll see how you feel . . . When I first caught sight of you at the Cooksons' house – remember? – I asked Robert who you were . . . You seemed very young then, but so lovely. Barely sixteen as I recall. Your birthday's soon, though, isn't it?'

'Next week. I'll be seventeen next week.'

'Seventeen's not too young, is it?' Their eyes met again and held.

'No. *I* don't think it is, Lawson.'

'So how do you feel, Sarah?'

'About you? . . . It's funny, I've always fancied you. I thought you was a god.' Sarah laughed as she recalled it. 'I was that peeved when Rhianna told me she was meeting you on her nights off. I could've killed her.' She uttered a little laugh of self-mockery. 'Honest I could.'

Lawson squeezed her hand affectionately and sighed. 'If only I'd known what I know now . . . Of course, if you *were* my girl there'd be no reason at all to evict you, would there?'

'Are you saying then, that you want me to be your sweetheart?' Sarah felt breathless at the prospect. It was what she'd secretly hankered for. She risked glancing at him again and caught his eyes upon her, intense, brooding.

'That's exactly what I'm saying. I'd like nothing better. And with Rhianna gone it sets me free . . . Otherwise I wouldn't dream, of course . . . Be my sweetheart, Sarah, my little love, and I'll treat you to the nicest dresses and hats and shoes. You'd never find me ungenerous. What do you say?'

She looked at him in awe, her small hands clammy inside her

gloves, trembling within his. She needed his final reassurance. 'You're sure, Lawson? I wouldn't want to do the dirty across our Rhianna.'

'She did it across me . . .'

'You're sure she's gone to live with another man?'

'John Gibson. An artist. She's taken up with an artist, Sarah. Can you believe that?'

'She must be mad.'

'But her loss is your gain. Meet me tonight and I'll take you out somewhere. What do you say? Have you got a nice frock you can wear?'

'Yes . . .'

'Good. Meet me at the top of Oakeywell Street, where it joins King Street, at eight. Don't tell your mother and father you're meeting me, though. But tell them not to wait up, eh?'

Sarah smiled conspiratorially and nodded. 'All right. Eight o' clock. And I won't breathe a word.'

'First, though . . . If you hear your mother and father talking about being evicted, it means Rhianna's been and told them she's left me. Whatever reason she's given them, ignore it. Think nothing of it. If you like, you could say, "Oh, he'd never do that, he's too soft-hearted" – which I am of course. But say nothing else. She'll very likely tell them a pack of lies anyway to justify her own shenanigans. Just say nothing. Offer no opinion. Never appear to be on my side particularly. Otherwise they might twig that we're sweethearts and they mustn't know. It must be our secret . . .'

'I won't breathe a word,' Sarah whispered, feeling a blaze of excitement sear through her breast at this new, dangerous, but utterly irresistible intrigue with her own brother-in-law.

'Now let me taste those lovely lips of yours again, to keep me going till later . . . Mmm! . . . I intend kissing you a lot more, my love . . .'

*   *   *

Sarah was not at the appointed place come eight o' clock, so Lawson flicked the reins and headed slowly towards Paradise. After only a few yards he saw a slight female figure, silhouetted by a gas lamp, hurrying in his direction and he smiled to himself. He halted Docker and she crossed the street, stopped at the gig.

'Sorry if I'm late, Lawson. Our clock's wonky.'

'You're not late, my angel. I just thought I'd save those lovely legs of yours the extra distance. Hop on.'

She climbed into the cabriolet beside him with admirable energy and youthful grace. He turned the carriage around and Docker set off at a steady trot, the clip-clop of his hooves and the rumble of the iron-rimmed wheels the only sounds in their ears.

'Where are you taking me?'

'Somewhere respectable for a quiet drink and a cosy chat. The Dudley Arms.'

'Ooh, I say!' Sarah was impressed.

'Did your folks say whether Rhianna has been to see them?'

'Never mentioned it. I don't think she's been a-nigh.'

'Well, fancy . . . Maybe she's too ashamed.'

'I reckon she must be, Lawson. I've been thinking about it ever since you went. She's a fallen woman, in't she?'

'Oh, entirely so.'

'Are you going to divorce her?'

'In time, when I'm ready to marry again, yes . . .' He engaged her eyes with a look of tantalising promise.

In the comfortable upstairs saloon of the Dudley Arms, where less than a year ago he had wooed Rhianna, Lawson called for a bottle of champagne and two glass flutes. He placed them on the table with a flourish and popped the cork, laughing and making a great show of it to overawe his young companion. He poured and when the bubbles had subsided he handed her a glass and raised his.

'To us, Sarah. To a tender, lasting and fulfilling relationship.'

Imitating him, she raised her glass. At his reassuring words,
hot blood was surging ever faster through her body.

Lawson was enchanting, charming and teasing. Sarah could
barely sit still as he spoke, wriggling her bottom in her chair,
crossing and uncrossing her legs as she giggled and laughed
at his outrageous, tantalising suggestiveness. Seldom had she
enjoyed herself so much as she was doing now, with this man
who was at least fourteen years her senior. It was hard to
believe she was alone with Lawson Maddox, that this was
the romantic tryst she'd longed for from the moment she first
cast eyes on him. Funny how things happen. How wonderful
that Rhianna and he had parted. How thankful she was.

'I hope you won't be like your sister,' Lawson said with a
provocative flick of one eyebrow.

'How do you mean?'

'I hope you'll be sweet and passionate, instead of stiff and
constricted, like she is.'

She laughed, half embarrassed at what he implied, half
delighted. 'I'll try. I promise. I don't want to be like her, do
I?'

'Here, let me fill up your glass . . . You know, you do look
like a very young angel come down from heaven.'

Sarah laughed happily. 'Do I really?'

'The only thing missing is a halo. But I hope you never
warrant one.'

'You mean it's more fun being wicked?'

'You don't have to be entirely wicked. Just a little bit
naughty – naughty having fun. We'll have fun together, Sarah.
We'll be naughty, you and me, shall we? There's nothing
wrong with having some fun, is there?'

'I wouldn't have thought so . . .' she said longingly.

'Trust me, we'll have so much fun without even laughing.
Just the two of us . . .'

They stayed in the Dudley Arms till about half past nine. Lawson suggested they go somewhere more private and Sarah agreed without hesitation. He bought another bottle of champagne to take with them. Outside, they boarded the cabriolet and he drove to his house in Meeting Street, Netherton.

He unlocked the back door and, taking Sarah's hand, led her inside. She was pleasantly surprised to see a fire burning welcomingly in the grate in that comfortable room as he opened the door. He took a spill from the mantelshelf, ignited it in the fire and lit an oil lamp.

'Whose house is this?' Sarah asked.

'Mine,' Lawson said as he trimmed the wick. 'As you know, I own a lot of houses.'

'And nobody lives here? I mean, it's not where you live.'

'Nobody lives here. It's my private den that nobody knows about. I came earlier and lit the fire. To make it warm and comfortable for you. Why don't you take off your coat and hat and make yourself at home while I get two glasses?'

Sarah smiled, took off her hat and coat as bidden and patted her hair, sneaking a look at herself in the mirror while Lawson was in the scullery. She sat down on the sofa and waited eagerly for him to come back. He returned with two champagne glasses and opened the bottle. The cork popped energetically and, with expert precision, Lawson aimed the effervescing liquid into one of the glasses without losing a drop. He filled it and handed it to her.

'Bottoms up!'

'Bottoms up.' Sarah sipped it and felt the bubbles tickling her nose. 'All this champagne is going right to my head.'

'Doesn't it make you feel nice though?'

She nodded, smiling amenably.

When Lawson had filled his own glass he sat next to her and put his arm around her. 'Oh, it's so nice to be alone with you at long last. I've dreamed of this moment.'

'Honestly?'

'Honestly. Kiss me, little Sarah.'

She offered her lips in a pout and he kissed her gently, lingering a second or two. He relieved her of the glass and placed it on an occasional table between them and the fire grate.

'Kiss me again, my angel, but this time part your lips. It's much nicer that way.'

She obliged, grateful for his teaching, and he pressed his lips into hers more fervently. After about a minute they broke off.

'See what I mean?'

'Oh, yes, Lawson. You do kiss nice.'

He handed her the glass again. 'Here, have another drink of champagne . . . Now, when we kiss this time I want to feel the tip of your tongue against mine. I want to taste the champagne in your mouth.'

'Are you sure?' Sarah asked dubiously, putting her glass down again.

'Quite sure. You'll like it. It's the nicest way to kiss.'

She was a little shocked at first, slightly repulsed, but after only a few seconds she was enjoying the other deep-rooted sensations it bred. The very intimacy of his tongue touching hers raised her to a new, different, untried plane of sensuality and excitement. For some minutes they kissed, her desire igniting and fanned into consuming flame as his hands caressed her body over her dress. When Lawson broke off she was breathless.

'I bought you a present,' he whispered intimately. 'I'd like to give it to you now.'

'Oh?' She was taken by surprise.

His hand went to the inside pocket of his jacket and he pulled out a small, prettily-wrapped packet. 'Here . . . Specially for you. Open it.'

'What is it?'

'You'll see.'

Filled with curiosity, Sarah opened the packet and pulled out the contents. 'Silk stockings!' she exclaimed with delight. 'Oh, thank you, Lawson.'

'Just the first of many presents, my love.'

'Lord, you're so generous. Rhianna always said you were generous.'

'Let's put them on now . . .'

'Now? This minute?'

'Yes. But I have to do it for you . . . Take off your boots.'

She obliged and he knelt down before her. He lifted the hem of her skirts and lay them above her knees. Sarah was in two minds whether to resist but, on balance, considered it might seem mightily ungracious if she did, after such a kind and thoughtful gift.

'I see you garter above the knee, Sarah. I like that.' Lawson placed his fingers inside the garter of her left leg and pulled it gently down till it slid over her dainty foot and was off. He repeated the exercise with the other garter. 'You have a fine pair of legs, my angel. Lovely neat ankles.' He drew his fingers and the palm of his hand gently down the back of her slender calves.

As he slipped his fingers in the inside of her stocking he felt the smooth, warm flesh of her unblemished thigh. Slowly, deliberately, all the time holding her gaze with the utmost devotion, he pulled off the first stocking, rolling it fastidiously down her leg while savouring the smoothness of her youthful skin.

He removed the other stocking with equal ceremony and, at the closeness of the moment, Sarah's heart was pounding so hard she felt sure he must be able to hear it. But weren't these intimacies so unbelievably exhilarating? He raised the hem of her skirt even higher. Her smooth thighs glistened like polished ivory in the soft yellow light of the oil lamp. He ran his hand over the back of her calf again and squeezed the soft flesh gently. Then he took the first of the white silk stockings, negotiated her left foot and carefully pulled the stocking up. He put the garter over her foot and slid that up her leg sensuously, letting it rest, gripping above her knee as before. Then he did the same with the other leg.

'Beautiful,' he breathed, running his hand gently over the smooth stocking. 'Don't they look sensational? Don't they feel grand?'

Sarah nodded her agreement with a panting smile. 'They feel so cool. I never had silk stockings before. And you have such a soft, gentle touch.'

'Show me your gratitude with another long, wet kiss.'

She leaned forward and flung her arms about his neck with abandon. Lawson's hands were still on her thighs, the hem of her skirt still up. He moved his left hand higher, stroked the soft skin of her inner thigh. His other hand he slid under her buttock. His left hand roved upwards until he felt the sparse tuft of soft hair at the bottom of her belly and the warm, moist place sheltered there. As he caressed her he heard her sigh and she held him tighter still, parting her legs to their mutual benefit. Her breathing and his became faster, more erratic.

'This lovely, soft, warm place is so inviting, Sarah,' he whispered. 'I'm going to kiss you there . . .' He bent his head, nuzzled his face between her thighs and his tongue found her. His hands went under her small, round buttocks and he pulled her towards him to increase the sensation. This new pleasure made her gasp. Her heart and her body called out to him as compulsively as a spring cuckoo calling for a mate. How on earth had she survived almost seventeen years without these simple yet totally exotic sensations she was experiencing now? Her hands gripped his head, fingers kneaded his dark hair for fear he might move away. She pulled his face more firmly into her hitherto secret place, now drenched with her earnest desire for him.

'I'm going to take you to bed, Sarah,' Lawson whispered and stood up.

Obediently, she stood up. It was consent enough. The hem of her skirt fell around her in a whisper of shifting cotton. She teetered slightly – the effects of the alcohol – and took his hand, allowing herself to be led. He downed what was left in his glass and grabbed the champagne bottle in the same hand.

'Can you bring the lamp?'

'Yes,' she answered breathlessly. 'And my glass?'

'Yes.'

Letting go of his hand Sarah followed him upstairs, his bulk casting a huge dancing shadow in front of them both. In the bedroom she looked round for somewhere to place the oil lamp and decided to put it on top of a tallboy. Nervous about what was to befall her, she finished off what was in her glass and looked at Lawson attentively. She was perfectly willing but unsure how to proceed.

'Let's undress,' Lawson said softly. 'It's so much nicer to feel skin against skin.'

He began to take off his clothes and she hers, till she was in just her chemise and new stockings and he was utterly naked.

'Take off your chemise as well, Sarah, my angel.'

She slipped it over her head and sat on the bed, what remaining modesty she possessed illogically inhibiting her from displaying more of herself. She looked at him naked standing before her, unable to take her eyes off what she saw. He went over to her, sat beside her, embraced her. Once more they kissed and they lay down, and she felt the magic of his skin against her. He took her hand and placed it between his legs. She took him in her small hand, showing her passion and willingness by gripping him firmly.

'Gently,' he said . . . 'Doesn't he feel nice?'

'Oh, yes.'

After too few tantalising minutes he shifted, snaked his body over hers. She found his lips and kissed him with unbridled abandon.

'Now . . .' Lawson said, whispering reassuringly as they broke off. 'I promise I'll try not to hurt. But it might at first. A bit . . . It usually does the first time.'

'I don't mind, Lawson . . . I want to . . .' She felt him tentatively probing her and winced at his first insistent push. 'Ow! . . . Ooh . . .' She whimpered again. 'Ooh . . .' Gradually, she felt him fill her up and move lusciously inside her. 'Oh, Lawson, I love you so . . .'

'And I love you, my little angel.'

He spoke no lie. He truly loved a virgin when he was taking her.

21

It was on 21st October, a Monday, that John Gibson received a letter written in the elegant swirl of a practised, professional hand. The elaborately headed notepaper bore an ominous string of names: Bowdler, Dickens & Moy, Solicitors and Commissioners for Oaths. He scanned the letter quickly, then slumped back into his chair at the breakfast table, overwhelmed with disappointment.

'Well, here it is, Rhianna. What we've been expecting. Although I must say I didn't think it would be delivered in the form of a solicitor's letter.'

Rhianna looked at him anxiously, unsure how this attack on their love affair would affect him. 'Do you want to read it to me?'

John raised it up in front of him. 'It says, *Dear Mr Gibson, I am instructed by your father, Alexander Gibson Esq., to advise you that, due to your unacceptable involvement with the wife of Lawson Maddox, Esq. and your subsequently enticing her away from the good offices of her spouse, the said Lawson Maddox, he has devised a new will. To summarise, the sole beneficiary of his estate on his death will be your sister, Mrs Cynthia Gale, with special provision for your mother, Mrs Ruth Gibson, in the event of her outliving your father. I am also instructed to advise you that the executors are named as Jeremiah Cookson, Esq. and the aforementioned Lawson Maddox, Esq.*

'*Furthermore, your father has terminated the arrangement he made with Lawson Maddox Esq. for the renting of the property in Windmill Street, which you currently occupy, with effect from Saturday 2nd November 1889. I remain, dear Sir, Yours faithfully, W V Bowdler.'*

John slapped the letter down on the table and looked at Rhianna. 'It begins . . . The victimisation.'

'Let it begin,' Rhianna responded defiantly. 'We don't want to live in any house of his and feel beholden to him.'

'So you don't mind?'

'Mind? Let's go away as soon as we can. There are plenty of houses to rent.'

'Or buy,' he said. 'My pictures have been selling. Already I have earned enough money to buy a modest house.'

'And I still have a nest egg . . .'

'Oh?'

Rhianna told him about the money that remained in her possession; the winnings from her betting on the cockfighting main with Lawson – nearly two hundred pounds of it. 'He never found it, never asked about it,' she added. 'It's ours to do with as we will.'

'Then we're not so badly off.'

'No, we're not so badly off at all.'

'What about your own mother and father?' he asked. 'I take it you haven't told them yet?'

'I haven't had the heart. I suppose next thing, they'll be receiving a letter from Lawson's solicitors, instructing them to leave the house in Paradise. I must go and tell them what's happened. But I'm dreading it.'

'Go today,' John advised. 'Go today and get it over and done with. And while you're gone I'll visit my mother and try and make my peace with her.'

'How do you think she'll receive you?'

He shrugged. 'I have no beef with *her*. But, for the sake of propriety, I've no doubt she'll side with my father. The appearance of respectability is everything.'

'But, John, what about your father?'

'My father? That pompous twit? I would expose him but for my mother.'

'What do you mean, expose him?'

'For what he is . . . Let me tell you about my *respectable* father,' John said, the scorn he felt for him manifest in his tone. 'When I was about twelve years old we had some relatives of my mother come and stay with us from Exeter for about a month. My Aunts Augusta and Dorinda, with Dorinda's youngest daughter, Stephanie. Stephanie was about fourteen at the time and a pretty girl. She and I were good friends, we had fun together. Well, I was in our garden one day, looking for Stephanie, when I heard whispered voices and giggling. Curious as to who it was, I crept towards the summer house where the voices were coming from, making sure nobody could see me. As the entrance of the summer house came into view I could see my father sitting on one of the chairs and Stephanie was on his lap. Such a situation would not seem unnatural, you would think, a niece sitting on an uncle's lap. Except that her skirt was up around her thighs and his hand was up there too. Both were laughing – she was giggling, pretending to resist but not resisting at all – so it was obviously a very friendly encounter.'

'So what did you do?'

'Nothing. I was too astonished to do anything. It all seemed so queer. It certainly didn't seem normal. I mean, it's not the sort of thing you'd expect somebody who purports to be a respectable gentleman, least of all your own father, to do with his fourteen-year-old niece, is it?'

'You never mentioned it?'

'Not even to her. You are the first and only person I've ever told. But whatever they did, however it might have progressed, it would have been with her consent, it seems. She never appeared to shy away from my father at any time, as you would expect if he'd tried to force himself onto her. She never seemed short of pocket money either afterwards.'

'There's no doubt, John, that some girls are more forward than others. And, let's face it, when you were twelve all those years ago, girls of only thirteen were of a legal age to wed. At that age they know all they need to know about being bedded, and they are curious to try it. They talk about it between themselves and listen to the experiences of older girls and are fascinated by the prospect of having a man. I certainly was, although I was too prim and proper to try anything.'

He smiled at that. 'Although I have never actually caught him in flagrante delicto since, I have seen how his head swivels when he sees a pretty young girl . . . and I do mean young. I did once drop a hint to him that I was aware of his penchant for young girls. That painting of mine that Lawson has, that you admired so much . . .'

'You mean "The Daughters of Paradise"?'

'Yes. I was going to call it "Virgins" but I decided in the end that that was too provocative. Anyway, I painted it with the express intention of giving it to him. It was my way of saying "I know what you are like". As it happened, he evidently didn't appreciate it, since he gave it to your husband.'

'It would never have occurred to me that there was a hidden meaning to the picture,' Rhianna said. 'It just seemed beautiful to me. All that sunshine and a calm, blue sea in the background.'

'Symbolism, my love. I suspect virginity – innocence – is all sunshine. Perhaps only when it's taken – perhaps only its loss – creates grey skies and consequences we can't always account for nor control . . . Anyway, we have a lot to do, Rhianna. We must visit our families and then we must find somewhere to live.'

That same morning Rhianna took the omnibus into Dudley. From the town centre she walked along Oakeywell Street and Prospect Row and reached Paradise. This visit to her mother and father she had not looked forward to making, but she had an obligation to let them know what had transpired in her marriage, for it was bound to affect them directly. Indeed, she would be surprised if they hadn't had a visit from Lawson already. She let herself in, kissed her father on the cheek and enquired of his health.

'Where'n yer bin?' Titus asked. 'Yo' ai' bin a-nigh for a wik or two.'

'I've been busy,' Rhianna replied. 'And I don't have the horse and gig any more.'

'Oh?' Mary uttered as she peeled potatoes at the stone sink. 'How come?'

'I was getting too independent for Lawson's taste. Have you seen him lately?'

'He ai' bin a-nigh neither.'

'I'm surprised. I imagined he would've been to see you.'

'Why's that then?'

'Because I've left him.'

There was a stunned silence while Mary and Titus looked at each other with open-mouthed incredulity.

'But you'm a-going back?' Titus goaded.

'I'm never going back.'

Rhianna explained about his infidelity, how she'd actually caught him in the act. She confessed her burgeoning friendship with John Gibson and how Lawson had finally made it plain he didn't want her in the house any longer because of it. She told how she'd fallen in love with John Gibson and how she was now living in the same house, even confessed to sharing his bed. Mary listened with increasing agitation and disgust while Titus sat and shook his head sagely. Nothing in this life surprised him any more.

'Yo'll be the talk o' the town,' Mary asserted acidly, unwittingly wagging a knife at her daughter.

'Well, while they're talking about me they'll be giving somebody else a rest.'

'Yo' ought to be ashamed,' Mary said, her contempt increasing as the information and its disturbing implications sunk in.

Well, at least it was an honest response, Rhianna thought. 'Why should I be ashamed, Mother? Don't you think that *he* should be ashamed after what he's done?'

'Men will always have their mistresses, Rhianna,' Mary said. 'It's up to a woman to accept that with dignity when it happens, turn a blind eye and rise above it.'

Titus looked at Mary with a puzzled frown. 'So, if I'd have had a bit on the side yo' wouldn't have complained?'

'Huh!' Mary replied impatiently. 'There was never any fear of you a-straying. Who in their right mind would suffer yo' climbing all over 'em?'

'Hey, I had me chances, Missus, I'll have you know. Just 'cause I never took 'em there's no need to look down on me and fling insults.'

'Well, I'm not about to turn a blind eye and rise above it, Mother. I've left him, I'm living in sin with a kind, decent and honest man who I love very much. And I'm not about to move out.'

Mary's face was like thunder. 'I don't admire you, Rhianna,' she said with utter disdain. 'To think as a daughter of mine would stoop to such degradation. You'm a fallen woman and I'll have nothing more to do with you. What d'you think will happen to you when you'm pregnant and he wants to get shut of yer, eh? Why, you'm no better than a common prostitute when you've got a husband who thinks the world of you and has been as good as gold to you – to all of us. You must want your head looking.'

'That's a point,' Titus exclaimed. 'Is Lawson gunna suffer we living here in his house because of yo' leaving him for another mon?'

'Oh, I doubt it, Father. He'll have you out in no time. I'm surprised he hasn't already. I've offered to pay rent till we find somewhere else for you. I've got a little bit of money put by.'

'I want nothing more off you,' Mary rasped. 'I won't be beholden to a whore, daughter or no. We'll tek our chances, me and your father. If we get turned out, then it'll be on your conscience. We'll manage one road or another. We managed afore.'

'I'm sorry you think like that, Mother. I just wanted to help. I wanted to make amends.'

'You can mek amends by going back to your husband – if he's saft enough to still have yer. Unless you do, never set foot in my house again.'

Rhianna looked at her father for support. 'She means it,' she said with hurt surprise.

'Oh, ar, 'er means it,' Titus quietly affirmed.

'What about you, Father? Are you on her side or mine?'

'I'm taking no sides. But remember, I have to live with your mother. And yet yo'll always be me daughter, my wench . . . But yo've med your bed . . . Yo'm the one who has to lie in it . . .'

Rhianna trudged back to Windmill Street in a miasma of frustration and disappointment. It was difficult to grasp that her own mother had disowned her for her affair with John; Lawson's affair meant nothing and was to be tolerated. Now, as a result of her confession, if Lawson had them evicted, it must be on her own conscience as Mary had said, even though she was willing, anxious to help alleviate any hardship. How unreasonable people were in such situations, especially family; only concerned about their respectability and what other people might say. Why no support?

She arrived home but John had not yet returned. She went to the studio to look at the painting he was currently engaged on. It was of herself reclining on a marble bench, looking lovingly at the ring on her wedding finger. A tiger skin was beneath her, a large purple cushion resting her head. She was wearing a long dress of very thin blue cotton gauze and around her hips to protect her modesty, she wore a cream-coloured stola decorated with large orange and gold polka dots. Already, it was turning out to be the finest painting John had done.

The blue sea in the distance, the fascinating umbrella pines and the overall feeling of tranquillity elicited a sigh from Rhianna. With all this trouble they had brought upon themselves and which had been wrought upon them, this tiny piece of Italy that had so obviously been conceived in John's imagination looked so wondrously beautiful.

There was lots to be done. John had several paintings that were ready to be shipped to his art dealer in London. Within the next day or two they would have to be packed up and sent to the railway station. He would have to uproot his studio again, store all his paints and other accoutrements and get ready to move to another house. Their clothes, shoes, hats, kitchen utensils, pots and pans, crockery – everything – would have to be packed ready for the move. They would need tea chests. And the furniture? Well, maybe they should burn it, such as it was; save the expense of hiring a carter to shift it.

Presently, when Rhianna was making up the fire, John returned, looking agitated.

'What happened?' Rhianna asked anxiously.

'I am ostracised, disinherited, disowned. What about you?'

'I'm ostracised, disinherited and disowned as well,' she said.

'We still have each other.'

'Yes,' she said with a smile. 'And never did we realise we would need each other so much.' She put the coal scuttle down, washed and dried her hands and turned to face him. Her arms went around his waist affectionately, his went around her shoulders. 'And we have work to do if we are to vacate this old house.'

'Yes,' he answered. 'I know.'

'First we must let your art dealer have whatever paintings are ready. That at least will save us from carting them with us.'

'Yes,' he said again.

'Then we have to pack everything ready for the move.'

'Would that we had somewhere to move to, Rhianna.'

'I know . . . Nobody wants to know us any more. We're miserable sinners who have no right to love one another. We might as well move miles away from here where nobody knows us, where nobody can point fingers at us.'

'That would be ideal. And you're prepared to go to those lengths?'

'Wouldn't Italy be nice?'

'Italy?' he laughed. 'Are you serious?'

'It was just a thought. It looks so vivid in your paintings.'

The very next day, Rhianna went out of her way to intercept Sarah coming home from work. She felt an urgent need to make her peace with at least one member of her close family. To be at odds was unthinkable, especially with her poor father suffering as he did. Sarah would understand, she would not condemn her for what she had done. Sarah might even be able to persuade their mother and father that she had done the right thing, that she really had no alternative but to leave Lawson if she did not relish the prospect of a life of anxious wondering and perpetual unhappiness.

She waited at the corner of King Street and Oakeywell Street and, from her vantage point, eventually saw Sarah crossing Hall Street with another girl.

But Sarah looked beyond her sister and walked past without acknowledging her.

'Sarah! . . .'

Despite the compelling entreaty, Sarah continued walking, continued to ignore her. Rhianna, incredulous, ran after her.

'Sarah! . . . Why are you ignoring me? We have to talk . . .'

Sarah stopped, turned and looked at Rhianna, and rolled her eyes with scornful impatience.

'I have to speak with you, Sarah. Would your friend mind if we talked alone for a few minutes?'

'I'll go, Sarah,' Maggie said diplomatically. 'See you tomorrow.'

'I don't see as we've got much to say to each other,' Sarah said with disdain.

'You as well?' Rhianna said, her heart heavy. 'Are you going to disown me as well, just because my husband was making me unhappy and I left him?'

'Lawson is a good, kind and generous man, our Rhianna and one thing's for certain – you didn't deserve him. But he's well rid of you now. You can go and live in sin with your artist chap. None of us admire you for that.'

'I'm not asking for anybody's admiration. I'm asking for your understanding. But a little bit of succour wouldn't have come amiss. It's been difficult enough—'

'You don't deserve no succour, our Rhianna . . .'

Rhianna tried to hold back the tears that were rimming her anxious eyes. 'Look, as regards the house . . . I wanted to help the three of you. I'm quite prepared to pay the rent for you till you find somewhere else to live. I know Lawson wants you out of there.'

'Oh, no,' Sarah said with a supercilious air. 'That's all been sorted out. I told you Lawson is a kind and generous man. Well, he's agreed that we can stay. Rent-free, same as before. He says why should we suffer because of you.'

'He's been to see you all then?'

'Oh, yes. You don't think he'd leave us in the lurch, do you? Not Lawson. I think that's very good of him. Especially the way you've treated him.'

'The way *I've* treated *him*? That's rich. Did he tell you why I left? Did he tell you I wasn't prepared to put up with his shenanigans with our Irish maid?'

Sarah shook her head with scorn, as if she was anticipating being fed a pack of lies and excuses. 'Oh, he was right about you. You'll make up all sorts of wicked lies to justify running off with your artist. Well, I don't believe a word you say, Rhianna. I'm ashamed that you'm my own sister.'

'Well, he's really got to you and *no* mistake. I just hope you come to realise the truth someday.' Rhianna sniffed, pulled out a handkerchief and wiped her eyes. 'In the meantime, if you're so certain I don't need to worry about you, I won't,' she added with a defiance she did not feel.

'I told you. Lawson will look after us. Goodbye, Rhianna. I hope I never see you again.' Sarah turned her back on her and walked away.

'You might not,' Rhianna cried huffily, trying to disguise the hurt she felt from this absolute rebuff by her beloved sister. 'But don't be so stupid as to put all your trust in Lawson Maddox.'

'Oh, good riddance, Rhianna,' Sarah called impatiently.

22

After visiting Messrs Thomas Miller McLean in the Haymarket on 31st October and depositing several paintings there, Rhianna and John arrived at Folkestone at about midday the following day. She looked at him with a reassuring smile as their train slowly traversed the Railway Pier which divided the harbour into inner and outer.

'Well, the sea looks nice and calm,' she said brightly, looking towards the outer harbour past the funnels of several steamships, then at the inner haven where sailing colliers were berthed.

'Let's hope it stays that way. I'm sure if that ferryboat rocks more than an inch I'll be seasick.'

Rhianna laughed. 'Of course you won't.'

The locomotive crossed the swing bridge that allowed ships passage in and out. The train stopped briefly, its line of carriages lying bowed in the left-hand curve of the Harbour Station before slithering like a snake in a sharp right-hand arc that straightened out at the steamer berths on the New Pier. They alighted from their carriage and for the first time Rhianna could smell the sea and feel the stiff south-easterly breeze on her face. The air had a distinct autumnal nip and she shivered as she looked up at a crane that would hoist containers full of registered luggage onto the ship. Rhianna was glad to board the large paddle steamer, the *Louise Dagmar*, and find a seat by a window fore of the paddle wheels, where they would have a decent view of the English Channel, uninterrupted by spray. The sea, to John's satisfaction, remained calm. On arrival at Boulogne they had time to eat prior to their onward journey to Paris.

From London, it had taken less than eight hours to get to Paris; a tribute to the enterprise and efficiency of the South Eastern Railway. In Paris Rhianna and John left the train, went through the custom house without trouble and took a cab. With his limited French, John made the cabman, whose blue hat with red cockade amused Rhianna, understand that they needed a decent hotel for the night. They were not due to catch their next train until Saturday evening so, next morning, at John's insistence, they visited the Louvre and later the cathedral of Notre Dame. Rhianna was interested in seeing the new Eiffel Tower, especially since Lawson had mentioned it, and was struck by its intricate tracery of ironwork and how delicate it looked from a distance. During the late afternoon they walked along the banks of the Seine, hand in hand, bought some provisions for their journey, including a bottle of wine, then returned to their hotel.

After a long drive across Paris they reached the Gare de Lyon where they were to board their overnight train. They had a compartment to themselves and were able to settle comfortably for the night. When they awoke from a sleep that had not been particularly tranquil, daylight was filtering through the carriage windows and they were hurtling through Macon. As the morning progressed and the miles stacked up behind them, both were taken by the landscape of regimented vineyards, placid lakes and distant mountains covered in snow. After another customs stop and a change of train at Modane, they arrived in Turin in the early evening, deposited their luggage at the station and found a suitable hotel.

Rhianna was disappointed with the first Italian city she set foot in. The light of that November morning showed her Turin was modern, lacking in the classical columns and cupolas she had anticipated. It was also snowing and cold. Why had they come to Italy when winter was knocking at the door? It was as damp and miserable as England. But they were impressed by the food and wine in a trattoria, and bought fresh provisions for the train journey for Rome that evening.

Turin to Florence was a long haul, some two hundred and fifty miles. But at last the exquisite dome and towers of the beautiful old city were evident in the distance. There was time to stop for breakfast before continuing the journey.

In Florence, the sun ceased to hide behind clouds, which retreated for the rest of that day. As Rhianna and John resumed their journey, they were transfixed by the majestic scenery. This was more like the Italy she had expected. The River Arno, which they travelled alongside for a while, was flowing brim full in a broad brown flood between hills freckled with villages and churches. Snow-capped mountains beyond were festooned with curling clouds, like elaborate wigs woven round the heads of eccentric granite giants. The area around Arezzo and Lake Trasimeno was sufficiently beautiful to put what seemed like a permanent smile on Rhianna's face.

And then, at last, as the winter sun hung low and orange in the sky, Rome, the Eternal City, manifested itself in its splendour of steeples and towers and roofs and, high above them all, the dome of St Peter's. The train passed the old walls and soon halted in the heart of the city.

'You realise what day it is?' John remarked as they boarded the omnibus that would take them from the station to their hotel.

'The fifth of November,' Rhianna answered. 'I think.'

'Gunpowder, treason and plot . . .'

She gave a dazzling smile. 'I see no reason why Rome in this season should ever be forgot.'

They laughed at that.

The hotel was a temporary residence. They had decided before they left England that they would need to take rooms suitable for John to work in. In the magnificent Piazza di Spagna next day they found a letting bureau run by an Englishman called Johnson who gave them a list of available apartments.

'But it's November and the winter is our busiest time,' Mr Johnson warned. 'Consequently our range of available rooms won't improve until May when most of the tourists disappear.'

Rhianna was tired after the long days of travelling and sleeping in strange beds, so they decided to return to their hotel and rest.

The following day, they decided to combine an inspection of a couple of apartments around Piazza Navona with a visit to St Peter's. From a distance, the Vatican looked enormous but, as they approached, seemed but a cluster of ornate buildings. Rhianna gasped and clutched at John's hand when she saw the beauty of the Piazza San Pietro laid out before her, with its central obelisk, its sparkling fountains and elaborate baroque colonnades.

Inside the basilica, the initial burst of majesty and glory, especially as she looked up into the Dome, was an experience Rhianna swore to John she would never forget. Its impressiveness did not affect her in any religious way, however. To her it was an immense and extraordinarily beautiful edifice, with so many wonderful images and artefacts to distract her, but not particularly revealing of its real function as a place of worship.

John was keen to show her the Raphael Rooms, to tell her about the work and the influence of this man who was possibly the greatest artist ever.

'My work seems so insignificant compared to his,' John said.

'But your paintings are so much smaller,' Rhianna replied consolingly.

He laughed. 'It has nothing to do with the size. More the emotion and sense of movement he achieves.'

Next day, John wanted to show her the Colosseum, so they took a fiacre to the Forum.

'I was overcome by the sight of it last time I was here,' he said as they looked at the spectacular ruin. 'I imagined thousands of people yelling at the gladiators, all smeared in blood in the arena below, the dust swirling round, the clash of swords, the smell of sweat.'

'You have a vivid imagination.'

'I know. I'm an artist . . . It's a remnant though, isn't it? This great pile, crumbling inch by inch, year by year. A remnant of the old mythology. A poignant reminder of the lack of regard the Romans had for human life. People and animals were butchered here.'

'Talking about butchering . . . did you see those porcupines hanging in a butcher's window earlier?'

'I understand porcupines are very tasty,' he answered flippantly.

'Well I don't fancy eating one . . . They eat some strange things here . . .'

They spent the morning sightseeing and, by virtue of its name, the Arch of Titus reminded Rhianna sadly of her father. She decided that later she would write to her family, seeking forgiveness and reconciliation. She and John wandered hand in hand, unconcerned about the time, along the Appian Way, through stretches of ruined tombs and, here and there, a deserted house uninhabited for years, into countryside. To their left they saw the distant Apennines, and miles of redundant aqueducts, their rows of supporting arches a picturesque pattern receding into the hills. Rhianna was surprised to see shepherds so close to the city; a very ragged fraternity, leaning on their sticks, motionless except for their nodding or shaking heads as they agreed or disagreed with each other. Old women and old men drove tired donkeys or led unwilling goats through olive groves and between lemon trees.

Tired they returned to their hotel. The apartments they had seen were unimpressive. Next day they inspected some more, in the Trastavere, which turned out to be unsuitable, and then decided to take a stroll in the Pincio Gardens. Young men, beautifully dressed, seemingly with nothing better to do, preened themselves under the shade of umbrella pines. They admired the unattached young women who pretended to ignore them as they lounged alone in their barouches, balancing or twirling their parasols to protect their delicate skin from the autumn sun. It was Friday and, in the Pincio's main square, a band was playing. Rhianna and John sat on a bench and listened as they watched the exchanges between the great unoccupied. When the band finished playing they decided to view the panorama of the city from the Pincio's elevated terrace. It was then that a man, who had suddenly appeared behind them, spoke to them in English.

'John Gibson, as God's my judge!'

John swung round to see who was addressing him. 'Good Lord! Edward Proctor. You're still in Rome.'

The two men greeted each other warmly and John introduced Rhianna.

'Have you returned here to work?' Proctor enquired.

'Yes, but in all honesty it was Rhianna here who prompted it.'

'Are you still painting Grecian ladies on marble patios, John?'

John smiled at this well-intentioned mockery. 'With a model like Rhianna, is there anything else worth painting?'

Proctor looked at her approvingly. 'Yes, I do see what you mean.'

'We arrived on Tuesday, Edward. We've not yet found rooms, though we've looked at a few. I've had little chance to do any work.'

'So, you're seeking rooms. What about a studio?'

'A studio would be fine, as long as there's somewhere decent to live.'

'I know the very place. A couple of minutes from here.

The Villa Strohl-Fern. A purpose-built artists' colony, and I happen to know there's a studio available. With living accommodation. If you're seriously looking for somewhere, I'd go and see it at once. Once word gets around . . .'

'Tell me where it is, exactly.'

'I'll do better than that, I'll take you. I rent a studio there myself. Have you got fifteen minutes?'

John looked at Rhianna, who nodded her consent.

'Lead on,' John said.

They reached the Villa Strohl-Fern from the Piazzale Flaminio, up the steep and curling Via de Ruffo. Beyond the iron gate the main house stood on the left, like a gatekeeper's lodge fronting the wild, uncultivated grounds that were surrounded by steep cliffs on one side and a high, impenetrable wall on the other, and dotted with Roman sculptures. Gigantic magnolia trees stood alongside umbrella pines, Lebanon cedars, alders and cypresses.

'This looks wonderful,' John commented.

'See the studios before you make a final judgement,' Edward suggested. 'I'll take you directly to the owner and he can show you around.'

Soon, they were standing at the door of Alfred Wilhelm Strohl-Fern. Edward tapped the door.

'A candidate for number three, Alfred,' Edward said when the man answered.

Strohl-Fern and John Gibson conversed for a while, discussing John's application for residence. The villa owner declared that he was a lover of classical antiquity and the exchange that followed seemed to forge an immediate bond between artist and landlord. Eventually, he agreed to show John and Rhianna the vacant studio.

It was a flat-roofed building annexed to the main house, of decent quality and on two floors, comprising a bedroom, a living-room and small kitchen, with a large window to illuminate the studio itself – perfectly self-contained and ready furnished, although in spartan fashion. Rhianna nodded her head in approval and John and Strohl-Fern agreed the rent.

The next few days saw them buying soft furnishings and household implements. John located an artists' colourman close to the Pincio from whom he could obtain all the materials he needed, and they were soon all set up. They left their hotel on 14th November and took up residence at Studio 3, Villa Strohl-Fern.

That same evening, tired after a hectic day of settling in, Rhianna wrote to her family:

Dear Mother, Father and Sarah,

Just a note to let you know that John and I are in Rome in Italy where we intend to make our home. As I'm sure you understand, we had no alternative but to leave, but neither did there seem much point in staying. I am only sorry that you could not see your way clear to giving us your blessing. My hope is that in time you will see things my way and that you will welcome me back into the family. I want nothing more. You can't imagine the sorrow it has caused both John and me that our love for each other should cause such a rift. But he is my future, the love of my life. He is such a kind, considerate and gentle person. He is very shy and sensitive, not a bit like Lawson. I know you would love him dearly if only you would give us both a chance.

I hope you are all keeping well and Father especially. Please give my love to our Sarah. She told me that Lawson is letting you stay in the house and I suppose that's very decent of him. It's certainly a load off my mind.

Please write to me to let me know that you are well. I beg you to tell me as well that you understand why I have done what I have done. Then my happiness will be complete. I shall write to you as often as I can.

I love you all dearly,
Rhianna.

In Rome, John's painting attained a higher level of quality. His pictures glowed with colour, he took more risks with his compositions and they acquired a boldness and a confidence that only enhanced them. His representation of the female form became ever more adept, ever more reverential. He and Rhianna were a formidable team and this was remarked upon by several of his fellow artists. He maintained a steady flow of work to his art dealer in London and received a steady flow of cheques in return, which he paid into MacBean's Bank where he had opened an account.

Rhianna had offers of modelling work from several other artists but she was only interested in sitting for John. They were comfortably off in Rome, though by no means wealthy. A couple of nights each week they would go out to dine, usually at a trattoria they liked in the Via della Croce, a short walk from the Villa Strohl-Fern. Sometimes they tried new places. Although John was fairly fluent in Italian, he advised Rhianna to learn the language as well, and accompanied her to the home of a Signora Biagiotti who gave lessons. Signora Biagiotti was a middle-aged lady who took a shine to them. She always sent them on their way with a stiff measure of grappa inside them, and a bag of oranges or lemons.

During the following weeks and months, the love Rhianna and John had for each other became more firmly established. Their mutual admiration and respect increased. They seldom exchanged cross words, but laughed together frequently at the little things that happened and enjoyed being together. Although John was shy, Rhianna soon discovered he had a sharp sense of humour. Few nights passed when they did not make love, and the profound contentment they found in each other only served to strengthen their bond.

During this time Rhianna continued to write weekly to her mother and father, telling of her very different life in Rome but not once did she have a reply. Each morning she hurried to collect any post from the post box, hoping there would be something, but each morning she was disappointed. Contact with her family was the only thing lacking in her life.

Life in Rome seemed to be one long series of fiestas and carnivals from Christmas and New Year onwards. Rhianna became caught up in one in February. She had been to buy meat and vegetables one morning in the Via Cola di Rienzo, one of the busy shopping streets on the other side of the River Tiber, when she heard a commotion. A procession came into view headed by mounted men in Moorish dress and chain mail, followed by Moorish women, conveyed in palanquins. A troop of archers preceded the French Academy's carriage, which was filled with students in beautiful white mediaeval dresses, and a comic procession of cooks clowning about on a cart was drawn by six men wearing horses' heads. Masked men and women walked alongside children who were screaming and shouting with glee as they threw confetti over spectators. It was all very good-humoured.

On Good Friday they made the effort to go to the Colosseum to watch the Procession of the Cross, led by the Pope. The city was overrun with visitors who had come to hear the Pope's Easter Sunday address outside St Peter's basilica. As the spring flowers bloomed and the temperature reached very comfortable levels in April there were concerts in the Piazza di Spagna, and Rome's birthday was celebrated with typical Italian flair on 20th April.

The only blot on Rhianna's contentment at the Villa Strohl-Fern was the immoderation of some of the artists there. Many seemed undisciplined and anarchic. Some drank to excess, reeked of tobacco smoke and some, John reckoned, were addicted to opium. One of the artists, a painter called Henry Wainwright, had a live pig brought to his studio for a painting he was working on. Unfortunately, the pig would not keep still and Henry, being a slow and very methodical painter, could not record it properly on canvas as a result. So he decided that the pig should be slaughtered, which would solve the problem of its inability to stay still. This however, created another problem. Because Henry was such a laborious worker, the porcine corpse began emitting odours that were none too savoury. As the spring temperature rose, it was impossible to escape the stink anywhere in the confines of the Villa Strohl-Fern. Eventually, a deputation, led by Herr Strohl-Fern himself, insisted that the rotting carcass be removed before the health of the entire community was seriously jeopardised.

It was becoming evident to Rhianna that life there was not idyllic.

'John, can we find somewhere else to live?' she ventured as they retired to bed one night. One of the artists in the colony, a Russian, a habitual drunkard, could be heard shouting aggressively in the grounds, a regular occurrence. 'I don't know if I can put up with the behaviour of some of these people much longer.' She nodded towards the window. 'I suppose he's got one of his whores with him again and he's arguing the price.'

'I do sympathise with you,' John replied. 'But where would we go?'

'Anywhere away from here. For six months I've put up with seeing him and that Dutchman molesting their women in full view of everybody, and I'm sick of it. It's as if they can't wait till they get to the privacy of their rooms. I'm sick of the way they leer at me when they come here to borrow things – which they never bring back, by the way. They look me up and down as if I were a piece of meat in a butcher's window. I'm surprised you haven't mentioned anything before, John. I know how you loathe such behaviour.'

'I do, and I agree with you. But it's very handy here.'

'Handy or not, I'm sure we could find somewhere to ourselves. Why don't we try the coast? Most of your paintings are set overlooking the sea. Wouldn't it benefit you to work in such a place?'

'As you know, Rhianna, I'm not a gregarious person and

I'd much prefer to work away from other artists. It's not as if I wish to be influenced by any of them, or that I thrive on their plaudits . . .'

'Then let's get away from here. If only for a short time.'

'Yes,' said John thoughtfully, anxious to do the right thing for her. 'I suppose we could take a break from here if you wish. I've been to the Bay of Naples before. It's quite beautiful. We could go there for a while and see what's available. It could be a holiday for you.'

'It sounds perfect.' Rhianna smiled her thanks.

He extinguished the flame in the oil lamp and snuggled into bed beside her. 'Tomorrow,' he whispered, taking her in his arms, 'I'll make the arrangements. Now kiss me . . .'

23

The road from Castellamare to Sorrento wound its way between vineyards and lemon groves, allowing tantalising glimpses of the Tyrrhenian Sea, which shimmered blue and turquoise by turn beneath the cloudless sky. The high stone walls that lined stretches of the white and dusty road were bedecked with white daisies and trailing purple wisteria and morning glory. Umbrella pines lavishly covered those precipitous slopes that had not been reclaimed for cultivation. At the whim of the gentle breeze, the leaves of the olive trees shimmered from neutral green to a soothing grey as soft as the feathers of a dove. Wildly luxuriant vines overhung rocks and gorges, their leaves trembling, eternally fanning themselves, throwing traceries of subtle shadows as cool as they were pale. Orange trees and lemon trees grew amid the vines, the vivid golds and yellows of their fruit as bright as lamps.

'I can so easily picture the times of Homer,' John commented. '*The Odyssey, The Iliad*. The ancient Greeks occupied much of this area in their day.'

'I can't imagine anything more dream-like,' Rhianna said over the rattle of the carriage wheels and the clip-clop of the pair of red-plumed, piebald horses that hauled them at a rapid trot.

'How hard they work these horses,' John commented. 'They whirl along at the same pace, up and down these hills. Driven by the desire to shift as many tourists as possible, I expect.'

Another carriage passed them in the opposite direction, with luggage strapped to it. No railway had whistled round the undulating curves of this Eden beyond Castellamare. No railway had tainted its exquisite remoteness with smoke and the stench of steam cylinder oil.

Rhianna said, 'I shall look on this as our honeymoon, John. I can't imagine any place more romantic . . . Oh, look at those children . . .' A band of ragamuffins, running barefoot like wood nymphs in the white pumice dust, ran to greet them, waving flowers and laughing. 'Oh, throw them a few soldis, John.'

John felt in his pocket and tossed his small change to them.

'Grazie, signore, grazie!' they called in response.

'It's a bit wearing having so many beggars everywhere,' he remarked. 'But their sun-flushed, smiling faces are a delight.'

They drove on, past long-forgotten Roman settlements, past fishing villages that nestled hidden within the curves of the shore far below. They skirted an unbroken chain of enchanting bays through this long range of thickly-clad hills that sloped steeply to the sea. Near a place called Meta, they crossed a bridge that spanned a wide ravine before the road turned inland, only to switch back in the opposite direction towards the sea. At the little town of Sant' Agnello, whitewashed shrines to the Madonna and Child, set in the corners of sunny walls, hid under the trellises of cascading roses in full bloom and dense curtains of wisteria.

Eventually, the carriage descended the gentle slope that led down to the shelf overlooking the Bay of Naples, on which stood Sorrento. They arrived at the Hotel Tramontano, a fine house perched on the very edge of a high cliff and with a large, well-tended garden. John paid the driver, who unstrapped their luggage, and it was taken in by a concierge who came running out to greet them.

At the east side of the Hotel Tramontano, between it and the church and monastery of San Francesco, lay a garden with a terrace poised high over the Tyrrhenian Sea. Rose bushes luxuriated in the shade of huge umbrella pines and ancient olives. To the right, a steep path zigzagged down to the Marina Piccola where small boats bobbed between the rocks. John sat at his easel with a box of watercolours, a jar of water and several brushes, painting. Rhianna was relaxing in the shade of one of the picturesque umbrella trees, immersed in the early chapters of Trollope's *The Way We Live Now*. Behind them, at the rear of the church, stood a *caffè* with tables and chairs laid out before it, shaded by another cluster of trees.

John looked purposefully out over the blue sea. Across the bay to the north-east stood Vesuvius, serene and majestic. Its conical sides, clad in spring greenery, belied its potential for havoc. Almost directly north lay the Isle of Ischia and its smaller neighbour Procida, both indistinguishable from the mainland from this viewpoint. John marvelled at the transparency of the light as he put the finishing touches to a study of the striking vista in front of him.

It was 18th May 1890, Rhianna's twenty-fourth birthday.

'For my birthday, please tell me that we can spend the rest of our days here.'

He laughed, turning his head to catch her expression. 'What is it especially that you like about this part of Italy? What makes you want to come and live here?'

'I'm surprised you need to ask when you see the answer before you? It's everything. The beauty of it, the sunshine, the warmth, the atmosphere—'

'The light?' he interjected.

'If you say so. But the people as well, John. Most are as poor as church mice but they are still so generous with what little they have, and so hospitable.'

'And the food doesn't disagree with you?'

'I love the food. You know I do.'

'Even that sausage you had yesterday, made with donkey meat?'

'What sausage? Oh, I wish you hadn't told me that. I'll never eat sausage again.'

He laughed. 'It's not in all sausage. Only certain sausage from the north, from Tuscany, I think.'

'So what about you?' she asked. 'What else besides the quality of the light would make you want to stay here?'

'The pleasing lack of impressionist painters. Damned French.'

'And you don't like the French, do you?'

'I don't like impressionism – all those dots . . . And it's nothing to do with Fernanda's husband, if that's what you're thinking. Although he did muck about with that impressionist stuff.'

The sun's insidious journey across the sky had left Rhianna bathed in sunshine.

'I'm getting hot. I shall look like a farm worker if my skin gets tanned. Shall we have a drink at that *caffè*? It's still in the shade, look.'

'Give me five minutes. I just want to put the finishing touches to this.'

Presently, John left his easel where it stood, with the painting still upon it, his colours lying on his folding stool, and took Rhianna's hand. The owner of the *caffè* was a tallish man in his mid-thirties with sparkling blue eyes and a moustache that swirled at the ends and made him look exceedingly dashing. As soon as he saw Rhianna sitting at one of his tables his eyes lit up and he made his way towards her purposefully, the very essence of Neapolitan charm. Rhianna asked for orange juice and John ordered a glass of white wine. He returned to deliver both drinks to their table and his smile for Rhianna lingered warmly as he asked if they would like to eat.

'Bruschetta and salami for me,' John replied.

'Is the salami made with the meat from a donkey?' Rhianna queried in her stilted Italian.

The Italian roared with laughter. He leaned back and yelled into the kitchen, 'Concetta, is the donkey still out the back? . . . *Sì?* . . . Well, my donkey hasn't gone missing, signora.'

Rhianna laughed with embarrassment and hid her face to hide her blushes.

'I assure you, only the finest pork goes into our salami. No donkey meat.'

'Very well, I'll have salami and bruschetta too.'

'Very good. And you may stop blushing now,' the *caffè* owner teased her with a broad grin.

He quickly brought their food and, when John ordered more drinks, he dallied at their table. He introduced his wife, a handsome-looking young woman with hair the colour of burnt sienna and eyes to match, whom Rhianna estimated to be in her mid-twenties. She and an assistant attended to other customers, from time to time stopping by to join the conversation her husband was conducting.

'So, you are from England. How long have you been in Italy?'

'Since last November.' John explained. 'We have been living in Rome. We are visiting the Bay of Naples for a couple of weeks. The problem is, we like it so much here I think we want to stay. I can just as easily work here as in Rome. I am an artist, you see. I paint.'

'You paint? Oh, *si, si*. I did not know there were any English artists. I thought all artists were Italian.'

John smiled tolerantly.

'Are you a good artist?'

'Only Raphael is better,' Rhianna proclaimed, in her limited Italian. 'But that's his opinion, not mine.'

'Oh, splendid! Your wife believes you are better than Raphael!' He laughed good-naturedly. 'What a wife to praise her husband so. What is your name, signora?'

'Rhianna.'

'Rhianna . . . Rhianna . . .' He allowed the word to swirl around his mouth, savouring the sound of it. 'And yours signore?'

'John.'

'May I call you Gianni?'

'Of course.'

'I am Pasquale. My wife is Concetta. I would like to see some of your work, Gianni.'

'If we find somewhere to live close by you could see masses of it,' John answered.

The man threw his arms out in an expansive Italian gesture, suddenly serious. 'I have a house. You can live in it. The rent is very cheap to an English artist.'

'You have a vacant house?' Rhianna queried. 'Near to here?'

'You want to see it? I can take you. See if you like it.'

John turned to Rhianna and said in English. 'It'd be a good idea to rent first to see if we really take to the area.' Then in Italian, he said, 'Yes we'd like to see this house. Is it far?'

'About half an hour from here.'

'Do we walk there?'

'We can go part of the way in my cart.' He looked at Rhianna mischievously. 'It's a happy coincidence that my donkey did not end up in the salami . . . since we need him to pull the cart now.'

Rhianna chuckled and John left to fetch his painting from the terrace.

'You are a very beautiful English woman,' Pasquale said while John was out of earshot. 'Such skin as you have is made for stroking.'

'Thank you, Pasquale,' she answered. 'John already makes quite an occupation of it.'

He laughed aloud at her candour. 'I am very glad to hear it. Otherwise it would be such a waste. Do you have children?'

Rhianna smiled and shook her head.

'But you will. Soon.'

'Soon enough, I daresay.' She blushed at his directness. 'And you? Do you and Concetta have children?'

'We have a young son. His name is Alberto. He is with my wife's mother today.'

John returned with his painting and his equipment, which Pasquale invited him to leave at the *caffè* for safe keeping. The three of them then trooped across the garden. The donkey had been standing in the shade with its nose in a trough. Pasquale hitched it up to his antiquated cart and invited them to jump aboard.

After weaving through narrow cobbled streets they crossed the main road, high above the Tyrrhenian Sea, that wound its twisting way through the peninsula to Amalfi and Ravello.

'Your wife's name,' John said to Pasquale. 'Concetta . . . It sounds Spanish.'

'It is of Spanish origin. But the Spanish ruled this part of Italy for three centuries. It is not surprising they left some legacy.'

'How old is your son?' Rhianna asked.

'He is nearly three years old. Maybe it's time we had more children. But in a morning my wife is keen to get out of bed and put her silkworms next to me for warmth. before I have the chance to make another baby.'

'Silkworms?'

'Yes. Every May she takes the seeds and tends them as if they were children. They are most precious. She wraps them in fine linen and puts them in our bed to keep them warm. Not a breath of breeze is allowed to flurry them. When the seeds are hatched they are fed on fresh mulberry leaves. They are better looked after than me. We have a whole room taken up by trays of these hatched silkworms, all eating mulberry leaves. You wouldn't believe the quantity they eat. But it's woman's work, Gianni, breeding silkworms.'

They began a steep ascent inland and Pasquale stepped down from the cart. John did likewise.

'It is kinder to my donkey if we walk now. But not you, Rhianna. You must stay on the cart so that your legs don't grow too big from all this climbing steep hills. Gianni will thank me for that,' he added with a wink to John.

By this time they were travelling along a winding mule track with limestone walls on each side. Behind, lush vines clung to rough wooden pergolas among the lemon trees on the stepped hillsides. They passed smallholdings, one after the other, in various states of disrepair, but the delicate scent of lemons was all-pervading. Goats and mules grazed on anything they could get their tongues around in the heat of the day. Chickens flapped lazily and small lizards scattered in all directions out of the way of the travellers.

'This track is called Via Montecorbo,' said Pasquale after they had travelled some distance, climbing higher and higher. 'Eventually it would take us to the town of Massa Lubrense.' He pointed to his left. 'That track leads to the house of my sister and brother-in-law . . . And this track to my right leads to the house of my father-in-law.'

'It's good that you all live so close,' Rhianna commented.

'Oh, *si* . . . And up that hill is where I live with my Concetta and Alberto . . . Now . . . the house that is empty . . . is just here on the left . . .'

He stopped the cart, Rhianna stepped down and looked about her. A gate set in a limestone arch was the only evidence of the house. Pasquale opened it and they walked together up a steep path in the cool shade of an olive grove through which a gentle breeze wafted, rustling the leaves. Vines grew in abundance as they did everywhere, clothing the rough-hewn pergolas in a dense green coat and already bearing tiny bunches of grapes. Then the house came into view, high on the hill. It was a two-storey affair constructed of limestone and did not look in exceptional condition, but it had a magnificent view across the Bay of Naples. Its roof was of red clay tiles, typical of the region. A tiled patio abutted the house, shaded by a pergola of vines which cast a dappled shade that danced to the rustle of a light breeze blowing from the south-west.

'Here is *paradiso*, eh? I will show you inside. It is very spacious.'

After entering through a heavy wooden door that was not locked, Pasquale led them into a large room. The stone walls had been whitewashed and needed doing again, but it was quite habitable. A primitive wooden table, which Pasquale referred to as a *madia*, and used for making pasta, had four chairs already set around it. In one corner was a stone fireplace with a chain extending up the chimney, from which hung a copper pot. Pasquale made the comment that it could be cold and damp up here in winter. Alongside the fireplace, and also built of stone was what Pasquale referred to as a *fornello a carbone*, a charcoal-burning stove.

The solitary window looked south-west towards Capri – the first full view they had had of the island. Beneath the window was a stone sink that emptied through a pipe to the outside world.

'Who lived here before?' Rhianna asked.

'My mother,' Pasquale replied solemnly, making the sign of the cross. 'She died a year ago.'

Rhianna expressed her regret as they followed him outside, in order to get upstairs by way of the stone staircase that ran up the side of the building. There were two rooms, beamed and raftered, divided by a thin plastered partition. The front bedroom opened onto a wooden balcony. John and Rhianna stepped out onto it together. Below, to their left, they could see the Isle of Capri, its sheer cliffs thrusting up from the sea in two distinct areas, like the two visible humps of a submerged camel. Straight ahead, but at a much greater distance, lay Ischia with its less spectacular topography. To the right of Ischia the plain of Naples rose gently to blend with the cone of Vesuvius. Surely, this was the most outstanding view in all the world.

'I think I could happily wake up to this every morning,' Rhianna commented in English and John heard the catch of longing in her voice. 'Oh, John, I think it's perfect. Can we have it?'

'But we haven't seen it all yet.'

'We don't need to. I just know it's ideal for us. As Pasquale says, it's paradise.'

He smiled with deep affection. First let's see how much rent he expects us to pay.'

Reluctantly, she nodded her agreement and they followed Pasquale across the dusty wooden floorboards into the back bedroom. From there, he marched them back down the stone steps to another room at the side of the house. It turned out to be a type of outhouse and in it was a collection of old tools, a stack of wine barrels and a rack of old, empty wine bottles. From hooks in the wall hung other tools; a scythe, a rake, a triangular spade with a long handle, an axe. In a corner stood an old wine press.

'Now I'll show you the *palazzo*,' Pasquale said with a gleam in his eye and led them to a small, roofless, stone-built construction that stood in the shade of an orange tree at one end of the plot. He pushed the door open and its hinges creaked in protest.

'The privy!' Rhianna chuckled, at which Pasquale smiled.

Pasquale led them away and they stood either side of him in the garden. 'I myself have tended these vines . . . They will yield a good harvest. Naturally, the wine from the grapes that grow here would be yours. Also, the olives. You would need plenty of olive oil to cook with and as fuel for your lamps.'

'We rather like this place, Pasquale,' John said. 'I think we would like to rent it. You would have no objection to us renovating it to our liking?'

'It needs some work, I agree. But it's not a problem.'

'Where would we get our water?' Rhianna enquired.

'From the roof. It is collected during rainfall and stored in a cistern.'

They came to an arrangement on the rent that suited both.

'When would you like to take occupation?' Pasquale asked.

'First we shall have to return to Rome to wind up our affairs and arrange for our belongings to be brought here . . . Can we say the thirty-first of May?'

'Of course. When you arrive I will introduce you to the rest of your neighbours.'

'Mostly your family, it seems,' John commented.

The Italian laughed. '*Si*. My family and my wife's family.'

Back in Rome, all arrangements had been made to leave the Villa Strohl-Fern. Their belongings had been packed up and a carter was due to collect them the following day for onward transmission to Naples.

John had had an idea for a new painting. Rhianna was posing with a bowl in her left hand, her right arm outstretched, supposedly dropping crumbs into an ornamental fish pond.

'How long before I can rest, Gianni?' she asked. She had taken to the Italian version of his name as used by Pasquale, and John did not object in the least. 'My arm's aching, holding this bowl out so long.'

'Rest now if you're tired, my love.' He put down his blacklead and stretched. 'Now is as good a time as any . . . We'll have a drink and then I want to take you somewhere.'

'Oh? Somewhere nice, you mean?'

'Somewhere rather special.'

'Somewhere far to walk?'

'Somewhere close by, actually.'

'Tell me.'

He chuckled. 'No. You'll very likely think me mad. You'll see when we get there.'

'I'm intrigued . . . In the meantime, what do you want to drink?'

'Some tea, I think.'

'I'll make some. Then I'll get changed if we're going out.'

'Wear something very special,' he called as she went inside.

After sorting through what was not already packed, she reappeared in a high-necked cream-coloured blouse in light cotton and a matching skirt, her dark hair piled up on her head beneath a straw boater.

'Oh, very elegant.'

'Thank you, Gianni. Are you going to tell me where you are taking me?'

'You'll see.'

Hand in hand, they left the grounds of the Villa Strohl-Fern and, within minutes, were walking across the Piazzale Flaminio towards the Piazza del Popolo.

'Here . . .' He pointed. 'This is where we are going. This church. Santa Maria del Popolo.'

It looked nothing from the outside; just a whitewashed baroque façade that, compared to the splendid architecture that surrounded it, seemed insignificant.

'This church was designed by Raphael, whom you insist is inferior to me.'

'Well, this is nothing to shout about, is it?'

But, when she saw inside, Rhianna gasped, her breath taken away not only by the beauty of the place but also the quietness and cool sanctity. They were all alone in there, and her footsteps on the stone flags and marble memorial slabs echoed through the nave, many times amplified.

'This place is a treasure-trove of masterpieces,' John whispered reverently. 'I came here the other day on my way to the bank. I thought you should see it before we leave for Naples.'

'It's magnificent, Gianni. It makes me want to cry.'

He smiled at that. 'Beauty should never make you cry. Beauty should always be uplifting.'

'But once you've experienced something like this it breaks your heart to let go of it. And yet we must. It's even more beautiful than St Peter's basilica.'

'Here, look at this painting . . .' He stopped at a side chapel and pointed. 'It's by Caravaggio. "The Crucifixion of Saint Peter".' John stared at the painting for what seemed ages, then stood for another age admiring the other Caravaggio, 'The Conversion of St Paul'. 'It's amazing how, in all these churches, you come across masterpieces as if they are nothing.'

Rhianna wandered into another annex, another chapel, one of the many commissioned by illustrious families and decorated in appropriate splendour. It could so easily have been the setting for one of John's paintings with the sweep of its intricately carved marble and the niches in which stood exquisite statues.

'That statue is by Bernini, who designed St Peter's Square,' John whispered when he had caught up with her. 'The other, there, is by Lorenzetto. Masterpieces all. Absolute master-pieces.'

'I've never heard of Lorenz— who?' she said.

'Lorenzetto. Well, I'll forgive you.' He looked into her eyes and took her hand. His face bore an earnest expression and she could tell that something was on his mind.

'What is it, Gianni?'

'Come and sit over here . . .' He led her to a pew nearer the altar and they sat down. 'You are going to think me utterly stupid . . . but forgive me, Rhianna my love. I have to do this . . .'

Tears welled in his eyes and she was moved to weep herself as she watched him intently. He had evidently reached some crisis of emotion and was about to tell her of a decision he had made that would radically affect her. At once her heart began beating faster with apprehension.

He took both her hands in his as he sat beside her. 'I am so afraid of losing you, Rhianna . . .'

The old uncertainty. The irreconcilable lack of confidence.

She sighed profoundly, looking straight into his eyes. 'You are the world to me, Gianni,' she whispered. 'The sun, the moon and the stars. You are never going to lose me. I won't let you. You make me happier than I've ever been in my life. I'll never let you go.'

'I'm happy to hear it.'

'I'm happy to declare it over and over. So what are you trying to say to me?'

'Just that . . . if we were wed . . .' He coughed to clear the lump in his throat. 'If we were wed I would feel more a part of you. You would feel more a part of me in turn. We have to be married to make our union complete, to complete the circle of our love.'

'But I'm already married. And Lawson won't divorce me until and unless it suits him.'

He was nodding his acknowledgement as she spoke. 'I know all that, my love. Of course I know it. I know you can never be my wife in the eyes of the law while you are married to him. But I'm going to marry you anyway! . . . Right here, right now. In this most beautiful of churches. I think it's very appropriate that I should marry you before God in this famous and wondrous church of Santa Maria del Popolo . . .'

'I don't see how we *can* marry yet, Gianni.'

John smiled mysteriously, almost dreamily and took from his pocket the Book of Common Prayer, which he opened up at the Solemnisation of Matrimony.

'I don't suppose the Catholic ceremony differs greatly from the Anglican,' he said taking her hand again. 'So here goes . . . *I take thee, Rhianna, to my wedded wife, to have and to hold from this day forward, for better for worse, for richer for poorer, in sickness and in health, to love and to cherish till death us do part, according to God's holy ordinance; and thereto I plight thee my troth.*'

'Oh, Gianni,' Rhianna sighed, exquisitely moved.

'Now you say this part . . .' He turned the prayer book towards her.

She ignored the book, looked directly into his soft eyes with love oozing from hers, and recited softly by heart, '*I Rhianna*

take thee, John Mallory, to my wedded husband, to have and
to hold from this day forward, for better for worse, for richer
for poorer, in sickness and in health, to love, cherish and to
obey, till death us do part, according to God's holy ordinance;
and thereto I give thee my troth.'

John fished in the pocket of his jacket and pulled out a gold
ring. Gently, he slipped it on the bare, slender third finger of
Rhianna's left hand and looked into her eyes, which were
brimming with tears.

'With this ring I thee wed, with my body I thee worship,
and with all my worldly goods I thee endow.'

She held her hand out to look at the ring. She put it to her
lips, kissed it, smiled at him and then wept. He took her in
his arms and she buried her face in his shoulder, overcome by
the spontaneity of this most unexpected, ultimately meaningful
gesture. Nothing more needed to be said. Both understood it
was a symbolic act of the utmost significance, though it bore
no legal weight. It was simply a very private and personal vow
made between them to endorse the love and commitment they
had for each other. In their eyes, however, it was as binding
and as real as if it had been conducted by the Pope himself in
the sanctity of St Peter's.

After some minutes, Rhianna took a handkerchief from the
sleeve of her blouse. She wiped her eyes and blew her nose,
looked at him and smiled, tearful but very happy.

'I do love you, Gianni. Oh, with all my heart . . . I'll never
forget this day . . .' She sniffed and wiped her nose again. 'I'll
have no conscience ever about calling myself Mrs Gibson from
now on.'

24

On the day of their return to Sorrento, John and Rhianna booked into the Hotel Tramontano once more, making it their base while they acquired enough furniture to make their new home comfortable. As soon as they unpacked the clothes they would need, they headed for the *caffè* of Pasquale and Concetta.

'Ah, *molto bene*!' Pasquale exclaimed when he saw them, and Rhianna saw the genuine delight in his eyes. 'You have returned. I'm so happy to see you. And you, Rhianna . . . You are more beautiful than ever.'

'Thank you.'

'Gianni, you are a very fortunate man to have so beautiful a wife.'

'You are right on both counts, Pasquale . . . Well, we are here . . . ready to commence the business of living in the hills overlooking Sorrento and the Bay of Naples.'

'Concetta!' Pasquale called, and Concetta appeared from the back room, a radiant smile on her face as she greeted them. 'I am taking Rhianna and Gianni to the house. Look after the *caffè*.'

The ride up into the hills was not unfamiliar now. Every twist and turn in the mule track that took them to the house was no longer a surprise, half remembered from the first time they had travelled it. Pasquale was full of good humour and it was not difficult to take to his easy-going, charming ways. He took them first to his own house and, whilst they were there, they were obliged to drink a glass of his wine, from last year's *vendemmia* he said, and to see the trays of silkworms that were consuming mulberry leaves at an absurd rate.

'But they are so noisy,' Rhianna said incredulously. 'I can hear them chomping away.'

Pasquale handed John the key – made of iron, large and extremely ornate – to *Paradiso*, for that was what they had decided to call this new home.

'Even the keys are beautiful in Italy,' John said in English to Rhianna as he handled it sensitively.

'Let us go on to your house now,' Pasquale suggested. He insisted that Rhianna ride on his cart while he led the donkey.

Very soon, they were walking up the shaded path that led through the garden of *Paradiso*. Something seemed different, Rhianna thought. Everything was tidier. The ground had been dug over, the weeds were gone. The vines were trained more deliberately over the pergolas.

'Somebody has been busy,' she commented.

Pasquale smiled dismissively. 'My brother-in-law and me. His name is Pietro. You will meet him later.' They arrived at the house. 'You will not need the key, Gianni. The door is not locked. We are no longer troubled by marauding Barbary pirates.'

'Perhaps I should carry you over the threshold, Mrs Gibson,' John suggested.

'I've already been over the threshold,' she quipped. 'Save your strength.'

Inside, the house was a revelation and Rhianna gasped with delight. 'The walls have been whitewashed . . . and the ceiling. The floor has been cleaned and . . . Oh, Pasquale, you have been very busy. Thank you. We didn't expect this.'

'I could hardly rent a house to an English gentleman and his beautiful wife if it was not fit for my donkey to live in. Upstairs, too, we have been at work as you will see.'

Upstairs, too, they *had* been at work. The beams and rafters had been swept off, cleaned and painted, the walls had been whitewashed, the floorboards had been cleaned and freshly varnished, the window frames painted. A handmade rug lay on the floor of the bedroom that looked out over the Bay of Naples, and Rhianna commented on it.

'It is a gift from Francesca, my sister-in-law. She made it when she knew you were coming here to live.'

'That's really kind. And she doesn't even know us.' Rhianna was taken aback by all this kindness and consideration, which she had not anticipated. She looked at John, who also seemed overwhelmed. 'These folk are so hospitable,' she said quietly in English.

John nodded and said to Pasquale, 'Today we have to decide what furniture we need to buy before we can live here. Most important is a bed.'

'Oh, yes,' Pasquale answered with a knowing look. 'I agree. A bed is most important, especially when you have such a beautiful and pleasant wife to put in it. But tonight you can sleep at my house. We have a bed for you. We have to pay a tax on it – it might as well be used.'

Rhianna looked at John, then at Pasquale. 'Oh, that's not necessary. We wouldn't dream of putting you to all that trouble. We have an hotel room waiting for us in Sorrento.'

'But it's no trouble. It's all arranged. Tonight you are to be my guests. We shall eat, Francesca will sing for us and Pietro will play his *fisarmonica*. It's all arranged.'

Rhianna and John felt entirely at ease with Pasquale and Concetta Amitrano and Pietro and Francesca Bellaria. It was a warm evening with just a light breeze coming over the headland from the south-west. Conversation and laughter never stalled during that glorious evening at the table on the patio which looked out onto the Bay of Naples.

Rhianna thanked Francesca for the gift of the rug, and Pietro for helping Pasquale with the work on the house. 'I think we shall be very happy here with neighbours like you,' she said. 'And to be so lucky in finding a place with such a view.' For an instant she mentally compared it with the grim view from Lawson's front-room window overlooking the slag heaps and the Union catch pound. She shuddered at everything else that the association invoked and quickly shut if from her mind. How different life was now.

The Italians wanted to know about *Inghilterra*, if the weather was ever this good, if the food was this good, if the *vino* was this good. They wanted to know whether Queen Victoria was still in mourning over her Albert and was it true that the Prince of Wales was a regular Casanova. They wanted to know if there were any railways in Britain and Concetta gossiped about a young widow in the village who'd had a daughter two years after her husband had passed away.

'It's a *miracolo*,' Francesca declared naïvely. 'A gift from God.'

'It's no miracle,' Pasquale said disdainfully.

'But the child is so like her husband. Of course it's a miracle.'

Pasquale laughed heartily. 'That's because her husband's brother is the father of the child.'

'No!' Francesca protested in disbelief. 'But she's not that sort of woman.'

Pasquale threw his hands into the air in a gesture of despair at Francesca's naïvety and they all laughed. 'Everybody knows it. Everybody knows he has been calling on her to give her *consolazione*. Everybody knows it except you, Francesca.'

'No, I don't believe it. The child is a gift from God for being a good Catholic. It's no different to the Immaculate Conception.'

'Have some more *vino*, Gianni, Rhianna.'

The children – four in all since Francesca and Pietro had two sons and a daughter – had eaten with the adults. Earlier they had been the centre of attention but now, while the grown-ups talked and drank wine, the children played in the garden amid the vines, the lemon trees and the olives, their excited voices from time to time punctuating the peace and tranquillity.

As the swollen red orb of the sun hovered over the sea in a cloudless sky, Rhianna imagined they were her own children playing safely there. The time must come when she and John would be so blessed; it could surely not be too long. They would be Italians, her children, born and bred in Italy, though of English parents of course. They would grow up steeped in Italian culture, in Italian values, in Italian traditions. Rhianna had no qualms about that. What she had seen of the country and its people had only delighted her. She had every admiration for them, rich and poor alike. She fondly recalled her own childhood, compared it to what she might expect for her children. She thought about her father, the mutual affection which they had enjoyed throughout all those happy years. Now it was spoilt, destroyed because her mother and sister refused to understand *her* feelings, *her* position. They even sided with her scoundrel of a husband. Well, they were pitifully misguided; soon enough they would discover what Lawson Maddox was really like, the roguery of which he was capable.

She pondered some of the incidents that had peppered her childhood and was lost in a pleasant reverie of nostalgia for her father. She did not hear the animated Italian voices and penetrating laughter; not until Pasquale had called her name three times.

'What are you smiling at, Rhianna?' he said. 'You see how she is smiling, Concetta. But it's at something inside her head.'

She looked at Pasquale, at Concetta, then at John and took his hand. 'Oh, I was miles away. Back in England when I was a little girl.'

'Please tell us about it,' Concetta entreated.

In her middling Italian Rhianna said, 'You asked whether

the wine in England is as good as it is here. My father used to make wine from all kinds of fruit and from flowers . . .'

'Because it's difficult to grow grapes in the English climate,' John interjected.

'Well,' Rhianna went on, 'I was just thinking about a time once when I was helping him. We had been to the fields and picked some blackberries – we can make wine from blackberries – and he asked me to add the sugar to the must, but I added washing soda by mistake because the bags looked alike.'

They all roared with laughter.

'And was your father angry?' Francesca asked.

'No. He didn't stop laughing for a week.'

'*Bravo!* He sounds like a typical Italian,' Concetta commented.

Rhianna did not feel inclined to discuss her family further for fear she let slip anything about their rift, and about Lawson, so steered the conversation away by asking about Pasquale's late mother. For half an hour, his family was discussed and then Pietro, who had been missing for five minutes, returned carrying an accordion.

'*Bene*, let's sing. Do you know how Italians love to sing, Rhianna?'

The sun was about to drop into the sea, to be quenched like a blob of molten glass. The sky above the horizon was aflame but overhead it was darkening.

They sang.

Oh, magical songs, magical harmonies underlying magical Italian melodies. Pasquale had a fine tenor voice, Concetta a vivid soprano. Francesca's voice was a rich contralto and Pietro's a robust bass. And how they used them. Rhianna and John listened spellbound to this impromptu but pure singing which matched the setting, the weather and the perfect evening. Rhianna looked at John and smiled, the sunset's orange glow casting a golden richness onto her skin. He touched her hand. There was something about this moment she would never forget. This wondrous place, this *Paradiso*. This flawless weather. This wonderful song. This compelling company. Oh, this extraordinary new way of life. It was people working with nature to provide perfection. Never had she been so happy. Never had she been so content. There was such a future here to look forward to with the man she loved. And she loved this delectable man with a passion she would have thought impossible . . .

They stayed only one night with Pasquale and Concetta. To have stayed longer – even though they would have been welcomed – would have been an overindulgence, so royally were they treated. Next day, Sunday, when they arose, their Italian hosts were dressed ready to go to church.

'Are you coming with us?' Concetta asked.

'Not today,' John replied. 'We have to go back to our hotel. But some other Sunday, yes.'

'You are not Catholics?'

'Protestants,' he said.

'Ah, *protestanti*,' Concetta replied as if he was afflicted with some sort of disease. 'But we like you all the same. We must convert you . . .'

Rhianna and John returned to the Hotel Tramontano, anxious for the next day to arrive, when the shops would open and they could buy some serviceable furniture, utensils and provisions. By Tuesday, their chattels had arrived from Rome and, by Wednesday, enough of what they had purchased was delivered, including a bed and bedding, and they spent their first night together at *Paradiso*.

By Friday, John was anxious to recommence working. His latest picture remained unfinished, so he set up his easel on the patio under the *pergole* and painted.

That evening, Pasquale and Concetta called in with their son, Alberto on their way home from the *caffè* and brought with them a pot wrapped in paper which they handed to Rhianna.

'A present for you,' Pasquale said proudly. '*Gnocchi*. You should eat them tonight while they are fresh.'

'Thank you. But only if you will join us and share them with us.'

'We would be honoured, providing you have time,' Concetta said. 'But you must be very busy.'

'I have all the time in the world.' She took the lid off the pot in which Concetta had delivered them. 'Anyway, what's the best way to cook them? I've never had *gnocchi* before.'

'*Gnocchi* are easy but so nice to eat. I will show you what to do. As a matter of fact, I will help you with everything.'

'You're so generous, Concetta, you and Pasquale.'

'Concetta!' Pasquale called, interrupting them. 'Come and see this . . .' He had wandered onto the patio and seen John's painting for the first time. Concetta joined him and stood at his side. Rhianna followed. 'Concetta, look at this. Have you ever seen anything so beautiful?'

Concetta gasped. 'Gianni . . . This is *your* work?'

John nodded.

'Oh, it is a masterpiece, Gianni,' she said excitedly. 'It takes my breath away. I have never seen anything so beautiful, so perfect . . . Look, Pasquale. That is surely Rhianna . . .' She pointed to the figure in the painting, clad in a flowing blue dress.

'Your wife was to be believed when she said you were better than Raphael, Signore Gianni,' Pasquale said with renewed respect. 'Of course, I thought she was exaggerating your ability . . . But now . . .' He paused to admire the image of Rhianna again. 'Your Madonna is far more beguiling.'

'But I paint my Madonna in different situations, Pasquale. As a Catholic, I hope you approve.'

'Oh, yes, Gianni. Michelangelo, Raphael, Caravaggio . . .' He hunched his shoulders and held out his hands in a typical

Italian gesture. 'They all painted their Madonnas. I doubt whether the Vatican approved of them all. But me? I am not so prudish. Your Madonna is the essence of femininity and beauty, but she seems unaware of the power of either. If I am any judge, it seems she has no desire to exploit her charms. That makes her all the more fascinating.'

John smiled. 'Thank you, Pasquale. I am happy that you approve. But credit must go to Rhianna. She is an excellent model.'

'She is very beautiful, as I have commented many times . . . Oh, I love this painting, Gianni.'

'Then it is yours. I would like you to have it.'

'But Gianni . . .'

'Please. I insist. It can never repay your kindness to us, who were strangers in your country.'

'Oh, you were strangers here but once,' Concetta said kindly. 'We are so happy to have you as our friends.'

'We are also happy to accept your gift,' Pasquale said. 'Thank you, my friend.'

Rhianna felt her eyes fill with tears at these touching expressions of amity. She had said nothing, only listened, watching the reactions of the Italian couple to John's work, how John responded. He was at ease with them, which said much. And she was glad of it. Now she pushed back the tears, smiled and said, 'I'll get started with the food.'

Next day, Rhianna felt compelled to write to her family. She was entirely happy and wanted to declare it and share her happiness with them.

Dear Mother, Father and Sarah,
I do wish you could be with me if only for one day to experience this Place where John and I have decided to live. It is indeed Paradise on Earth, so much so that we have decided to call the house Paradiso, *which is the Italian word. It is such*

a strange coincidence, I suppose, that we should call it by the same name as where you live in Dudley. But this is truly the Paradise of Eden and nothing about dear old Dudley could influence our choice of name. We overlook the Bay of Naples if you want to find it in your Atlas. As we look out of our bedroom window we can see the Island of Capri with its steep cliffs on one side and Mt Vesuvius (which erupted only 2 years ago, they say) on the other.

Our neighbours are the kindliest of people and have made us very welcome. I must say that all the locals are gentle and gracious and so polite. I imagine they would like us even better if we were both men, since so many have left the area to seek their fortunes in America and Argentina. There certainly seems too many unmarried girls for the available men. The weather is unbelievably warm and sunny, but the breezes are cooling and very welcome.

John is inspired to paint and I know he will produce his best work ever here. Although I have told you before how shy he is, he is not so with these people who have been so kind.

There is so much for me to learn here. We have our own vineyard with orange trees and lemon trees growing through the pergolas. They tell me that they harvest the oranges and lemons in December and April, so we just missed the last harvest. The blossom and the leaves give off a lovely scent all the time. We have olive trees as well, which we shall harvest in October after the grapes. Of course, I shall have to tend all these while John is busy working. Olives are so plentiful that they even use the oil for burning in the lamps. I have developed quite a taste for olives now. The grapes we are due to harvest in late September and Concetta and Pasquale, our friends have promised to help us make our own wine.

If you could see the tan I've got you would swear I was a farm-worker, which I suppose I am now. And yet I love it. I have never been so happy as I am here in Sorrento with John. I have taken to wearing typical Italian dress – a cotton

*handkerchief around my neck, white linen sleeves tucked up
at the elbow, a short-waisted little bodice, a wide apron
and a cotton skirt that is very light and shows my shins.
Of course it is too warm to wear stockings here and none
of the women do. Some don't even wear shoes, just twisted
cloths tied around their ankles.*

*You might find it hard to believe but since coming to Italy
I have learnt to speak Italian. It's true. There is no choice
really because so few Italians speak English that you can
understand. I am nowhere near as fluent as John but I am
getting better all the time and I understand everything that
is said to me. In this part of Italy though, they speak with
an accent that is harder to grasp and some of the words they
use are different to those they use in Rome.*

*Mother, if you could see me, you would not begrudge me
my contentment. Please make it complete by getting our
Sarah to write to me. Overlook your prejudices and give
me your blessing at last. I hope you are all keeping well
and that Father's gout is not too painful. My love goes to
Sarah and I hope she is still enjoying working at Hillman's.
If you happen to see Lawson you may tell him I'm well and
very happy.*

Your ever loving daughter,
Rhianna.

Summer came and went in an endless series of perfect days
and heady nights. Rhianna and John acquired a cow and
Concetta taught her how to milk it. They acquired chickens
and thus a continuous supply of eggs. Rhianna tended the vines
conscientiously and took an obsessive interest in the grapes,
watching them grow fatter and sweeter by the week. Next
year they would plant more, although they would not reap
the benefit of such planting for another three years at least.
She cultivated a herb garden near the patio, grew tomatoes
that were big and round with a soft, mellow taste, and peppers

that were succulent. She learned how to make pasta, how to bake delicious breads in the charcoal oven, and was amazed at how much olive oil Concetta used in everything. No wonder they all grew their own olives. She continued to write to her family every week, walking down to Sorrento town to post her letter, taking advantage of the arduous walk to buy meat, flour, cheese and other provisions. And, while engaged in all these domestic and horticultural activities, she still found time to sit for John whenever he asked her to.

John continued to send work to his dealer in London and a steady stream of cheques flowed back. Pasquale asked him if he would consider using Concetta as a model in one of his typical settings and he would buy the subsequent painting. John assented and Concetta turned out to be a good subject. Out of respect for Pasquale and Alberto, John suggested she dress in garments less revealing than those Rhianna sometimes wore for his paintings, but Concetta had different ideas. She defiantly fetched a filmy red silk dress she had made herself, and was adamant she wear it. She was blessed with vivacious Italian looks – not quite beautiful but better than pretty – a round, expressive face with full lips and dark eyes that had the soft and wild look of a young doe. There was mischief in the sweetness of her smile, but an innocent mischief tempered by the constraints of her religion and the gentle community of which she was a part. Her lush black hair she wore in the becoming fashion of ancient Greece, which her Greek ancestors brought with them to Sorrento, divided at the back into two plaits, braided round her head like a crown, then fastened with black ribbon and a long silver bodkin she called a *spadella*.

Concetta had a younger brother, Serafino, nineteen years old, who was a waiter at the Hotel Tramontano. He had spotted Rhianna when she first arrived there with John. When he was not at table he fell into the habit of coming to the house and helping her with the heavy garden work. He had fallen hopelessly in love with Rhianna and would have done anything for her, always making excuses that he would come tomorrow and do this job or do that job. Concetta alerted her to Serafino's partiality and, subsequently, Rhianna was always very polite and chatty with him in her steadily improving Italian, but without giving him any encouragement at all.

Towards the end of September, Rhianna noticed that there were suddenly deliveries of huge barrels to the neighbouring houses. Pasquale explained that they were for the grape harvest. One day he called in to *Paradiso* on his way home from the *caffè*.

'Tomorrow we are holding our *vendemmia*,' he said with his usual bright smile. 'We would like you to join us if you can. The weather is set fair and it will be most enjoyable.'

'Of course, we would be delighted,' John replied.

'Good. Come at about half past six.'

'In the evening?' Rhianna queried.

Pasquale burst out laughing and his moustache widened across his handsome face. 'In the evening? Are you serious? No, half past six in the morning of course. But the early start will be well repaid, I promise you.'

'Don't worry, we'll be there.'

He touched Rhianna's arm affectionately. 'Wear your oldest clothes, *cara mia*. We don't want you to ruin your best outfit.'

'I suspect it's a compliment to be asked to a *vendemmia*,' John remarked when Pasquale had gone. 'They see us as honest and hard-working. Besides, I understand they make quite a thing of the grape harvest.'

So, at half past six next morning, John and Rhianna presented themselves in suitable attire at the house of Pasquale and Concetta. Rhianna wore an old cream blouse that buttoned down the front, with long sleeves to protect her arms from scratches, together with a long brown cotton skirt that had seen better days. On her head she wore a scarf in the style of the local women. Yet, even in her ancient, rustic garb, she looked wonderful, with her waist so slender and her back elegantly erect. Her hair was piled up on her head and held with pins, which gave a graceful set to her neck.

The sun was already climbing, though as yet it was still hidden by the hills, but the dawn sky was clear and the air was warm. It promised to be another good day.

Pietro and Francesca arrived with Concetta's brother, Serafino, who looked longingly at Rhianna and smiled. Others followed, neighbours, friends and relatives, people Rhianna did not know, all there to help. As they laughed and talked, Concetta stepped outside bearing a tray on which were mugs of coffee. She handed them round and Rhianna sipped hers.

'Good Lord!' she exclaimed. 'What's in this?'

'*Grappa*,' Concetta told her and laughed. 'Enjoy it.'

'It's strong. It will set us up for the day and no mistake.'

Everybody took a large basket and followed Pasquale, who had loaded his cart with ladders and the huge barrels. As they trooped behind the cart the air was perfectly still and the smoke rising in perpendicular columns from the cooking fires of the farmsteads that peppered the downward sweep, vied with the tall cypresses of the more ornate gardens.

In a few short minutes they were walking through green tunnels of vines, heavy with dew. The pergolas that formed these verdant galleries seemed overburdened with grapes. Pasquale unloaded some of his barrels and they began setting up the ladders for picking, and tables for sorting the grapes. Everybody was handed knives and John was posted with a ladder to a particular pergola and began cutting bunches of black grapes from the underside. Rhianna began gathering from the sides and putting the cut bunches into the basket she had been given. As soon as she had filled it, Serafino collected it and emptied it into one of the barrels before sheepishly returning it to her. On one occasion she plucked a grape from a bunch and flirtatiously put it to his mouth. His blush was vivid, but he opened his mouth and she, laughing, popped it in.

'Eat as many grapes as you like,' Concetta called, also laughing, having witnessed the exchange.

It was not long before the sun ascended over the hills bathing everything in a warm yellow glow, and the baskets and boxes began to fill up with grapes. Pasquale and Concetta stood on opposite sides of the table sorting them, discarding any bunches afflicted by mildew, keeping those with a velvety bloom on them – which was the yeast and bacteria that together would trigger the fermentation. These good grapes, stalks and all, went into the barrels which, when full, were loaded onto Pasquale's cart to be hauled up to the ground-level cellar at the house, to be crushed. As they were pressed, the juice flowed into other barrels that had been specially prepared, while empty barrels were returned to the table to be refilled with more sorted grapes.

After about three hours of intensively stripping vines, Rhianna turned to John who was working close by. 'Do you think those are Concetta's sisters carrying those hampers?'

John looked up. 'There is a facial resemblance.'

'I think they have food for everybody. Look, they're laying a table.'

'Break time,' John surmised. 'Thank goodness. I could do with a rest. No doubt you could too. It's hard work, this. But it seems to me that the vines are all but done now.'

Indeed, the work was soon afterwards declared finished and everybody was invited to take some refreshment. They were offered fresh bread, home-baked in a charcoal oven and still warm, cheese, mortadella and salami, tomatoes and fresh fruit. Jugs of red wine from last year's harvest appeared and everybody sat around on the ground, taking advantage of the break.

Then, the whole army of workers gathered up the equipment and headed for the house of Pietro and Francesca, and the whole process was repeated. Another picnic was supplied, everybody rested, then, to the complete surprise of Rhianna and John, they all moved to *Paradiso*. John complained that he had made no arrangements for the large barrels they used, but Pasquale had. And while the small army of tireless, willing workers stripped the vines and converted the grapes that were oozing juice into an unappetising mish-mash of dark liquid containing skins, stalks and pips, Rhianna began to panic that she might not have enough food to feed everybody afterwards, for that seemed to be the custom and the expectation.

She sought Concetta's advice.

'Don't worry. Do you have any *prosciutto*?'

'Ham? Yes, I have a whole leg of ham.'

'*Bene!* We can slice it into strips and put it into a sauce of tomatoes, onions, herbs and garlic. Served with cheese and pasta it will be a feast fit for your Queen Victoria. I will help you. And don't worry if you have no wine. We still have a whole barrel from last year.'

'Concetta, I don't know what I'd do without you.'

'You would cope easily. You are a born survivor.'

The two young women gossiped like old biddies, laughing as they worked together preparing the feast. Concetta talked about her silk harvest the month before, then told Rhianna about her sisters and their husbands, one of whom had gone to America with the promise that he would send for her when he was settled; that was more than a year ago and she hadn't heard from him since. She talked about their children, their in-laws, other neighbours. Rhianna was picking up the local accent, which amused Concetta, who taught her how to curse in Italian, this had them both chuckling.

'Tell me how you go about getting married in Sorrento,' Rhianna said, slicing tomatoes.

Concetta's eyes widened at Rhianna's apparent ignorance. 'But you are already married.'

'I am,' she replied, telling no lie. 'I mean the girls here. What is the custom?'

'Oh, the mother of the young man does the proposing.'

'The mother?'

'*Si*. She goes to the girl's mother and says, "I want this girl for my son". Then the girl's mother talks it over with her husband, both pairs of parents settle the money question, then it's up to the young couple to agree to the match.'

'I take it you and Pasquale had no trouble agreeing.'

'I have known Pasquale all my life, Rhianna. When I was a young girl he was a grown man and I idolised him. I have always been in love with him. For as long as I can remember.'

'And he with you.'

'Since I was about sixteen, I think. Else he would not have asked his mother to approach mine.'

'Did he not ask you first?'

'Yes . . .' Concetta smiled her mischievous smile. 'But such is the custom here, that the official approach had to come from his mother . . . I think I was lucky with so few men left . . . Also, I liked the house we were promised . . . The house we live in now . . .'

It was about seven o' clock by the time the *vendemmia* was finished. The sun, in a gold and rosy glow, dipped behind the umbrella pines on the hills to the west and darkness fell. One last barrel remained at the side of the patio, three-quarters full of black grapes waiting to be crushed.

'We shall finish it afterwards,' Pasquale said dismissively.

So the host of workers, all friends by this time, sat at the tables Rhianna and Concetta had made ready and they served the food. Jugs of delicious wine passed from one to another as everybody filled and refilled their glasses. Conversation was loud and animated and laughter rang through the cleared vines that Rhianna had tended so conscientiously. When they had all eaten, Pietro fetched his accordion and then the singing and dancing began.

'I don't know where they get their energy after such a hard day's work,' Rhianna commented to Pasquale.

'Oh, everybody has reserves of energy . . . as you will find out very soon,' he added mysteriously.

The moon came up, a silver crescent in a deep purple sky. Everybody danced. Everybody danced with everybody else in traditional Neapolitan whirls that had been performed for centuries. Pasquale sang. Pietro sang. Concetta sang. Francesca sang, then they all sang together. And then everybody sang.

'Now,' said Pasquale, interrupting the festivities. 'We have a special ceremony to perform . . . Rhianna and Gianni . . . Will you come to me, please?'

Rhianna and Gianni looked at each other puzzled, she shrugged but, hand-in-hand, they presented themselves in front of Pasquale. Everybody looked on, nudging each other, benevolent grins on their expectant faces.

'You must take off your shoes, both of you,' Pasquale instructed.

Both bent down and obediently took off their shoes.

'Now you must tread the grapes in the old-fashioned way.' He grabbed Rhianna around the waist and lifted her up to a round of cheers.

She shrieked with laughter. 'Put me down!'

He deposited her feet first in the barrel that still contained uncrushed grapes. 'Gianni, I will not lift you. You must get in without my help.'

Everybody laughed and applauded as John climbed inside the barrel with Rhianna. Her skirt and petticoats floated on top of the mass of grapes, which were becoming wet and pappy around her feet. As the skins burst with their marching on the spot, she could feel the juice warm and sticky against her shins as she sank deeper into the barrel. The upward pressure of her knees as she raised her feet broke the skins of the grapes towards the top and she could feel the fluid trickling down her thighs. Pietro struck up with a lively tune and everybody clapped in time with the music. Rhianna and John, laughing with joy and without embarrassment, trampled the grapes to the rhythm of Pietro's accordion until they were crotch-deep in a bath of dark red, sloppy liquid.

'You see?' Pasquale said after they had taken the barrel to ferment with the others. 'I told you you would find reserves of energy.'

After this unexpected finale everybody thanked everybody else and began drifting away. Rhianna and John cleared away the soiled plates and empty glasses.

'We can wash them in the morning,' she said. 'Right now, I'm going to wash myself. My legs are all sticky and clammy with drying grape juice and my skirts and drawers are soaked. I swear the stuff's already fermenting on my skin.'

'I'll lick it off if that's the case,' John replied flippantly.

'I fear you'd have a swarm of fruit flies in competition.'

'On second thoughts, let's both take off our clothes. If your drawers are anything like my trousers they're ruined. I feel sticky in the most embarrassing places. We can wash with pails of water from the cistern.'

He began undressing. In no time he was standing naked before her, moonlight outlining his sinuous body. 'Now you . . . Do you want some help?'

'If you want to . . .' she whispered.

She unfastened her blouse and he gently pulled it away from her, down her arms, then tossed it onto the table on the patio. She unfastened her juice-stained skirt and slipped it, along with her petticoats, down her sticky legs.

While she took off her chemise and her drawers he went to the downpipe and filled two pails with water. When he returned to the patio she was standing naked in the moonlight, shaking out her hair, which she had just unpinned. He lifted one pail and poured it all over her.

She gasped as the shock of the cool water cascaded over her head, her shoulders, her breasts, down her back, over her belly and down her legs. As she stood dripping in a pool of it she felt suddenly indignant that he had surprised her thus.

'I'll get you for that,' she shrieked. At once she grabbed the other pail and emptied the water over him, determined to get her own back. It drenched him and he laughed.

'Oh, just you wait,' he said good-humouredly.

He ran to the downpipe and quickly refilled the pails. She was hiding behind a pergola, laughing now. When he returned she made a grab for one of the pails and he allowed her to have it. They threw water over each other simultaneously but this time she squealed with joy. It was turning into a game and besides, she was expecting this last drenching, so it came as no shock to her glowing body. Rather, the cool, clear water was refreshing and she felt it rinsing away the cloying grape juice and debris of broken skins from her legs and her crotch.

'Let's fetch some more,' she suggested, dripping wet.

They refilled the two pails.

'Let me trickle the water over you,' he suggested 'and I can rub you down.'

She stood still while he poured water down her back and rubbed away the grime of the day, gently stroking her taut, smooth skin with the palms of his hands. She turned to face him and he trickled water across her shoulders and watched as it spilled over her. Her breasts glistened tantalisingly in the pale, silvery light of the moon that, with the reflection from the sea, imbued a suffused lambency to the night. Her nipples hardened in response to the water's chill and he stroked each tenderly before pouring more water over her. He swished it over her gently rounded belly and the soft curve of her hips, and the crystal clear droplets sparkled like diamonds in the silky setting of her dark curls. Gently, but too briefly, his fingers caressed her and she uttered a little sigh of pleasure.

'I'll wash your legs,' he whispered.

Rather than pour water directly, he dipped his hands in the pail and splashed handfuls of water over her thighs, sensuously stroking them with a smooth up and down motion to remove the sugary stickiness. But this sensual intimacy was, not surprisingly, having another effect. As his left hand stroked her thigh and returned inevitably to the soft, warm place between her legs, teasing her again, she saw that he had grown hard for her which, in turn, aroused her the more. While he bent his head and took a nipple between his lips she ran her fingers through his wet hair, pulled his face more firmly into her breast and sighed longingly. This night was no different to any other night with regard to her desire. She wanted him tonight as she wanted him every night. Only the circumstances of this night were different; the starlit sky was a roof, the sickle moon a lamp, perhaps the patio for a bed . . . What was it about him that made her yearn for him? He only had to touch her and she melted. He only had to look at her with those soulful, liquid eyes that told of his desire and her heart beat as fast as if she had run a mile.

As John raised his head he left a trail of kisses on her wet neck and found her lips, cool, moist, soft and accommodating. He pressed himself to her and she felt him hard, insistent against her belly as rivulets of water trickled through her soft curls and between her legs. The spittle in her mouth thickened . . . She took him in her right hand, closed her fingers around him and stroked him gently, to and fro. *Oh, everybody has reserves of energy . . . as you will find out very soon.* Did Pasquale mean *this*?

She parted her legs and guided him into her as she stood. His hands cupped her firm buttocks and she let out a little gasp of expectation as she felt him enter and draw her close to him.

Mother, if you could see me, you would not begrudge me my contentment . . .

They stayed like that for a few minutes, gently moving, teasing the pleasure out of each other with slow, gentle thrusts that intensified each other's appetite inexorably. The passion grew but the position was limiting. They needed the expanse of a bed to roll about and give full vent to their fervour. If only the patio could be soft and kind to her back she would sink onto it and take him with her.

'Oh, Gianni, don't ever stop wanting me.'

'Nor will I ever,' he breathed.

At that, he pulled away. As he scooped her up in his arms and carried her bodily up the stone steps to their bedroom, her dripping wet body gleamed tauntingly. He placed her on the bed and they writhed together like otters, the sheet soaking up the water that still lingered on their bodies.

Oh, everybody has reserves of energy . . .

25

Salvatore Vinaccia regularly travelled from his home in Bologna in the north to Sorrento in the south. A prosperous merchant, he dealt in the intricate cameo jewellery and the beautifully crafted furnishings and knick-knacks made of olive wood and decorated in *tarsia* – inlaid pieces of stained wood – that were peculiar to the Sorrento area. It was the last Tuesday in January 1891 and cold and wet. Desirous of something warming inside him at the end of his working day, he decided to call on his old friend Pasquale Amitrano at his *caffè* next to the monastery of San Francesco.

The two men greeted each other affably. It had been three months since last they'd met.

'No wonder the tourists don't come to Sorrento at this time of year,' Salvatore said. 'I swear it's damper and colder here than in the north. Even without this rain.'

'You may be right, dear friend. Having never travelled further north than Napoli I wouldn't know. But damp it certainly is . . . What will you have? Coffee?'

'And a stiff measure of *grappa* to warm me, if you don't mind.' Salvatore unbuttoned his overcoat, took off his hat and sat down at a table. He lit a cigarette and waited.

Pasquale delivered his coffee and a glass of *grappa* and sat at the table with him. 'Has this visit yielded any treasures yet, Salvatore?'

'There are always interesting pieces to be had.' The man from Bologna spooned sugar into his coffee and stirred it. 'But no more nor less than usual. Whatever I acquire, you may be sure there are always plenty of ready customers. How is your wife, Pasquale? Is she here?'

Pasquale shook his head. 'As you say, Salvatore, we are bereft of tourists now. All is quiet. If I need help I can call on Signora Rispoli. There's no need for Concetta to venture down from the hills. Besides, she enjoys the extra time she has with Alberto.'

'Ah, Alberto. How is the boy?'

'Growing up too quickly, as children do.'

'Have you had any photographs taken of him?'

'Not yet.'

'You should.' Salvatore sipped his *grappa* and licked his lips. 'Photographs are a wonderful record. Wonderful to pore over in years to come . . . especially on winter nights like these. I regret that I never had my own daughters photographed when they were younger.'

'How are your daughters? Did you not say that one was about to marry?'

'The eldest, yes. She married at Christmas . . . to a fine young man. I am content with the match.'

'And was she photographed in her bridal dress?'

'Oh, yes. I must remember to bring a print with me to show you next time. She is a fine-looking girl. They are all fine-looking girls, even though I say so myself. They take after their mother, of course.'

'Concetta was never photographed when we married,' Pasquale said regretfully. Then his eyes lit up. 'But I have had a painting done of her – by an English artist I know. Would you like to see it? I have it here. I'm so proud of it I'm inclined to keep it by me to show everybody.' He lowered his voice. 'Let me tell you privately, Salvatore, that not only am I proud of the painting, but I'm proud of my wife's striking looks as well.' He smiled as he stood up, and made his way to the back room where he took the painting out of the case he'd made specially to carry it about. When he returned he lit another oil lamp and held it close to the picture for Salvatore to admire it the more. 'Is she not a beautiful woman, Salvatore?'

'Indeed so, my friend,' Salvatore remarked, holding the painting at arms' length. 'This work is most impressive. It's the very image of your wife. The artist has caught her look perfectly. And I love the classical Italian setting . . . Marvellous . . . An English artist, you say?'

'Yes. A very talented English artist, wouldn't you agree?'

Salvatore looked closely at the signature. 'John Mallory Gibson,' he said thoughtfully. 'You say you know him?'

'I have come to know him well. He rents the house my mother and father used to live in. Him and his wife.'

'I would like to meet this John Mallory Gibson, Pasquale. Can you arrange it?'

'I don't see why not. If you can call here again tomorrow morning at about eleven I will try to make sure he is here to talk to you. You have a proposition to put to him?'

'Who needs mundane photographs if you can have magnificent paintings like this of your loved ones? My daughters would love to see themselves represented so.'

When Pasquale returned home that evening he called in to see John and arranged for him to visit the *caffè* next day.

'I will go with you down to Sorrento,' Rhianna said. 'I need to buy meat and tea – a whole basketful of stuff. I could meet you at the *caffè* afterwards and you can help carry everything back up those steep hills.'

At the *caffè* next morning, Pasquale introduced John to Salvatore. For good measure, Pasquale had also taken the painting of Rhianna that he owned and had that available as well to show off to Salvatore.

'It is so much better to see them by the light of day,' Salvatore remarked, 'even though it's so overcast again. These paintings make me yearn for warmth and sunshine.'

John smiled unsurely.

Salvatore continued. 'I am profoundly impressed by your work, Signore Gibson, and I have a proposition to make . . . I am the proud father of six daughters. Their ages range from fourteen to twenty-three. All of them are quite beautiful. I will pay you handsomely if you will paint each of them in this style, with a classical Italian setting.'

'Do you mean altogether in one painting or a separate painting for each daughter?' John asked, to clarify in his own mind what was required.

'Oh, a separate painting for each. They would not be satisfied with less once the idea has been planted. How much time would you need for such an undertaking?'

'It depends on how big you want the paintings. I paint everything in the most minute detail, Signore Vinaccia, as you can see. It all takes time. It can't be rushed.'

'Let's say the same size as this one of my friend Pasquale's wife, Concetta.'

'Then I would need at least a week – possibly two – for each.'

'And how much must I pay?'

John hesitated. He wanted to give the right answer, to be fair to his potential client and to himself. 'I think that is something I must first discuss with Rhianna. She will be here soon if you don't mind waiting a little longer . . . Would it be your intention to bring your daughters to Sorrento?'

Salvatore laughed good-naturedly at the idea. 'They would not be content to stay anywhere less than the Hotel Tramontano. No, much more convenient and much less of an expense if you travelled to Bologna. Of course, I would pay such expenses in addition to your fee.'

'That would mean my being away from home – from Rhianna – for anything between six and twelve weeks.' The thought did not appeal. The idea of leaving Rhianna to her own devices in a foreign land, however kindly the neighbours, did not appeal at all. Unless she could accompany him. 'I really must talk it over with her before I commit myself.'

'I understand,' Salvatore said. 'I have arranged to see an

artisan this morning about some cameos. When I have completed my business with him I will return and you can let me
know your decision. Shall we say one hour from now?'

John nodded. 'All right. One hour.'

Rhianna eventually returned and, over a cup of coffee, John
explained to her what was involved in the proposition. After
considering it, she said, 'I don't think it would be possible for
me to go with you, Gianni, much as I'd like to. There's the
cow to milk, the chickens to tend to and a thousand other
jobs that have to be done. Oh, I shall miss you dearly, my
love, but I think you should accept the offer and go alone. It
would help your career. Commissions for work, especially by
word of mouth, could be very lucrative, and I bet this Signore
Vinaccia knows plenty of other wealthy Italians who could
commission you. I imagine the Italian wealthy are no different
to the British when it comes to paying handsomely for their
elegant daughters to be painted. Especially in the manner that
you can portray them. It's vanity after all, isn't it?'

He sighed. 'I'm not sure I'm prepared to leave you for
so long.'

'Why?' She looked into his anxious eyes. 'I shan't stop loving
you. I'll survive. I'll have plenty to occupy me. And we shall
write regularly, shan't we? Take the commission, Gianni, just
so long as it's worth your while. Have you thought how much
to charge for six paintings?'

'I suppose it must at least equal what I would get for six
paintings sold by my dealer.'

'Naturally. So it's easily worked out . . .'

John and Salvatore Vinaccia agreed a fee and John at once
took half of it in cash, the balance to be paid on completion
of the paintings. It had been arranged that he would live in one
room at Salvatore's house and work in another. On the day of
his departure, the last Friday in January, John was morose.

'I am loath to leave you, Rhianna.' He stood hovering at the door of *Paradiso*, clutching his easel, six prepared canvases and all his paints, together with a box containing his clothes.

Rhianna smiled, tears filling her eyes, for it touched her to see him leave her so reluctantly. 'Go!' she breathed, and bent her head so that he should not see her watery eyes. She put her arms around him and hugged him tenderly. 'The time will fly.' She knew it to be a blatant untruth; alone with nobody to hold her in bed, cold through the damp winter nights. 'In no time you will be back and it will be spring. And this is a golden opportunity for you . . .'

'If you're sure . . .'

'Yes, Gianni, I'm sure,' she said in her calmest, most reassuring voice. 'I can cope here. If I need help there's always Concetta.'

He nodded, but he was not convinced. He had not counted on ever being parted from the woman he worshipped. It had always been his biggest fear. 'All right,' he said reluctantly. 'I shall miss you more than I know and possibly a lot more than I can reasonable tolerate. I'm certain of it. But if you're confident . . .'

'I told you, I shall be all right. You will too. Just don't forget to write to me with your address as soon as you arrive in Bologna.'

'Of course.'

'Then *arrivederci*.'

'*Arrivederci, cara mia.*'

Absence, it was said, makes the heart grow fonder. Well, thought Rhianna, as she watched John disappear down the path to meet Pasquale and his waiting cart, she did not see how she could become any fonder of John than she was already. But if it had that effect, she would not complain.

The following day, Nunzio the *postino* called. Rhianna was leaving the hen coop, having just collected eggs, one of which she intended having for her breakfast, when she saw his squat figure ambling up the path between two newly constructed pergolas already planted with young vines.

'*Buon giorno, signora,*' he hailed, clutching a letter in his hand and already waving it at her. 'This is addressed to somebody at this house called Maddox.'

'Maddox?' she repeated, flushing at being reminded of the name she had endeavoured to hide and tried her best to forget. 'Ah . . . Somebody's evidently got mixed up . . .' she said inventing a plausible explanation. 'It was my name before I married Signore Gibson.'

'Ah. Your maiden name.'

He handed her the letter. 'Thank goodness it is for you, signora. I was worried that it might have been wrongly addressed. If it hadn't been yours, it might have taken me all day to find the right person. I am relieved it's you. You've save me a lot of walking.'

'Thank you, Nunzio,' she said, briefly inspecting the hand-writing on the envelope as she took it.

'It's from England, eh? Somebody there remembers you.'

'Yes, it's from England,' she said pensively.

Nunzio evidently wanted to chat but she was anxious to open her letter so she bid him goodbye, turned her back on him and headed inside with her eggs and the envelope. As she walked away she tried to discern who the familiar, spidery, unpractised handwriting belonged to.

As she opened it, her heart leapt into her mouth and her hands began to tremble. Could it be that her prayers, her pleas to her family for understanding and forgiveness were answered at last?

It read:

Dear Rhianna,

Mother is very sick and has been for some weeks now. She has gone to nothing and Dr McCaskie says he don't give much for her chances. He says she has a growth in her bowel which he reckons is a cancer. She keeps asking for you, Rhianna. She says she wants to make her peace with you before she dies. All the while she is on about you. She blames herself that you left with your artist chap after angry words. I know from your letters that you've been asking for her forgiveness. Well, now it's yours for the taking. If you could see your way clear to coming home to see her I think you should. But you had better be quick. Father misses you as well. He is not well neither but at least he isn't laid up in bed yet. He never moves from his chair. He's mythered to death about poor Mother though. He says he rues the day he allowed you to leave after that argument what you had. He forgives you everything and he wants you to come back as well and never shuts up about how Lawson must have treated you for you to have left him. They both send their love. Please come back, Rhianna. We love you dearly but with Mother being so ill, please come soon. We need you.

 Your loving sister,
 Sarah.
 P.S. I am not well myself either.

Rhianna sat down, astonished. Why couldn't this letter have arrived yesterday before John left, when she would have had the chance to discuss it with him? Why did they have to wait so long to let her know this terrible news? Why now? Why not a week earlier if her mother was so ill? Why not sooner than that? Her mother's illness was evidently not a sudden thing if she had a cancer of the bowel.

What should she do? It put her into such a quandary. Of course she should return to England to see her dying mother. But she had responsibilities with the livestock, with the horticulture. She had to be here to receive John's first letter, else how would she know where to write to him, to let him know what had occurred?

Her first thought was to seek advice. So, she donned her hat and coat and, clutching the letter, braved the stiff breeze that was blowing over the headland as she hurried to the house of Pasquale and Concetta.

'In one way it's come at a convenient time with John away in Bologna,' Concetta remarked.

'Yes, but with so much work to do and the cow and the chickens to look after I don't see how I can go. If Gianni was still here of course . . .'

'You must go, Rhianna,' Concetta advised. 'If your mother is dying and asking for you, you would regret forever not being there at her side. Go quickly. Francesca and I can share the work of looking after things for you. You must not even think about staying here. And who knows, you will almost certainly return before Gianni.'

Rhianna nodded at her sage advice. 'You're right, Concetta. I knew you would put it into a proper perspective for me. Just so long as you don't mind. So long as you understand my position.'

'Of course I do.'

'But Gianni's letters . . . Until I receive his first I shan't know where to write to him. I will write down my mother's address in England for you. When his letters arrive, if you could forward them to me . . . I'll leave some money for the post.'

'Don't worry about a thing. I will send them to you. When shall you leave?'

'Monday. I daren't leave it later. It'll take nearly a week to get back to England.'

'Pasquale will take you and your luggage to Sorrento town, where you will be able to take a carriage to Castellamare. Let us have your address in England when you leave.'

'You are both so kind, Concetta. I shall never forget your kindness.'

Rhianna arrived back in Dudley on Sunday 8th February 1891 more than a year after she'd left. In Station Drive she pulled up the collar of her coat and shivered as she told the driver of a hansom cab where she wanted to go. Once inside, she sat back, her mind awhirl now with apprehension over how her mother, her father and Sarah would greet her after such a long absence. No doubt things would be strained at first, but she would welcome their arms about her again, their reassuring hugs. She longed for their forgiveness, for the inner peace that reconciliation would bring. She longed for the chance for them to meet John at some later time, for she knew how they would come to love and admire his quiet, reserved ways.

The wind was blowing the rain in squalls. Through the windows of the hansom everything looked depressingly drab; even more drab than when she left. The trees that lined Castle Hill were bare as they yielded to the wind, branches swaying wildly. The keep of the old castle, high on her right-hand side, looked even more dilapidated, deathly grey against a miserable sky. The cab driver turned left into Birmingham Street and the huddles of houses and filthy courtyards became more squalid the higher they ascended the hill. Where it met Hall Street, two groups of drunken louts were shouting angrily and squabbling as they turned out of the public houses. Nothing had changed.

They turned into Oakeywell Street and the horse broke into a trot as the driver urged it on. Rhianna was poignantly reminded how Sarah had finally turned her back on her at that very spot. Sarah . . . eighteen last October, going on nineteen now . . . She would be quite the young lady, blossoming into beautiful womanhood. Maybe she was courting seriously, contemplating marriage. She hoped he would be worthy of Sarah, whoever he was.

Rhianna's heart started pounding the closer she got to home. It would be only a couple of minutes. Without stopping, the hansom whisked her over the junction with Constitution Hill and into Prospect Row, its wheels rattling over the potholes. The familiar reek of the gasworks . . . The rows of houses came to an end on both sides, a little workshop on the left, then fields. Prospect Row dwindled to a muddy track. Her excitement increased, as did her uneasiness.

They turned left.

Paradise. Could any place be more inappropriately named after where she had been? Allotments on the left-hand side – no vines, no pergolas, no oranges, lemons or olives. Nobody was working there this desolate, windy day. Then there was the row of houses on the right. The hansom drew to a halt. In mere seconds she would be with her mother and father again . . . and Sarah. She felt in her bag and asked the driver how much she owed. Fivepence. She gave him sixpence and told him to keep the change. He took her case and put it on the pavement, mounted the cab, turned round and, with a touch of his hat, drove off.

She lugged her case up the entry, wondering whether to go in without knocking. But she desisted. She could not take things entirely for granted. So she knocked . . . and waited. She knocked again . . . nothing. No point in standing on ceremony . . . She put her thumb on the latch . . . pressed it down, apprehension mounting. It disengaged and she pushed the door open gingerly. The raw-boned figure of her father was sitting in his armchair asleep in front of a dying fire, his gouty foot still on a cushion in a washing basket, a dirty shawl around his shoulders. Nothing had changed . . . Nothing . . . But his face was pale and drawn, he was thinner even than before she left. As the door shut, he opened his rheumy eyes and looked at his daughter vacantly as she put down her case.

'Father . . . It's me . . . Rhianna . . .' She stooped down, put her arms around his shoulder and hugged him. She saw a tear roll out of one eye. Give him a chance to wake up and come to his senses. 'Father . . . It's me . . . Rhianna . . .'

He clutched at her hand in recognition and held it tight. 'Me babby,' he muttered weakly. 'Oh, me babby . . . Thank the Lord yo'n come back . . .'

She caught the smell of his stale breath as she affectionately rubbed the thin, scrawny hand that reminded her of a bird's claw. 'How have you been, Father? Oh, I've missed you . . . There hasn't been a day—'

'Have yer come back for good?'

'No, not for good, Father . . . Just for a while. To look after you for a while . . . and Mother . . .' She stood up and poked the fire. It flickered into a flurry of half-hearted flames. 'How is Mother?'

The old man closed his eyes and turned his face upwards. He had not shaved in days, his grey hair was matted and greasy. There was an unsavoury smell about him. Tears squeezed out of both eyes now.

'How *is* our Mother?' she repeated.

Titus shook his head slowly. 'Your mother's jed and buried, my wench . . .'

'Oh, no . . . *NO!*' Her hands went to her face in a gesture of horror.

She was too late.

Damn it all, she was too late. Dear God in heaven, why?—

She cried, her face an icon of misery and regret that the last she had seen of her mother was during a needless argument. They had never become reconciled, never had the chance to say how sorry they were.

Oh, how she cried.

She'd missed her mother's blessing over John, her forgiveness for leaving Lawson. She wanted to tell her mother how much she loved her, how much she'd missed her, how upset she'd been at their stupid, needless rift. Now it was too late. Why could she not have waited for Rhianna to arrive before dying? Why could she not have died in Rhianna's arms?

'When did she pass away, Father?'

'A wik a-Monday.'

'So when was the funeral?'

'Last Monday . . . Up at Top Church.'

So she had been buried the day Rhianna left Sorrento.

'Did she die peacefully?' Rhianna blubbed through her handkerchief.

'Oh, at the end . . . But the pain . . . Her suffered unmerciful. In the finish it was a blessing.'

'I'm so sorry I didn't get here in time, Father. Oh, I'm so sorry . . . I'd have given the world . . .'

'Her knew as yo'd come. Her wanted to mek it up wi' yer. Her tried to hold on till yo' come but . . . but in the finish the Lord decided to tek her . . .'

'And you miss her . . .'

'Oh, Christ, ar. I miss her, our Rhianna. And I've missed yo' an' all.'

'But I'm back now . . . For a time anyway . . . So where's Sarah? How is she?'

He pointed upwards and she looked at him with a puzzled frown.

'A-bed,' he said and shook his head ominously.

'In bed?'

Titus nodded and more tears trickled down the lines of his face like rivulets in a series of gullies.

'I'd best go up and see her. She said in her letter she wasn't well either. Then I'll make up the fire.'

She opened the door and ran up the narrow staircase, her footfalls loud on the hollow wooden stairway. She shoved open the door to Sarah's room and saw her younger sister, a mere shadow of the belle she used to be, dozing on her side, her face turned towards Rhianna. Her long hair was tangled and unkempt, her face was drawn and as pale as death. Her bright, adolescent beauty was gone. And it was cold in there. So cold.

'Sarah!'

Sarah opened her eyes and stared wildly.

'Sarah, it's me, Rhianna . . .'

What had she come back to? What unspeakable evil had befallen this household that was once vibrant?

The younger woman twisted round to lie on her back and, with difficulty, raised herself on her elbows. At once, Rhianna saw her distended belly, an ominous mound under the bedclothes.

'Sarah!' she said in alarm. 'My God . . . You're pregnant!'

Sarah squealed with agony as another searing contraction convulsed her.

26

'How long have you been like this?'

Sarah sighed feebly and shrugged. 'About nine months, I suppose.'

'No, you fool. How long have you been having the contractions?'

'I dunno . . . Three hours. Maybe four . . . I dunno . . .'

Rhianna put the backs of her fingers to Sarah's brow to see if there was any fever. The girl was sweating but her face felt cold.

'Why didn't you call on somebody for help as soon as you knew?'

Sarah closed her eyes again and turned her face away.

'Why, Sarah? Why?'

'Because I want to die, Rhianna. And I want my baby to die with me.'

'Well you're not going to die. Neither you nor your baby. Why didn't you alert one of the neighbours? Somebody would've gone to fetch the midwife.'

'Don't bother with me, Rhianna,' she said pathetically. 'I'm not worth it. Leave me be. Just let me die.'

'I'll do no such thing.' She ignored the self-pity. 'Pull yourself together. What you're about to go through will be no picnic, but you're going to be all right. Now hold on . . . I'm going to get help.'

Rhianna rushed downstairs and looked at her father, slumped again like a rotting corpse in the chair. She knew then that if she had not arrived when she did, he and Sarah, as well as the unborn child, would surely have died through lack of attention. Titus huddled under his blanket, seeking relief from the cold and she looked again at the fire. First she must rekindle it. They would need a fire to boil lots of water. She lit a candle and, with the scuttle went to the cellar that was almost devoid of coal barring some debris and a few shovelfuls of slack. She managed to scrape together a few small pieces, enough to make one fire.

When she'd washed her hands, Rhianna put on her coat and ran out of the house toward the home of Old Mother Bowen in Constitution Hill. Rhianna was not sure that the old lady was still alive, much less which house she lived in but, after a couple of enquiries, somebody pointed it out. She hurried up the entry and knocked on the back door.

'I need Mrs Bowen to attend a birth,' she said breathlessly to a whiskery old man in a collarless shirt and twisted braces.

''Er ai' 'ere, my wench. 'Er's gone to lay out that Sol Poole what popped 'is clogs last night. Dost know 'im?'

'No.'

'Gentleman, 'e was. Never do yer a bad turn if 'e could do yer a good un. Scarlet fever's what got 'im.'

'I'm sorry to hear about him. So how long do you think she'll be?'

''S 'ard ter say. Another 'alf hour, mebbe. Mebbe an hour.'

'Have you got a piece of paper and a blacklead and I'll write down the address. Ask her to come as soon as she can, will you? Please? It's my sister and she's already started in labour. Three or four hours ago.'

The old man went inside and it seemed like ages before he returned clutching a scrap torn off a sugar bag and a stumpy blacklead. Rhianna scribbled down the address.

'That's no good any road,' the man said. 'I wun't bother.'

Rhianna looked at him questioningly.

'Ne'er un on we can read. Why as yer doh just tell me where it is and I can tell 'er when 'er comes back?'

She told him.

'Yo' mean Paradise just off Prospect Row?'

'That's it.'

''S nice down theer, ai' it?'

'Yes, lovely. But please tell her to come right away.'

'I'll tell 'er. 'Er'll charge thee seven an' six. Yo' know that, doh yer?'

'That's all right . . . Tell her, if she hurries I'll double it to fifteen shillings.'

Rhianna headed back, not certain that she had sufficiently stressed the urgency of the matter. It would not be so bad if she had previously attended a birth herself and knew what to do. But she hadn't . . . She only knew what people had told her and it sounded terrifying. If she was faced with it alone, she had no idea how she would cope. But she told herself that if she had to cope, she *would*. Sarah needed her more than at any time in her life. She must not let her down.

As she hurried back to Paradise Rhianna pondered whose child Sarah was carrying. Whoever the brigand was, he evidently had not stood by her. Maybe he had made the excuse, like so many young men those days who wished to escape the responsibility of fatherhood, of deciding at the last minute to emigrate, promising falsely that he would send for her when he was settled and had found work in the New World. And Sarah could be so easily led . . .

She arrived home and heard Sarah emitting another chilling scream. The fire was burning bright by this time. To damp it down a little, to make it last, she threw on half a shovelful of slack then went to the brewhouse and filled a pan and the kettle with water. She put them to boil and went upstairs.

In her agony Sarah was gripping the brass bedstead behind her as if her life depended on it. Her knuckles were white, her face contorted.

'Breathe deeply and relax,' Rhianna suggested.

'Relax? How the bloody hell am I supposed to relax?' Sarah shrieked. 'It's as if a big dog's got his head inside me and he's trying to rip out my insides.'

The spasm passed and Sarah quietened down again.

'I've sent for Old Mother Bowen,' Rhianna said calmly, mopping Sarah's brow. 'She should be here soon. Take it easy while you've got the chance . . . But tell me, Sarah . . . Where's the father? Who *is* the father?'

Sarah shook her head and her face contorted in pain once again. 'It's coming, Rhianna,' she wailed. 'I swear it's coming . . . Oh God . . . Oh, I'm soaking wet now . . .' She kicked the bedclothes away and looked between her legs. 'Me waters have just broke . . .'

Rhianna immediately got up and went to a drawer to find towels. There were no clean ones.

'Where are the towels, Sarah?'

'There's only some dirty ones. In the washing basket in Mother's room.'

They would have to do. She fetched them and Sarah lifted herself while Rhianna placed them beneath her.

'Whoever the father is, Sarah, I wish he could see you now. Are you going to tell me who it is?'

'No . . . I ain't. I'll never tell you. Nor nobody else, for that matter.'

'Is it somebody I know?'

Sarah shrugged as if she didn't care. 'Don't expect me to talk about it now . . . Don't you think I've got enough to contend with?'

'Of course. I'm sorry. It's just the shock of arriving back here and finding you giving birth, Father at death's door and Mother already gone.'

'You should've come sooner.'

'You didn't let me know sooner.'

Sarah yelled out again in her agony. 'Help me, Rhianna . . . Help me . . . Please . . .'

Through the piercing screams, Rhianna heard a knock on the door downstairs and ran down to answer it.

'Come in, Mrs Bowen. Thank goodness you've come.'

Mrs Bowen stepped inside. 'How often am the contractions a-coming?'

'Often. Her water broke a little while ago. She must have been in labour four hours at least.'

'It still might be some time yet, my wench. Doh thee fret. I'n 'ad fifteen meself so I should know . . . Have yer got plenty wairter on to bile?'

'What you can see there. But we've got no more coal.'

'No more coal? Then yo'd best get on and see if yo' can borrer some from next door while I see to the poor wench upstairs. We'll need a load of it.' Mrs Bowen cast a professional eye over Titus sitting propped up in his chair as she opened the stairs door. There would be another easy fifteen shillings before long, by the looks of him, she thought . . . to lay him out.

Sarah's baby, a boy, was born shortly after seven o' clock that evening. It weighed less than four and a half pounds, a scrawny, screwed-up little bundle.

'It's the most puny thing I'n sid in many a year,' Old Mother Bowen said downstairs as she pocketed her fifteen shillings. 'I doubt whether it'll see the wik out. Even if its mother can feed it.'

'I'll get Dr McCaskie in to examine it,' Rhianna said.

'I should . . . And while he's here, yo'd best get him to look at the young madam an' all. Oh, there's no bleedin', nor nothin' like that – I doh think as 'er's got an ounce o' blood left in her. I'n never sid anybody more anaemic. Your sister, is it, did yer say?'

Rhianna nodded. 'I've been abroad fifteen months, Mrs Bowen. I got back today . . . To all this . . .'

'Some 'um-comin', I'll be bound. Well, 'er needs to stop

a-bed an' rest. Get some sweet stout down her neck and plenty eggs and mate. There's no flesh on her boones. I'n sid more fat on a butcher's apron.'

'Do you think she's not been looking after herself properly, Mrs Bowen?'

'I'd say it's bin a damned long while since her had a good meal.'

Rhianna sighed. 'My mother died just a fortnight ago. I suspect Sarah was looking after her till the last – neglecting herself.'

'Oh, this is longer neglect than that, my wench. 'Er ai' looked after herself properly for months. Any road, yo' can tell by the weight o' the babby. The poor little bugger's starved to jeth an' all while 'er's bin a-carryin' 'im.'

'Are you sure, Mrs Bowen?'

'Ask Dr McCaskie. I used to see yer sister knockin' about. Pretty young thing, I always thought.'

Rhianna thanked Mrs Bowen for her attendance.

'I'll pop by termorrer and have a look at 'em both. All part o' the service.'

Rhianna had been able to borrow a couple of buckets of coal from next door while Mrs Bowen was attending to Sarah, so they had some heat for a while. She had lit a fire in Sarah's bedroom so that she and the baby could benefit from the warmth. Tomorrow, she would go to the coal yard and fetch a hundredweight, providing her father's old handcart was still serviceable. She found some potatoes that had started sprouting, some flour, butter and some cheese and made a cheese and potato pie. Titus ate it though not heartily, and Sarah woke up to have a little. Then, when she'd cleared up, Rhianna decided to get her father upstairs and give him a bed bath in order to reduce the malodours that were an invisible but eminently perceivable aura around him. She took Sarah a hot drink and wondered if the baby would take any food yet.

The mite hadn't stirred. One thing was certain, Sarah would have to try and feed him soon and to do so, she must feed herself first.

When she felt she had done as much as she possibly could, Rhianna went to bed. She lay weeping and could not stop. She wept over many things; the loss of her mother, the state of her father and Sarah. Was this terrifying predicament that afflicted them the result of her leaving them in anger and despair more than fifteen months earlier? Was this the direct consequence of that decision? She could hardly have foreseen it. Surely, she could not be blamed entirely. She could hardly be blamed for her mother's cancer. Her mother had seemed fit and well and perfectly capable of looking after her father when she left. Sarah, too, was settled in a new, well-paid job at Hillman's, and excited at the prospect of meeting a decent lad.

She heard a faint cry from the baby and pulled the pillow over her head. Sarah must look after the child herself. Her stupidity – or had it been good intentions? – had resulted in her pregnancy, so she must shape up and take the consequences.

But all these tears . . . Everything was made worse because she was also missing John so acutely. She missed him beyond belief. When she'd arrived at Turin on her way back to England she'd looked on a map in the railway carriage and seen how relatively close Bologna seemed. If she'd had his address she would have called on him, surprised him, explained that she was going to pay her last respects to her dying mother and that she would be back at *Paradiso* long before him. Whatever happened now, it would be at least another week before his first letter arrived. *Oh, Gianni . . . Are you well without me by your side? Are you missing me as much as I'm missing you? Oh, Gianni . . .* She wanted so much to return to Italy, to John, to the idyllic life they had made for themselves; the sunny, kindly, generous, easy-going life in the hills of Sorrento. She wanted to hear the constant roar of the sea, feel the sun and the warm breeze on her face, look forward to seeing Gianni's next painting. She wanted to see that intoxicating, perplexed look on his face when he was unsure of himself, as he so often was. She wanted to see her vines growing, her lemons, her oranges, her olives, her tomatoes. She wanted to receive the affectionate smiles and greetings of Concetta, of Pasquale, of Francesca, of Pietro . . . and of young Serafino.

Being away from her loved one made her feel love all the more acutely. Yes, absence did make the heart grow fonder. She could never take for granted what was normally there to enjoy. Now she found it hard to see herself as she used to be – living her cosseted yet mundane and ultimately deceived existence with Lawson Maddox. That was another lifetime, she was somebody else then. Having discovered this life with John she could not conceive of anything different. But now, suddenly, life was different and the cruel difference was inducing this endless weeping. Oh, she wanted to help her poor father and her unfortunate sister, there was no question about it, but she also wanted to return to John. The last thing she wanted was to lie sobbing in this unaired bed because of them.

Rhianna wiped her tears on the pillow and heard the child mewling again. Perhaps she should go and investigate, try and encourage Sarah to deal with it. So she slipped out of bed, lit her candle and tiptoed into Sarah's room. Experimentally, she put the knuckle of her forefinger to the baby's mouth and he tried to suckle it. Rhianna was astounded at the instinctive reaction of an untutored child. Of course, he was hungry at last. She roused Sarah. Sarah awoke, drowsy.

'Your baby's hungry, Sarah,' she whispered. 'You must try and feed him. It's time.'

'I can't, Rhianna,' Sarah bleated meekly. 'I'm bone weary. And I feel all hot. Can you open the window?'

'Yes, I'll open the window. But you must sit up and try to feed the baby.' Rhianna slid the sash down a couple of inches.

'There . . . Come on, I'll help you sit up.' She put her arms under Sarah's armpits with the intention of lifting her. 'God! You're ringing wet with sweat.'

'I told you . . . I'm so hot.'

'Hot or no, try and feed the child.' Rhianna lifted the baby out of the half-open drawer in which it was lying and put it into Sarah's thin arms.

Sarah unbuttoned her nightdress and watched as the baby suckled her meagre breast. For the first time since her return Rhianna detected the faint flicker of a smile on Sarah's prematurely aged face.

The next morning, Sarah seemed no worse. She was still hot, pale and complained of sweating, she was still weak and lethargic, but Rhianna was convinced she was on the mend. She went downstairs to light a fire while Sarah fed the child again, but whether the child was actually drawing milk she did not know, and Sarah was not certain either.

Rhianna left them to rest and got her father up. With a struggle she helped him dress and with further difficulty managed to help him downstairs to his chair, his drawn face an icon of agony.

'Maybe you should stay in bed, Father,' she suggested, aware that her work would be cut down if he did.

'Folk die a-bed,' he replied curtly.

She made toast and brewed a pot of tea. Titus messed his breakfast about unenthusiastically and Sarah ate only part of hers with an equal lack of interest, although she finished her cup of tea. When she had cleared everything away and made up the fire Rhianna put on her hat and coat and went to the town to buy groceries. First, though, she made her way to the churchyard of St Thomas's church – Top Church – with the intention of finding her mother's grave. She found it, near the black wrought iron railings that separated the churchyard from High Street at its junction with Stafford Street. The grave was just an elongated mound of earth with her name burnt into a rough wooden cross that had been hammered into the cold ground at one end. Rhianna knelt in the damp, muddy earth beside it and wept. Why could her mother not have lived until she returned?

But then ... what if she had lived? What if she had survived, merely to witness the heartbreaking state of her younger daughter in such a distressing decline and suffering the agonies of bearing a bastard child, her first grandchild? Had the knowledge of the trouble Sarah was in hastened Mary's demise? Well, it could not have helped.

'God bless you, Mother,' Rhianna whispered, tears streaming down her soft, round cheeks that were cold from the wind and the rain. 'Please forgive me for not being with you when you died. I'll do my best for Sarah and for Father, but he's grieving terribly. God bless you, Mother.'

Rhianna stood up. She would return as soon as she could and bring some flowers. She would make sure a suitable headstone was erected, bearing an appropriate inscription.

When Rhianna returned to the house, Sarah had thrown off all her bedclothes. She was groaning, talking to herself unintelligibly in her unconsciousness. Rhianna felt her brow. It was hot, clammy, sweaty. She went downstairs and brewed a pot of tea, handed a cup to Titus and took one upstairs to Sarah, rousing her from her troubled sleep.

'I've brought you some tea, look.'

Sarah nodded, singularly indifferent. Rhianna placed it on her bedside table.

'Do you want me to make the fire up?'

'No,' she mumbled. 'I'm boiled.'

'Why not try and feed the baby again?'

Rhianna helped Sarah to sit up and went to hand her the child. But the baby was soiled and needed cleaning and changing. When Rhianna had tended to it, she handed him over to Sarah who put him to her breast. But as she was feeding, she dropped off to sleep again.

This can't be right, Rhianna said to herself.

Mrs Bowen called. Rhianna mentioned Sarah's fatigue, her sweating, her feverishness. The midwife pulled down the bedclothes and lifted up Sarah's nightdress.

'Milk leg, see? There's no milk gone to her bresses. It's all in her legs. Dover's Powders am the thing. Her needs some Dover's Powders. Keep an eye on the wench. If 'er gets any wuss, fatch the doctor to 'er.'

'I will,' Rhianna replied.

Rhianna went out again. She shoved Titus's old handcart, its wheels squealing for want of oil, to the coal yard in Bath Street by the gasworks. There she paid for a hundredweight of coal which was tipped into the handcart by a man who was black with coal dust. Oddly, she considered how difficult it would be to have an illicit affair with him without giving the game away through being contaminated with his ample smuts. Before she left to shove the loaded cart up Constitution Hill's steep and rutted incline, she requested and paid for a further five hundredweight to be delivered to the house by horse and dray.

When Rhianna arrived home, she paid back the coal that she owed next door, then went to tend her three patients. None of them seemed vastly different to when she went out. All three were depressingly ill. Sarah had had diarrhoea, just to add to her ailments.

During the night, Rhianna felt that Sarah had taken a turn for the worse, so first thing next morning, she visited the surgery of Dr McCaskie.

'Indeed, I was not aware your sister was pregnant,' the doctor said defensively, as if she was blaming him. 'However, I must confess that each time I called on your poor mother, the girl was not in attendance.'

'Not?'

'I never saw her. She was never there when I was.'

'Whether or no, she's in a bad way now,' Rhianna said. 'I'd like you to see my father as well. He's not half the man he was before I left for Italy.'

'Your father's condition, of course, is a deleterious one. And at the stage it's in, you must never expect him to be any better. He will only ever get worse.'

'All the same, I'd appreciate your having a look at him. I mean, not only is he ill, but he's grieving over Mother.'

'Of course. I'll call this afternoon . . .' Dr McCaskie hesitated. 'But, er . . . I'm afraid there's also the small matter of my fees for the last three visits . . .'

'Oh,' she responded in embarrassment. 'I'm sorry, Doctor. I didn't realise . . . I'll pay what's owed when you call.'

By the time he called, Sarah seemed even worse. Her breathing was laboured, she was running a high fever. She was sweating profusely, shivering and was a sickly grey. The child had given up crying and Rhianna suspected that Sarah had had no milk to give him after all.

Dr McCaskie examined her and shook his head. 'Puerperal fever,' he said gravely. 'Childbed fever. I shall prescribe a combination of calomel and Dover's Powders. Who delivered the child?'

'Mrs Bowen from Constitution Hill. But she seemed very able. She was very concerned for the health of both of them.'

'Did she come directly from home?'

'She came from laying out somebody who died of scarlet fever the night before.'

The doctor shook his head again. 'And no doubt she didn't bother to change her clothes nor wash properly afterwards. I do wish these people would take the trouble to understand basic hygiene. Especially when they are attending a parturition. Your sister could have picked up the infection from Mrs Bowen. You see,' he explained, 'germs so easily enter the raw surface of the uterus after separation of the placenta.'

'So she has scarlet fever as well?'

'No,' he answered firmly, 'she has childbed fever.'

'I, er . . . I had to put dirty towels under her, Doctor, when her waters broke,' Rhianna admitted sheepishly. 'There were no clean ones in the house. Could that have caused it?'

'Hmm . . . Well, you see, that's not ideal either, Miss Drake.'

'Maddox. Mrs Maddox.'

'Despite that, the girl is a shadow of what she used to be. And it's not entirely due to giving birth. I do remember her, a healthy young girl, bright and breezy, always with a cheerful smile. Never thin. What has brought her to this? Do you know?'

Rhianna shook her head.

'You only have to see the condition of the baby to see that she's neglected herself, or has been neglected for a long time – months. She is acutely anaemic. Iron is what she needs to rectify that, so I shall put her on a course of Blaud's pills.' He leaned over Sarah and spoke quietly to her. 'Tell me, Sarah, have you been taking any opiates regularly?'

'Opiates?'

'Yes. Morphia or laudanum for instance?'

Sarah shook her head, looking confused . . . Then understanding made her change her mind and she nodded. Dr McCaskie looked ominously at Rhianna.

'What have you been taking, my dear?'

'I dunno exactly . . . Some sort of powder. They call it *dope*.'

'By mouth or by hypodermic syringe?'

'By mouth.'

'How often?'

'Almost every day.'

'For how long?'

'Six or seven months, I s'pose.'

Dr McCaskie sighed. He turned to Rhianna. 'It's as I feared.

All the signs are there. Your sister has become what the medical profession calls an habituée of opiates. How and why she has, we need to understand. The drug has had its effect in several ways. It has suppressed her appetite, so she is now very thin and undernourished. Not only that but the relentless seeking to acquire it has taken priority over everything else, including her eating. No doubt she has spent whatever money she earned in paying for the stuff, and fed her craving till she was no longer capable of working. Since she has not had the drug for perhaps some days she is now showing the symptoms of deprivation. Certainly, she is hardly capable of looking after her child.'

'But how on earth did she get like this?'

'I would dearly like to know,' he said earnestly. 'One can only hazard a guess. But there's more, Mrs Maddox . . .' He looked at Rhianna with sympathetic eyes. 'Her poor child is also in a state of narcomania – the effects of deprivation, that is – through your sister, naturally. I suspect it is already suffering these effects in the same way she is. I fear it will not have the strength to survive the week.'

'So Sarah not only has childbed fever, but this . . . this deprivation as you call it?'

'Precisely. She is going to need quite some looking after, believe me, if she is to get over either.'

'Can you give her something to alleviate her suffering? The baby, as well?'

'I could administer an appropriately small dose of morphia which would relieve at once the anatomical effects of the deprivation in your sister, although I do it against my better judgement. However, I do believe she warrants some respite to help her get over the childbed fever. The Dover's Powders will help, of course. They do contain a small percentage of opium anyway. Once – that is, if – she recovers from the childbed fever, I am of the opinion that she should be left to overcome the narcomania without resorting to the source of it. And I think she will overcome it providing she has the required grace and grit. Thankfully, it is only a recent habituation, not of long standing. There is every chance that she will overcome it. Meanwhile, she will feel extreme anxiety, depression, headaches, severe stomach pains and suffer recurrent bouts of diarrhoea. She will sweat profusely so she must be given water to drink frequently else she will dehydrate.'

'She's already had diarrhoea, Doctor . . .'

'I am going to prescribe chloral hydrate and bicarbonate of soda for the pain. She must also be allowed alcohol – port wine is ideal, especially during frequent warm baths so that she may sweat the toxins out of her system. Once she gets over this fever she must never be allowed to come into contact with opium ever again . . .'

The doctor searched in his bag, withdrew an evil-looking hypodermic syringe and part-filled it with morphia. He located a vein in Sarah's wrist and injected it. It all looked decidedly painful.

'Give your sister as much to drink as she will take. Fight the fever by keeping her cool, keep a window open. She will sleep peacefully now but when she awakes, she must try to eat something and drink water – for the sake of the child as much as for herself. And give her the medication as I shall prescribe.'

Rhianna nodded her understanding. 'So what about the baby?'

'All I am going to prescribe for the baby is Mrs Winslow's Soothing Syrup or Street's Infants' Quietness. Both contain a small amount of opium, so either should give the child some relief. We have to give the mite some comfort even if its chances of survival are low. However, it cannot go unnourished so I am going to find a wet nurse. I believe I know of somebody. Expect her within the hour. The poor little thing is already critically ill.'

'Now, what about my father?'

'Yes. Let's tend to the old man now.'

A wet nurse arrived, a young woman about the same age as Rhianna, who said her name was Rose. Rhianna sat her down on a chair behind her father while she fetched Sarah's baby from its drawer upstairs. She handed it to Rose. Rose unfastened her blouse to expose a plump, white breast and the child began sucking hungrily.

'The poor little soul must be clammed,' Rose commented. 'See how he's goin' at it? Like a pig at a tater.'

Rhianna smiled at Rose's lack of inhibition. 'He's had barely anything since he was born. I don't think my sister's got much milk for him. The doctor doesn't think he'll survive.' Rhianna explained how she had arrived home from Italy only the day before and found that her mother was dead, her sister was in the advanced stages of labour and her father was starving and incapacitated with grief.

'Struth! It must've been terrible for yer.'

'And now Sarah's got childbed fever, the doctor says. The trouble is, she's been taking opium or something and got herself and the baby habituated – that's what the doctor called it. I don't know what I'm going to do.'

'Ain't she wed?'

Rhianna shook her head.

'Who's the father?' Rose asked.

'She won't say.'

'P'raps she don't know.'

'Oh?' The thought and what it implied troubled Rhianna. 'What makes you say that, Rose?'

'Sounds just like a friend I used to have . . .' She rocked Sarah's baby gently as she fed him. 'Got mixed up with a right crowd – not that I'm saying your sister has, o' course. She had a chap who used to make her have laudanum regular. I 'spect it was 'cause 'er'd let him do whatever he wanted with 'er when she was half-baked. There's some evil sods about.'

'Oh, I'm sure Sarah would never do anything like that, Rose. She was always brought up to abhor anything like that.'

'No, I'm sure you'm right. I was just saying about me friend . . .' She looked down at the tiny head of the child. 'He ain't taking no more. He ain't had an eyeful either. Still, his little stomach must be full.' She drew him away from her nipple.

'Maybe he's got some wind.'

'I daresay.' Rose lifted the baby so that he was upright against her shoulder, his head was lolling over it, a grimace on his tiny face. He emitted a little burp and Rose smiled. 'There, that's better. Shall we try some more now?'

'It puts you off having babies,' Rhianna remarked. 'But when they're as sickly as he is you can't help feeling for them. You can't help doing your best for them.'

'Oh, you have to do your best and no two ways.'

The child seemed sated and Rose wiped her nipple. 'I think that'll do him for a while.'

'When shall you come back, Rose?'

'This afternoon. Just afore teatime.'

Rhianna smiled. 'Thanks. I'll have the kettle on and we can have a cup of tea together.'

'That's the idea . . . I do hope the little chap survives. It's a shame. He didn't ask to be brought into the world like this, did he?'

27

Two weeks passed. There were some anxious days with Sarah, and even more anxious nights when Rhianna sat up, watching over her sister, but eventually the fever abated. What remained were the debilitating, unbearable symptoms of early opium deprivation. The child, whom Sarah had decided to call Harry, had gained scarcely any weight at all but so far he had survived. He took a little food, just enough to sustain his tiny body, but he too, despite the soothing syrups Rhianna administered to him, was plagued by the lack of opium, to which his mother had unwittingly addicted him. His spasms of crying, his pale, cold sweats and his freakish, uncheckable shivering were heartbreaking to behold. Nothing could be done to help him. Only time would cure the awful, unimaginable craving and pain that poor Harry must endure.

It was almost a full-time occupation looking after Titus, let alone the other two invalids. The only relief Rhianna had from the interminable drudgery was when she had to go out to buy provisions.

As dinnertime approached one Tuesday towards the end of February, Rhianna was glad to escape the confines of the little terraced house and the incessant and frequently unpleasant demands on her. She decided to walk to the town and put some flowers on her mother's grave. So keen was she to leave that she failed to take proper note of the dark clouds amassed in the sky that threatened a thorough dousing.

She bought some anemones from the florist in High Street and made her way up to Top Church. To get to the grave she had to pass the vestry and, as she reached the top of the steps on the path that led to it, the heavens opened. She had brought no umbrella, and tried the vestry door with the idea of sheltering from the downpour, but it was locked. So she hurried round to the front of the church and entered by the main door. She was not the only person with the same idea and she smiled resignedly at a poorly dressed, elderly woman who had decided to share with her the lofty main entrance beneath the granite spire.

'Damned weather,' the old lady declared and her profanity reverberated up the wide curling staircase, echoing in the high void that led to the gallery and the organ loft.

'Yes, damned weather,' Rhianna agreed, but disinclined to engage in a lengthier conversation. She looked down at the floor, fixing her eyes on the pattern of tiles and thought of John. She had received no word from him yet. It had been her ardent hope that she would have heard from him within a week of her return to England. The post from Italy obviously took longer than she imagined. If it took John twelve weeks to fulfil his obligation to Salvatore Vinaccia in Bologna, it would not matter too much; she was very likely to be stuck in England, nursing Sarah and her father back to health for at least that long. She could not leave them to their own devices. Not at all. Sarah was in no fit state to look after herself, let alone a seriously ailing child and a father rendered decrepit from the effects of chronic gout and galloping consumption. No, for the time being, her home was that unutterable place which belonged to her husband, stuck between untidy allotments and the spoils of mining that came up to the railings like a tide. There was no escape.

'Who's the vicar here these days?' the woman asked.

'I'm not sure,' Rhianna answered politely. 'The Reverend Cosens, I think.'

'I remember the o'd vicar. Cartwright.'

Rhianna nodded. She had never heard of him.

''Twas 'im as married me.' The old woman's words echoed

and rang off the cold stone walls. 'And afore 'im was Luke Booker. He was the one as christened me. It was just afore I had the cholera. They dai' think as I was gunna live, but I showed 'em. Me fairther died o' the cholera an' all. He was on'y thirty. 'Twas the wairter, yo' know. Yo' daresn't drink it unless yo' biled it fust. Good thing the guvamint did summat about it.'

'Yes,' Rhianna said.

'The wairter, I'm on about.'

'Yes.'

'Them anemones yo'n got in yer basket am bostin', ai' they?'

'They are. But they cost enough.'

'For a grave, bin 'em?'

'Yes, if it ever stops raining.' At the natural prompt, Rhianna opened the church door and peered outside. 'Oh, it looks as if it's easing up now.'

'Thank the Lord.'

Both stepped outside and looked warily up at the sky. The old woman turned left at the bottom of the steps and Rhianna turned right. She returned along the path that led round the back, passing the vestry. Beyond the vestry the path petered out and she trod carefully, trying to avoid the puddles and patches of mud. She could smell the brewery close by, a smell that she liked and disliked at the same time; she liked the fact that it reminded her somehow of potatoes boiling but disliked how hungry it made her feel. Hawthorn trees were bare and stunted in the winter's chill, but the grass beneath her feet was long and its cold wetness seeped uncomfortably through her dainty boots.

She put down her basket and stooped beside the grave to remove the flowers she had left on her last visit. Holding her coat and skirt up a little to save getting them wet, she made her way to the water butt at the back of the vestry and replenished the enamelled grave vase. She returned to the grave and set about arranging the fresh anemones, admiring them for a second or two, smiling with pleasure at their bright colours. She ignored the crack of a fallen hawthorn twig some way behind her, until the swish-swish of footsteps dragging through the wet grass made her turn round. A hideously familiar figure was striding towards her.

'Rhianna. I thought it had to be you.'

'Lawson!' She stood up, unsure how to react. She would rather have encountered some rotting corpse dragging the remains of its mouldering shroud.

'As I drove up from Stafford Street I could see this figure through the railings bending over a grave,' he said affably, as though no rift had ever developed, as though they had never been apart. 'There was no mistaking *you*. I could barely let pass the opportunity to speak. Although, believe me, I have no intention of intruding on your grief. It goes without saying I was sorry to hear of the death of your mother. Please accept my heartfelt condolences.'

'Thank you.'

'However – on a brighter note – it must be said, you look very well.' He smiled in anticipation of her accepting the compliment.

'I *have* kept *very* well, thank you,' she replied, unsmiling. 'Italy seems to have had a beneficial effect on me.'

He had changed not at all. He was as handsome as ever, bright-eyed, smiling warmly, charm oozing from every pore.

'It's wonderful to see you,' he continued, raindrops glistening upon the shoulders of his coat and on his hat. 'Do you intend to stay in England now? Or is this just a fleeting visit?' There was no rancour, no enmity.

'I don't intend to stay longer than necessary,' she said, relieved by his affability and reasonableness. 'But there's the question of Sarah . . . and my father, of course. If you knew about my mother, no doubt you are also aware that Sarah has had a baby?'

'I heard she was pregnant, yes.'

Rhianna shrugged. 'She had a son a couple of weeks ago. They didn't expect the poor little mite to live. So far it has, though God knows how. She's not married either. It's a tragedy in a girl so young. She had so much to look forward to. She could have taken her pick of any number of decent lads, instead of one who let her down . . .'

'I understand how you must feel, Rhianna,' he said, his voice gentle and full of sympathy. 'I know you thought the world of her.'

'Still do . . . Even after she sided with you when I left. Even after she shunned me.'

'Perhaps the less said about it the better, eh? What's done can't be undone, Rhianna. If she's one of the unlucky ones now, all the regrets in the world won't change it. But time can diminish the cruellest hurts . . . So how is John Mallory Gibson?'

'Very fit and very well, thank you . . . last time I saw him.'

'Oh? He hasn't come back with you then?'

'He's still in Italy. He's got a very lucrative commission to fulfil . . .' She knew at once that she'd said too much. She looked self-consciously at the toes of her wet shoes poking out beneath her long skirt, then looked searchingly into his eyes. 'Lawson . . .'

'Yes?'

'Lawson . . . Despite what happened between you and me, I feel bound to thank you for your kindness to my mother and father, and our Sarah . . . I mean, for allowing them to stay in the house . . . I would gladly have paid the rent for them. I did offer.'

He waved his hand dismissively. 'It was the least I could do and honestly, it was of no consequence. Why should they have been punished just because you and me didn't see eye to eye at the time.'

'It's just that, at one time, you said something about them having to get out.'

'Heat of the moment, I expect. We're often sorry for things we say in the heat of the moment. Don't you think?'

She nodded guiltily. 'I daresay . . . Sometimes. I daresay I'm as much to blame as anybody.'

'We all are. We wouldn't be human if we weren't . . .'

It started raining again. Rhianna looked up at the sky as if it would yield a clue as to how long it might continue, and felt the cold spots on her face. She wrapped the collection of tired old flowers she was holding in the paper wrapping from the fresh.

'I'd better go before I get drenched, Lawson. Thanks for stopping to say hello.'

'There's no need for you to get drenched, Rhianna . . . Let me give you a lift. Remember there's a hood on my cabriolet.'

'So you still have the cabriolet?'

He smiled disarmingly. 'And the same horse – Docker. Oh . . . maybe it's time I settled down to something less racy. Maybe I should buy a clarence or a brougham and employ a liveried driver.' He gently took her elbow and looked into her eyes appealingly. 'Let me give you a lift. For old times' sake.'

'Thank you, but there's no need. I'm quite happy to walk. Even in this weather. The fresh air will do me good. Besides, I've got some shopping to do. Things to buy.'

'No matter, I'll take you wherever you want to go. I insist. It would be very ungallant of me not to offer you that courtesy.'

'Since when has your gallantry ever applied to me?'

'Oh, that's unfair, Rhianna,' he said smoothly. He picked up her basket and carried it as he led her away. 'I was never aware that I was ungallant.'

She did not want to discuss that. 'I have to go to the bin to throw these old flowers away,' she said, veering from the path.

He unhanded her and watched her dispose of the rubbish, her face flushed as she avoided a muddy patch. 'I've missed you, you know, Rhianna,' he said when she returned.

'I don't want to know,' she replied.

He laughed affably as he took her arm again. 'No, I don't suppose you do. But it's quite true. You left an indelible mark on me.'

She uttered a little laugh of derision. 'Lawson, it's me you're talking to, not one of your young floozies.'

He laughed again, amused at her coolness. 'No, maybe I shouldn't expect you to believe it . . .' They descended the steps and reached the pavement where his cabriolet was parked. He handed her up into the passenger seat. 'Are you comfortable?'

'Yes, thank you.'

'As I was saying . . .' He sat beside her, covered their legs with a waterproof leather carriage apron and flicked the reins. 'I *have* missed you. Much more than you would have imagined. You were a good, decent girl and I was a feckless fool for driving you away. Fifteen months of us being apart has made me realise it.'

'Lawson, I said I don't want to know, and I really don't,' she said bluntly. 'Oh, I appreciate your friendship, your kindness to my family. But it's over between *us*.'

'Except for the small matter of our still being married . . . Where do you want to go?'

'Lipton's.'

The rain was coming down in splintering rods that hammered on the taut hood of the cabriolet. The horse trotted on over the cobblestones, oblivious to the tumult that was swilling the mire of High Street into the gutters on either side. There were few folk about now. Those that were, were evidently sheltering in the warmth of the shops.

'Are you happy, Rhianna?'

'Very, if you mean am I happy with John.'

'I envy him . . . I never imagined I could . . . But I do . . . Having you . . . His having some sort of ability to make you happy.'

She looked straight ahead, ignoring his comment as she felt his eyes fixed upon her. They fell uncomfortably silent, stuck for further conversation till they pulled up outside Lipton's store.

'I shouldn't be long. I doubt whether it will be very busy. But you don't have to wait.'

'I'm in no rush.'

If she could have escaped from him she would. But there was only one way in and out of Lipton's. So she bought what she needed and resigned herself to him driving her home. At least she would stay relatively dry. But fancy seeing him. His affability had quite disarmed her. She might have expected some aggression, some antagonism, but there was none. Only his obvious pleasure at seeing her again and his admission, which she was interested in hearing despite her denial, that he had been a feckless fool. Well, his feckless foolery had cost him her love.

'Lawson . . .' she began tentatively as soon as she got back in the cabriolet. 'I need to discuss divorce with you. You know I can't afford to petition for divorce.' Might as well mention it first as last.

'Divorce?' As he flicked the reins he looked at her earnestly. 'I have no intention of divorcing you, Rhianna. There's no doubt in my mind that this diversion of yours with John Mallory Gibson will eventually fizzle out. My only wish is to welcome you back when that happens.'

She sighed. It was not going to happen, this fizzling out. As each day passed the bonds of love between her and John grew stronger. Just because they were apart right now did not mean he was absent from her thoughts. Far from it. He was constantly on her mind in spite of the grief and distress at home. But how could she let Lawson know that without antagonising him? He was dangerous when he was antagonised.

'How can you not wish to divorce me?' she said vehemently. 'I've been grossly unfaithful. I've been sleeping regularly with another man.'

'But I was unfaithful as well. The one cancels out the other. So there'll be no divorce. I can say that with certainty.'

'Look, Lawson, can't we talk about it . . . reasonably? We haven't lived together as man and wife for what? Nearly a year and a half? And I'm sure there must have been other women in your life since. Doesn't that suggest it's unlikely we shall live together any more?'

He shrugged his shoulders as he clutched the reins. 'Well, we can talk about it, of course we can. Though I don't understand this obsession of yours with divorce. It can only lead to contempt for you. You know how society disdains divorced women. And divorce won't be recognised in Italy, you realise that, don't you? You wouldn't be allowed to remarry in Italy either . . . But have dinner with me one evening and let's discuss it. There's a grand little restaurant opened over the billiard rooms in High Street. We passed it earlier. It would be good to have your company again over dinner.'

They turned into Hall Street, and its narrowness compelled Lawson to rein in the horse to a cautious walk lest somebody stepped or slipped off the stone kerb.

'What chance have I got to go out when there are three invalids to look after?'

'I'm sure they wouldn't miss you for just a couple of hours. You could make sure they were all settled for the night before you went out.'

'I don't think it's such a good idea, Lawson.'

'Frankly, I think it's an excellent idea. You're the one who wants to discuss divorce. What better chance? And in a very civilised atmosphere . . . over an excellent dinner.'

It was tempting. To get him to agree to divorce meant

everything. 'Just so long as you understand that I prefer you as a friend, not a husband. I have no intention of becoming reconciled.'

'Yes,' he laughed. 'I understand that you have no such intention.'

'All right,' she said. 'If nine o' clock isn't too late. I believe I can have them all settled by then.'

On the Friday, Dr McCaskie called. Sarah, he proclaimed, had got over the fever remarkably well considering her other difficulties. The calomel and the Dover's Powders had done their work. The course of Blaud's tablets was having a beneficial effect on her anaemia too, as far as he could judge, but she remained listless. It was the opium deprivation, he said, but eventually her body would readjust to normality. Then there was the question of her thinness. She had to be built up. Large amounts of food would outface her so she was to be given small nourishing meals, and often. This same regime would not hinder Titus's health either, for he was like a bag of bones. And it was no more difficult to cater for two as it was for one.

So Rhianna spent a great deal of time cooking. Dr McCaskie gave her a pamphlet with suggested recipes and she decided she would use them. There was calf's foot broth, chicken broth, eel broth and a restorative soup made from veal knuckle that was thickened with arrowroot. Eggs featured strongly, coddled, scrambled, poached in milk, or made into omelettes. She produced jellies from beef, cow heel, Irish moss, orange and port wine, and nourishing puddings such as arrowroot blancmange, baked custard, curds and whey, and semolina cream. Almond restorative made a wholesome drink, as did albumenised milk, and milky coffee enriched with the beaten yolk of an egg.

Harry, however, remained ill, barely gaining weight. Rose, the wet nurse, was still engaged to attend but as Sarah regained some strength, it was evident that with what little feed he took, she was able to provide a little sustenance herself, so Rose came only twice a day, at midday and at teatime.

Rhianna decided to keep secret for the time being her arrangement to have dinner with Lawson. When it was over she would hopefully be able to announce that he'd agreed to divorce her as soon as the law allowed it. On the Saturday night before she went out, she made a beverage of eggs and brandy for Titus and Sarah which, Dr McCaskie assured her, was a powerful restorative and would give a restful night's sleep taken at bedtime. She put Titus to bed, made sure Sarah and the child were comfortable and, after changing into her best dress, she awaited Lawson's arrival.

In a strange sort of way she'd looked forward to it. Seeing him again had triggered memories of the good times they'd had together and she'd pondered them a great deal. She recalled again that first tryst when he'd taken her to a cockfight. She should have realised then what type of person he was, but his roguish yet harmless disregard of the law was attractive to a girl who had spent all her adult life in the sheltered monotony of domestic service and the Girls' Friendly Society. She had profited from that illegal cockfight, too; that money she won had been a godsend. And still was.

She heard the sound of the horse's hoofs on the hard, rough surface of the road outside and, checking that the fire was safely banked up and guarded, she locked the door quietly behind her and left the house. The carriage lamps illuminated her as she climbed aboard Lawson's cabriolet.

'My life, you look astonishingly beautiful,' he said sincerely. 'I am going to be so proud of being seen with you again.'

'Who is likely to see us who matters?' she enquired.

'I shall delight in the admiring glances other men flash in your direction. It doesn't matter who.'

Very soon they arrived at the restaurant, which occupied the first floor over one of the town's billiards rooms. They had lamb cutlets fried in breadcrumbs and then Dutch apple pie followed by cheese. Lawson ordered a bottle of Burgundy but Rhianna took only one glass, realising she must keep her wits about her. Throughout the meal she told him of the troubles she'd encountered since her return home. She explained Sarah's problems and wondered how she had got into such a state. She told him how sorry she was to have arrived after her mother had passed away and told of her anxiety for her father and poor little Harry. Lawson listened attentively making sympathetic noises at appropriate times, until he'd had enough morbidity.

'I want to cheer you up,' he said when they finished eating.

So he reverted to how he used to be. Having got her troubles off her chest with the telling, she seemed glad of the opportunity for some mirth at last. He talked bawdily but wittily, which amused and, to her surprise, excited her. This was the Lawson she had fallen in love with; dashing, daring, funny, indelicate, ribald. This was the unconventional Lawson who had swept her off her feet.

Encouraged by her easy laughter and the way she looked at him, he squeezed her thigh beneath the table.

'Lawson! We happen to be in a restaurant!'

'Nobody can see. The tablecloth hides us. I have a bloody marvellous erection too . . . Give me your hand . . .'

'I most certainly will not.'

'Nobody will see. Go on . . . Feel it.'

'I won't.'

'It's a miracle of hydraulic engineering, this doodle of mine. You don't know what you're missing. Its ability to stand up and defy gravity amazes even me. Go on, feel it . . .'

'As I recall, it's more like an unreliable pistol that can only fire one shot at a time and takes at least an hour to reload,' she said disparagingly.

He chuckled at that. 'Half an hour,' he riposted. 'Only ten minutes with you.'

'Even if that were true, it's nothing to boast about.'

'You think not? . . . But you must admit it's pretty . . .'

Talk veered towards sex in their marriage, to Rhianna's unease. He reminded her of the first night they made love in that hotel at Bath, several days into their honeymoon.

'I thought it was never going to happen. I wanted you so much I was getting depressed . . .'

'Oh, spare me the reminder, Lawson.'

'I still want you, you know. You must realise it by now. I'm still deeply in love with you. Come back to me. I need you more than ever. I'll change. I want to change. I want to make you happy.'

She sighed and finished what remained of her wine. His lack of understanding of her feelings frustrated her. Did he really believe she would go back to him after his behaviour when they lived together?

'The only reason you want me back is to thwart John.'

'To hell with John. Come back to me and I promise I'll stop seeing other women. We'll have maids that are repulsive and an ugly cook. You can have another gig, and another pretty mare like Blossom—'

'I'll never forget the way you had Blossom stolen from under my very nose.'

'To bring you to your cake and milk. You were being unfaithful.'

'Not then, I wasn't. But you were . . . With our maid-of-all-work. Caitlin . . . Do you still bed her?'

'No.'

'So who are you bedding these days? Can you count them on the fingers of one hand?'

'I'm not bedding anybody.'

'So I'm your target till you find somebody, am I?'

'You *are* my wife,' he said, his indignation rising. 'Let's not forget that. There's nothing unusual or controversial in a man bedding his wife.'

Or his maid, Rhianna thought but did not say it. Instead, she said, 'Except that in our case it's not going to happen.'

'Why not, pray? I have the right. And am I not an excellent lover?'

'Quite right, Lawson. You are *not* an excellent lover.'

'Ah, and now you have enough experience to judge,' he commented disdainfully.

Rhianna twirled the empty glass by the stem between her fingers. She wanted to make no further comment. She had goaded him and he'd had too much to drink. Already, by the tone of his last remark, he was spoiling for a fight.

'I'd like to go home now,' she said.

'Go home? You haven't earned your supper yet, my dear. The only home you're going to see tonight is our marital home. And you know what to expect when you get there . . . You're no different to other women – you'll love it anyway . . . Why put on this absurd charade of resistance?'

She got up from the table. 'Charade, is it? I don't think so, Lawson,' she said with a calmness that was false. '*You* might consider yourself God's gift to womankind, but I don't. I know you too well. Thank you for the dinner . . . That at least was excellent.'

'Wait! . . .' He stood up, took out his wallet and dropped a banknote on the table. 'I'll take you home.'

She was conscious that their raised voices had attracted the attention of the other diners. Discreetly, she swept out of the room, grabbed her coat from the stand and skipped down the stairs, knowing that Lawson would follow as soon as the waiter had taken his money. Outside, she turned right, past his parked cabriolet, heading towards Top Church as she put on her coat. He appeared, looked left and right, saw her and ran after her.

'You'll get manhandled walking alone at this time of night,' he called, his breath a cloud of steam in the February cold.

'I'll get manhandled if I ride with *you*,' she retorted. 'I'd rather be manhandled up an entry by some drunken miner.'

'Or miners . . . plural.'

'Better still.'

She turned and hurried away. Thankfully, he did not follow, but she heard him uttering obscenities as he climbed into his cabriolet. By the time he had clicked to the horse she was fifty yards away and she hid in a shop doorway until he disappeared in the other direction. When she was sure he had gone, she stepped out again into the dimly-lit street and hurried towards home.

Oh, her refusal had done her no favours, but she could never allow herself to be used and abused again by him. Who did he think he was? What sort of woman did he think she was? Did he believe her to be as fickle as him? She had John now. She loved John. She would never, *could* never be unfaithful to him . . . Oh, John . . . Gianni . . . What was he doing right now? Was he sleeping, or looking up at the stars in a clear Italian sky wondering if she was watching the stars too. She looked up. If the sky was not swathed with dark storm clouds she might be able to see the same stars as he. Even the clouds were conspiring to prevent that elusive, tenuous communion.

She turned the corner at Top Church and looked about her. There was no sign of Lawson. Well, maybe she had put him off sufficiently to stop his pestering her any more. She might have known he would behave like that. It was in his nature. Despite all his fine words he could never be faithful; not when that thing between his legs ruled his head; that thing of which he was so proud and so fond of talking about, that was such a miracle of gravity-defying hydraulic engineering. Somebody else was welcome to it. Anybody was welcome to it who was stupid enough to fall for his suggestive talk.

She turned into Paradise, treading carefully over its uneven surface. There, at the bottom, she could just make out a horse and gig, its lamps unlit in the darkness. Her heart lurched to her mouth. There would be no escaping him. If only there was some other decent soul about whom she could turn to for help. She turned back along Prospect Row, reached Constitution Hill and scoured its dimness. At the bottom of the hill two hundred yards away she could see the figure of a man in a cape silhouetted against the light from the gasworks. He was walking towards her. She would wait for him, seek his help. Better the devil you don't know . . . She glanced behind to make sure Lawson was not coming. As the man got closer she saw with the utmost relief that it was a bobby on the beat. As he approached she went to meet him.

'Oh, please officer, will you help me?'

'It's time you were tucked up in bed, eh, young lady?' She thought she detected some sarcasm in his voice. 'It's a bit late for walking the streets in this neck of the woods.'

'Please, I need your protection,' she entreated.

'Protection? Hey, don't try that on me. I'll take you to the station and lock you up if you don't get on home quick. You'll find precious few customers about up here.'

'Listen, I am not a prostitute,' she said indignantly. 'I'm a decent, respectable woman and I'm asking for your protection. You're a police constable and a man is pestering me.'

'Where? I can't see no man?'

She explained her presence there and that the man was waiting for her outside her home in Paradise.

'Very well, miss,' he said grudgingly. 'I'll give you the benefit of the doubt.'

They walked on unspeaking, along Prospect Row and down the hill. As they turned into Paradise, Rhianna pointed. 'There. Can you see him? That horse and gig. That's where I live. He's waiting for me.'

'Yes, I can see him,' the constable said without enthusiasm. 'Come on, we'll have you home safe and sound. When you get in, just lock your door, eh?'

As they walked towards the horse and gig, Lawson lit the

coach lamps and stepped down into their light. He smiled at the constable.

'Good evening Albert.'

'Good evening, Mr Maddox, sir. I thought I recognised the gig.'

'That's a fine specimen you have there, Albert.' He nodded towards Rhianna.

'A lady, to hear her talk. Yours, is she?'

'Oh, she's mine all right. She's my wife.'

'Your wife? Ah . . .'

'We live apart . . . at the moment. A temporary arrangement.'

'Is that why she reckons she don't—?'

'You don't need to get involved in a dispute between husband and wife, Albert. It'd be a waste of your time. We can sort out our differences ourselves.'

Rhianna, seeing which way the tide was turning, crept away in the shadows while they were talking. Before Lawson realised she had gone, she was at the top of the entry. As he went to follow, he heard the back door close and the key turn in the lock.

'Better sort it out another day, eh, Mr Maddox?'

'Yes, I suppose so . . . Can I give you a lift, Albert?'

'That's very kind of you, sir.'

'Women!' Lawson said disparagingly. 'Are they worth all the effort we put in for them, all the kindness?' He felt in his pocket and pulled out a handful of coins. He picked out a sovereign and handed it to the constable.

'Thank you, Mr Maddox, sir. That's very kind. I hope I didn't put my foot in it when I asked if she was one of yours.'

'Not at all. She knows there have been other women. It's the reason we're not together now.'

'Well, sir, there's plenty more fish in the sea, I always say.'

'It's teeming with them, Albert.'

*   *   *

When Rhianna entered the house she was surprised to see an oil lamp burning on the table. It could only mean one thing: Sarah must have come downstairs. One of the cupboards at the side of the grate was open; the cupboard in which she stored all their medicines and pills. She picked up the lamp and held it up to peer inside. Everything had been moved, a couple of bottles had been knocked over. Her heart, already thumping over her escape from Lawson, now started pounding harder. Sarah . . . Opium . . . Where was the green bottle of laudanum? Oh, God, no . . .

She had to see if Sarah was all right. She opened the stairs door and screamed. A pale, thin body, naked from the waist down, slid down the bottom stairs, and slumped onto the cold quarries with a dull thud.

'Oh, Sarah, Sarah! I knew I shouldn't have left you.'

Sarah half opened her eyes and a brief, dreamy smile told of the peace she had found in some other paradise.

28

Sarah was feeding her child as she sat propped up in bed one morning in early March. The incident with the laudanum was past though not forgotten. In some ways it had been a blessing, bringing Sarah's dependency into the open. Rhianna had had a long talk with her, explained what the opium had done to her and to Harry, and how she must avoid it at all costs in future, irrespective of how she felt without it meanwhile.

'I love you dearly, Sarah,' Rhianna said, 'and I'll help you get over it. But you must promise me you'll put all your willpower into avoiding it in the future.'

Sarah nodded earnestly, but was unconvinced of her own conviction.

'Dr McCaskie says the craving will disappear in time—'

'How much time, Rhianna?'

'He didn't say – but eventually your body won't require it. For a time though, he says, you'll feel ill for want of it, but you mustn't give in to it.'

'I do feel ill. My stomach feels all knotted, I get cramp in my legs, I'm having to do number twos all the time. I've got no strength, Rhianna.'

'You must never give in to it, our Sarah. If you do, when I've gone back to Italy, you'll end up in the workhouse and that would break my heart. So I'll help you all I can.'

'But poor Harry seems to get no better,' Sarah said, gently squeezing the fragile bundle to her breast.

'Look after him, nurture him, let him feel your love and I'm sure he'll pull through.'

'If he feels as bad as I do, then God help him.'

It had been a month since Rhianna left Italy and still she had not received a letter from John. If he had written, and she was certain that he would have done, he in turn would be concerned that she had not replied. That would set him fretting, wondering. It would almost certainly affect his work, for she was well aware of how sensitive he was. He would become preoccupied, depressed. He would be in no position to know what had really happened, unaware that she was in England and still yearning for his love and his first letter. Maybe she should write to Concetta asking why she had not forwarded his letters. As each day passed she became ever more concerned, ever more convinced that something was amiss. What if he was dead? No . . . Don't even think about that . . . But what if he was ill? What if an accident had befallen him? What if he was lying in some strange bed injured, unable to move? How would this lack of correspondence from the woman he loved be affecting him? She should be with him. But how could she leave her father grieving so morbidly? How could she abandon Sarah and her baby?

'So when are you going back to Italy, Rhianna?'

'When I can see that you're better. When Harry shows some signs of getting stronger. When I'm sure that you can look after him . . . and Father as well.'

'Couldn't you take me to Italy with you?'

The baby finished sucking and Sarah wiped her nipple. She lifted the child to encourage him to bring up any wind.

'But what about Father?' Rhianna said. 'He couldn't make the journey to Italy. And would you like to see him in the workhouse for want of care?'

Sarah shook her head.

'It's one of the reasons it's so important you keep off that stuff and get better.'

'I will get better, Rhianna. I promise. But when I am, what will happen about money if you're not around? How shall I be able to work with a baby to look after?'

'Yes, I know,' Rhianna said quietly, sadly, for it looked as though she would be trapped in England for many months yet. Maybe for ever. Maybe they would have to give up their *Paradiso* and live permanently in England. John would have to return to live and work in Dudley. They would have to find a suitable house here and that would be that. The sad end of a most wonderful dream. How they would miss Italy. How they would miss Concetta and Pasquale, Pietro and Francesca. How they would miss the warm, sunny days, the balmy nights, the spectacular vista from their bedroom window, the suppers under the pergola on the patio . . .

'Would you like me to put Harry back in his new crib?'

Sarah nodded. 'He needs changing. He's messed himself again.' She offered Rhianna the child. Rhianna wiped his mouth and laid him on the bed. She unfastened the soiled napkin, peeled it from him and put it aside ready to be boiled.

'Tell me about John,' Sarah said.

'John? . . . Oh, he's the most unassuming person imaginable. He's the sort of man you would pass by in the street and never bother to give a second glance to. He worries a lot. He imagines he's going to lose me all the time, he's so unsure of himself, so lacking in confidence.' She gave a little chuckle. 'And yet he's the kindest, gentlest, most considerate person I've ever met in my whole life.'

'He's an artist, isn't he?'

'The best. His paintings are a sort of reflection of him. Precise, soothing, inoffensive. Just beautiful.'

'Is he handsome?'

'He's certainly not ugly, but I wouldn't call him handsome particularly.'

'Not like Lawson?'

Rhianna reached over for a clean napkin that was lying on top of the tallboy. 'He's as far removed from Lawson as it's possible to be. Which suits me fine.'

'You love him dearly, don't you, our Rhianna?'

'With all my heart and soul. I'd die for him.'

'Tell me about Italy. Would I like it?'

'I imagine you'd love it. It's different to England. The weather, for a start. The summer is months and months of warm sunshine and soft breezes. The evenings are warm and everybody eats their meals outside. We grow our own grapes, olives, lemons, tomatoes – everything. We make our own wine . . .' For a second, Rhianna sidetracked herself, recalling the night she and John trod grapes after their *vendemmia,* and how their playful washing had led to a particularly passionate lovemaking afterwards. She halted her reverie and fastened the clean napkin on Harry, pulled down his nightgown and laid him back in his crib. 'There aren't the factories in Italy, either. Not like here. People work on the land. Most of them are very poor. And yet they're all so kind and hospitable.'

'I think I *would* like it, Rhianna. Are there some nice young chaps there?'

'Not too many, as it happens. A lot of the young men left to make their fortunes in America and Argentina. The girls are always going on about the lack of men . . . But there's Serafino . . .'

'Serafino? That's a funny name. So who's Serafino?'

'Oh, the brother of my friend Concetta. He's about nineteen, maybe twenty by now – a handsome lad.' There was a flicker of interest in Sarah's eyes that died when she realised she had nothing to offer any young man. 'Concetta reckons he's carrying a torch for me.' Rhianna laughed as though the idea were preposterous.

'For you? I think you have all the luck, Rhianna . . . Tell me, what sort of clothes do they wear in Italy? Are they like ours?'

'More or less. The styles are a bit different. Skirts are a bit shorter, showing your ankles. Nobody wears stockings, especially in the summer – it's just too warm. The girls sometimes wear light linen blouses with a separate lace-up bodice . . . I'm sure I told you.'

'Can't you show me something?'

'Yes . . . I have a dress I can show you. I wore it when I left Italy.'

'Oh, put it on, Rhianna. Let me see what it's like.'

Rhianna smiled. It was so encouraging to see Sarah take an interest in something, instead of the moping, sleepless suffering, the miserable cold sweats and the shivering. Perhaps she was making some progress, though doubtless, there would be relapses.

The metallic clunk of the letterbox downstairs distracted her. Maybe it was a letter from John at last. She ran downstairs, almost knocking the washing basket that protected Titus's accursed foot, and through to the front room. A letter was lying on the linoleum by the front door. She picked it up, but saw that the stamp bore a profile of Queen Victoria. Her heart sank. It was not from Italy. Disappointed, she ran her thumb under the flap and opened it.

What she read took her breath away. She had seen a letter like this before, almost identical. It was from Bowdler, Dickens & Moy, Solicitors and Commissioners for Oaths. Lawson's solicitor. By noon on Friday 13th March 1891 they must be out of the house in Paradise.

Seven days notice to quit.

How could he be so callous?

Of course, he didn't mean it. How could he? How could anybody be so cruel to their fellow beings, especially ailing ones? He knew how ill they were. It was just a ploy, a threat, merely a device by which he could get her to return to him. Well, she would give it the treatment it deserved and ignore it.

She went back upstairs.

'We've just had notice to quit this house,' she told Sarah. 'By a week on Friday.'

'From Lawson?'

'From Lawson's solicitor. Lawson obviously told him to send the letter.'

'He said he'd never do that. He promised me.'

'Oh? He promised *you*? When?'

'Oh . . . I don't know.' Sarah lowered her eyes guiltily. 'Ages ago.'

Rhianna looked at her sister suspiciously. 'You know, Sarah, you've never been able to lie or hide your guilt. You're hiding something from me. What is it?'

'Nothing,' she protested. 'Why should I be hiding anything?'

'Because I can tell.'

'I'm not hiding anything, Rhianna. I've got nothing to hide any more. Look at me, my life is an open book now.'

'Yes, except that you won't admit who Harry's father is . . .' At once Rhianna connected the two issues and the awful possibility struck her. 'It's not *him*, is it? Oh, tell me it's not Lawson. Tell me you haven't been so *stupid* . . .' She looked at Sarah aghast while she awaited her answer.

'I told you . . . I'll never tell you who it was.'

For more than a week Rhianna harboured her doubts. She knew Lawson well enough to realise that he considered no woman was out of bounds. His vindictive streak would hardly inhibit him from seducing his errant wife's younger sister. Lawson and Sarah . . . It had an irresponsibly vengeful twist to it that was typical of him. But it was too puerile to even contemplate, even for Lawson. What grown man could ever stoop to such perverted immaturity? No, *this* was more in Lawson's line; this letter giving notice to quit that she could see standing on the mantelpiece where she had mockingly given it pride of place. This was how he punished people who didn't fulfil his wishes. Notice to quit indeed. Well, she could hardly wait to see what he was going to do about it. For her part, she was doing nothing.

'Tell me, Father?' she said on the Thursday afternoon as she sat with Titus in front of the fire. 'Do you have any idea who the father of Sarah's baby might be?'

Titus shook his head. 'I wished I knowed, my wench,' he croaked weakly. 'I'd go and beat seven bells of shit out of the bleeder.'

'But she must have gone out regularly. Didn't anybody call for her?'

He shook his head ruefully. 'I never sid nobody. 'Er was off out all the while. Every night 'er'd be out till pig squayling. Then it started as 'er never come 'um. Up to no good I always reckoned, but 'er never took no notice o' me, nor your mother. 'Er was beyond reach after a bit.'

'When she got addicted to opium, you mean?'

He nodded almost imperceptibly and looked around him. 'To think as her's come to that. To think as a daughter o' mine has come to that . . . I would never have believed it possible.'

Rhianna put her hand over his. 'But we had some good times, Father. Think about those and thank God for them.'

'If on'y your mother was still here . . .' Titus's thin face screwed up, his chin trembled and tears began to fall from his rheumy eyes. 'Oh, I do miss your mother, our Rhianna . . .'

'I know,' she breathed. 'We all do . . . We all do . . .'

She let go his hand. She could not grieve for him and it was futile to try. Her own grief, her own heightened, tortured emotions were enough to contend with. So she left him to grieve alone as she went upstairs to tend to the baby.

'Has he taken any feed today?' she asked Sarah. 'He doesn't seem as well today.'

'You've seen him at the nipple, Rhianna, but he ain't had hardly anythink. I'm just as full. They'm startin' to hurt a bit.'

'Look at the poor little devil's face. He wants to cry but he hasn't got the strength. God alone knows what he's feeling . . .'

'Pain, I suppose. Oh, I do wish he'd perk up a bit. It's as if we'm fighting a losing battle with him.'

'How do *you* feel, Sarah? Tell me what you feel?'

'You know how I feel. Weak as a kitten. I only have to get up to sit on the jerry an' I feel as if I'm gunna faint. I'm no good for nothin', our Rhianna, and I'm fed up with it.'

'You're better than you were. I can see an improvement. That diet sheet Dr McCaskie gave us has helped. You're not as thin as you were.'

'I don't know what I'd have done without you, Rhianna,' Sarah said tearfully. 'I'm so glad you came home. I missed you so much while you was away. I had nobody to turn to.'

'I missed you as well.'

'Did you? Honest?'

Rhianna nodded. It was obvious to her now that the letter Sarah sent asking her to come home was a desperate plea for herself, just as much as it was a plea to visit her dying mother.

Every morning Rhianna slipped into the same routine. First job was to rake out the ashes in the grate and make a fire. When that was roaring, she would hang a kettle over it and brew a pot of tea then take a cup each to Sarah and her father. Back downstairs, she would cook bacon and eggs and make a fresh pot of tea then serve the invalids breakfast in bed. While Sarah fed Harry, Rhianna would then get her father out of bed, help him to the jerry and dress him. She would struggle to get him downstairs and settle him in his chair, then pass him his razor, his soap, his shaving brush, his tot of hot water and a towel so that he could shave. Back upstairs, she would gather the foul slops from three jerries, empty them then wash them out. There was crockery and cutlery to wash up, laundry, cleaning, preparing food, cooking, coal to fetch from the cellar, fires to make up again, rugs had to be beaten, floors swept, condensation cleaned from windows. A bowl of warm water to take upstairs so that Sarah and the baby could be cleaned.

Thus it promised to be that Friday morning. Rhianna got

up at seven and peered out of the window at the dismal world outside. It had been officially announced that the land abutting the south of Paradise, which had been acquired by the council, was going to be turned into a park next year. At last. Well, that would certainly be an improvement on the pit spoil that looked greyer than ever in the insistent rain that was lashing it. She washed, dressed and went downstairs. She lit her fire and brewed her tea as usual and returned upstairs with two mugs. He father rustled in his bed and snorted as she placed a mug on his bedside table.

'What's the weather up to?' he muttered.

'Raining. Just for a change.'

She opened the door to Sarah's room and went in. As she peeped into the crib she could see that the baby was peacefully sleeping. Sarah stirred, her colour white and sickly. She levered herself to the sitting position and Rhianna puffed up her pillow and placed it at her back.

'Drink this while it's hot.'

'Ta. Is Harry awake?'

'Not yet.'

Rhianna went downstairs. The fire was burning bright. She hooked the dutch oven over the cast iron bars of the fire basket and hung some strips of bacon on the hooks to cook and drip their fat into the collection tray at the bottom. The bacon started to spit but the smell was wonderful. It was one of the smells of home that she truly missed when she was in Italy – until she managed to get some unsmoked bacon in Sorrento once and Nunzio the *postino*, who was delivering mail at the time, alerted the neighbourhood to the wonderful aromas of her English cooking. She broke three eggs into the fat that was bubbling in the base of the dutch oven. When all was ready she kept it warm while she dipped slices of bread in the liquor from the bacon and toasted it. Plated, it was ready to serve.

She helped her father sit up in bed to eat his, then delivered Sarah's, handing her a knife and fork. While Sarah ate,

Rhianna sat on the bed and peered into Harry's crib. The child had still not stirred. She put the backs of her fingers to his little face and felt it with the intention of gently waking him. His face felt cold and rubbery. She pulled back the wraps and felt his body . . . Stone cold . . . Oh, dear God . . . Yet another crisis. The icy chill of even more anguish ran up and down her spine.

'Sarah . . .' she whispered, dreading telling her what she must tell her.

Sarah looked up.

'The baby's dead.'

Dr McCaskie came at once. Apart from issuing a death certificate there was nothing else he could do. He offered his condolences to Sarah, but in private to Rhianna afterwards he declared he was surprised the child had lived this long.

'I can see how you are situated,' he said kindly. 'Would you like me to arrange for the body to be collected? I know an undertaker who will do it providing you use him for the funeral. I assume there *will* be a formal funeral?'

'Oh yes, of course. Thank you, Doctor. That will be a big help.'

While she awaited the undertaker she consoled Sarah before getting on with her household chores. She wept for the child. Like any new-born baby you can't help but wish to protect it and see it thrive. So it was with Rhianna. But the child suffered so much through no fault of its own and she felt so sorry for it. It did not have the experience or the words to tell her how it felt, how it suffered. She dearly wished they could have nurtured it, but what sort of life would it have endured? Perhaps it was a blessing after all.

At about half past twelve she heard the sound of carriage wheels and the clip-clop of horses' hoofs, followed by hurried footsteps echoing through the entry. The undertaker. She opened the door in readiness.

To her alarm, she was grabbed by a man and hustled down

the entry. Although severely shaken, she protested volubly, asking why she was being treated thus, but it made no difference. In the street three more men were standing in the rain, huddling inside their coats to protect them from the blustery wind. To her horror, she saw that one of them was Lawson; his face was a stranger's. The man who was holding her by the arms marched her in front of Lawson as if she were a criminal brought before a judge.

'These men are my bailiffs,' he said stiffly. His look was cold, resentful. 'Since you have not complied with my notice to quit, you are being evicted.'

'Now?' she shrieked, incredulous, the rain slapping her face like an unforgiving schoolmarm.

'Yes, now. You have had ample warning. You had till noon today . . .' He turned to the man who was hurting her wrists. 'All right, let go of her and get back inside . . .'

'What right have you got to evict us?'

'Non-payment of rent. I have every right.'

'But we have a baby dead in the house and two invalids who are incapable of walking?' she yelled angrily. Rain was soaking into her dress and through her hair, her skirt was billowing in the wind. 'You never wanted any rent. You agreed they could live here rent-free.'

He laughed derisively. 'You'll have a hard job proving any such nonsense. Landlords don't provide houses rent-free. We're not charities.'

'Nor are you charitable, Lawson Maddox. I'll pay the rent. You know I will. How much is owed?'

'You can pay the rent if you like but it won't make any difference. It's too late. I've got folk who'll pay good money to live here. Folk who *won't* default. I can't afford to house you and your pitiful family any longer. Already I've been too tolerant, lost too much revenue.'

'I can't believe you're doing this,' she hissed. 'What are you going to do?'

'Turn round and see.'

She turned around. Her father was being carried out, by two burly men, still in his chair. They set him awkwardly on the pavement in the pouring rain while he protested, feebly flailing his arms and cringing at the massive pain that was suddenly afflicting his blighted foot. As she tried to go to her father to help, Lawson grabbed her and held her back.

'You absolute swine,' she screeched. 'You could stop this. It's cruel – brutal. Have you no pity? Can't you see he's a sick man? Sarah's no better either. Are you so vindictive that you can show no mercy? Your quarrel is with me – not them. Leave them be. You can have your rent.'

'Their well-being is nothing to do with me,' he said disdainfully, his face like frozen marble, his voice as sharp as a splinter of broken glass. 'They are not my concern.'

'Let me help my father,' she pleaded, changing tack as she struggled to break free. 'For God's sake, let me put a coat over his shoulders. *Let go of me* . . .'

She began kicking and he slapped her face.

'Calm down, you damned harridan. I am only taking back what is rightfully mine.'

Rhianna was momentarily stunned into silence. She put up her hands to ward off further blows, but none came. The unexpected fear she felt at the first blow receded.

But she knew she was beaten.

Nothing that she could say or do now would save them from Lawson's vindictiveness.

It had not been a good morning and the rest of the day promised to be even worse. Sarah was brought out, but at least the bailiffs had allowed her to put on her dressing gown. She stood for a few seconds but had to sit down and there was nowhere else but the ground with its rain-stippled puddles. The cold and wet seeped through her clothes to her skin and she shuddered. She looked as though she was about to protest, to take issue with Lawson, but the words failed to come out of her tight drawn lips. Another man followed bearing the crib, still with the dead child in it. He thrust it heavily onto the uneven pavement, jarring the lifeless infant.

'Have you no respect?' Rhianna said to the man.

Lawson peered at the dead child with a curiosity that to Rhianna appeared compulsive, then turned away with deliberate disinterest. She was sceptical of his reaction, wondering what his thoughts were at that precise moment. What did he know about this child? She would love to know.

The men started bringing out the furniture. To Rhianna's surprise, they began loading it up onto the cart. At first, she believed it was so that they could move it elsewhere for them, until she realised that Lawson was not nearly so charitable.

'Where are you taking that?' she asked him.

'It's going to be sold, to recoup some of my losses. Not that it's worth a fat lot. Look at it, for Christ's sake. Have you ever seen such tat?'

'If it's worth so little why don't you leave it?'

'I want it out of my property. What would you do with it anyway? Would you walk around with it on your back like a packhorse while you found somewhere else to live? They won't want it in the workhouse, because that's where you're going to end up.'

'Never,' she said defiantly.

More and more things found their way onto the cart. One of the men was tying it all on, oblivious to the driving rain. Titus was shivering on the chair they had allowed him to remain on, and Sarah was weeping uncontrollably on the ground, her thin, helpless figure pathetic in the dressing gown that was absorbing water like a sponge. Her hair was bedraggled, the rain dripping though it and mingling with her futile tears.

Rhianna shivered in the cold. 'Now that you've taken all our chattels, will you at least allow me to go back inside to get our clothes?'

'All right,' he said. 'I'll go with you.'

She went upstairs and from under her bed withdrew the suitcase she had brought with her from Italy. While Lawson inspected the paintwork, the walls and the ceilings of his precious property she stuffed as many clothes and shoes as she could into the case. She went into Sarah's room and collected up her meagre belongings then her father's bits and pieces, which didn't amount to much either. Her mother's things she would have to leave; there was no way of lugging all them about as well. As she struggled to shut the case she could sense Lawson, like the hunted senses the hunter.

'Well?' he said, filling the door frame.

'Would you help me by shutting this case, please? Then I'll be out of your house forever.'

He stooped down beside her, pressed on the lid and snapped it shut. As he flipped the catches on he turned to her. 'You could have prevented all this.'

'Ah! So it's my fault.'

'Of course it's your fault.'

'Naturally . . . It's funny how you can never be blamed for anything. Whatever happens, whatever goes wrong, it's always somebody else's fault. Never yours. You really are quite a remarkable man never to be at fault.'

She stood up and then reached down to pick up the case. She thought he might have the courtesy to carry it for her, but courtesy was not his strong point where she was concerned. So she lifted it by herself with great difficulty and grappled with it down the stairs, Lawson behind her. It crossed her mind that he might shove her down the stairs, so she held tightly to the handrail with her free hand till she reached the bottom.

Outside in the rain, the loading of the cart was finished and one of the bailiffs asked permission to haul it away. Lawson gave it and Rhianna, Sarah and Titus watched the furniture that had served them so well disappear up the hill. He gave the instruction to one of the others to change the locks then mockingly touched his hat, stepped up onto his cabriolet and flicked the reins.

'Good riddance,' Rhianna muttered under breath. She turned to Sarah. 'Decent chap isn't he, eh, Sarah? Exactly the sort every girl should aspire to marry.'

'What are we going to do now?' Sarah asked, shivering with cold.

'Well, we can't stay here. I'll hurry to the station and find a hansom. We'll have to stay the night in an hotel till we can get settled.'

'We'll have to take the baby with us, won't we?'

'Yes, unless the undertaker comes before I get back. I'll try not to be long.'

Before she went, she asked Titus to stand a second or two while she shifted the chair that Lawson had allowed him to keep into the shelter of the entry. Then, she carefully manoeuvred him onto it.

'I won't be long, Father. I'm going to get a hansom to take us to a nice warm hotel.'

29

They took lodgings at the Castle Hotel in the town, but for how long Rhianna did not know. What money she had would not last indefinitely. There was a funeral to pay for next week, no doubt her father would require Dr McCaskie to call after the nightmare of eviction, and perhaps even Sarah . . . On their way to the hotel in the hansom they detoured to deliver the dead baby at the undertaker's in Hall Street; it would have precluded them acquiring rooms had the corpse of a child accompanied them. The landlord was inclined to refuse them anyway at the sight of Sarah in her dripping wet dressing gown and Titus having to be supported as he walked, both seemingly at death's door. Only Rhianna's poignant supplication and her earnest appeal to his commercial nature, by ensuring he had sight of several gold sovereigns in her hand, swayed him. At once Titus took to his bed, glad of clean, dry sheets, blankets and a warm eiderdown, relieved to be out of the bitter March wind and the rain. The ordeal had been more than he could take.

Rhianna's priority was to find a furnished house to rent. Meanwhile, at least they were warm. She bought a copy of the *Dudley Herald* and scoured it for available accommodation, but few were being offered furnished. One, however, looked promising. It was in Bond Street, just around the corner from Campbell Street where they had lived before. Next morning, she made her way to the address to which she had to apply and presented herself to the landlord, a Mr Willetts. He escorted her to Bond Street, ranged on each side with a long row of terraced houses with smoking chimneys lined up like sentries. He showed her around the house. The rooms needed wallpapering, the scullery needed a coat of whitewash, there were damp patches on the ceiling in two of the three bedrooms and the fire grate was none too special, but it would do. It was certainly no worse than the house in Paradise. The furnishings were not exceptional either, but she hadn't expected them to be. Just so long as they could live there till Sarah was better, without the expense of spending more money. She paid a deposit and took the key.

On the Sunday, she went to the house to light fires to air the place; a little coal remained in the cellar from the previous occupant. Fortunately, clean bed linen was supplied, which she took from the cupboard Mr Willetts had shown her, and made up the three beds. She cleaned the windows and polished the front step and looked forward to some peace at last, some respite from Lawson Maddox's vengeful antics.

Suddenly, like a bolt of lightning, it struck her that she would not be able to retrieve John's letters when they arrived. She must write to Concetta at once to let her know this new address. Maybe then she would resume contact with the man she earnestly loved and missed so much. She longed to be free of the pain of emptiness and longing and grieving for his absent love.

It occurred to her that if any letters arrived at Paradise meanwhile, Lawson would collect them; he would realise who they were from and destroy them . . . But an even more terrifying thought struck her – he was evil enough to reply to John. He was malicious enough to write saying she had no further need of him since she'd returned to the sanctity of her marital home. A lump came to her throat. Would he really stoop so low?

It was precisely the jolt she needed. As soon as she returned to the Castle Hotel, she wrote a quick note to Concetta, unsure of the spelling of any of the Italian words. It might be a couple of weeks before she got a response; another couple of weeks wondering and worrying. Worrying not just for herself but for John as well. He must be at his wit's end for want of a letter.

All this worrying was taking its toll. The death of the baby, the obvious deterioration in her father, Sarah's distressing ups and downs. She was feeling peculiar herself sometimes. It was a real effort to get up of a morning. Even after a good night's sleep she felt tired and drained. Nor was it lack of food; she was eating well. Maybe it was to be expected looking after her invalids; they were hard work.

Monday arrived. She put on her hat and coat and slipped out to post her letter. The March wind was boisterous, biting as it seared through Dudley Market Place. Smoke from the chimneys twisted one way then another. She walked down Wolverhampton Street, with its exotic furniture stores, jewellery shops and public houses, to the little post office on the corner of Priory Street. Inside, she handed over her letter and paid for the stamp.

'How long does it take to get to Italy?' she enquired anxiously, recalling how long it had taken her and John.

'Five or six working days at least,' the assistant told her.

A week, in anybody's language.

On her way back from the post office Rhianna secured a hansom. She asked the driver to take her to the Castle Hotel and explained that her sister and father, who had to be taken to a house in Bond Street, were both infirm. He was most obliging, assisting Titus and Sarah, whose clothes were several sizes too big for her, into the house. He helped Titus upstairs and settled him into the clean, bed that awaited him, then lugged the heavy suitcase upstairs. He wished them the best of luck as Rhianna sent him off with a generous tip.

Sarah said she would sit up a little while. As Rhianna unpacked their clothes, Sarah decided to help but was overcome by a feeling that she was going to faint so lay on her bed and watched, incapable of helping more.

'You were going to show me that Italian dress you wore,' Sarah said. 'Remember?'

Rhianna rummaged through the case and found it. Smiling, she held it up. 'This is the one . . .'

'Oh, put it on, our Rhianna. I'd love to see what you look like in it.'

Rhianna stripped to her underwear and slipped the dress over her head. It was made of linen and a rich crimson in colour, with a rounded neck that swooped tantalisingly close to her cleavage. The sleeves were close fitting and three-quarter length and it was tight at the waist. She shoved her hands into the pockets on either side of the skirt and twirled around.

'Oh, it's lovely, Rhianna. It don't half show your figure up.'

'It's an Italian style for Italian women. Italian men like to see their women to best advantage.'

'But the poor folk you told me about wouldn't wear a dress like that, would they?'

'They probably wouldn't buy one, but maybe they'd make one similar.'

'Can I try it on, Rhianna?'

'I think it would swamp you at the moment. Let's wait till we've built you up a bit more, eh? Then you'll look a treat in it.'

Sarah smiled. 'Yes, I need to fatten up a bit more, don't I? I'm still too scrawny.'

'Oh, you're on the mend. You'll soon fill out.'

Inside one of the pockets Rhianna felt a scrap of folded paper. She withdrew it and looked at it, puzzled. She opened it up. As she read it she felt her insides drop. It was the address in England – in Paradise – that she should have handed to Concetta so that she could divert John's letters. How on earth had she forgotten to hand over anything so important? No wonder she had received nothing. Concetta wouldn't know where to send the mail. Yet in another way it was also a blessing; Lawson would pick up none of John's letters. At least John would be safe from his vindictive fancies.

One of the first things Rhianna had to do was buy some provisions. At the market place she stopped to buy vegetables and oranges. She made her way to Devis's the butchers and bought some liver, to Lipton's for tea, sugar, butter, cheese, lard and a loaf of bread until she could intercept the baker's van. As she came out of Lipton's, a wreck of a girl passed in front of her carrying a child. Yet another ailing young mother – and she had the look about her of being unmarried. The girl turned and spoke to Rhianna.

'Mrs Maddox . . . It's yourself, is it not?'

Rhianna looked at the waif horrified; she recognised her. The thin, haunted look had not totally destroyed what was once a pretty face; the eyes were still wide and alert. 'It's Caitlin, isn't it? Caitlin O'Flanagan.'

'That's right, ma'am. I'm pleased you still recognised me.'

Rhianna did not know what to say. Although the girl was carrying a baby it seemed too intrusive to mention it. Odds were that Lawson was the father. But Caitlin was a bag of rags, pale and emaciated. It could have been Sarah she was looking at.

'I got a baby, ma'am,' she said, stating the obvious.

Rhianna smiled uncertainly. 'I was just about to ask whether it's a boy or a girl.'

'A girl. Seven months old.'

'She seems quite small for seven months, Caitlin.'

'Oh, that she is. I didn't think I was going to rear her. But I was lucky. She pulled through. We both did.'

'Were you ill as well then?'

'Oh, you could say that, ma'am. But I'm getting better.' She smiled affably, putting Rhianna at her ease. 'We both are.'

'And your husband?'

'I'm not married, ma'am.'

Rhianna was itching to ask whether Lawson was the child's father but it was too soon, and too personal a question.

'Please, ma'am . . . I know it might be awkward for you, meeting me like this, especially after . . . you know . . . But I'm so glad I've seen you. You were very fair to me in the short time I worked for you . . .'

'I was in service myself once,' Rhianna said kindly, taken with Caitlin's sincerity. 'I know what it means to have a considerate employer.'

Caitlin lowered her eyes. 'I'm so sorry for the way it all ended up, ma'am.'

'Water under the bridge, Caitlin.'

'I understand, ma'am . . . that . . . that you and Mr Maddox went your separate ways . . .'

'Yes, we did.'

'Best thing you could have done, if you don't mind me saying so.'

Rhianna shrugged non-committally. After all, what business was it of Caitlin?

'Oh, ma'am, please don't mind me askin', but would you take me for a cup of tea and a bite to eat? I've not eaten for two days, and my baby . . .' There was an impassioned plea in her expression that Rhianna found impossible to resist. 'And there's so much I'd like you to know. So much I can tell you . . .'

Rhianna was suddenly intrigued and pondered where they could go. It was afternoon, the dinnertime rush was over. 'All right. Let's go to the Fountain Dining Rooms across the road.'

'Wherever you say, ma'am.'

'What name have you given the baby?' Rhianna asked conversationally as they headed towards the eating house.

'Rhianna, ma'am. After you.'

'Rhianna?' Rhianna smiled, pleasantly surprised and of course flattered. 'You named her after me?'

'Yes. As a reminder of what a decent, sensible woman should be like. I look up to you, ma'am. I always did. I admired you from the outset. I just got a little bit sidetracked by your husband along the way.'

'I suppose that's one way of putting it.'

'But I didn't know he was your husband at the time,' she said defensively. 'Otherwise I would never . . .'

They quickly arrived at the Fountain Dining Rooms. The place was empty but for a youngish couple who were whispering sweet nothings to each other in a distant corner. Rhianna chose a table far from them and they sat down.

'How's your mother?' Rhianna asked while they waited to be served. 'Is she still a cook?'

'I don't know, to tell you the truth, but I imagine so. I don't see her. She's a devout Catholic, you know, ma'am. She disowned me when she found out I was pregnant.'

'Just when you could have used her help and support.'

Caitlin sighed. 'Indeed I could've. I know that only too well, ma'am.'

'Please call me Rhianna,' she said with a smile. 'I'm not the lady of the house any more.'

'Thank you. Thank you, Rhianna.' The baby roused and murmured so she rocked her gently in her arms. Caitlin smiled, her large eyes creasing pleasantly. 'She's sleeping well today.'

'So what is it you want to tell me? What is it you think I should know?'

'Well, first, that your husband is the father of my child – if you hadn't already guessed it.'

Rhianna gasped. It still came as a shock.

'You seem surprised.'

'And yet I shouldn't be, should I?'

'Oh, but that's only the beginning. I don't think you ever knew what he was like, did you? You couldn't have, else you would never have married him, I'm sure. A decent lady like yourself.'

445

A waitress arrived at the table and asked if they were ready to order.

'Have whatever you fancy to eat, Caitlin. Have a dinner if you're hungry.'

'If you're sure you don't mind.'

'Of course.'

'You're very kind.' Caitlin looked up at the waitress who seemed to have distanced herself from the girl, as if she might catch a whiff of something unattractive. 'Do you have a beef dinner left?'

The waitress said she believed so. Rhianna ordered a slice of fruit cake for herself and a pot of tea for two.

'What about the baby?' Rhianna asked.

'Oh, if she wakes up she'll take some of my potato if I mash it up, that she will.'

'Fancy meeting up with you again, Caitlin,' Rhianna went on. 'You were the last person I expected to see.'

Caitlin looked guiltily at Rhianna. 'I'm so sorry, ma'am – Rhianna I mean – over what happened . . .'

'Please, no more apologies, Caitlin. Apologies aren't warranted. You were the second best thing that ever happened to me.'

Caitlin smiled, more comfortable with Rhianna after her reassurance. 'The second best? . . . Ah, I suppose the first best was your artist friend?'

'You're well informed.'

'Lawson kept me informed . . . then . . . At the time, I was pleased that you left. I thought it would leave the door open for me. How stupid I was . . .'

'So where are you living, Caitlin? It must be difficult for a young mother on her own.'

'Oh, I rent a room.'

'And do you work?'

'No . . . I have to beg. I'm one of the dregs of society.'

'You beg? Oh, Caitlin . . .'

'But I've not always begged. When I left your house Lawson found me a job as a maid at his bawdy house—'

'Bawdy house?' Rhianna repeated questioningly. 'You mean that house he kept in Netherton for his goings-on?'

'No, not that one. He has this house in Downing Street, by the castle . . . Didn't you know? He rents the rooms by the hour to the well-to-do men who need somewhere to do their dirty business with their fancy women. It's a bit like an hotel. There's a couple of small dining rooms where they entertain their women before they take them to bed. There's always drink available . . . other things too . . .'

'I never heard of such a thing,' Rhianna exclaimed. 'I knew he had some properties other than the ones he rented to families. I didn't know he had a bawdy house.'

Caitlin looked at Rhianna with sympathy in her expression. 'Goodness, Rhianna, you don't know anything, do you?'

'So which well-to-do folk go there – to this bawdy house – with their fancy women?'

'Oh, I don't know them all for sure. Important people who expect absolute discretion. There was a lawyer, I was told. One or two bigwigs from the town hall . . . wealthy factory owners . . .'

'Did you ever hear of a man called Alexander Gibson?'

'Oh, *him*! Yes, I remember him. He was often there. He liked very young girls.'

'Mmm. That is no surprise . . . What about Mr Jeremiah Cookson?'

'He used to go there as well . . . and his son, Robert Cookson . . . Though they never seemed to be there at the same time. I expect Fanny used to see to it that they never encountered one another. I guess it could have been embarrassing.'

'Fanny? Did you say Fanny?'

'Yes. Fanny Lampitt. She was Lawson's housekeeper there. She ran the place for him.'

The waitress returned with Caitlin's dinner, Rhianna's piece of cake and the pot of tea, and placed them on the table. Rhianna thanked her.

'Caitlin, would you like me to hold the baby while you eat?'

'Oh, would you mind? That's very kind.'

She passed the baby to her and Rhianna cradled her in her arms, looking down at the child curiously to ascertain whether it bore any resemblance to Lawson.

'I remember Fanny Lampitt,' Rhianna said looking up again as Caitlin sprinkled her dinner with salt and pepper. 'The very first night I met Lawson she was with him. She spent a lot of time that evening with Robert Cookson.'

'Yes, I understand he was one of her favourite clients.'

'Clients?' Rhianna queried.

'Yes, she was a prostitute. As well as looking after the bawdy house she plied her trade there as well. Only very select clients though, you understand. She wasn't on her back all the time, like some of the girls I knew.'

Rhianna looked astounded.

'Didn't you know?'

'Caitlin, I don't know anything. Please tell me. What has been going on?' Caitlin was ravenously tucking into her meal . . . 'No, it can wait till you've finished eating.'

'Besides the bawdy house, Lawson runs three brothels,' Caitlin announced when she'd finished her food and wiped her mouth.

'*Three* brothels?' Rhianna was aware that in her astonishment she was repeating everything Caitlin said.

'Oh, yes. Scattered about the borough, so they are. Well, as I think you know, I fell head over heels for Lawson. I met him at a cock and hen night in the town and we got talking. I learnt later it was before you married him. Well, to be sure he was great fun and he had such a way with him . . . It was the first time I'd ever been with a man and till that moment I was more wholesome than the blessed Virgin herself. He took me to that house in Netherton. After that my life was changed. I was besotted and I couldn't wait till the next time he took me there. I expect he could see how much in love with him I was, that I'd do anything for him . . . Then, one night – it was after you'd left him and I was working as a maid in this bawdy house – he said he didn't think I loved him. He was testing me, of course. I see that now. When I said, "Of course I do", he said I was to prove it.'

'And how were you to prove it?'

'He wanted me to go to bed with somebody else. If I would do that, it would be proof, he said. He said there was a man in the house – a friend of his – who wanted me. He said if I wouldn't, it'd be proof enough that I didn't love him. "How can I go to bed with another man?" I said. "I only want to go to bed with you. I love only you," I said. "What if I want you to?" he said. "Won't you do it for me?"'

'Well, Rhianna, I didn't know what to do and that's the gospel truth. I was torn. Anyway, he pulled out of his pocket this little packet containing powder – dope, he called it – and mixed it with some gin we were drinking. "Drink that," he said, "it'll make you feel all nice and relaxed. Like being in Elysium," he said. I remember his words so well. So I drank it. Before I knew it I felt so nice, just like he said I would – different to how I'd ever felt before. I can't describe it. The world seemed so warm and benign and I felt as though nothing could harm me. It was such a lovely feeling, Rhianna. I felt like a contented kitten that really had found its perfect home. And I had the urge to make love as well, like never before . . . He took me to this room and said I was to do whatever his friend wanted. After a while this man came in. I didn't know him from Adam. I never saw him again after, either. But he stripped my clothes off me and I just lay there, smiling contentedly – I was in paradise, remember, this Elysium, so warm and comfortable – and he took his own clothes off as well. He lay on the bed with me and he messed about with me for ages, feeling me all over, kissing me everywhere . . . It was nice . . . Then he had me . . . I was quite happy for him to have me. As I recall, it was very pleasant. And nothing could harm me, remember – I was cocooned from harm.

'Next day I woke up and thought it had all been a pleasant, erotic dream. Then Lawson came in and kissed me and thanked me for going to bed with his friend. I looked around me. The bedroom was strange – not my room – but I did have this recollection of spending the night there. I really can't remember how I felt when Lawson thanked me though – whether I was pleased I'd proved my love and that he was appreciative, or what. But I knew one thing for certain – I wanted some more of that dope.

'Of course, it happened again quite soon after. And so that I could have some more dope I agreed to it readily. It wasn't long before I was pleading for dope. Lawson said I would have to earn it. I can see now that he wasn't interested in me for himself any more. So he moved me from his bawdy house and took me in his gig to another house that was obviously one of his brothels. There I spent most of my time on my back underneath some of the most grotesque creatures imaginable. In my lucid moments I realised I had descended to the level of a whore, but I felt no shame. It was worth it, Rhianna. It was worth being poked up hill and down dale till I was sore, by all those disgusting men, just to get my dope.'

'So if you were working as a prostitute, Caitlin,' Rhianna said, 'I presume he paid you? Some folk reckon it's a job of work, after all.'

'I never got a penny. But I didn't need money. Everything was found, my food, my drink. I was warm, I had my own bed which I shared, as I said, with every filthy, dirty Tom, Dick and Harry in the borough and beyond. But most of all I had my regular dope which he was happy to provide for as long as I earned money for him. Quite a few of his girls were on dope as far as I could see. Once decent girls, like me I imagine, who'd fallen for his evil charms.'

'How many girls were there in his brothels?'

'Oh, Lord knows. Eight in the house I lived in.'

'Eight?'

'But then, Rhianna, after a while, it was obvious I was pregnant. One or two men liked me with a big belly like that, and he kept me on for a while. But as my time drew closer he threw me out. He said I was no use to him any more.'

'Nothing surprises me any more about Lawson Maddox,' Rhianna proclaimed indignantly. 'Then what happened?'

'Well to be sure I had nowhere to go. My mother had disowned me, remember. Eventually I was picked up out of the gutter, a pathetic, stinking mess of pain and shivering incontinence. They took me to the workhouse. I had my baby there and they helped me to overcome the awful, painful craving for dope. They explained that my baby was just as addicted as I was. I endured hell, Rhianna, and so did she . . .' Caitlin looked lovingly at the child back in her arms again. 'There's no hell like it when you can't get it, believe me. But I was determined never to touch that stuff again. I began to realise what a whore it had turned me into. I was never brought up to live my life like that. We were a respectable, God-fearing family. After a few months they could see I was getting better and they agreed to discharge me, providing I gave up prostitution, kept off the dope and could find proper work. Well, I stopped all that . . . Mind you, I could so easily go back on the dope if I could afford it, but I'm determined not to. Never . . . But I haven't found work yet. So I have to beg . . .'

'How can you be sure the baby is Lawson's, after so many men?'

'I just know. I was pregnant even before he made me lie with other men. I hadn't been with anybody else then. You know when you're pregnant, Rhianna. And it could only have been his child.'

'I take it Lawson doesn't provide for the baby?'

'What a joke!' Caitlin said sarcastically. 'He wouldn't even acknowledge her existence.'

'Well, perhaps he should . . . Tell me . . . Did you ever come across a girl younger than you called Sarah Drake?'

'The name doesn't ring a bell.'

Caitlin's ignorance of Sarah was not proof that Sarah hadn't been subjected to the same ordeals but the symptoms they shared were sadly too similar to be discounted. Caitlin was perhaps luckier; she'd reared her baby and seemed to have successfully broken the opium habit. But Lawson's callousness, his utter lack of concern for the well-being of the girls he seduced, was criminal. Surely she could have him arrested. He would surely stand trial. And a conviction might even ensure a speedy divorce.

'Would you do me a favour, Caitlin?' Rhianna asked.

'I think I owe you one.'

'It's my opinion that Lawson should stand trial for what he's done, not only to you but to other girls as well. And I think I know another, besides you. Would you come with me to the police station tomorrow? I want to report him. I want to make sure he pays the penalty for what he's doing.'

Caitlin looked reticent. 'Oh, I don't know, Rhianna . . . Once they know I've been a prostitute they'll arrest me, to be sure.'

'No, they won't. Not if you give evidence against him. You're a victim, Caitlin. You're also a witness. An important witness. Meet me at eleven outside here. I'll buy you dinner again later.'

Caitlin smiled. 'Very well . . . You see how important my dinner is to me now. When I was taking that stuff I barely ate at all. I must be getting better.'

'Well here's a half sovereign to buy you some supper and help you to continue with your recovery.'

'Thank you, Rhianna,' Caitlin said, taking the small coin. 'You're so very kind. There'll be no dope, though. Not any more. I have a baby to care for.'

30

Rhianna returned home and put away her shopping. She went upstairs and checked, first of all, on her father. She was concerned about him. His breathing had become laboured, he was feverish and refusing to eat.

'Would you like a cup of tea, Father?'

Titus nodded from his pillow, failing to open his eyes.

Back downstairs Rhianna brewed a pot of tea, poured out three cups, added milk and sugar, put them on a tray and took them upstairs. She took one to Sarah, then one to her father and sat him up. Still he did not open his eyes, as if to do so would bring into view the viciously disappointing world from which he was anxious to escape.

'If you're no better tomorrow I shall ask Dr McCaskie to call,' she told him as she pressed the cup gently to his lips.

Titus sipped indifferently at the hot, sweet tea, and some dribbled down his chin. Dr McCaskie could not cure him now. Nothing could cure him. He had suffered enough over the years; consumption, severe gout, the painful rift in his family, a once-decent daughter turned slut and opium addict. But the worst suffering of all was this unbearable heartbreak over the loss of his beloved Mary. If such was the joy of living he would rather be dead. He would much rather be dead . . .

Rhianna knew she was not going to get any conversation out of him. He was not interested in conversation. He inhabited his own world these days and evidently preferred its seclusion. She spoke to him as she would to a child, expecting no reply, while he slurped the tea little by little. Afterwards, she held his hand briefly and felt a faint squeeze of affection from him.

'I'm going to see Sarah now, Father.' She relieved him of the empty cup, put it back on the tray, and settled him in his bed again. She picked up the cup she had poured for herself and took it with her to Sarah's room.

'I met somebody today in the town I hadn't seen for a long time,' Rhianna said conversationally, sitting on the edge of Sarah's bed with her tea cup held between two hands.

'I thought you seemed a long while.'

'Well, we had a good long chat. It was very enlightening.'

'Oh? Who was it?'

'Do you remember me mentioning a maid I employed when I lived with Lawson in Himley Road? An Irish girl called Caitlin O'Flanagan?'

'Vaguely.'

'She was the one I caught with Lawson at that house in Netherton. She was the reason he and I parted.'

'Oh, that one . . .'

'Well, when I discovered she and Lawson were . . . you know . . . lovers . . . I thought of her as the most despicable kind of Jezebel. Funny, isn't it, how incidents tend to change your perceptions of somebody? I mean, when I first met her she seemed such a decent, honest girl. I took to her at the time, and what happened afterwards made me change my mind. But after talking to her today I'm sure my first impression was right. I believe she *is* a decent, honest girl after all. She was just cruelly misled. Shall I tell you what happened to her?'

Sarah shrugged with uncertainty, avoiding Rhianna's eyes. She had an uncomfortable suspicion where this might be leading.

'Well, Lawson made her pregnant, you know. She was madly in love with him and he knew it. Anyway, one night he asked her to prove how much she loved him. He told her that if she truly loved him she'd be prepared to do anything for him, even sleep with another man if he asked her to. And he did ask her. Can you believe that, our Sarah? Caitlin refused at first, but to persuade her he gave her some dope. She said the dope made her feel all nice and cosy and safe and she didn't mind his friend doing all those things to her. When Lawson asked her again, she was glad to do it because it meant she would have some more dope. When she asked for more, he said she had to earn it and he put her in one of his brothels. She reckons she had to have sexual intercourse with as many men in a day and night as wanted her. Can you believe that, our Sarah? Don't you think that's terrible?'

Sarah nodded half-heartedly, biting her bottom lip as she studiously avoided Rhianna's eyes.

'By the time she was due to have her baby, Lawson kicked her out because she was no further use to him. And you know what happened to her?' Sarah shook her head. 'She was picked up from the gutter and taken to the workhouse. But you know, through all her trouble she was determined to raise her baby and stop using dope forever. I think she's been very brave, very determined. She had nobody, Sarah. Nobody. All she has now is her baby, and she loves that child with all her heart.'

'I loved Harry, Rhianna. I still love him.'

'Oh, I know that,' Rhianna said gently. 'But I thought what a coincidence that both of you should have had a baby, and both of you had this hankering for opium.' Rhianna looked at her sister knowingly. 'It's quite a coincidence as well that both of you knew Lawson . . . Isn't it?'

Sarah looked down at her fingers, which were fiddling nervously with the edge of the sheet, her loose hair falling forward, half covering her face. She sniffed, but said nothing. She sniffed again and with the back of her long, slender hand wiped her right eye. Conscious that Rhianna was watching her she looked up.

Rhianna saw the tears streaking down her face and knew for certain that this was exactly what had happened to Sarah. She too had been one of Lawson's innocent victims. She shifted across the bed and slid her arms around Sarah, drawing the girl to her. The younger girl's head rested against Rhianna's chest and, as she gave her a reassuring hug, Sarah began sobbing. She sobbed for a long time, neither girl speaking, apart from Rhianna's whispered consolations. It was good for her sister to cry like this. It all helped to get the hurt, the guilt, the grief of losing the child, out of her system.

'It doesn't matter to me that you had an affair with Lawson,' Rhianna said when Sarah's blubbering had subsided. 'Feel sorry for yourself, not for me. Don't you see, he's a cad. He keeps a bawdy house and brothels. He puts girls like you through hell to feed his vile self-conceit and fill his wallet with money they've earned. He's the worst kind of parasite. He should be locked up . . . I suppose he promised you the earth?'

Sarah nodded as she dabbed her reddened eyes with a handkerchief. 'He told me he loved me, Rhianna. I thought he wanted to marry me. And I idolised him.'

'You poor, poor fool.' She consolingly ran her fingers through Sarah's hair. 'Why don't you tell me all about it. Get it off your chest. It's something we have to discuss. Tomorrow I'm meeting Caitlin again and we're going to the police station. I'm going to report him. I'm going to get him put away. He won't get away with it.'

Sarah sniffed and sighed, dried her eyes. 'It was when you'd left him to live with your John Gibson. He met me from work one afternoon, told me he was glad you'd gone, that it was me he'd loved all along. He said we should start courting and we could all stay in the house in Paradise for nothing. He took me to that house he keeps in Netherton and . . . well . . .'

'He seduced you . . .'

'It was my first time, Rhianna, honest. I'd never been with a man before that.'

'Caitlin said the same thing . . . Maybe he's got a passion for virgins. Why would that be, I wonder? I would've thought he'd prefer girls with some experience . . . But then there's always the chance of picking up some venereal disease, I suppose.' It was then that Rhianna realised she'd been a virgin too. She recalled Lawson's glassy-eyed delight at the prospect of waiting till their wedding night to savour her virginity. 'And then I bet he asked you to prove you loved him by agreeing to go to bed with other men. Is that what happened next, Sarah?'

'Yes, but not till we'd been courting for a while.'

'Till he'd got tired of you . . .'

Sarah shrugged. 'Maybe . . . But I didn't want to go with anybody else. I was in love with him. I only wanted him. But he gave me the dope. Same as he did that Caitlin.'

'And then you realised you were pregnant?'

'Yes . . .' Her voice tailed off. Then, more earnestly, she said, 'It's funny you mentioning about virgins, Rhianna . . .'

'Oh?'

'Well, he couldn't get over how young I was . . . I was still only sixteen – no – just gone seventeen, but he said I looked even younger. I heard him say he could get more for me if I pretended to be a virgin . . .'

Rhianna uttered a laugh of derision. 'Well, how can you pretend to be a virgin when you're not? Either a girl is a virgin or she's not. Men can tell the difference, surely.'

'Oh, it's easily faked, Rhianna. It's something he made the younger girls do.'

'How? I don't understand.'

'I had to squat over a bucket of hot vinegar and water with myrrh and acorns in it. Every day. The steam off it was supposed to tightened me up.'

Rhianna tutted in disgust and disbelief. 'And did it?' she asked, her curiosity getting the better of her.

'It seemed to . . . Then, before I saw the client, I had to shove up a scrap of sponge that'd been soaked in blood, to make it look as though I'd bled after.'

'You mean, so that when he entered you, the pressure would squeeze out the blood?'

'Yes. All I had to do was yowk a bit, to make it sound convincing. It seemed to fool 'em all.'

'And Lawson made you do all that?'

'Yes.'

Rhianna shook her head. 'He's unbelievable. Every time anybody speaks about him it exposes new depths of his depravity. Do you remember anybody called Alexander Gibson? You might remember him from your days at the Cooksons.'

'Yes, there was a man who was familiar to me. A real swell. Getting on a bit.'

'I bet that was him . . . But it must have been awful for you . . .'

'Oh, it wasn't so bad, our Rhianna. Some of these chaps were quite nice. Some did it ever so nicely. I quite liked it . . .'

'Sarah!'

'It might sound awful but it's true. You want me to tell the truth, don't you? I had my regulars who liked me. I didn't have to pretend to be a virgin with them after the first time . . .'

Rhianna sighed. 'But as your belly got bigger, he could hardly pass you off as a virgin anyway.'

'No, that's when he made me work as an ordinary prostitute.'

'And what did he pay you for this *work*?'

'Nothing. He never paid me a penny.'

'But you'd given up your job at the leather works by this time, I suppose.'

'Oh yes. I didn't have no time for that.'

'My God, it's a wonder you didn't catch anything.'

Sarah shrugged again. 'Well, I don't think I did.'

'Do you think we should get Dr McCaskie to examine you?'

'I din't catch anything, Rhianna,' Sarah insisted. 'I just told you. He had me checked regular.'

'Oh, Sarah, my poor little sister.' Rhianna hugged her again.

'After all that, doesn't your own determination make you want to win through and put it all behind you?'

'If I could just get through one day without aching for some dope I know I'd soon get well again.'

Rhianna reached for her cup and finished the rest of her tea which was only lukewarm by this time. 'I have an idea,' she said. 'I have an idea that I'm sure would help you . . .'

Next morning early, Rhianna called once more at Dr McCaskie's surgery. She told of her concern for her father and he promised to call later that day.

'Can you make it late afternoon?' she suggested. 'I'm going to the police station when I leave here.'

'The police station? May I ask why?'

She told him what she had discovered during her meeting with Caitlin, and Sarah's subsequent confession.

'That man should be brought to book,' he replied.

'I couldn't agree more. That's why I'm going to the police.'

'You can count on my support, Mrs Maddox. If you need a witness I'd be happy to stand. You can't go around ruining the lives of decent young women, like he has. Good Lord, I've seen the proof of it and no mistake.'

'Thank you, Dr McCaskie. But somebody – presumably a doctor – is checking these girls for venereal disease. If we knew who it was he could be a valuable witness too.'

'It might not be any doctor we know of. Any unqualified quack could do it if he knows what to look for. But let's hope it's no quack.'

Rhianna left the surgery and was just in time to meet Caitlin with her baby. Caitlin smiled amiably when she saw Rhianna and they made their way to the police station, while Rhianna told her Sarah's story.

Dudley police station and lock-up in Priory Street was a parody of the old Norman castle which overlooked it, built in local brick. Its square, ivy-clad towers were castellated and decorative arrow slits adorned the adjoining walls. Beyond the wrought-iron railings that protected it from the marauding public lay a broad path that mimicked a drawbridge which, in turn, led to a gate that was meant to resemble a portcullis. Together Rhianna and Caitlin walked beneath the jutting blue lamp and the coat of arms, through the heavy gate. Through a door across the inner courtyard, they were greeted affably by a constable at the counter.

'I'd like to see an inspector, please,' Rhianna requested sombrely.

'An inspector, eh. Well, I think the inspector on duty might be a bit too busy to see anybody right now, ma'am. If you'd like to tell me what it's all about, I daresay I can help.'

'It's something I'm only prepared to discuss with an inspector,' she answered, remembering the too-friendly greeting between a police constable and Lawson the night he lay in wait for her. 'I have a very serious complaint to register that needs urgent police attention. Please ask an inspector to come and talk to me. We shall not move from here until one does.'

Caitlin watched Rhianna with ever-increasing regard as the constable left the desk and sauntered through a doorway behind him. A few minutes later he returned with a poker-faced inspector and indicated the two women who wished to see him.

'Inspector Marsh at your service.' He looked at Caitlin and her baby suspiciously. 'How can I be of help?'

'Can we go somewhere a little more private?' Rhianna suggested, looking round her. 'What I have to say is not for delicate ears. I would hate it to be overheard.'

'Very well,' the inspector said reluctantly, intrigue getting the better of him. 'Come with me . . .'

They followed him to a room that was lit by an electric light and furnished with four chairs and a desk strewn with papers. On the wall were pinned up various notices, most of which were out of date. A fire was dying in its small cast-iron grate on one side of the room. The inspector poked the fire, picked up the scuttle that stood on the hearth and tipped on a few lumps of coal.

'Please sit down,' he said as he rubbed his hands together to get rid of the coal dust. He lit a cigarette. 'Now . . . How may I help you ladies?'

Rhianna began at the beginning. She told all, explaining in explicit detail about Caitlin and Sarah and their ordeals at the hands of Lawson Maddox. Inspector Marsh listened attentively, eyes focused on Rhianna as he drew repeatedly on his cigarette. He finished it and lit another. His expression giving nothing away apart from glancing at Caitlin curiously from time to time.

'And you maintain that this young woman here, this Miss O'Flanagan, worked as a prostitute for Mr Maddox against her will?' Scepticism was evident in his expression.

'Against her will and against her nature.'

He looked at Caitlin again with distaste. 'Where was that, miss?'

'I . . . I'm not really sure where it was . . . I was doped when he took me there you see. I was barely sensible.'

He rolled his eyes disdainfully. 'I would need an address. No address, no evidence.'

Rhianna recalled that she had seen the evidence, but she did not have it. The list of properties she found in his desk once gave the addresses that could indict Lawson. But she could not recall them. If only she'd been more curious. If only she'd made a note.

'So . . .' the inspector went on, looking disdainfully at Caitlin. 'You claim you were not taken willingly to wherever it was?'

'How could she be willing if she was under the influence of that vile drug?' Rhianna asked testily. 'She's just said she was hardly aware of what was going on.'

'But she put up no resistance either?'

'How could she?'

'I am merely trying to establish this, madam – if she did not resist, then by definition she went of her own free will.'

Rhianna sighed with frustration. 'Is there somebody of higher standing we could see? I can see you're not very sympathetic to what we're saying. A man out there is breaking the law, making the lives of certain decent young women miserable and wretched, not to mention breaking the hearts of their families. And you act as if you're totally uninterested.'

'No, hold your horses, madam. Of course I'm interested. But in order to bring a case before the courts we need evidence. Hard evidence—'

'Isn't Miss O'Flanagan evidence enough? Is not my sister at home evidence? Her doctor has seen the proof of what we're saying. He is quite prepared to give evidence. Besides, how can you not *already* know these places exist? It's beyond belief. You are the police after all, the guardians of the peace.'

The inspector shrugged. 'With respect, how do I know Miss O'Flanagan here and your absent sister haven't got a vendetta against Mr Maddox? How do I know they're both not making it all up? If they were doped how do we know it wasn't all a dream?'

Rhianna tapped her index finger on own chest repeatedly. 'I'm married to the beast. I know him. I know what he's capable of . . .'

'The tone of your voice illustrates precisely my point, Mrs Maddox. How do I know *you* don't have a vendetta against him? How do I know you're not seeking revenge for something he might have done against *you*?'

'Be assured, Inspector Marsh . . .' She struggled to stifle her indignation. 'But this is getting us nowhere. We are wasting our time here. If you won't do anything. If you won't arrest him . . .'

'How can I arrest a man merely on what you've said. Where

is the evidence? I need to know where these so-called brothels are. We need to raid them and catch people in the act. We need to have the proof that he owns the properties. Thus we would need a warrant to search his house for the deeds to these places. You are making very serious allegations. Before we do anything we need to be sure of what we're doing. We need to plant police officers in these places, who can find out what's really going on and report back.'

'Oh, they'd enjoy that, no doubt,' Rhianna responded caustically. 'They'd enjoy being drawn into Lawson Maddox's net.'

'You do our officers a disservice, ma'am. They are not corrupt, as you imply.'

'Nor corruptible either?'

'Nor corruptible either.'

'I have my doubts,' she said scornfully, recalling the illegal cockfight at the Old Bush when Lawson implied he paid off the constable to turn a blind eye.

'Have you considered bringing a private prosecution against Mr Maddox, Mrs Maddox?' the Inspector asked, changing tack.

'Do I look as if I could afford it? In any case, this is surely a police matter. An opportunity to rid the community of this evil. Why should it be left to me to pay?'

'It was just a suggestion.'

Rhianna stood up. 'Thank you for your time, Inspector Marsh. But I don't think you have heard the last of this.'

As she had promised, Rhianna stood Caitlin dinner again in the Fountain Dining Rooms. Before they ate, the young Irish girl went to the new water closet that had been installed recently and changed the baby's napkin. That done, she opened the front of her blouse and fed the child, hidden from the eyes of strangers. She returned to the table and Rhianna told her she had ordered their food. Caitlin settled the baby in her arms, rocking her gently to try to get her back to sleep.

'She's a good soul, you know, Rhianna. Hardly a murmur from her.'

'You're lucky. Not all babies are as placid.'

'Especially after what I put her through . . .'

Rhianna straightened the knife and fork in front of her, making sure they were parallel to each other. Caitlin watched her and smiled, recognising it as a habit come from being in service.

'I have a proposition to put to you, Caitlin.'

'Oh?'

'Yes. Something that would benefit all of us, I think.' Her eyes met Caitlin's. The candour of Caitlin's expression told her that although the girl's body had been defiled and abused, the quintessence of womanhood and the innate graciousness she had once possessed remained intact. 'I would like you to bring the baby and come and live with me and Sarah – for the time being at any rate.'

'Oh, Rhianna, that's very kind of you, but surely—'

'Before you accept or decline, let me just explain a couple of things that might sway you. Whilst it would benefit you, inasmuch as you wouldn't need to beg any more, and you would have a roof over your head that would cost you nothing, you would be helping me.'

'As a maid, you mean?'

Rhianna laughed. 'No, not as a maid. I don't want to employ you. In any case I couldn't afford to employ you right now. But Sarah, as I explained, is still struggling to beat this addiction that you seem to have overcome already. You have so much in common the two of you. You've suffered the same tribulations. I think it would help her back to good health if she had a close friend she could share her troubles with. You'd be somebody she could look up to. I'm sure you could become very good friends as well. As a matter of fact, I believe you would be a crutch for each other. Certainly, it might restore her interest in life with a baby in the house again. Then there's my father . . . He's an invalid now and I have the distinct feeling he's willing himself into his grave, he's so heartbroken over the death of my mother. If I could leave them both, knowing they're in your hands when I go out to work, I would feel a bit more at ease.'

'You're going out to work?'

'I have to find work, Caitlin. The money I had is all but gone and I have the baby's funeral to pay for, the rent on the house, the doctor's bills . . .'

'Oh, Rhianna, I'd love to be of help. To be sure, living with you would make my life so much easier. But I don't want to be a burden. I couldn't afford to pay for my lodgings and you have enough on your plate . . .'

'I'm hoping you'd take some of it off my plate. And I don't want money off you for your keep. Do you agree? Will you come?'

'Oh, yes . . .' Caitlin raised her eyes as if in supplication to the Lord. 'Thank you. Of course I'll come.'

'Good. Today . . . We'll collect your things from your room later.'

'There's not a lot to collect, Rhianna.'

'But first, let's go to the offices of the *Dudley Herald*. After the lack of interest from that police inspector, I'm even more determined to bring Lawson Maddox to book. I'm sure they'd be glad to expose his wickedness in the paper. Then the police will be forced to do something. The public will demand it.'

'Rhianna, there's . . . there's something I should have told you, but until now the time hasn't been right . . . That police inspector . . . Inspector Marsh . . .'

'Yes?' Rhianna looked at Caitlin, puzzled.

'I think he recognised me. He was the first man I told you about. The very first man that Lawson wanted me to . . . to go with . . . The one I had to prove my love by sleeping with.'

Rhianna groaned inwardly. 'Oh, Caitlin. Are you quite sure? Remember you were drugged.'

'Drugged or not, I'm quite sure. It was him.'

'No wonder he wasn't interested, if he's a friend of Lawson.'

'I bet Lawson knows already that you've been to report him, Rhianna.'

'I bet he does. All the more reason to get the newspaper to expose what he's up to.'

After they left the Fountain Dining Rooms, Rhianna and Caitlin went to the offices of the *Dudley Herald*. Mr Joshua Hatton deigned to see them and she told her story again, citing Caitlin as a victim of the vile trade in young girls by which Lawson Maddox was profiting.

'As the publisher and printer of the *Dudley Herald*, I'm afraid I could never allow such accusations to taint the pages of our newspaper, Mrs Maddox,' Mr Hatton replied. 'Such stories, such sordid details, would most definitely offend our readers' sensitivities. The church leaders, the town councillors, indeed all the dignitaries of the town would clamour for my blood if such degenerate reporting ever saw the light of day.'

'But you report all other crimes and court cases in the borough,' Rhianna argued.

'Indeed we do, including the arrest of the occasional prostitute plying her trade on the streets of this respectable Black Country town. But such as you're suggesting, never. It's more than my position is worth.'

'Do I take it then that you are either in favour of this corrupt abuse of young women, or are a regular visitor to such places that sell their services?'

Mr Hatton leaned back in his chair patiently and clasped his hands together in front of him. 'Mrs Maddox, I can assure you that I have never set foot in such a place,' he said calmly, and Rhianna knew she had overstepped the mark. 'And such remarks are not the way to ensure my co-operation.'

'I'm sorry,' she said. 'But something has got to be done about this and I thought you might like to be of help.'

'Mrs Maddox . . .' He leaned forward as if to divulge a great secret. 'Respectability is the framework into which our society fits its life. That very respectability dictates that we protect our readers, more especially the wives and daughters of the borough, from such abominable, unspeakable events. They would not make pleasant reading and I would be called to account for publishing such material that many would find offensive. Hypocrisy and the evasion of morality of course exist within society, we know that. But it is not the purpose nor aim of my newspaper to report such alarming and astonishing goings-on.'

'I am surprised and very disappointed,' Rhianna said evenly. 'Those very wives and daughters you mention are the ones I am most anxious to protect. And I'm not so sure they're as squeamish as you make out. But if they're not made aware of the danger's existence, they can't be on their guard, can they? If the pretty daughters of the area have to be served up as dainty morsels to titillate rich and morally incontinent men, then let them at least be of an age that they can understand the nature of the sacrifice they're asked to make . . .' She paused for breath and to garner more thoughts. 'Oh, I know that not all prostitutes are unwilling – some revel in it. But those that are unwilling should be allowed the same protection that you demand for your readers.'

'I take your point, Mrs Maddox, and I do sympathise. However, let me remind you of the fuss and palaver caused as recently as 1885 by a certain Mr W. T. Stead, the editor of the *Pall Mall Gazette*, a London evening newspaper. Do you recall the *"Maiden Tribute of Modern Babylon"*?'

'I don't think I do. Possibly I was protected from exposure to it then in the way you believe respectable girls should be protected.'

'Then at the risk of being indelicate, let me enlighten you. In

1885, the age of consent, as you may recall, was twelve years old. Mr Stead, with the help of a Mrs Josephine Butler ... You might remember Mrs Butler. She was the reformer who campaigned against the Contagious Diseases Act, which placed prostitutes under police supervision. Anyway, this Mr Stead ... with the backing of Mrs Butler, the Salvation Army, Cardinal Manning and the Archbishop of Canterbury, he exposed a trade in virgins by arranging to have one procured for himself.'

'You mean he abused the poor young girl himself?' Caitlin asked.

'No, indeed he did not. He merely wanted to show that this traffic existed. The girl in question was certified intact before and after the events that provided the research for his claims. Stead ran six pages of vivid sexual disclosure following his research, under such sub-headings as "*The Violation of Virgins*", "*Strapping Girls Down*", and the like. That evening people were paying up to a shilling for a newspaper that normally would have cost a penny. W. H. Smith helped his cause by refusing to handle what he called filth, thus enhancing its appeal. So the Salvation Army sold the copies instead. London was in uproar. But there were two sides to the coin ...

'A rival newspaper, the *St James's Gazette*, complained about Stead for openly dealing, in the plainest of language, with what they called the vilest parcel of obscenity. In their eyes, the offence was not the abduction and rape of young girls but raising the issue in public—'

'But that's ridiculous,' Rhianna interrupted. 'It's absurd.'

Joshua Hatton shrugged his shoulders. 'It's the society we live in, Mrs Maddox. Let me tell you ... MPs vilified the *Pall Mall Gazette* as the very worst of the gutter press. One MP even demanded that Stead be imprisoned. I remember the Home Secretary telling the House that his countrymen were determined to uphold the purity of their homes, meaning that they must close their doors to the likes of Mr Stead's article.'

'And close their minds, too,' Rhianna commented.

'For three days, Mrs Maddox, Stead ran more stories, giving more insights into the virgin trafficking and the goings-on in the underworld, and the hierarchy continued to be disgusted. Respectable people were appalled. His offices were besieged, newsboys selling the papers were arrested. The series, however, was syndicated in America and across Europe. He achieved notable success condemning the morals of some of his countrymen. It was said by some that he was merely the herald declaring this depravity. The government wanted to prosecute him nonetheless, until somebody realised that by doing so they might be seen as sympathisers of the virgin violators.

'Petitions came in to Parliament thick and fast from Stead's supporters demanding the age of consent be raised, and the Salvation Army blasted Westminster with several brass bands to reinforce the message. A major scandal had developed, Mrs Maddox. Meanwhile the Home Secretary declared that the publication of any obscene writing was a misdemeanour if so judged by a jury. Indeed, Mr Stead taunted the government further and evidence was contrived against him. He was indeed prosecuted and duly served his time in prison.

'So you see, Mrs Maddox, I am not quite prepared to put my neck on the block when legal precedents have been set. Although I do earnestly sympathise with your cause.'

31

'Caitlin, don't you think it's beyond belief that Lawson Maddox should be allowed to prosper unchecked in his crimes?' Rhianna was agitated as they left the offices of the *Dudley Herald*. They crossed Priory Street near the Saracen's Head where she used to meet Lawson in the early days, and headed towards the market place. 'I feel we're up against some sort of male conspiracy, as if they're all conniving to protect, even deny the existence of what male society has created.'

'Female too,' Caitlin said resignedly. 'Some women are as bad as the men. Those who exploit men, wilfully selling their bodies.'

'Oh, some women too, I daresay ... But that police inspector ... no wonder he didn't want to help if he'd been favoured with a free visit to Lawson's bawdy house and a night cavorting with you. But he needs exposing as well. He's just as corrupt as Lawson. His wife should be told—'

'But that newspaper man,' Caitlin interjected. 'I can understand his reluctance if there's a chance he would go to jail for printing what we told him.'

'I know. It says a lot for the society we live in when publishing the truth can be a crime, but those who perpetrate the real crimes, those who abuse and violate decent girls, are overlooked and get off scot-free.'

'So what can we do, Rhianna?'

'I don't see how we can do anything more. Nobody wants to talk about it. Nobody cares. Lawson will continue to get away with murder.'

They walked on, ploughing through the shoppers in the

market place. They walked down Castle Hill disheartened, and Caitlin led Rhianna into Fisher Street on their right, a narrow, crumbling ravine of red-brick oppressiveness.

'You walk around here by yourself?' Rhianna queried. 'At night?'

'Not at night if I can help it. In the day, though. I have to.'

They hurried on and turned right into Birmingham Street at the Brewer's Arms avoiding a drunk who called after them from across the road. When they turned left almost at once, into a gruesome alley called Guest's Fold, Rhianna shuddered. A gutter running with foul, stinking slurry cut across the uneven brick paving of what amounted to nothing more than a squalid courtyard. Washing lines, slung between the dilapidated houses, bore poverty-stricken garments that flapped raggedly in the blustery March wind. Pieces of card-board filled empty spaces in the windows left by broken panes. Roof tiles were missing, chimneys leaned precariously. These dwellings had been condemned as unfit for human habitation long ago yet still they stood, a blight on human dignity, a canker on the landscape. Children peeped warily from behind wooden doors that had not seen a lick of paint in sixty years, their curious, innocent eyes and dirty faces masked by sores and running noses.

'You can't live here, Caitlin,' Rhianna said, appalled.

'I know.'

On the left was a decaying terrace of small houses rendered in crumbling cement, green with lichen. Caitlin opened the door to one of them.

'Don't come in with me, Rhianna,' she pleaded, turning back to face her. 'You won't like it. I'll just get what's mine and tell Mrs Froggatt I'll not be back.'

'Let me hold the baby for you.' Caitlin handed her the baby. 'Do you have enough money to pay any rent that's owing?'

'I pay a week in advance, Rhianna.' Caitlin went inside.

Rhianna looked about her warily while she waited. The grudging eyes of Guest's Fold seemed to be upon her and her decent clothes, watching from behind old and limp net curtains and doors that clattered on their hinges. An urchin, a boy of about eight years, although it was difficult to determine exactly, approached and asked her for a penny. She was inclined to oblige him but knew that if she did, she would be besieged from all quarters when already she felt intimidated. She shook her head and the boy, scowling, let her be. Then, the shrieks of an embittered woman rang from a dwelling across the alley and a child wailed.

Caitlin at last emerged, carrying her scant possessions wrapped in a sheet tied up at the four corners. They set off for Bond Street. Although Bond Street was far from salubrious it was a world away from the corrosive poverty of Guest's Fold and the whole warren of insanitary courtyards around Birmingham Street. Rhianna wondered how far she herself had been from such a grisly existence if Lawson had subjected her to the same traumas that Caitlin and Sarah had undergone? How fortunate she had escaped his grip, married or not, for surely he had as little regard for the institution of marriage as for anything else.

The first thing Rhianna did when they arrived home was to make up the fire, which had almost burnt out. While the kettle heated up she told Caitlin to make herself at home and led her upstairs with her baby to meet Sarah. Sarah was sitting on her bed trimming her toenails.

'Sarah, this is Caitlin, the girl I told you about. Caitlin – Sarah . . .' The two girls greeted each other guardedly. 'And this is Caitlin's baby, Rhianna . . .'

At once, Sarah asked to see her, to hold her, and Caitlin laid her in Sarah's eager arms. The baby, it was obvious from the outset, would be the catalyst that Rhianna had hoped for.

'How old is she?' Sarah asked, gently moving the child's blanket from her face so she could gain a better look.

'Seven months.'

'She's beautiful. Oh, look at her eyes, they're so blue . . . Look, Rhianna, she's smiling at me . . . She's a lovely little thing.'

Rhianna the elder smiled to herself. This was going to work. Already she could feel it. 'You two have a lot in common and a lot to talk about. Do you mind if I leave you while I tend to Father? I need to see to him before the doctor gets here. Then I'll make that cup of tea.'

Titus had hardly stirred. Rhianna gently touched his forehead with the backs of her fingers. He felt hot, feverish. His face was flushed, his breathing was laboured and he was shivering. When he realised she was beside him, he muttered that he had a pain in the side of his chest.

'Dr McCaskie will be here soon.'

He nodded feebly. In the weeks that she had been home, Titus had lost weight. He was thin to begin with; now he was emaciated, his frail body waxy and ashen. He had rapidly worsened.

'I'm making a cup of tea. Would you like some?'

He nodded again, eyes still shut.

'I won't be long.'

The kettle was bubbling away when she arrived downstairs. She brewed the tea and was putting it to steep when she heard a knock at the back door.

'Dr McCaskie! You've timed it right. I've just brewed a pot of tea.'

'Excellent,' he replied and smiled admiringly. 'Shall I see the patient first?'

'Yes . . . And I should forewarn you, Doctor . . . we have two new family members. One is Caitlin O'Flanagan, the young lady I told you about who alerted me to Sarah's suffering. The other is her seven-month-old baby. Considering what they've both been through they seem well on the road to recovery. But if you have time to examine them, I'd be grateful.'

'What responsibilities you take on for yourself, Mrs Maddox . . .'

'I'm counting on Caitlin taking some of the responsibility away from me, to tell you the truth. I'm hoping she'll be able to look after Sarah and Father for me. I need to find work. What money I had is either gone or accounted for . . .' She smiled reassuringly. 'But there's enough to meet your bill and the baby's funeral.'

Dr McCaskie regarded her kindly. 'Don't worry about paying my bill till you've found work, Mrs Maddox. I don't believe there's anything outstanding.'

'Except your bill for this visit.'

'There's no rush. Let it not be a worry. I'll make my way upstairs then . . .'

When the tea had steeped Rhianna laid five cups, saucers and spoons on a tray, along with the pot, a jug of milk and a bowl of sugar. She carried it up the twisting staircase and set the tray down on the dressing table that stood under the window of Titus's room. Dr McCaskie put his stethoscope back into his bag and looked up at Rhianna ominously, shaking his head. Things did not augur well.

'I'll take a look at your new guest and her baby. I take it they're in Sarah's room . . .'

As Rhianna raised her father up she heard the doctor introduce himself and start talking to the girls as he closed the door behind him. She heard Caitlin and Sarah laughing at comments he made and it struck her that already there was some rapport between the two girls. Thank God. The only thing she hadn't yet decided was where Caitlin should sleep. Let her decide that herself.

She put the cup to Titus's lips and saw to it that he took some liquid. Conversation seemed superfluous. He had her care and that seemed sufficient. She tried to pick up scraps of conversation she could hear coming from the other bedroom. Even though she couldn't make out everything that was said, their voices were lively.

The doctor emerged smiling from the girl's room just as Rhianna had fed the last drop of tea to Titus. She gently laid him down, smoothed the bedclothes across his chest and led the doctor downstairs.

'So what do you think, Doctor?'

'The girl and her baby have both made a remarkable recovery. Her influence on your sister can only be beneficial. If that's the purpose of your bringing them together then I applaud you for your foresight. But Sarah is also making progress. She is certainly much brighter than she was last time I saw her, and gaining weight, I fancy. She tells me the pains of opiate deprivation are also somewhat reduced, as is the craving, and her bowel movements are more normal now.'

'I noticed.'

'This is excellent progress, Mrs Maddox. We must be thankful, considering the state she was in.'

'And my father, Doctor?'

'Your father, Mrs Maddox, has pneumonia. No doubt brought on by the trauma of being evicted into the pouring rain and cold over the weekend. With his primary condition, it's hardly surprising. How long did you say he's been like this?'

'Well, he took to his bed Saturday afternoon. As soon as we got to the hotel.'

'Hmm . . . I'll be blunt. I can't imagine him making a recovery. He's weak to start with.'

'And grieving over my mother.'

Dr McCaskie rubbed his chin. 'That too. Is he eating anything? Drinking anything?'

'Very little. He refuses most things. But I've just given him some tea.'

'You're doing all you can. That much I know. But be prepared for the worst, Mrs Maddox . . .'

'Oh dear . . .'

'He's going to need some careful nursing. I'd best call tomorrow to see how he is.'

Not only the fever, but the liquid that was filling Titus's lungs meant that the continual gasping for breath was too much for his heart to cope with. On the Thursday morning, when Rhianna went in to see him as soon as she got up, he opened his eyes and smiled.

'Yo'n just missed your mother,' he said lucidly, despite his breathlessness. ''Er's on'y just gone.'

'You mean she was here?'

Titus nodded.

'Oh? How was she?' Rhianna asked, humouring him.

''Er looked well. 'Er said to gi' yer 'er love.'

'Give her mine next time you see her, eh?'

Titus nodded and closed his eyes. Evidently he and Mary had arranged something between them, for he died later that day.

The funeral for Sarah's son Harry was postponed, so that both Harry and Titus could be buried together in the grave Mary already occupied.

On the day of the funeral, Maundy Thursday, the Reverend Cosens conducted the very private service at St Thomas's church. The wind was reinvigorated, blowing cold from the east and the dark clouds unleashed their burden of rain. The hawthorn trees rustled and the bunches of daffodils that had been lovingly arranged on surrounding graves swayed in sympathy. When they went out to the grave, Rhianna and Caitlin stood together, overlooking the hole in the ground in the lee of the church, and shivered. Caitlin had barely known Titus, Harry not at all, but she understood the grief Sarah must be feeling for a child she had known only a fleeting moment. Compounded with the grief of losing a father and a lover, she was surprised Sarah had retained the will to live at all. Rhianna meanwhile pondered sadly some of those moments of pleasure she had shared with her father.

'*Man that is born of woman hath but a short time to live, and is full of misery . . .*' intoned Reverend Cosens into the teeth of the wind.

Rhianna wept silently, surprised that she still had tears left to cry. God knew she had shed enough already over her mother, over Sarah, over Harry . . . over John.

'*In the midst of life we are in death: of whom may we seek for succour but of thee?*'

The first phrase stayed with her . . . In the midst of life we are indeed in death. Why had these dreadful things happened? Who was to blame? Was she herself to blame for defiantly going against Lawson's will in the first place? If she had stayed, would Sarah still be the same sweet, naïve young girl she had been before? If they had not been evicted, would her father still be alive? Would their mother still be alive if Rhianna had not broken her heart by defying her and Lawson, and eloping to Italy with John? Or was Lawson the only true cause of all these troubles? Yes, it was Lawson. Of course it was Lawson. Everything that had happened was a consequence of his depravity. What other man could be so vile, so evil, so immoral? What other man could knowingly, wilfully crush decency and innocence as if they were vile insects unworthy of life? Her eyes behind her black veil were seething with hatred. He was as guilty of murder as he was of adultery. She could happily see him hanged for it. Her frustration over his reckless wickedness and her hopeless inability to bring him to book, were overwhelming. She was utterly helpless to do anything at all.

'*Forasmuch as it hath pleased Almighty God of his great mercy to take unto himself the souls of our dear brothers here departed, we therefore commit their bodies to the ground; earth to earth, ashes to ashes, dust to dust, in sure and certain hope of the Resurrection to eternal life . . .*'

The damp, black earth thudded onto the lids of the two coffins and Rhianna swayed against Caitlin, who held on to her steadily. She shivered at the awful sequence of events that had plagued her since her return to Dudley. Lawson had caused these things. Lawson was responsible. Only he could account.

She wished she had talked more to her father. She wished she could have drawn him out of his grief. She wished she had done more for him. Now he was gone, gone to his beloved Mary. But he was happy again and she did not begrudge him his happiness. This was what he'd wanted above all else these last two months.

In her gloved hand Rhianna was already holding a small lace handkerchief. She lifted her veil and dabbed at the hot tears that were once more stinging her eyes, and felt another squeeze of sympathy from Caitlin. The wind gusted, she held on to her black hat and looked out across the churchyard, through the railings. Men were coming and going from the Three Crowns opposite. Despite everything, life went on. In the midst of death there was in fact life. As close as they were, other people were unaware of the suffering she had seen, the suffering that affected her. Beyond the Three Crowns and the Windmill Inn behind it, a billowing cloud of white steam from the Gypsy's Tent brewery mingled, instantly dispersed, with scattered steam from the brewery of the Peacock Hotel. So many breweries, she pondered illogically, so many public houses . . .

In the midst of death there was certainly life. And where there was life, there was hope . . .

Two months . . . It had been two months since Rhianna had seen John, two months since she had last lain with him and enjoyed the warmth of his body against hers. It had been two months since they had made love and she was aching for him. Where was he now? Was he still in Bologna, or had he completed his commission and returned to Sorrento? If only she knew. If only there was some way of knowing. Her letter must surely have reached Concetta by now. Hopefully, he was aware by this time of the events that had compelled her to return to England and detained her. At least he would know. It would at least reduce his worrying. If only she knew how he was.

Caitlin and her baby had been living with Rhianna and Sarah for two weeks. It had been the finest tonic Sarah could have had. With a baby in the house she was enjoying a renewed interest in life, a reason to drag herself out of the mire of wretchedness in which she had been drowning. Sarah was growing stronger, her face was becoming round and pretty again, her figure was filling out nicely. Most mornings she left her bed and got dressed and took a greater interest in everything around her. The grief of losing her baby, together with the guilt she felt, which Rhianna now realised overshadowed the grief of losing her mother and father, was diminishing and she was smiling again. Maybe it helped that she had known the child but a brief time, Rhianna did not know. But she was thankful to see this signal improvement in Sarah's health and demeanour.

She felt confident that she could leave the two girls together with the baby to occupy them while she found work. And she found work that same Easter Tuesday afternoon, producing brass stampings at a factory in New Mill Street, just two minutes walk from Bond Street. She was to commence her employment next day. It was not work she had done before, or even entertained, but they needed money now. Until she heard from John, until Sarah was fully recovered and she was sure she would never relapse into opium taking, she would have to stay in England and work. That much she sadly accepted.

32

Rhianna did not enjoy very much her first day at Town Mills Stampings. The work was too repetitive, the whole place reeked of tallow, and the small stampings she produced from the thin coils of brass were too small and fiddly to handle easily. Several times she cut her fingers as she lifted the tiny pressings from the pattern. It would take some getting used to. As she swung the handle of the hand press there was little of joy to contemplate, only its annoying squeak and the awful sequence of events that had overtaken her since her return to Dudley, which played over and over in her mind.

At half past twelve the hooter blew and, following the example of all the other girls in the workshop, Rhianna stopped working and ate the sandwiches she had brought, and flipped the stopper off the bottle of tea that had long since gone cold. Two other girls, Minnie and Maude, suggested she draw her stool alongside theirs and eat with them. She was glad of their easy company and their ready smiles. She listened to their bubbling enthusiasm for their lives and their loves and hoped they would never suffer the outrages she had seen. Of course, she told them nothing about her own life; when she knew them better she might. There would be plenty of time.

At one o'clock the hooter blew again and they all returned to their workbenches. Her spirits were more elevated. She relived the wonderful months she had shared in Italy with John and she tried to imagine it now; the Bay of Naples in all its brilliant springtime glory, its bright, warm sunshine, its exotic umbrella pines, its blue skies and bluer sea. How she missed it all, how she ached to be back there and experience unimpeded contentment again with John. She longed to hear Concetta's infectious laughter and talk of her silkworms, Pasquale's forward yet guileless charm. She fondly remembered sitting out late beneath the stars with John at her side, drinking wine and listening to Pietro's music, Francesca's singing and the impromptu harmonies they all produced, that sent shivers up and down her spine. But none of these things affected her quite like her love for John. Dear, intense, reserved John.

Well, what of John's work in Bologna? She wondered how close he was to finishing it, what they had made of him there, how the family had treated him. One thing for certain was that he would be surrounded by girls, the daughters of Salvatore Vinaccia. If he became grossly involved in his work maybe he would not worry too much about not hearing from her. Maybe the girls would divert him. She hoped they liked him, that they felt they could include him in their domestic lives and make him feel at home. She had no worries about his fidelity. His fidelity was assured . . . and wasn't it good to know it?

A man wearing a greasy overall came and stood at her side, interrupting her thoughts. He had come to pick up the tray of finished stampings.

'Do you have the time?' Rhianna enquired.

'Yes, my flower.' He looked her up and down admiringly. 'And the inclination . . .'

She smiled patiently. 'So what time is it?'

'Five an' twenty past.'

'Five and twenty past what?'

'Five.' he said, amused that she was not aware of the hour.

'Is it as late as that?'

'It is, my flower. Yo'm a fresh un 'ere, ai' yer?'

'I started today.'

'Wha'n yer think? Dost think yo'll tek to it?'

'It's a job of work,' she replied. 'I don't do it for love of it. Just for the money.'

'Well, there's sod-all new in that, eh? What's yer name?'

'Rhianna.'

'Bist married, Rhianna?'

'Oh, yes, I'm married.'

'Pity. I could tek to a likely wench like thee. Always too late, me. Somebody always gets theer fust. What's his name?'

She hesitated. Never again would she admit to being married to Lawson Maddox. 'His name's John.'

'John, eh. Well, I'm George. We'll be seeing quite a bit of each other, Rhianna, as I do me rounds.'

Rhianna smiled and George turned to walk away. 'Tell me, George,' she said, halting him. 'Are you married?'

'Me? No, not proper married. Could never afford a weddin'. But me an' me wench live together as man and wife. What's being married, other than havin' a bit o' paper that says so that I cor read any road? 'Er's still got a ring on her finger and 'er's took me name. I defy anybody to say as we ai' wed.'

'What's her name?' Rhianna asked.

'Em'ly.'

'Have you ever been unfaithful to her?'

'Me? No. But I'm always game.' He grinned at her with increasing interest.

'You've never been with a prostitute?'

'Christ, no. I couldn't afford it. Any road, why pay good money for summat as I get for nothing at 'um? . . . Don't tell me as yo'm a pro, Rhianna,' he added disbelievingly.

Rhianna chuckled. 'Lord, no. Oh, it's all right, George, I'm not propositioning you either. I was just curious. I just wondered what sort of men go with prostitutes. That's all.'

'Them as have got a shillin' or two to spare I reckon.'

'Is that all? Just those that can afford it?'

George shrugged. 'Mebbe them as am fed up wi' their missuses an' all. Them as have wed ugly buggers. Them as

483

think they can get away with it. Them as cor 'elp theirselves . . . 'Ave yer put your card in here saying how many stampin's yo've done?'

'Sorry . . . Here it is. I don't seem to have done that many. I daresay I'll get quicker.'

'Course yo' will . . . Well, I'll be on me rounds, Rhianna. See yer tomorrer.'

Shortly after six o' clock Rhianna stamped her time card and walked home. Caitlin had begun preparing a meal while Sarah played with the baby. As she entered, Rhianna could smell lamb chops cooking in the oven at the side of the cast-iron grate, and the rich aroma made her mouth water. A pan of potatoes was boiling on the hob next to another pan containing shredded cabbage.

'Has everybody been all right?'

'We've been fine, is that not so, Sarah?'

Sarah smiled and turned the baby to face Rhianna. 'She's cutting a tooth,' she said excitedly. 'She's been a bit grumpy today and when I put me little finger around her gums I could feel this little sharp lump. She's cutting a tooth. See if you can see it, Rhianna.'

Rhianna stooped down obediently and tried to coax her namesake into opening her mouth, but to no avail.

'Here, let me have her a while.'

Rhianna took the child and sat down in the armchair her father used to sit in. As she bestowed hugs and baby talk on little Rhianna she watched the two girls. They were like two mothers looking after one child, both devoted to it, though neither competing for its attention. Even though the poor baby didn't have a decent father who could be present, it did not lack for love and attention. The very presence of the baby in the house had had a magical influence on Sarah. Each girl had found a friend.

As Sarah began making gravy, Rhianna heard the sound of

horses' hoofs outside and the rattle of carriage wheels. There was a knock at the door.

She froze.

Lawson.

What could he possibly want?

She decided to ignore it. Another knock, more impatient this time. Warily, she got up and peeped through the hole that the latch went through. Nobody was in the narrow angle of sight. Curiosity got the better of her and she lifted the latch, still holding the baby. She opened the door a fraction. At once, she thought she was going to faint and gripped the door handle firmly with one hand while she held on to the baby with the other.

As she flung open the door, a familiar face looked at the baby, its expression changing from concern to puzzlement. 'I didn't think we'd been apart that long.'

'John! . . . Oh, John!'

She could say nothing more. Tears of joy filled her eyes as she fell into his arms. 'You're here. My God, you're here. How long—? When did—? Why did—?'

'All in good time . . .' He hugged her tight and kissed her longingly on the lips. 'God, I've missed you.'

'No more than I've missed you.' She stepped back to look at him, to feast her eyes on this man she loved so much and had not seen for far too long.

'Are you going to invite me in?'

She chuckled at her forgivable oversight. 'Yes, come in . . . Can you manage your case?'

'Yes, I can manage the case. Can you manage the baby?'

'The baby . . .' She laughed again, stepping aside so he could get past her. 'You didn't think it was ours, did you?'

'I was trying to do a quick mental calculation.'

'It's Caitlin's.'

'Caitlin's?'

'Oh, it's a long story. But let me introduce you . . .'

The two girls had already ceased their tasks so they could witness this long overdue reunion. They nudged each other and smiled, and said how pleased they were to meet John after hearing so much about him.

'Welcome to this house of three women and a baby,' Rhianna said.

John put down his case, took off his hat and looked around unsure of what he had turned up to.

'Let me take your hat and coat . . .'

He gave her his hat and unbuttoned his coat. When he'd slipped it off, Rhianna took it. 'I'll put them in the front room . . . Come with me, Gianni . . . Caitlin, can you hold up tea for a while? I must talk to him first. Have we got enough food?'

'There's plenty for all.'

Rhianna turned to him, her affection, her relief at seeing him and being with him again, brimming over in her eyes. 'There's so much to tell you. So much has happened. Oh, John, I've missed you so much . . .'

He stood close, facing her in the chilly front room and took her hands. 'That's all I wanted to hear,' he whispered tenderly. 'My God, it's been hell without you. I've been demented with worry.'

'I was afeared you would be. Didn't you enjoy Bologna?'

'Bologna? Oh, the Vinaccias were hospitable enough – very kind, in fact – and Bologna's a beautiful place. But I missed you. I learnt one thing, Rhianna – I can't live without you. When I received no replies to my letters I was beside myself . . .'

'My stupid fault for forgetting to give Concetta my address. Although I think it was for the best, as it's turned out.'

'How can that possibly be?'

'Don't worry. I'll explain later.'

'How is your father, by the way?'

'He passed away as well, John. Pneumonia and a broken heart. Just over a week ago. It's all been so sad.'

'I'm so sorry, my love,' he said with earnest sympathy. 'When you needed me most I wasn't here.'

'And how I've needed you . . .' Rhianna leaned her forehead against his chest and he sniffed her hair as he stroked it.

'What's that I can smell in your hair?'

She looked up at him curiously. 'Smell? . . . Oh no! It must be tallow you can smell. I started work today in a factory. I bet it's seeped into my clothes and everything.'

'Why are you working?'

'We need money. What money I had has all gone. Why else?'

'You poor, impoverished girl . . .' He smiled contentedly, as if her lack of funds was of no consequence. 'So tell me all that's happened.'

'It'll take a fortnight . . . Why don't we eat first and then I'll tell you everything? I bet you're hungry from your travels.'

'I'm starving. I've not eaten since this morning in London.'

'We can unpack your case afterwards.'

'Actually . . . I'll open my case now. I bought a couple of bottles of Pasquale's wine. He insisted – you know Pasquale. Do you think the girls would like a glass of wine with their dinners?'

'I don't think one glass would hurt them.'

As they ate, Rhianna told John everything; not in great detail, for that would unfold over time and as it became relevant.

'When I saw Concetta and she told me you'd rushed back here to be at your mother's side you can't imagine how helpless I felt, not being here to support and console you. Mind you, I was relieved to know why you hadn't answered any of my letters.'

'Fancy me forgetting to give Concetta my address in the first place. I can't get over it. But I take it you'd finished working in Bologna, if you actually saw Concetta.'

'I confess I hurried the last two paintings. I was anxious to get back to Sorrento to find out what was wrong, to find out why you hadn't written. I left Sorrento as soon as Concetta told me. Apparently, she'd only just heard from you a day or two before.'

'So how did you get on with the family in Bologna?' Rhianna turned to Caitlin and Sarah. 'He was commissioned to go to Bologna to do paintings of the six pretty daughters of some wealthy merchant we met in Sorrento, you see. I'm interested to know if I had competition.'

John's eyes crinkled into a smile. 'I got on very well, my love. They are a fine family. The girls are all very handsome too, as their father had said. They were good sitters, but inclined to ceaseless chatter – to me, not to each other. Each sat alone with me. Supposedly to inhibit their chattering. But to no avail.'

'I bet you got to know them well.'

'Their dreams, their fears, their laments. I think I became a *confidente* to each.'

'But there was only one married, wasn't there?'

'And two more spoken for. The others all had their eyes on somebody or other.'

'As long as they didn't have their eyes on you.'

'No, but I think their mother did,' he said, tongue in cheek, and they all laughed. 'They said they would like to meet you, I told them so much about you.'

He poured more wine, then Caitlin and Sarah told their stories.

'It doesn't surprise me about Lawson,' John commented when they had finished.

'It doesn't?' Rhianna said.

'I knew all along he was involved in prostitution.'

'You did? You knew and yet you never told me?'

'It was none of my business, Rhianna. Besides, it was evident you had no idea at all. If I'd told you when I first got to know you, doubtless you wouldn't have believed me and might have thought it malicious of me to suggest such a thing. I didn't want to alienate myself.'

'But how did you know?' Rhianna asked. 'You were in London, miles from his sordid world.'

'Because I knew my father was involved as well.'

'Your father?' Rhianna's expression was one of realisation. 'Of course . . . I know you said he had a hankering for young girls . . . and there always seemed to be some mysterious tie-up with Lawson.'

'I despise my father,' John exclaimed for the benefit of Sarah and Caitlin. 'He was definitely in partnership with Lawson. Covertly of course. It wouldn't do for it to be known that one of the town's most eminent personages was involved in prostituting young girls.'

'So how is he involved?' Rhianna questioned.

'He owns or owned a couple of the houses that Lawson runs as brothels.'

'I thought Lawson owned them all.'

'Some, yes. Not all. And the reason I know is that I happened upon the deeds once when searching for something in his study. I was curious and made it my business to find these places. When I saw the number of men rapping on the front doors with their canes and looking furtively about them, it was very quickly very obvious what was going on. Of course, he could have sold the houses to Lawson since. That I wouldn't know.'

Rhianna shook her head in disbelief at the mounting evidence against Lawson, the man she had so foolishly and impulsively married, the man she had failed to bring to book. 'But your poor mother,' she said. 'Are you going to try and become reconciled with her while you're here?'

'I think I should try, but I don't hold out much hope.'

'I think you should. And talking about reconciliation . . .' She looked earnestly at Caitlin. 'I think it would be a good idea for you to seek reconciliation with your family.'

Caitlin shook her head. 'My mother won't have anything to do with me. And my father won't, in case he upsets my mother. I know them. They're funny old sods.'

'How old are you, Caitlin?' John asked.

'I'm just twenty-one.'

'Why?' Rhianna asked. 'What's her age got to do with anything?'

John leaned back in his chair. 'Well, Rhianna, it's my intention that you and I go back to Italy just as soon as it's feasible. However, I understand that you wouldn't care to leave Sarah here and not be able to oversee her complete and absolute recovery. But it seems obvious to me that Caitlin and her baby have become an integral part of your family as well. So what I propose is this . . . We all go to live in Italy.'

The three women cast glances at each other, each to witness the reaction of the others. All were smiling their approval.

'Go on, John,' Rhianna urged.

'Well, we have room enough at *Paradiso* – we could even build extra rooms if we needed to. The climate and the way of life will suit Sarah and Caitlin. You, Rhianna could do with a bit more help there and I'm sure they'd be willing to give it. And lastly, we can afford it. I happen to have won several more important commissions – friends of Salvatore Vinaccia – and my dealer in London is clamouring for more paintings.'

'That would solve all our problems,' Rhianna responded enthusiastically. 'Oh, thank you, Gianni. It's more than I could have hoped for. How do you feel about that, Caitlin? How do you feel about living in Italy?'

'From what you've told me I think I'd love it. And as for the lack of men . . . Thank God for it!'

'One step at a time,' John counselled. 'Even though Caitlin is twenty-one, it's only common courtesy to seek the blessing of her parents before we take her abroad.'

'Since I am twenty-one, I'm already of an age when I can make my own decisions,' Caitlin said eagerly.

'Nevertheless, I'll go and visit your mother,' Rhianna asserted. 'I'll explain everything. If she is so keen to alienate you, then I don't foresee any problem. If, on the other hand—'

'I don't care what she says. I'm going to Italy with you. She didn't stand by me when I needed her. None of them did. Oh, sure I have a brother who still speaks to me once in a while, but nobody else. You're the only person that's ever helped me anytime, Rhianna.'

The following evening, Rhianna and John together walked to King Edmund Street where Mrs O'Flanagan lived with her husband, Padraig.

'Maybe it's not a good idea for them to see you with me,' Rhianna suggested. 'If they're as strait-laced as Caitlin makes out, they'll frown on both of us . . .'

'I see what you mean.'

'So let me go in alone. If I want you to come in, I'll call you. Don't wander off too far.'

He nodded and disappeared from view as Rhianna knocked on the door.

After just a few seconds the door opened and an astonished Mrs O'Flanagan asked her to enter. She exhorted the several inquisitive sons and daughters that loitered, to vacate the little scullery while she had a chat with her important guest, whom she had not seen in an age.

'I heard you were abroad, so I did. Will you not sit down and tell me all about it?'

Rhianna sat down and painted a verbal picture of Italy that she hoped would stand her in good stead, considering her purpose there. Mrs O'Flanagan listened with wide-eyed awe.

'I've actually called about Caitlin,' she said when she reckoned she'd given enough information, short of divulging all about John.

'About Caitlin?' Mrs O'Flanagan's expression changed. 'I know nothin' about Caitlin, Mrs Maddox. I don't even know where she is. She turned her back on her family and the Lord above, and turned to wickedness.'

'She's living with me in Dudley at the moment, Mrs O'Flanagan. She's well looked after, her and her baby.'

'Her and her bastard, you mean, Mrs Maddox, God forgive me for my language.'

'Caitlin was the victim of a very ruthless man, Mrs O'Flanagan. Whatever she's turned out to be in your eyes, she's a good and loving mother and a born survivor. You should be proud of her.'

'How can I be proud of anybody – my own daughter included – who steals from her employer and gets herself dismissed, who foolishly gets herself into trouble with a man who wouldn't or couldn't marry her?'

'She never stole anything from me, Mrs O'Flanagan, if that's what you mean.' Stealing her husband did not qualify; Caitlin had done her an enormous favour by doing so. 'On the contrary, I know her to be scrupulously honest. I'd stake my life on it.'

Mrs O'Flanagan looked at Rhianna questioningly. 'If she never stole anything, why was she dismissed from your house?'

'It was my husband's doing. He wanted her out of the house. I employed her without his consent or prior knowledge. It was my fault in the first place.'

Rhianna was determined to protect Caitlin's integrity. Evidently, Mrs O'Flanagan was not aware that Lawson had been having an affair with her.

'But that makes no sense at all, Mrs Maddox. Because he employed her afterwards at that guest house he runs in Downing Street.'

Guest house! Is that what Caitlin had called it?

'I don't know the whys and wherefores, Mrs O'Flanagan. By that time, Mr Maddox and I had separated. But that's another story and I'm not here to discuss it. I'm here to discuss Caitlin. After what she's been through you should be proud of her.' Rhianna was aware she was sounding like the lady of the house again and realised she should moderate her tone. 'I'm sure you'd want to help her in some way. I'm certain that if you were prepared to forgive her she would love to be reconciled. She misses you, Mrs O'Flanagan. She misses her father and her brothers and sisters. She's a fine girl . . . You have a beautiful granddaughter besides . . .'

'I can find it in my heart neither to forgive nor forget, Mrs Maddox. She was never brought up to have loose morals. She allowed herself to be defiled.'

'She's not the first, nor will she be the last.'

'Be that as it may, I can't condone such feeblemindedness and lack of decency in me own daughter. She's defied all our ideals. She's reaped her just desserts and it serves her right.'

'But she was young, Mrs O'Flanagan . . . Maybe a little bit impetuous . . . And she was in love.'

'She should have kept herself to herself. Pure till the time of her marriage. That's how she was brought up.'

'Mrs O'Flanagan, I have befriended Caitlin once again and my life is all the richer for it. I would very much like to employ her again in some capacity or other. I haven't quite decided how yet. But I have to tell you that it's my intention to return to Italy very soon and I would love to take her with me, baby and all. It would please me no end if she could go with your blessing. She's a single girl trying to do her best for a child she loves. If I don't take her she has nobody she can fall back on for help . . . What I'm trying to say is . . .' She looked at Mrs O'Flanagan earnestly. 'I went to Italy without my mother's blessing. She took ill while I was away and maybe the worry of my going without being reconciled had something to do with it. But by the time I got back here to make my peace she was dead. We both wanted to heal the rift, Mrs O'Flanagan, but it was too late. We never had the chance and it was heartbreaking. Now, I feel robbed of her pardon for what I did because, like Caitlin, I was never a perfect daughter either, in her eyes. Maybe her soul is still restless for want of reconcilement. I would hate any of that to happen to you.'

Mrs O'Flanagan sighed. 'Were you, too, a wicked woman, Mrs Maddox?'

'I didn't think so, nor do I still. But in her judgement I was.'

'I heard you left Mr Maddox for another man . . .'

'Yes, I did . . . Always, there are two sides to a story, Mrs O'Flanagan,' Rhianna petitioned solemnly. 'For this reason, I urge you to be sympathetic to Caitlin's plight. I urge you to hear her side of the story.'

'Very well. Send Caitlin to me. We'll try and make our peace as best we can.'

'Thank you, Mrs O'Flanagan.'

33

Baby Rhianna was at the centre of a tearful reunion between Caitlin and her family. Mrs O'Flanagan found it hard to let go of her new granddaughter once she had seen her. She held her in her arms and secretly wondered how she could have been so bigoted about an innocent baby, especially one so pleasant and so pretty.

'Be sure to look after this child, Caitlin,' she urged.

'That I will, Mother. You can be sure of it.'

'She's a beautiful baby, the image of your Aunt Berneen when she was the same age. Is she not, Padraig?'

'That she is, Maura,' Padraig answered.

'And keep yourself well. Look at you. You're a scarecrow. You must eat well to keep well, not skimp your meals. It's a sure certain sign you've not had me behind you.'

'I'm eating plenty, Mother. Rhianna's been telling me about the glorious food in Italy. Plenty of fresh fruit and vegetables.'

'You mean Mrs Maddox.'

'That I do, but she's asked me to call her by her Christian name. We're friends now.'

'And she's a good friend. She thinks the world of you. Don't ever let her down.'

'Don't worry, Mother. I won't.'

'And who knows? In Italy you might meet a fine young man and settle down. It's a Roman Catholic country, so 'tis.'

Caitlin chuckled at the absurd notion that a decent Italian man would tell his mother he wanted to marry a girl who'd had another man's child out of wedlock. 'Oh, I want no fine young man, Mother. I'm done with men. Besides, what decent young man is going to want me? My baby and me will fare just fine with Sarah and Rhianna and her John.'

Mrs O'Flanagan nodded. ''Tis to be hoped so. But if things don't work out, you know we are here for you.'

Caitlin put her arms around her mother's neck. 'Thank you, Mother. That's all I needed to hear. I'll write regularly. And I shall come back and visit you anyway.'

'And this little mite will be grown up by then, I daresay. So when are you leaving?'

'On Sunday.'

'Will you come and see us again tomorrow before you go?'

'If you want me to.'

'Of course we want you to,' Padraig said stifling a tear. 'Of course we want you to.'

The rest of that week, Rhianna and John were busy preparing for the long journey to Sorrento. There were clothes to pack, extra medicaments to acquire for Sarah and Dr McCaskie's bills to pay. Rhianna felt she was due a rebate on the rent they hadn't used but John suggested she would get nothing, having paid in advance and agreed a minimum occupancy of the house. She informed her foreman at the stamping works that she did not require the job after all. She duly collected the small amount of wages owing her and said goodbye to Minnie and Maude, and George who collected the finished pressings.

On the Saturday, the day before they left, John went with the intention of making his peace with his mother. Meanwhile, Rhianna took Sarah, walking very slowly as she held onto Rhianna's arm for support, to buy a huge bunch of flowers to put on the grave that accommodated their mother, their father and little Harry. At the graveside, they wept in each other's arms in mutual consolation, thinking their own thoughts, invoking their own images of their dead family. They wept for different reasons. Rhianna mourned the loss of a dear mother and a father who had suffered too much in life. Sarah keened over her easy virtue, and at her begetting a bastard child by a villain who could not be brought to book. She wept especially over the loss of that poor, innocent victim that had been in her care but a short while.

Afterwards, they shopped for bread, cooked meats, cheeses and pickles for sandwiches to sustain them for the first part of their journey.

'I think John's ever so brave, offering to take me and Caitlin to live with you in Italy,' Sarah said as they walked slowly home.

'But that's John. He realised I wouldn't be able to leave you behind.'

'Not like Lawson Maddox.' There was palpable scorn in Sarah's voice.

'Not like Lawson Maddox.' Rhianna turned to look at Sarah. 'But I'm glad you're all coming. I'll be able to keep an eye on you. On Caitlin as well. I daresay it'll all turn out for the best. I know Italy will be kind to you. You'll make a complete recovery in Italy. That's what John's counting on. For Caitlin as well – she's still vulnerable, you know.'

Sarah nodded. 'I know. But she's stronger than me. I'm trying hard to be like her . . . to be like you as well, our Rhianna.'

Rhianna smiled. 'If I'd stayed with Lawson, who knows how I might have ended up. There but for the grace of God . . .'

'Can we stop a bit, Rhianna? I need a rest.'

They stopped and Sarah rested her backside on the window sill of a drapery shop in Hall Street which was, as always, bustling with shoppers. She took several deep breaths.

'Can I ask you something, our Rhianna?'

Rhianna looked at her puzzled, wondering what sort of

question required her permission for it to be uttered. 'Ask whatever you like.'

'I suppose you *have* been . . . you know . . . sleeping with John while you've been living with him?'

Rhianna looked at Sarah with open-mouthed incredulity, then burst out laughing at her apparent naïvety. 'What a funny question! What do you think?'

'I don't know what to think. I always think of you being very virtuous and above that sort of thing . . .'

Rhianna laughed again. 'Oh, I'm no angel, Sarah. I'm only flesh and blood.'

'So *have* you been doing it with him?' Sarah coloured at raising this sensitive and very private issue. 'I mean, you've shown no signs of being pregnant.'

'Funny you should mention it . . .'

'Oh?'

'I missed my last two showings . . .'

Sarah's eyes lit up and she flung her arms around her sister's neck. 'You mean . . . ? You mean you *are* pregnant?'

Rhianna nodded. 'I do believe I am.'

'But you said nothing.'

'No.' She shrugged. 'With everything else going on it seemed so piffling.'

'Piffling? It's the best news anybody could have. And we needed some good news to fend off the bad. Have you told John?'

'Not yet. Let it be our secret for now, our Sarah. I don't want to tell him till we're in Italy. We'll organise a party and invite our lovely neighbours and I'll announce it then. It'll be cause for some celebration, believe me.'

'Pity you're not married to John, Rhianna.'

Rhianna looked at Sarah intently. 'Who needs a marriage certificate? John and I regard ourselves as married to each other all the same. We took solemn binding pledges in Rome just between ourselves. Nothing that would be acknowledged by the church or by society . . . but private pledges that mean everything to us.'

'It sounds so romantic . . .'

'It was. He's the love of my life. I'm the love of his. I just thank God we found each other when we did.'

'I do, as well . . . Oh, I feel better now, Rhianna . . . Your news has done me the world of good . . .' Sarah smiled radiantly, the most promising smile Rhianna had seen her give. 'Shall we go on? I think I can make it back now.'

Sarah and Caitlin looked out excitedly at the drab Black Country world through the window of a hansom, as if they were royalty prepared to smile and wave at everybody they passed. But as everybody hurried to church in their Sunday best hats and coats nobody was interested in even casting a glance towards the carriage and its occupants travelling towards Dudley railway station. As they were driven down Birmingham Street with its foul, condemned courtyards, Caitlin glanced at Rhianna, acknowledging privately that her rival of old had saved her from the life of prostitution that would have inevitably ensued had she remained there. Rhianna smiled back knowingly. They turned right into Castle Hill and all Caitlin could see through the window on her side was the high wall that surrounded the castle grounds. Well, if what she had been told was true, the landscapes of Italy would be infinitely more appealing.

They pulled into Station Drive and, when the driver had unloaded all their baggage and handed it down piece by piece, John paid him.

'Have a good journey, sir.'

'Thanks. We hope so,' John answered affably.

They didn't have to wait long for the Dodger that would take them to Dudley Port. From Dudley Port they embarked on a further journey through mineral-ravaged terrain to Birmingham's Snow Hill Station where they must change again. At Snow Hill, the acrid smell of steam, scorched oil and smoke and people rushing about with travelling cases, was all vividly new to Sarah. Baby Rhianna was awakened by the dissonant roar of monstrous, liveried locomotives and the sibilant clanging of iron buffers as carriages and goods wagons were shunted around, and would not be settled. John bought two Sunday newspapers from Wyman's to read on the journey to London; the *Telegraph* and the *News of the World*. In Bologna he'd been starved of news, he said.

They boarded the half-past eleven for Paddington and found a compartment all to themselves. Caitlin laid the baby down on the seat and allowed her to kick her little legs and gurgle as she sat beside her. Sarah watched, amused and amazed that every day the child showed some evidence of having discovered something new – even one so young.

'So are you *very* disappointed that your mother still shuns you?' Rhianna asked John.

'Yes, I'm disappointed, my love. But I'm not surprised. She has no idea at all that my father is involved in Lawson's ignoble businesses. She's blind to the fact that compared to him I'm a saint. But I wasn't about to shatter her illusion.'

'Maybe one day she'll realise. She's having to demonstrate her loyalty to your father by shunning you. But as your mother, it must be breaking her heart.'

'She showed no signs.'

'But you don't know what's going through her mind, John.'

'That's true. I really don't.'

'I mean, look how Mrs O'Flanagan welcomed Caitlin back.'

Caitlin looked up at the mention of her name and smiled. 'And it's such a load off my mind. You can't spend your life at odds with your family.'

'I'm glad you and your family healed the rift, Caitlin,' John said. 'As for me, I wouldn't care if I never so much as crossed my father's *mind* again. But my mother is very vulnerable. She's living in cloud-cuckoo-land. I'll write to her when we get to Italy. Just to express more eloquently my side of the story. She'll read a letter. Maybe she'll begin to understand.'

After they had been travelling for a while they fell quiet. John, who was looking through the window at the greening fields and trees that were leafing up, complained that he was hungry.

'I wish we could get a cup of tea,' Rhianna said longingly as she unpacked the sandwiches.

'We might have time at Leighton Buzzard or Berkhamsted,' he answered. 'They can't be too far away now.'

They finished their sandwiches and sat companionably, talking about this and that. John eventually fell asleep to the steady rumble and roar of the iron wheels as they click-clacked over the track. His head rocked gently from side to side in concert with the swaying of the railway carriage. Rhianna watched him, full of love and reverence, and gratitude that he had come to England to take her back to Italy. He was her rescuer, her knight in shining armour. What would she do without him? She looked at Sarah; she too was dozing by this time. There had been such a noticeable improvement in Sarah over recent weeks. The worst was over. They would rear her, she would continue to improve.

Caitlin, who was feeding the baby, caught Rhianna's eye and smiled contentedly.

'Well I'm not tired, Caitlin,' Rhianna whispered, returning the smile. She picked up the *News of the World* and scanned the front page.

Irish home rule took up a great deal of space but the lingering scandal of Charles Stewart Parnell, 'the uncrowned king of Ireland', and his lover, the recently divorced Mrs Katherine O'Shea, was predominant. Salisbury's Conservative government was also preoccupied with the partition of Africa, and trouble loomed between other European powers, according to the number of references to it. But Rhianna was not interested in politics. The paper rustled as she turned the page.

She scanned the next sheet and a bold headline caught her eye: 'White Slavery Rears its Ugly Head Again.' Curiosity compelled her to read on.

An off-duty officer of the Brussels Police was horrified last week when a fifteen-year-old girl wearing only a negligée appeared in the Rue St Laurent and was immediately surrounded by a crowd of shocked onlookers. For her own protection the girl was detained by the policeman and taken to the police station for questioning. She informed the police that she had been forced, against her will, into a life of prostitution behind locked doors in a Brussels brothel. She had been unwittingly presented with the opportunity to escape and did not hesitate to take advantage of it.

The girl, who is English, gave her name as Flossie Kettle, and comes from Dudley in Worcestershire. She was later handed over to Belgian government officials who decided, in the light of past experience, to hand her over to the British Embassy in Brussels for repatriation. She was subsequently escorted from Brussels by two plain-clothes policemen from the Criminal Investigation Department of the Metropolitan Police and returned to Great Britain on Friday. She was taken to the New Scotland Yard headquarters on the Thames Embankment for further questioning.

A spokesman for the Metropolitan Police told our reporter that Miss Kettle claims her mother had been tricked into selling her for the sum of £5 to a woman posing as an officer for an employment agency that was recruiting young girls for domestic service in prestigious homes in London. In her sworn statement, she also alleged that she was subsequently taken to a house in Dudley where she was given a drug, believed to be chloroform, prior to being medically examined in order, she believes, to ascertain that she was a virgin.

From there, she was taken to Brussels, along with three other girls of a similar age, accompanied by a man who was well known to her.

The Metropolitan Police spokesman has since told our reporter that two people, a man and a woman, have been arrested in Dudley in consequence of these allegations. They are being held on charges of unlawfully abducting a young girl for the purposes of sexual exploitation. The couple are named as Miss Fanny Lampitt, also known as Frances Underhill, and Mr Lawson Maddox, both of Dudley.

The Belgians' defensive and prompt response is commendable and borne of a fear of history repeating itself. In 1879 a similar incident occurred, which led to a sequence of events that caused outrage in Belgium and Britain, and deep embarrassment to the Belgian authorities. The moral crusades that followed included the affair concerning Mr W. T. Stead and his legendary article 'Maiden Tribute of Modern Babylon', *which were published in the* Pall Mall Gazette *and caused unprecedented furore. Further revelations made by social reformer Mrs Josephine Butler in her famous Brussels court appearances culminated in the dismissal from duty of Edward Lenaers, Chief of the Brussels Morals Police and the sentencing of twelve brothel keepers. These events brought to public notice the fact that English, Scottish and Irish girls as young as twelve and thirteen were being sold to brothels in Brussels and Paris and traded for sex.*

The events culminated in the passing of the Criminal Law Amendment Act of 1885. The Act made provision for the protection of women and girls and the suppression of brothels. It contained legislation against procuration and defilement of girls under thirteen years of age, particularly by threats, fraud and administering of drugs. It raised the age of consent to sixteen, banned the abduction of girls under eighteen for the purposes of sex and made unlawful the detention of any woman or girl against her will with the intent to have carnal knowledge of her. Furthermore, the Bill gave Justices of the Peace the power to issue warrants to any person looking for a missing female, to search any suspected place.

The re-emergence of this kind of trafficking in young girls between the two countries is regarded by both governments as highly sensitive. Until this incident, it had been generally believed that the 'White Slave Trade' had been eliminated.

The police are continuing to gather evidence against Miss Lampitt and Mr Maddox and are confident that there will be sufficient to bring them to trial in the near future. Meanwhile, Miss Kettle has been happily reunited in Dudley with her widowed mother, Mrs Molly Kettle.

Rhianna slumped back in the seat, wallowing in the sweet relief and satisfaction that this astonishing news engendered. She could hardly contain her excitement. For weeks, ever since she had known of Lawson's abominable antics in prostituting Sarah and Caitlin, she had tried every means available to bring him to account. To no avail. Now, little Flossie Kettle had done it for them all and Rhianna was wild with hope. Lawson was getting his come-uppance after all.

As the train rattled on, she tried to relax in the knowledge that she was safe at last from Lawson Maddox and his further vindictiveness. He had wreaked his havoc. Now Sarah was safe. Caitlin was safe. So was Flossie Kettle. But this news was momentous and she could not relax. Her heart trembled with elation. If anybody deserved to be put away, he did. She only hoped that with the overwhelming evidence that had come to light through Flossie, further incriminating evidence would not be covered up by policemen or lawyers who had something to hide . . .

'Caitlin, let me hold the baby,' she said. 'You must read this. I think you'll find it very interesting.'

She handed over the newspaper as she leaned forward to

take the baby, then holding her in her arms, she watched Caitlin's changing expression.

'My God!' Caitlin exclaimed, her eyes wide with wonder. 'They've got him. They've got him, Rhianna. And we thought he would get off scot-free.'

'It was always a mystery to me what had happened to little Flossie Kettle,' Rhianna said. 'I'm so glad she's been found, she was such a sweet young girl. Her mother admitted to me that she'd sold her. But I never dreamed that Lawson could have had anything to do with it. I can't believe I was ever so naïve about him. There's no limit to what he's capable of, Caitlin. What's made him like he is, I wonder?'

Caitlin shook her head and said she could hardly imagine. Rhianna looked at John who was still dozing and prodded his thigh to wake him up. He had to know at once. John woke up and looked about him disoriented for a second or two. He looked at Rhianna. Her bright eyes were alight with an intensity he had never seen before. He smiled at her expectantly.

'What? Have we arrived?'

'No, not yet.' She eased herself forward on the seat excitedly and touched his hand. 'Quick, John, read this. You must read it at once. Tell me what you think.'

Rhianna handed him the newspaper and pointed out the article. She watched intently how his face changed as the import of the news registered.

'That's fantastic! My God! Serves the blighter right.'

'But what should we do, Gianni?' she asked animatedly. 'Should we go back and give evidence against him?'

He pondered a moment. 'No. It strikes me there'll be enough evidence already available to put him away for a very long time. Other folk are bound to come forward, possibly even your Dr McCaskie. We won't be the only people outraged at what he's done.'

'But what if your own father is implicated?'

'That's his affair. But somehow I don't think he will be. He'll have covered his tracks if I know him. I imagine he's already sold his remaining properties to Lawson anyway.'

'Do you think I would be able to get a divorce from Lawson on the back of all this?'

'I'd say it's doubtful, although I'm no legal expert. The two issues are unconnected, I would've thought. One is against the Crown, the other is a civil matter. I'd let him stand trial first and be convicted. Besides, any divorce application from you might only serve to confuse the prime case against him. Next time we return to England, in a couple of years or so, seek legal advice then. Who knows what might have happened by that time. In any case, divorced or not, it won't affect our lives together.'

'No, you're right, Gianni,' Rhianna answered with a happy smile, reassured. 'There is no rush. It can't make any difference to us, can it? I mean, not really.'